# . . . and mother earth wept

To Rhonda,
A kindred spirit and a great lady. This book is about strong women and healing – the writing of which saved my life.
Enjoy!
With Love,
Judy
J A Schrader
November 2007

a novel

by J.A. Schrader

Published by:
J.A. Schrader
10062 Sage Sparrow Court
Highlands Ranch, CO 80126
303-471-0644



*Registered - Library of Congress*
Schrader, J.A.
. . . and mother earth wept: a novel / J.A. Schrader. — 1st edition

ISBN: 0-9676464-0-5

Cover design by Nick Zelinger of NZ Graphics
Author photograph by Tate Brown

Printed in the United States of America
November, 1999

Acknowledgements

I used to think writers were the most powerful, smartest people that ever lived. All of our history is available to us because someone wrote it. Our journeys to other worlds and some of our favorite people were introduced to us in books. After completing this labor of love, I discovered that writing the book is the easy part. After the writing, the real work begins. There are many friends, family members and professionals that I would like to thank.

My family has always been my greatest source of support and my friends my personal cheerleaders, without whom I would not have been able to complete this book. I dedicate this to them. Specifically, I would like to list the following people who gave resources and endless hours of time:

Dan Mason for giving me permission
Rob Wendels and to Heather Schrader for providing the resources and opportunity to discover the real discipline of writing
Sue Brock for editing and English lessons
Maureen Christensen who encouraged me to write *MY* story
Pat Sladek who champions creativity in all of God's creatures
'Wednesday's Women' – you know who you are
Maureen Van Damme, Anne Nicholas, Janiece Anderson and Tina Pyle for edits, suggestions, and encouragement

First, last and always – to my husband, Ray, who read it, argued about it, edited it, and encouraged it. To my children who never doubted I could do it and always loved me exactly as I am. To my brothers and sisters, and to our parents, for giving me the greatest gift of all – the family.

Mamma, this one's for you.

*Mankind had his way with her*

*Her dysfunctional immune system became even weaker*

*World-watchers were prohibited from interceding,*

*as had been done throughout man's age*

*Now the Gods allowed man to reap what he had sown*

*And natural consequences set into motion*

*The catastrophic events that ushered in her baptism . . . again*

*She was forgiven for her sins . . . and mother earth wept*

## *Chapter 1*

The red Ford Mustang purred as she pulled into 7-Eleven at Speer Boulevard and Zuni.

"Hey, Jazz." He loved to call her by her *other* name to remind her that *he knew her when*. He worked the toothpick in his mouth and ogled her as she walked down the aisle.

"Class this morning, huh, Jazz? You know, you ought to quit smoking these things," he said, handing her the carton of Camel filters. "They're really bad for you."

She quickly paid and walked toward the door, fumbling in her purse for keys.

"Whoa, lady! Watch where you're going."

Two strong hands caught her shoulders and she looked up into laughing green eyes. Tall, rugged, cowboy hat, faded Levi's, worn boots and a pinch of smokeless in his lip. And that must be his horse idling away with the rifle in the back window, she thought.

"Well, what's the verdict?" he said, with an accent she couldn't identify – slightly British – not even close to real.

"I think you should get a different accent! Excuse me," she said, flipping her long blond hair and brushing past him. Damn! He even smelled good!

Getting into her car she put the Mustang in reverse, cut the wheels too hard and gunned it right over the rubber trash barrel with the swingy top. Slamming it into first, she roared out of the driveway as the cowboy laughed at her through the glass doors.

"I guess I showed him. Boy, was he nice looking." Now she was irritated that she hadn't stayed to strike up a conversation. "Well, I can always go back and run over the trash barrel again," she laughed. "That would impress him."

She pulled onto Speer and headed toward Auraria campus, satisfied she had dismissed him properly.

Her thoughts turned to school. Today was her last class before graduation in January and a bachelor's degree in Sociology. It had been a long four years.

Levi was already eleven years old. He was her sanity, her insanity, her boss, her love and her buddy. Yes, it was a sick dependency on her only child, but she knew that she may never know the love of a man again and was satisfied to feel the love for her child. It was hard financially, but the two most satisfying things she had ever done were to be Levi's mom and to stick it out in school.

After graduation they were moving to Albuquerque where she had accepted a high paying job with a big corporation. Two weeks between graduation and her hire date would be plenty of time for a short vacation to the reservation in Dulce, New Mexico, to validate him to his tribe – Jicarilla Apache. Levi was born in the same adobe room as his father. She wanted him to feel the pride of his people and know he belonged. His first words were memories of another time and she wanted him to know where the memories began. Shivering, she remembered her dream. The memory was morbid and barbaric with a menacing warning to protect her son. She pushed the flames and evil images away.

Speer was jammed, as usual. By 9:30 the traffic should be thinned out, but they were improving the road again. Should have stayed in the other lane, she thought, waiting for turning trucks to back up and get on with it. She waved at the girl holding the red flag, remembering her days as a flagger.

Science class started at 10:00 and it was only 9:40 – plenty of time. Today they would get their final grade. She was reminded of what Professor Nevens had said last Thursday; "You won't want to miss our guest speaker next week, if you want to get a passing grade in this class."

Must be a personal friend of his, she thought cryptically.

Driving to the farthest space in the student parking lot she saw the cowboy's horse parked a couple rows away – taking up two spaces. "Darned cowboys," she laughed. "How did he beat me here?"

She entered the classroom rummaging in her purse for a pen and heard, "Whoa, lady! Watch where you're going." The belly laugh she only saw through the 7-Eleven glass doors rolled through the classroom, bringing a bright rose color to her face.

"Well, I run into you again." Extending her hand as a sign of truce, he shook it firmly and long. Oh, he is nice to look at, she thought.

"Professor Ian Jayne, from Sydney, Australia, and the pleasure is all mine," he said, bowing deeply with hat in hand.

"Jane Jayne," she blurted.

"Oh, damn!" she said, as embarrassment burned her face again.

“I’m sorry. I’m Jane Abigail Zerlich. I apologize for my lack of respect for someone with such a wonderful name." She curtseyed in a mock show of subservience. "I am pleased to meet you and dying to know why you’re in my sociology class."

She loved the bantering, sarcasm and humor and couldn't wait to dissect this whole morning and relive every playful word. Her energy level was high and she was vibrant with his undivided attention.

Today she ignored the *too tall and too big* label she'd assigned herself. She'd worn her black leggings and white sweater, which accentuated her long legs and big bust. She was in the spotlight, and for once was comfortable there and wanted to stay.

As she started to say something clever, his attention was diverted to Professor Nevens who clutched his head in both hands, reeled forward and slammed face-down on top of his desk.

Professor Jayne raced toward him jumping over rows of chairs with the agility of an athlete. A deafening crash shook the building, hurled window glass the length of the classroom and knocked Jane to the floor. The next explosion was much closer and Jane desperately tried to get up, pushing chunks of glass farther into her palms and knees. Painfully, she pulled a jagged piece of glass from her calf and blood seeped through her leggings.

"Hold still. Don’t try to walk until it quits bleeding," said Professor Jayne, as he took a bandanna from his pocket. “Tie this around your leg. And stay put!”

Unable to shake the stunned feeling that enveloped her, she obediently tied the bandanna and hobbled to retrieve her purse.

Professor Nevens’ still form slumped over his desk – his lifeless eyes staring across the room. The student teacher lay on the floor clutching her stomach and Jane knew she was dead. The new boy with the pacemaker sat propped against the wall. There wasn’t a mark on him, but his eyes were open and fixed. Classmates fled in terror.

Another explosion – this time farther away. Jane knew they were under attack, but by what? Who was the enemy?

"My God, Levi! I’ve got to get to my car.” She tried to run, but the pain stabbed at her calf. “Damn!” Desperate to escape, Jane stumbled blindly into Professor Jayne. For all his heroic efforts, he too, looked on the edge of shock.

"I have to get my jacket and backpack," he said. "Wait right here, don't move. Don't go anywhere." He looked at her eyes, for some recognition of understanding.

"But I have to find my son." Her voice sounded foreign and

distant. She was about to lose her grip. He led her outside the door where she gratefully sat on the sidewalk.

"I'll help you find him if you'll wait for a few minutes." He quickly assessed her bandaged calf. "You'll need help with that leg."

"Okay," she said, strangely relieved. “I’ll wait.”

Racing back to the room, he rummaged through his backpack. Lifting Professor Nevens to a sitting position, he grabbed the leather pack under the desk and quickly surveyed its contents. He rummaged through drawers, taking papers and stuffing them into his backpack and Paul Nevens' leather pack. Satisfied he had what he wanted, he secured the packs and realized Jane was watching him through the open door. Her expression was uncomprehending. Good! There would be no need to explain.

"Let's get out of here," he said, helping her stand. Gratefully, she accepted, but why was he leading her away from the parking lot?

The sky was a pewter gray and plumes of smoke rose in all directions. Currigan Hall, which occupied a full city block, was engulfed in flames. What happened? Was it the end of the world and she was still alive to see it?

The need to run overpowered her as the panic rose. This stranger was forcing her away from her only means of escape and he became the enemy. Why did he take Professor Nevens’ pack? She struggled from his grip as hysterical screams erupted from her throat and his powerful arms encircled her. They fell to the ground and she fought him until exhausted.

"Please listen,” he said, gasping for air. “I can explain what has happened. I've tried to warn people for months, but nobody believed me. Only Nevens. He knew." Professor Jayne was talking rapidly, unable to stop the pent up emotion spilling out. In spite of her fear she listened and tried to block out the reality of his words. Was he insane? Or was she, for believing?

Suzan stared out the window of the Amoco Oil warehouse. Memory of her argument with Jesse replaced any thought of work. The computer was down, phones were dead, and the electricity had been off all morning and she still had the fuel usage figures to enter.

Her head pounded. Jesse's accusations crushed at her temples and hot tears burned a familiar path down her flushed cheeks. She cautiously looked around hoping no one had witnessed her latest flood of emotions.

“Grab the Kleenex, get some coffee, clear your head and get back to work,” she ordered herself. Too late! Marion, Suzan's boss and closest friend was already coming to the rescue.

“Marion, it’s no big deal – I don’t want to discuss it.” She wanted her rage. She wanted to justify her anger – to seethe for awhile. She was being too abrupt, but didn’t care.

She started to pour more coffee when the pain seared through her temples and she dropped her cup, reeling blindly for something to steady herself. "My God, Marion, what’s happening?”

"Suzan? What's wrong?" She could hear Marion, but the pain became unbearable and she couldn’t answer, unaware that the screams slicing the air came from her own throat as the pain crashed through her skull.

Open your eyes, will the pain away, breathe deep, relax, she told herself. She focused on a cat running across the parking lot, drivers running from their rigs and the sun shining. The pain subsided as quickly as it hit her. Cloudless winter day, cool, crisp air, airplane falling from the sky.

"Falling," she whispered hoarsely. The aircraft headed for the empty field east of the building. "My God! It’s falling!" tore from her throat as she tried to run. Marion stood paralyzed at the window.

The impact of the plane crashing to the ground burst through the window in a blinding flash, hurtling the two of them into the wall like limp rag dolls.

Several minutes passed before Suzan regained consciousness. Blood ran into her eyes from a deep, ragged gash on her forehead. Broken glass formed myriad abstract shapes and liquid colors, mingling with the spilled green and pink mints, the red rose and the broken picture of her daughters. Ignoring the shards of glass on the floor, she crawled to Marion’s still form lying in the corner and felt for a pulse. Lifting Marion’s limp arms, she pulled her through the broken glass to find somewhere safe. Suzan froze as a second explosion violently shook the building. Fiery reflections danced wildly on the office wall and she ran to the window to see the black churning cloud of the burning plane rise in a surrealistic rage.

Strangely detached, as if viewing a scene in a movie, she heard other explosions and saw several boiling clouds of smoke . . . three . . . four? There could be other planes, as the flight path to Denver International Airport was directly over them. Where were the fire trucks, the ambulances and rescue teams?

Running through the warehouse to the loading dock to escape, she heard the truck drivers screaming as they raced toward her, “Go back! Go back!”

The plane’s shadow covered the ground as it closed in on the nearby holding tanks. The impact was blinding and deafening. A blaze of liquid flames showered the parking lot like molten rain. The drivers thrashed wildly as the fire reduced their burning bodies to fiery spots on the asphalt.

Fuel in the semi-trucks and cars exploded as the flames formed a solid curtain of fire. Suzan saw vague images running from wall to wall, frantically searching for the door. Choking on the smoke-filled-air, she stumbled toward the back exit of the warehouse toward the vague light of the open door and reached it just as the loading dock collapsed in a heap of molten metal. The cool, crisp day turned into an inferno and Suzan fell to the ground fighting for breath until she felt her lungs would burst.

It was easier to breathe on the ground and after several minutes she stood, supporting herself on an old red station wagon. Where were her coworkers? How many of them got out and how many were still trapped forever in the pyre that had been their work place? "Oh, Marion," she whispered softly, vaguely remembering.

The macabre scene jolted her into false celebration. She was out! Alive!

The quiet neighborhood that bordered Amoco looked like a battlefield. People tried to put out fires with hoses that only trickled, as others gazed skyward in shock. Vaguely aware of the people, the voices, and what they were saying; phones down . . . no electricity . . . no water . . . cars won't start. All she could think was . . . I'm out . . . I'm alive.

Sobbing and shaking uncontrollably, she was freezing, even though she was singed and seared by the heat of the explosions. "I hope the police have a blanket with them. It's so cold." She was talking out loud and knew it, but the sound of her own voice was reassuring. "Where are the police? They should be here by now." she murmured.

She sat on the ground at the edge of the parking lot of the local elementary school where teachers lined-up outside with the children, fire drill style. Several people fiddled with battery cables, trying to start cars. What could have happened that prevented every car from starting?

Blood covered her pink cashmere sweater and hands. Her blood? Standing unsteadily, she looked at the reflection in the window of the red station wagon and saw a dark and eerie wild woman. She put her hands to her face and watched the image mimic her. There was a long ragged gash over her eye. Blood trickled down seared skin and into her long, singed hair. She was scary.

The sun cast muted clay shadows as it pried through the thick smoke cloud. She was roused from numbness as loud arguing erupted from teachers, children cried for their mothers, and they all became aware that the police weren't coming. A teacher pleaded with her to take the children who lived in the same direction she was going. Suzan's thoughts turned to her two daughters, Mira, in ninth grade, and Jacinth, in seventh. She prayed someone was at school to help them and agreed to walk with the four children, even though she felt light headed and dizzy. Soon, there were only two. She single-mindedly forced herself to continue. Physical shock did its magic and protected her; she didn't feel the pain from the deep cut on her forehead or the dehydration clawing at her throat and eyelids, leaving her tongue dry and skin hot.

Obsessed as she was to find Mira and Jacinth, she was drawn inside Pablito's, the little neighborhood grocery that had been there forty-three years. Dark inside, it took awhile for her eyes to adjust. Several young boys pried the meat locker with crowbars. A kaleidoscope of broken glass covered the floor. She gawked at bare shelves as if searching for items on a grocery list. Broken bottles of mayonnaise and ketchup lay in lumpy puddles with broken eggs, and tortillas with footprints – like Salvador Dali paintings – everything melted from its proper place. She froze, staring at the tall image reflected in the glass of the empty juice cooler. It frightened her. The watch on her wrist mocked her – Thursday, 9:47am, December 9. "It can't be right," she mumbled. "That was a lifetime ago." Time. A Lifetime. "Time – life," her parched throat tried to speak, her head throbbed and her vision blurred.

A loud victory shout erupted from the boys as they pushed the doors of the meat locker open. She automatically moved toward the sounds, stood at the dark space of the opened locker and felt the cold air enclose her.

Laramie Lea Zerlich lay frozen under her desk listening to screams coming from somewhere down the hall. Remembering the terrorist attack at the Los Angeles Airport and the whacko that bombed the Empire State Building, she didn't know whether to stay put, or bolt and run. Had terrorists attacked the building and were they now searching for hostages? She waited. Another explosion – further away this time – and another. "My God, what the hell is happening?"

She grabbed her purse and ran down the hallway to the fourth floor lobby where Corinne lay slumped over the reception desk. Laramie gently lifted her head. Beautiful, old Corinne – so full of soul and daring life to show her something she hadn't already seen. Her wise old eyes stared without life.

She ran to the elevators to escape the building and heard a woman's voice, crying for help. She moved closer to the walls and knew the cries came from the elevator shaft. How many floors below? She tried to open the doors, but they wouldn't budge and she kicked them in frustration. The screams became louder.

Laramie searched for something to use for leverage to pry the door. There – in the psychiatrist's office, the planter on the stand. Disregarding the shrink's twisted body blocking the door, she forcefully pushed it away and dumped the planter. She pried the elevator doors open with the wrought iron planter base and wedged her body between them using the strength from her legs and back to slowly open the doors. The elevator was stuck between the first and second floors. She ran down the emergency exit stairway to the first floor and pried the door. The terrified girl saw her and passed into a dimension of fear-induced insanity and couldn't grasp that Laramie was trying to help.

"Please don't hurt me. Let me out. I promise I won't tell. Please let me out."

"I want to help you. Please – I won't hurt you. You can come out now." Laramie tried to talk her out of the corner, but the girl was trapped in another memory. Laramie climbed up onto the floor of the elevator and slowly moved closer to the hysterical girl. Before Laramie could stop her, she jumped from the elevator and disappeared through the broken glass of the front door.

The scene at 8th and Sherman was haunting; cars frozen in place between garland draped street poles and silent red bells that mocked the coming holiday. No radios blared, no horns honked, no sirens screamed. Eyes exposed terror and mouths gaped wide. She would never forget these first moments of understanding that everything was different. And people died. Smoke burned her eyes as she walked across Sherman to the parking lot.

Aggressive young toughs systematically rummaged through cars and purses as owners stood by in the stupor of shock. She knew it was dangerous. Then she heard the sounds - forlorn wails of confusion and terrified screams of fear.

Three teenage boys approached as she found keys, opened the driver's door and quickly got in and locked it. They laughed, mocking and mimicking her fear. "You punky, pricks," she yelled through the closed window. Mad at her own show of fear, she flipped them off in mock courage. This was how the little dick-heads make people afraid and rule the neighborhoods, she thought. She heard her mom chide her for referring to people as body parts. "But, damn! Some people are just body-parts!"

She knew her car wouldn't start, but wanted the coat and snow boots she kept in the trunk in case the weather changed, as it often did in Denver. She also remembered the emergency kit she'd re-stocked just last weekend, and her backpack with various notebooks, pens, probably a pack of cigarettes and a couple of Snicker's candy bars. What do people take with them when an emergency happens and they have to walk home? And why did she have to walk home anyway? Why wouldn't the cars start? No one ever told her how to prepare for something like this. And what was this?

A foreboding fear overcame her and unsummoned tears rimmed her eyes. Her body shook as the fear intensified, and tears washed silently down her face, leaving streaks of black mascara. "What the hell is going on?"

A fist pounding on her window brought her back with a jolt. "My God, you scared the crap out of me," Laramie shouted. Shielding the glare from the windshield she saw an elderly man motioning to roll down her window. He talked in bursts and held a wad of money in his shaking fist. She rolled the window down a crack and saw relief come to his faded eyes.

"Please, Señora." The old Indian spoke in halted gasps. "Take my Dominic to the church . . . three more blocks . . . I'll pay you . . . take him to his mother." Laramie saw the ashen gray face and the hand clutching his chest as he fell to his knees, slumping against the car door, spittle bubbling from his throat and spilling down his chin. She was horrified! This old man was going to die right in front of her. Struggling with the door to move his body away, she got out on the passenger side and quickly ran to him. He was already dead.

She saw the small boy half hiding behind the bus-stop bench carrying a tightly stuffed pillowcase. Tears rolled down his face as he ran to his grandfather. He looked about five years old. He pulled on the old man's coat sleeve. "Come on, Pappa, we have to go to the church. Get up, Pappa, get up," he cried, pulling the limp sleeve.

Laramie gently touched his shoulder, but he pulled away and kept tugging and shaking the old man's sleeve – the money still clutched in the bloodless hand. Laramie took the money and stuffed it in the boy's coat pocket. "Your mother will need this, Dominic," she said, and she took his hand. Dominic pulled away. He didn't want to leave his Pappa.

"Dominic, listen to me." She gasped! His eyes startled her. She expected them to be dark. Dominic's coloring was the same as his Pappa's except for his sad, ancient, cerulean blue eyes. "We have to go to the church to get your mommie so she can get your Pappa. Show me where the church is, Dominic. Good heavens, there must be twenty-nine churches in this square mile," she said absent-mindedly. Obediently, he pointed up 8th Street. "Good, let's go find your mommie."

Remembering the items in her car, she opened the trunk, took off her heels, put on her running shoes and grabbed the backpack, stuffing in the emergency kit, snow boots, and her purse. She put on her down jacket, the one she always took camping. "Damn! I left my leather jacket in the office." She stared at the building. "Too bad - I'm not going back in there."

"Come on, Dominic." Bending towards him she zipped up his coat. He was looking right into her with those blue eyes, frightened tears spilling down his cheeks. "Oh, honey, it's going to be okay." She hugged him close, his tears leaving huge splotches on her new silk shirt.

Dominic tugged her up Grant toward 9th Street. "I didn't know there was a church up here Dominic. Do you live close by?"

Running now, he hollered, "My mother lives at the church. I live at home with Nanna and Pappa."

I guess it's none of my business, thought Laramie. "I'll take him to his mother and they can go to wherever they live and I'll go where I live." She looked at her watch – still 9:47. "But that was hours ago."

People filled the tinsel decorated streets; some screamed, some prayed, many were in shock. Dogs ran together down streets and cats were high in leafless trees. "What's wrong with this picture," she whispered. Dominic ran ahead and stood at the door of an old chapel at 10th and Grant.

Many people went to pray at the altar of the Virgin Mary. Saints on stained-glass windows watched as Dominic guided Laramie by the hand to the very first row and sat beside a huge man, reeking of alcohol and oblivious to all around him. Rosary beads fervently passed between finger and thumb as candles softly glowed and whispered prayers rose in chant, supplicating God for mercy. She sat beside Dominic and whispered, "Where is your mother?"

His little brown fist pointed a finger toward the marble statue. "There," he said smiling. Laramie strained to see where he was pointing. It was obvious to her that he could see his mother. She stood up to get a better look, maybe behind the statue. "Pappa and Nanna bring me here every morning and every night to see my mother."

She stared at his words. Surely she misunderstood. It was too bizarre! She looked again at the statue. She looked at Dominic. He adored the statue with his eyes and Laramie knew that's who he called Mother.

"Okay, we can do this," she mumbled. "Let's go find your Nanna, Dominic."

"No," he said, with a remembering look. "Nanna couldn't wake up this morning. That's why Pappa was taking me to my mother."

Laramie felt panicky. "What do you mean, Nanna couldn't wake up this morning?"

The boy was getting very frustrated with her lack of understanding. "Pappa tried to wake up my Nanna, but she wouldn't wake up."

"Okay," said Laramie, to calm him. "And Pappa was taking you to your mother to take care of you?"

"Yes," he replied, with a don't-you-get-it look on his face.

She did get it, but it was unbelievable and she didn't want it. "Well!" she looked around at the growing crowd. "Do you know anyone else here?"

"I know everyone here," he said, looking from face to face. "These are all my aunts and uncles."

"Oh, my God," she said out-loud, looking at the drunk man who stared at her from blood-shot eyes as if she were an evil demon.

"Dominic, let's go to your house," she said, trying to sound cheerful.

"I can't go back there," Dominic whispered. "Pappa and Nanna aren't going to live there anymore and I have to live with my mother now. Pappa is going to live with his mother, too. That's what he told me – he did," said the frustrated boy, trying to convince her.

She couldn't believe it! How in the world did an old man and old woman convince a little boy that a statue of the Virgin Mary was his mother?

"What in God's name were they thinking of? And where the hell is his mother, anyway?" Lifting her gaze upward, her voice ripped from her body in an angry outburst. "And what am I supposed to do with him now?"

Dominic took her hand, and with those clear blue eyes, looked into her face and said matter of factly, "If you don't have a mother, my mother will take care of you."

"Yea, well when does she make the peanut butter sandwiches? I'm starved." She grabbed his hand and angrily headed for the door almost tripping over the drunk's legs.

The air was cool outside and her head began to clear. Dominic stood very still beside her. Kneeling in front of him, she asked, "Do you want to come home with me?"

"Pappa said my mother would find me a new mother today." He placed his small hands on her cheeks and bravely asked, "Are you going to be my new mother?"

That was it – the floodgate burst and the tears flowed. Pulling him to her so he wouldn't see the heartbreak in her eyes, she tearfully choked, "I need to find my mother, too." She sobbed as she held him, there, on the steps of the church. They weren't an odd sight. People were in the streets and on the sidewalks – some to find solace, others to wreak havoc on the weak. As Laramie and Dominic left the church the robe shrouded preacher-man stood on the corner of 10th and Grant, lamenting the end of the world. Maybe he was right.

Everyone talked of airplanes falling from the sky, of the many explosions and fires. A doctor from nearby Denver General shared the scene of death when the electricity went out. Life machines stopped supporting, surgery halted and many died. A policeman told what happened at the jail; those behind the lock-up doors at 9:47 were still locked up, including guards, lawyers, clergy and staff – all trapped behind silent doors. Silent. The city itself was in shock – a scene that every survivor would tell over and over for generations to come.

Whether they believed in God or not, everyone prayed and pleaded that loved ones be alive. It's hard to remember that there is a plan, whether we acknowledge it, approve of it, or even care.

The devastated city confirmed what Professor Jayne tried to tell her. Jane knew life would never be the same and she was lucky to be alive. But why did he stay to help her? She said a silent prayer that Levi was still alive, too. Last night's warning dream returned. Why did it want recognition? She had to find him and protect him.

"Where is your son?"

"At school, about two miles from the 7-Eleven where I ran into you this morning."

"Embassy Suites, is near there. I'll grab my clothes from the room and . . . damn!" He pulled the electronic lock card from his pocket. "This thing won't do me any good now. Let's get your son and then we'll figure out what to do."

This is madness, she thought. I met this man only hours ago, and now everything's different and he's deeply involved in my life.

"Don't question madness, fate, or divine intervention," he replied.

"Did you say that out loud?" She was shocked. "It felt like we're talking to each other's minds."

"It's probably a phenomena of the energy field. It won't last long if that's the case, so enjoy it while you can," he joked. "But, now would be a perfect time to renew your belief in God."

"God?" What did God have to do with this? Talk of God always evoked anger from Jane, probably because she blamed Him for everything. From the things that happened in her own life, right down to all the tragedies in the world. That is - if there really is a God! And if there is, why does He allow suffering, death and cruelty to happen to the very creations He professes to love so much? Funny, how in desperation, her foxhole prayers always started with, *God, please*.

Jane suddenly remembered the sleeping bag and backpack in the car, since last weekend. What else was there that she might need? The backpack contained Levi's fishing pole, windbreaker, and high-top tennies, her canteen and a couple of peanut butter and jelly sandwiches. A cloudburst chased them off the lake early and a hamburger at McDonald's had soothed the disappointment of the short fishing trip.

"Professor Jayne, I have to get Levi's things from my car." She was anxious about Levi and hated the idea of backtracking, but knew she would never go back to the city.

"No more *Professor*, please. Call me Ian. I need to get my rifle, too," he said, angry with himself for not remembering earlier.

Fear stricken faces hurried by. Jane felt their fear and fought to keep it from becoming her own. A phenomena of the energy field? It was terrifying!

When they reached the parking lot, Jane understood why Ian had steered her in the opposite direction. Cars loomed with open hoods, students and staff stared dumbly, unable to comprehend why every car was dead. Bodies lay in the parking lot and slumped over steering wheels. Looters ran from car to car shaking door handles, snatching blankets and jackets, and forcing watches from wrists and rings from dead fingers. "My God, what happens to people?"

She opened the trunk and grabbed the sleeping bag and backpack. Grimacing at the week-old sandwiches and wrinkled apples, she was about to close the trunk when Ian appeared with his rifle slung over his shoulder, as well as a leather belt with neatly arranged bullets. Ian's backpack and Professor Nevens' leather pack were stuffed tight so several boxes of rifle shells were dumped into Levi's backpack.

"Save those," he said, pointing to the stale sandwiches and dying fruit.

"You're kidding," she said, lowering the trunk. Catching the lid, he snatched the sandwiches and apples and stuffed them in Levi's backpack.

"Trust me," he said, matter of factly. "They'll taste great to somebody. I've spent years thinking of this, and I hope I haven't overlooked any possibility. I didn't think it would happen so soon and I'm not as prepared as I hoped to be. Although, I don't know how anyone could have planned for this, no matter how much warning there was. I knew whenever it did happen, I'd be in exactly the right place to do what I needed to do, and it looks like you're it, lady."

"Is that why you pack your rifle half-way around the world with you?"

"No, actually, I've just come off a rather pleasant moose hunting holiday in Canada. I'm pleased as dinkum to have it with me now, though."

Four young men began circling, but Ian anticipated their plan and quickly shoved his packs to Jane and cocked the rifle. "Just walk slowly. I'm right behind you." They were not prepared for Ian's quick action and steady glare. "Well, get on with it!" he shouted. The young men backed away, not willing to die for the coveted gun.

Ian snapped the safety on, saw the tears streaming down Jane's face and put his arm around her, silently vowing to stay until she and her son were safe. She would never forget the comfort felt in that moment of silent communion.

*God, please* help me stay alive, she secretly prayed, and Ian gently squeezed her shoulder.

Who was this man who so abruptly became a part of her life? Or was he just passing through? It felt as though she had known him forever, but she only knew his name and that he was somehow aware of what was happening. No wonder they hadn't believed his warnings. Who wants to hear that life as they know it will stop? But that wasn't entirely true, something else happened, not all life stopped. What stopped? Time? Was time standing still?

"I'll bet Big Ben in London is standing still too," she said.

"What did you say about Big Ben?"

The puncture wound in her calf throbbed. She needed to rest. She needed a cigarette. Jane sat down on the curb as silent figures walked past. Ian sat beside her and lit them both a Marlboro from his shirt pocket, aware of the shadowy eyes darting to his rifle. He knew their fear and clutched it a little closer.

"I said, I'll bet Big Ben is standing still, too."

Sadness engulfed Ian. He wanted to be six years old again so he could cry and his mother would hold him in the old acacia rocker his father had made. He wanted to be back in Australia, the land he would never see again. An overwhelming grief and feeling of failure enveloped him.

He and Paul Nevens had researched the information together. The latest figures were in Paul's leather pack. They planned to compare their data after class this morning and take the evidence back to the science exposition in Sydney. There was only one more stop to make, the Seismic Activity Center in Boulder. He failed to pinpoint when it would happen. Everything boils down to a mathematical equation and Ian couldn't prove it mathematically. If he had just come to Denver one week earlier! Then what? If he had convinced a million scientists could anyone have done anything to stop it? No! The answer was no! Time ran out for man to change the course he had so recklessly taken. Man made his choices and earth obeyed. Simple! She didn't have a choice. But it didn't change how he felt at this moment.

Jane felt the weight of his extraordinary grief and put her arm around him. All pretense of self-consciousness disappeared as the common bond of grief united them. She didn't ask any more questions without answers. She knew their paths were bronzed together somewhere in time and everything was different. That was then, and this is now. THIS is how it is now.

"You're right about Big Ben," he said. "Time is standing still in London, too."

Levi! "My God, I've got to find Levi!" Jane jumped up and ran blindly through people milling about in shock. Ian grabbed the packs and chased after her. Speer looked like a parking lot. The awesome scene at the I-25 overpass paralyzed her.

Ian, panting to catch his breath, followed her transfixed stare. Cars, semi's, limousines and trucks, all assumed permanent places eight lanes across, as far as his eyes could see. A mournful chorus resonated as anguished survivors wailed at the death surrounding them.

Ian stood beside Jane allowing her to drink in the sight, knowing she needed to believe what he told her to survive. Words alone could not convince her, but this scene would live in her memory forever. A fierce cloak of devastation hung on the city. Fires burned and smoke-filled clouds filtered the sun lending an eerie rose colored haze to the air. Her pain-filled eyes told him she believed. The reality was harsh. Gently guiding her away, he knew this was only the beginning of the harsh realities to come.

"Where is your son?"

"What?"

"Your son," he repeated. "Where is he?" Ian looked at her pupils. "You're still in shock." He gently guided her to sit on the curb as people hurriedly passed by them – away from the city.

"Shock – yes, it's shocking."

"Where is your son?" he repeated to the terrified eyes that couldn't quite remember. "At school?"

"Yes! Yes, Levi's at school," she said excitedly.

Ian unwrapped the peanut butter and jelly sandwich from Levi's backpack. "Here, eat this and chew slowly."

"Damn!" I couldn't chew this fast if my life depended on it. I can't eat this - no more – please."

"Suit yourself," he answered as he ate the rest in two bites.

She obediently took a bite of the wrinkled apple Ian offered. "I didn't think I'd be the one to benefit by this old wrinkled-up thing."

"Chew slowly, there's plenty of time. When you're ready, we'll go find your son."

"Evee and Red live just a couple of miles from 7-Eleven. They watch Levi if I'm not at home when he gets out of school. I think I can handle it now," she said, tossing the apple core. "Let's go find Levi."

Looking at this man holding her hand and definitely in charge, she noticed again, his broad shoulders, his serious countenance, and his intense hazel-green eyes. She wasn't very often wrong in her male assessments, but he was more a man than any she had known, cowboys included, real or imagined. And there had been a few.

As they neared the 7-Eleven, more people flowed onto Speer toward downtown. Each wore the hollow mask of worry and fear with a definite, singular destination toward home and terror in their hearts for what they would find there.

The store was nearly empty. Shelves were toppled and empty cold case doors gaped open. No more vitamins, jerky, or chocolate Santa's lined the pay counter. The clerk lay on the floor with eyes staring, toothpick still tightly clenched in the crooked sneer on his face.

As Ian and Jane approached Navajo Street they saw Red standing just inside his motorcycle shop, *Two Wheelers*. Red's huge body filled the darkened frame of the doorway. A menacing figure without the shotgun, nobody would dare cross the threshold of his shop with that gun in his hands. Relief shot through his eyes and something else that Ian couldn't identify quickly vanished, replaced by immediate distrust of the stranger holding Jane's hand.

"Where are you taking this big, ugly guy?" The two men sized each other up, neither missing a thing in the other's glare. He sure didn't look like a baby-sitter to Ian. Red was eyeing Ian's rifle and Ian knew he was scheming on a way to make it his own, one way or the other.

"Oh, for God's sake, Red," started Jane, but Ian interrupted.

"We're trying to find her son, Levi."

Red's face softened at the sound of Levi's name. All the bikers liked the *Little Guy*. Red especially, because Levi's father and he had been partners, clubbers, brothers.

Red finally broke the locked eyes between the two, and to Ian's surprise, offered him his hand. "Any friend of Jane's is a friend for life. If you're trying to help Jane and the Little Guy, I owe you because they're my responsibility."

Red took a step outside and the filtered sun streamed into the shop and settled eerily on the two bodies lying neatly side by side, covered with the soft deer hide that usually hung on the wall behind the counter. Jane didn't have to be told who they were. A loud gasp escaped her throat as she lunged forward. Red and Ian both blocked her from entering the shop. She struggled against their hold and turned to Red with enraged tears streaming down her face.

"Who did this? Who would do this to them?" Jane demanded.

Red's eyes filled with tears too, he thought they'd all been spent. "No one did it to them. It happened right in front of me and I couldn't do a damn thing to stop it." The tears flowed freely down the giant's face and they could almost see his big heart breaking. "You know Evee had that heart murmur and Tad was born with one too. Whatever happened this morning was just too much for them. Tad died first and she carried him into the shop this morning, right after the electricity went out. I caught her just before she fell. She was still clutching Tad. Didn't loosen her grip on him one bit. You know how much she loved that boy. She died in my arms." The sobs came unabashed now, and he didn't apologize. He'd held her in his arms as the life drained from her body. "You know I loved that boy as if he were my own, just like the Little Guy."

It was true. Tad and Levi were Red's own blood as far as he was concerned, and he would have also died for their mothers. Jane always knew she could count on Red to be Levi's surrogate father, since he didn't have one anymore.

After the death of Levi's father, Red and Jane tried to be together and it just didn't work for them. Jane offered to move out of the big house, but Red wouldn't hear of it. He moved from the big bedroom to the smaller one next to Levi's. Red didn't blame her, always loved her, and always accepted her and the boy as his own to care for. And Jane let him. He was a good man.

Then Red met Evee. She came in with her son to buy a part for her broken down Harley and before she left, she had a new bike, a new man, a new home, and Tad had a new father. Red knew God sent Evee and Tad to him. Evee breathed life into a dead part of him and from that first day he worshipped the ground she walked on.

Jane and Levi moved out of the big house and into the little house, as Red and Evee insisted they stay close. All Red's clubber brothers accused him of having two women and felt he should give one up to the club. They only made that mistake once. There wasn't a problem once the rules were understood. Rule Number One: Evee was Red's woman and Tad was his son; not stepson, not Evee's bastard kid, but Red's son. Rule Number Two: Jane was Red's woman and Levi was his son. Everyone knew that Red killed Levi's father – accidentally, but dead just the same. Rule Number One was a matter of the heart. Rule Number Two was a matter of honor – an understanding between brothers. The death of Levi's father was never discussed. That's just how it was.

Red said a good woman stood next to the saints in heaven, and nobody messed with his women. He made Rule Number Two for Jane's sake. He was proud that she wanted to change her life and sad too because that meant someday she and Levi would probably leave him. He always knew it would be okay when it happened.

What he shared with Evee was a gift. "Rare," he said. "When it happens – grab it, hold on for dear life and never let it go." And it had been one hell of a ride for them. They lived life every minute – Tad and Levi, too. They went everywhere with Evee and Red. No babysitters for his boys. Red was somewhat of an enigma; a true brother biker – with innate traditional values who believed a mother should raise her own kids. He was proud when Jane decided to go back to school and it was just natural for Levi to stay with Red, Evee and Tad, when Jane was at school. Evee insisted and the boys were thrilled. Levi thrived in the safe-haven of their home and he and Tad were treated as brothers.

Oh Levi! How could she tell him Tad and Evee were dead? Jane sobbed in Red's arms, as she knew Evee had just hours before. The big man's arms enveloped her and absorbed her pain. He was back again – composed – solid.

Ian witnessed the scene with true compassion for Red's pain and knew he would have given his own life to save the boy and woman.

Levi was at school when all the lights went out and his teacher fell to the floor. Some of the kids started bleeding and screaming and he didn't know where to go or what to do. An explosion boomed through the school, shattering windows and knocking jars of tempera paint from shelves. Levi ran to escape when the Principal, Mrs. Thomas, grabbed him by the shirt.

"Levi, please stay. It's safer here than it is outside."

"But, some kids have blood in their eyes and coming out their nose and mouth."

Mrs. Thomas shook her head in understanding, trying to calm him. "Go in all the classrooms and shout as loud as you can for everyone to gather in the gymnasium. We can help everyone get home." She had to get the remaining children and teachers away from the frightening death masks that stared in every room.

Levi was on a mission and it helped to avert the panic and fear that gripped him. He watched Mrs. Thomas comfort and calm the kids and teachers, as they assembled in the gymnasium.

Levi loved Mrs. Thomas. Of course he loved his mom and Evee first. He spent a lot of time in the principal's office and sometimes would be disruptive in hopes of being sent to see her. He didn't know that Mrs. Thomas had known his father and that she had loved him, too. Levi never talked about him. No one did. It was Mrs. Thomas who'd arranged for Jane to receive several grants to pay tuition and other expenses to get her through school.

Mrs. Thomas loved Levi, too. He was so much like his father. Every time she saw him it was a reminder that she could have had a son like him, but she'd made her choice and now must be content to be happy for them. And she truly was. Levi loved to talk about his mom and gave Mrs. Thomas regular updates on how she was doing. Mrs. Thomas knew that change comes with the gut-wrenching, blood-sweating pain of defeat and the sweet taste of surrender when the struggle ends, and she knew Jane had survived the struggle.

The thought of never seeing Levi again broke her heart. She didn't know what was happening, but knew everything was different. She agonized about letting him go and thought of taking him with her, but she loved him too much to hurt him.

She did not want to encounter Jane today. She wanted to remain her anonymous benefactor. Emotions were too high and she didn't want Jane to remember the other time they had recognized the grief in each other's eyes. She wanted a clean slate, with nothing to cast a shadow on the good will that existed between them as Levi's mom and the Principal, Mrs. Thomas.

The morning wore away and only a couple dozen children remained. Tension and fear reached its threshold as the remaining teachers disappeared to find their own children. Mrs. Thomas decided to remain with the unclaimed children in the gymnasium.

She had no husband, she had no child, she had made her choice. She knew that some of the parents commuted quite far and would not be able to walk the distance in one day. The children would be safe here. There was food in the cafeteria, blankets in the nurse's office, and the children had their jackets. They would stay warm bundled up in the teepee the fifth grade class had erected in the gym as a social studies project.

Time was drawing near to say goodbye to Levi. She watched him read a fifth grade reader to a kindergarten girl and other children began to calm and sit around the circle. He is a natural born leader – just like his father. When the story was over, five of the younger children were asleep and the room was calmed. She silently prayed for his future and hugged him with the longing of an empty heart. At this moment she deeply regretted her life choices.

Levi was happy to be near her heart and she smelled good, like his mom. She told Levi to get his bike and ride straight home as fast as he could.

At the bicycle rack he unlocked the bicycle chain. Evee and Red bought him the bike. It was identical to Tad's. Red welded images of a Harley gas tank on them, with orange and red flames shooting out. Leather streamers hung from the handlebars just like the ones on Red's motorcycle.

Three older boys stepped in front of Levi. One opened a knife with a flip of his wrist and stood spread legged like in the karate movies Levi loved to watch. Levi turned the key, the chain came off and in one smooth movement he ripped the knife away from the boy's hand with a precision and force that even surprised him. Not expecting resistance, the boys stood gape-mouthed. Mrs. Thomas exploded from the classroom door brandishing a flagpole, charging straight at them and they scattered in defeat. Levi slipped the knife and chain into the pouch as Mrs. Thomas fastened his knapsack to the bike. "Hurry home, Little Guy. Hurry and find your mom."

Levi hopped on his bike and rode as fast as he could. He did not slow down, look back, or pay attention to the angry voices hollering, but he was not prepared for what he found at home. And it was just beginning.

Red caught him and Ian caught the bike as he tore around the corner. He reared his head back and looked at Red, then his mom, and buried his face in Red's neck as his body shook and tears soaked into Red's beard.

Red held him for a long time then handed him to Jane. "Here, Little Guy, take your mom home. I'll clear things out of here and be up to check on you soon."

Ian offered to stay and help haul boxes, and although Red wasn't much on accepting help, somehow he trusted this funny talking cowboy, and besides, he liked his rifle.

"If you could just help me get some of this inventory to the big house, the neighborhood can have the rest."

Of course, the first item of business was Evee and Tad, lying on the floor with the deer hide covering them. "I'll just take them up to the big house if you'll stand in the doorway, big and mean looking."

"I can give it a go."

"Yea, I'll bet you can."

Ian took his place in the door of the shop, allowing the big biker his grief, and honoring his privacy. Red disappeared through the back door carrying Evee down the alley, through Evee's rose garden, now sticks of remembrance for the cold winter day, through the kitchen door, down the dark hallway with the rose motif runner and into the bedroom.

Gently laying her on the bed they shared just last night, he performed the primal ritual of bathing departed loved ones, with water scooped from the toilet tank. He covered her with her favorite goose-down quilt and went back to the shop for Tad, repeating the process until mother and son lay clean in the bed, as peaceful looking as though taking a nap. There would be plenty of time to bury them after one last night in the comfort of the home they'd loved. And Red would have time to say goodbye.

The sounds came from far away – barely audible voices without words. A woman's voice became clear – "She needs stitches," and, "See if you can find some water."

A child's voice asked, "Did she say anything?"

Another voice – a man's, "Do you recognize her?"

The child again, "Gran, she's not from our neighborhood. This is the woman I told you about who walked with us from the school and helped us to come home."

"Ah," said the woman. "Madre de Dios. She is a mess."

Cold pressure on Suzan's forehead aroused her. "There now, let me help you. I just want to wash some of the blood and dirt from your face." Suzan's parched throat choked on the water offered as she gulped it down. "Ah, mi'ja, you were so close to the explosions." Suzan dazedly reached for something to help her stand. "Don't get up – not yet. You have a terrible cut on your forehead. This bandage will keep the dirt out and stop the bleeding." The woman tied the last knot and helped her sit on the nearby bench. Suzan's legs felt weak and leaden, and her head throbbed. She recognized the old woman and man as the owners of the store. The young boy was one of the children who had walked with her.

"We found you here on the floor." It was the woman speaking. "We asked some neighborhood boys to open our meat locker. When the electricity went out, we couldn't get the new door open. Darned electric door – we should have kept the old one."

The old woman was talking to no one in particular while rummaging through boxes in the dark room. "This will make you feel better," she said, handing Suzan a carton of orange juice. "Drink it slowly. There – that's good." Her head began to clear and she cried as images of death and fire returned.

The old woman rested Suzan's head on her heavy bosom and gently rocked and quietly told her how the explosions shattered the windows and her twin black labs both died. How strangers came and took things – things she would have gladly given them. How the neighborhood tough guys took all the money and medicine. She finally left her store and let people take what they wanted while she visited each neighbor to find many dead or dying.

"I have been left behind . . . God forgot to take me . . . but I've had many endings and many beginnings." Suzan heard her mother's voice comforting her through this old woman's body.

Walking outside together, the change of light momentarily blinded her. The smell of smoke hung heavy on the air, filtering the sun's rays. Had the whole city burned?

Standing in front of Suzan, holding her shoulders, the old woman looked deep into her eyes. "You talked about Mira, Jacinth and Jesse when we found you. You are stronger now. Go to them. You will help them survive this." Suzan looked into the pale eyes of the woman and again felt her mother's presence.

"God protect my children," she hoarsely whispered and the tears started. Immediately she thought of Jesse. Why did he always seem like one of her children?

*You're all my children.* The words were soft. Gentle.

Suzan's eyes darted to see who'd spoken and her knees buckled.

"Oh, honey – you're still so weak. Maybe you should stay awhile more."

"No," said Suzan, "I have to get home."

"Ah, yes. Vaya con Dios," said the woman, embracing Suzan for a long time. "I am an old woman and don't mind that I will not live much longer," she whispered. "God bless you."

While crossing the railroad tracks at 23rd and Market, unexpected tears filled her eyes and slowly trickled down dirty cheeks. Laramie could hear the children crying and knew their fear. She didn't know who they were, but they were close. They? How many? Why was the fear so strong now? Had she felt it earlier? What was happening to her? Where did the tears come from, and how did she know it was about children's fear? But she did know – she didn't know how, but she knew.

Dominic was also filled with questions. Pappa told him that questions and answers were never the same for each person. It depends on where you sit in the medicine wheel. Pappa said only he would know the answers to his questions, as they were for him alone. So he didn't ask Laramie for answers, just silently held her hand, trusting he was going the right way. Pappa said he would always be going the right way. He knew Pappa and Nanna were gone now, that aunts and uncles are everywhere, and you always know who your mother is. He knew that Earth Mother was sad sometimes because people didn't treat her with love – they forgot the way. Pappa and Nanna said he still understood the way when he was born. Pappa said that happens to all mothers' children . . . they forget the way. But children know. Then they forget.

Tears blurred her vision and she stumbled over the railroad ties. "Damn," she cried, brushing blood and dirt streaks across her black skirt. Her skirt was torn up the seam to mid-thigh and her nylons were shredded. Thank goodness her running shoes were in the trunk. Yes, thank goodness! Laramie believed that nothing happens by accident, and there aren't any coincidences, although she wasn't too sure about today. Now she was walking hand-in-hand with a five-year-old, blue-eyed Indian boy with a wisdom and acceptance she'd never experienced in a person – child or adult. Acceptance of life is one of those things she'd strived to acquire and was lucky to occasionally catch glimpses of it.

The quiet tears still flowed and fear from the child intensified – then she saw them – the children. They peered at her and Dominic through the diamonds of the chain-link fence. Large, fearful eyes. Staring. Waiting.

"Where's your mommy?" Fear stared back at her as she knelt to look in their large dark eyes. Looking past the girls, Laramie saw the black dog lying near a large outstretched body shadowed by the open door. Dried blood stained the wooden slats of the porch. "How many times will this scene be repeated?" thought Laramie, sadly.

Should she take the girls somewhere or wait with them for their father? "Where's your daddy?" She brushed ragged hair from the smallest girl's face. No answer. "Is he at work?"

Two small sets of shoulders hunched up in *I-don't-know* fashion.

"Does your daddy live here?" A negative head shake. "Do you have brothers? Grandparents? Anyone nearby?" No. Laramie opened the gate to go inside and find addresses, pictures, something to help identify them. Immediately the black dog guarding the body stood, growled, and barred its teeth, warning her not to approach. "Okay," she said, which seemed to satisfy him, as he circled his tail and assumed his original sentry position. It always amazed her that dogs circled their tails before lying down. Somewhere inside she knew it was a generational memory from the days of the tall grass when they circled the grass to flatten it down into an appropriate bedding area. It was curious, but they all did it.

This part of town was row houses with thin walls joining thin walls and small front yards enclosed in chain link fences. Knocking on the neighbor's door, she looked back at the children as Dominic slowly opened the gate and went inside the yard with the girls – the black dog didn't move. Laramie pounded again, calling into the dark house. She watched the girls and Dominic walk up the steps, around the body and the dog, and disappear in the shadowed doorway. Laramie ran back to the fence and the dog stood, again warning her she was not welcome. Must be a big-people thing, she thought. The children soon filed out with the girl's winter coats, boots, gloves, hats, and dolls – black, like them.

Seeing the shock on Laramie's face, Dominic quickly said, "They had to get their warm clothes so they can go with us."

"Go with us? Go where with us? If they go with us, how will anyone find them?" Dominic patiently looked into Laramie's eyes. Questions no longer had answers. She stuffed the children's boots, hats and gloves inside the backpack, and placed a quickly scrawled note with Suzan and Jesse's address under a rock inside the gate.

They all filed out, including the dog, so big and black that Laramie knew he was a Canadian Timber Wolf. Head hung low, he followed about twenty feet behind. Boy, if we don't look like a band of Gypsies, thought Laramie. My own heritage – Gypsies.

Gray bark clung to the wintered cottonwood trees arced over the banks of the South Platte River where green reeds refused to shed their color. It was seasonably mild, hard winter hadn't officially arrived yet. Laramie blessed the sun prying through the smoke filled air – it belied the cold nip that made noses run and eyes water. They passed others walking the river, but the black wolf warned all who saw them to beware.

Suspecting the children hadn't eaten since morning, she fished through the backpack for Snickers. The children crowded around to see what other treasures were inside and sure enough, they found four hawk tail feathers from her hike up Waterton Canyon. They were probably wild turkey or buzzard feathers, but she proclaimed them hawk feathers – *Messengers of the Gods* – and put one in each child's hair, as well as her own. "Now we look like real Gypsies," Dominic proudly announced.

Laramie would always look like a Gypsy, with or without the feather in her hair, the band of children following, or the black dog that looked like a wolf. Barely twenty-five years old, she had reached that mature young-woman place that allowed confidence to ripen and compliment the natural beauty of her long chestnut hair and large, wise, crystal-blue eyes. At 5'6", she wasn't as tall as her sisters, Suzan and Jane-Abbey, but all 130 pounds were exactly where they should be. Although all four of the Zerlich kids had naturally curly hair like their dad, even Laramie's sister's admired her gently cascading curls. When Laramie was around, women as well as men stopped to stare, and she didn't mind.

She saw herself clearly and liked who she was, secure in her femininity and womanhood. She knew how she felt about subjects from birth control and abortion to religion and politics. To say she was opinionated would be putting it mildly. But there was a price to pay. Most male egos couldn't tolerate her strong will and determination. She practically choked on words like, subservient, submissive, and obedient, and refused to be worn as an ornament, or be seen and not heard. She adamantly believed that the *right to liberty, freedom, and the pursuit of happiness,* meant women, as well as men.

While watching the children search for more treasures, she felt the empty space of yearning in her heart and knew there would be a man to love her exactly as she was, and they would have children, lots of children.

As they walked along the river they ate the Snicker's candy bars and even shared with *Black*, as Laramie affirmed the wolf's new name. Neither of the girls had uttered a word since found peering through the diamonds of the chain link fence.

"My name is Laramie and this is Dominic," she said, putting her arm around Dominic.

"What's your name?" She inquired of the oldest girl.

"Jen."

"Well, good, Jen – and what's your name?" She squatted down to look at the youngest girl – large black eyes staring back.

"Sara," answered Jen.

"Okay, Sara and Jen. How old are you?"

Jen held up eight fingers. "Sara's five."

"Great, Dominic and Sara are both five and Jen is eight."

"And what's your dog's name?" She looked from Sara to Jen, and they looked at each other like she must have forgotten already.

"Black," Jen and Dominic said in unison.

"No, not the name I gave him. What was his name before?" There was no reply, just three sets of eyes staring back at her.

"Okay, it doesn't matter, because now his name is Black. Reaching to pet the black wolf, she pulled her hand back as his eyes rolled – showing the whites.

Black suddenly froze in the trail. His head dropped, ears laid flat and a deep growl rumbled in his throat. Quickly turning, they saw the young man backing away, palms outstretched, slowly disappearing over the hill. "Well, okay, Black. Good dog! We can make friends later."

The smoke filled clouds stretched thin across the Front Range and the filtered sun cast a deceiving rosy hue on all it touched. The walk was long and the quick energy of the Snickers was soon replaced with weariness.

"Okay kids – I know you're tired, but we have to pick up our pace so we can get to Auntie Suzan and Uncle Jesse's before dark."

Daylight was quickly fading, but they didn't have much farther to go. The children were hungry and the hazy sun no longer took the chill off the air, as the little band of Gypsies and the black wolf reached the shopping center at 120th and Colorado Boulevard.

Dozens of silent forms carried armloads of groceries, hurrying by, lest they be mistaken for looters. Remembering the shopping she planned to do on her way home from work, she too chose to seize the opportunity and search out the items she needed. The children agreed to sit by the newspaper racks. They would be safe with Black.

As her eyes adjusted to the darkened store, she knew this would take all her courage. Dead bodies slumped over cash registers and lay in aisles. It seemed a sacrilege to step over someone's mother, brother or son. Did she really need the items? She shuffled through the dark shelves, thinking that tomorrow would be better, maybe the electricity would be back on, but something made her stay. She found feminine hygiene items, shampoo, vitamins, and picked up five cartons of cigarettes. Now, she felt like a looter, but dismissed it as necessity, even though she no longer smoked.

Fumbling through the dark, she found sacks for cartons of milk, eggs, butter, and several loaves of bread. She was getting greedy and berated herself, mentally trying to justify her actions, but knew there were no excuses and that she didn't care.

The children were waiting with Black, right where she had left them. After readjusting their loads, with each child carrying a sack, they headed north on Colorado Boulevard – only about a mile more to go.

It troubled Laramie that people just died. Like an inner explosion happened at the same time airplanes fell from the sky and watches stopped. Why did some die and others live?

Her mind wandered over the morning's events. Polo, her two year old Doberman, whined all morning as she did in the spring when an electric storm was coming, and Polo was never wrong. Her car acted up on the way to work – losing power, like the last sputtering from a dying battery. And the noises in her head started when she was on her way to work, again when she tried to call the mechanic, and just before the electricity went out – crackling sounds – like someone talking on a two-way radio. She wondered if she'd somehow heard other people talking? Did she just get a smaller dose of what killed others?

Relieved to see the opening in the fence, which surrounded the quiet suburban neighborhood, she led the tired children down the path between the houses as dusk cast its last whisper of light on their welcome destination. Dread smothered her as she stood hesitantly at the door.

"Auntie! We didn't know what to do! Where are my mom and dad? Patty and Tracy died at school and Mr. Davidson was bleeding from his mouth and nose, and Linda's mom had a heart attack. None of the flashlights work and there's no water." Both Mira and Jacinth bolted through the door and were talking at the same time, relieved, as they clutched Laramie.

"Whoa, slow down." She hugged the girls, entered the dark living room and dropped sacks, backpack and pillowcase to the floor. "Mira, get your mom's candles in the hallway closet, and, Jacinth, get the extra blankets your mom uses for camping. We'll get warm, and find something to eat while you tell me about your day."

Laramie searched outside. Black was curled in the far corner of the porch. "Good boy, I'll bring you something to eat."

Dominic, Jen and Sara stood silently huddled by the door. "Dominic, are you afraid?" asked Laramie as she knelt in front of them.

"I don't know where we are."

"Do you remember I told you we were going to my sister's house?"

"Yes, but now it's dark."

"Yes, it's dark, but you can still see me a little, and you can hear my voice, and you can touch me. See?" She softly spoke as she gently touched their faces and stroked their hair. "Do you feel me touch you Jen? Sara?"

"Yes," Jen whispered and Dominic hugged her neck.

"You won't leave us?" he whispered in her ear, his voice full of tears. "We won't have to find another mother?"

"No, you won't have to find another mother. I'll take care of you. You'll like it here and Mira and Jacinth will like you too, you'll see. Do you believe me, Dominic?"

"Yes. Everything is the right way, I remember now."

"That's good. Everything is the right way," she whispered, gratified by their trust.

"I could only find three candles, Auntie." Mira placed them on the kitchen table, the fireplace mantle, and the coffee table. The soft light from the candles lent a feeling of comfort to the chilly house but Laramie knew she would have to make a fire soon. Where were Suzan and Jesse and why was it taking so long for Suzan to get home? She should be home by now, unless . . . "God bless Suzan," was her silent prayer as she found cold spaghetti and cut up some apples.

Soon dinner was on the table, all the children knew each other's names and a cozy bed lay waiting. Mira designated a spot for each child, the smallest in the middle with Auntie Laramie and her on the outsides. "There's a mother in all of us," sighed Laramie, proud of Mira's ability to take charge and calm the children. She was glad she'd come here. It was the right thing to do – the right way, as Dominic had said.

Mira had turned fourteen in August, but her height gave the impression that she was much older. Everyone, including her parents, expected more from her. At 5'11" she was claiming her own beauty as the childlike roundness disappeared to make way for the chiseled features of the woman-child. Mira had always been a take-charge child. Now, she was eager to take charge and receive the praise from Auntie Laramie as reward.

It didn't take long for the spaghetti to disappear, apples to be eaten and sleepy heads to nod. Laramie, remembering the water in the toilet tanks, designated one bathroom for use during the night, but they couldn't flush. Catching the last drips of water from the taps, she wiped all the faces and hands and dressed them in sweatshirts and pants.

She brought wood from the garage and started a fire and the children were soon asleep. Finding a pair of Suzan's sweats, Laramie blew out the candles and snuggled under the blankets. She was exhausted. "God, bless Suzan and Jesse, Jane and Levi, Judd and Dani, and Mom and Dad," she whispered, allowing sleep to claim her.

Ian helped Red carry boxes of leather goods, clothing, metal work, glassware and motorcycle parts, back to the house and down in the basement where Red opened a hidden door. Red lit the Coleman lantern hanging on the hook for this purpose and Ian was dumbfounded. It was a concrete vault – at least 40' x 40' and filled with arms and ammunition. Red could outfit a small army from this room. Ian was speechless and the shock wasn't lost on Red.

"I'll tell you about it later."

Ian nodded numbly as they roamed through racks and boxes of everything from high powered rifles, revolvers, semi-automatic assault rifles, and he was afraid to ask what was in the boxes that weren't clearly marked.

"Only Evee and one man knew about this room. He was the man who helped me build it, and they're both dead now. I'll be damned if I'll tell the brothers. If they knew about it, they'd trade it all on the street for a twelve year old whore."

Ian was relieved when they walked out, the doors were secured, and he was on the outside with Red. Boy – a body left in there would stay forever – like an Egyptian tomb. Ian shivered with the thought and Red, recognizing the fear, slapped him on the back and laughed. "Let's go make a plan."

"Easy for you to say," shot Ian with relief.

Red and Ian went down the alley, through the rose garden, around the shared garage, and into the little house where Levi was asleep on the couch and Jane softly sang, "You are my sunshine, my only sunshine."

Red brought a six-pack of Coors Light in bottles from the concrete room and popped the lids on the kitchen drawer handle, handing one to Ian. Damn! An ice-cold beer!

"You make me happy, when skies are gray," sifted in to them as they sat in the dark kitchen, talking and drinking away the nightmare of the day.

Dark of night surrounded Suzan as she struggled to keep

focused. Today had been a long, hard journey – like walking through a different time. Shoulders silently bumped shoulders. Feet slowly shuffled – some hurried – all guided by an ancient inner force of homing. Fear was in all the eyes.

Why was it taking her so long to get home? She tried to quicken her pace, knowing that Mira and Jacinth were home alone. Jesse! Oh God! What if something happened to him? "Oh my God - no, no, no," she cried. "Don't let anything happen to Jesse." What if she never saw him again? "Oh God, no." What had they argued about? She couldn't even remember.

*"How important is it, really?"* The words were soft. Gentle.

"Who's there?" Dropping to her knees she crouched, eyes darting, quite expecting to see the culprit playing a cruel joke, trying to scare her. There was no one. She put her head to the cool concrete of the sidewalk and laughed until she cried. Feet hurried by – skirting around her – fear. "People will think I'm a loon, but what does it matter, really?"

She forced herself to continue. It would have been hard to tell where she was if it weren't for the stars shining so brightly. No lights streamed from kitchen windows or porches to light her path. Had there ever been so many stars before now?

Fighting the blackness that tried to overpower her, she strained to hear the words blowing on the night wind. "What?" she blurted, listening to see where the voices came from. She heard sobbing and cries for Mamma. The cries sounded like they came from a canyon, as they seemed to echo: *Mamma – Mamma – Mamma*. She remembered the child's voice calling Mamma in the dark. Yes – a child's cry – from a nightmare or fear of the dark. And she heard the laughing from the deranged mind that can no longer face the reality of the day – hysterical laughing that tries to stop, but cannot. And sometime in the night, Mamma picked her up and carried her home.

▮Flames dancing in the fireplace hypnotized her. The fire drew her in and she forgot about the cold, even though her body shook with chills. Soon, she slept the fitful sleep of the watch-guard, going into a shock-imposed dream-place while hearing reality from somewhere close.

She woke, startled by the sound of the front door opening and the wind gusting past the familiar figure standing there. The fireplace glowed as the wind brushed life into the dying embers.

Jesse Gant stood silently in the doorway, drinking in the familiar sight. It was as if nothing happened to this room. Cool white moonlight shone on the faces of those sleeping on the living room floor and his heart filled with relief. Thank God they'd survived!

He knelt close to Suzan where she lay curled in front of the fireplace and smelled the scent of smoke that still clung heavily to her hair and clothes. She heard his hard breathing and knew he had walked a long way. His trembling fingers brushed matted, singed hair from her face, cold lips touched her seared cheeks and his tears mingled with hers. She touched his lips and he pulled her close, unable to speak, just content to be in the familiar comfort of her touch.

How simple life becomes when time stops pushing the day. The moment grew long and tender, filled with gentle emotion.

It was dark when Jesse woke . . . and cold. He crept to the garage door and automatically flipped the light switch. "Damn!" The memory of yesterday quickly returned. Yesterday? He moved forward in the darkness, aided by the shaft of moonlight streaming through the glass panes. Standing at the window, he watched the stars and remembered how bright they shone while walking home last night.

Was it just yesterday that everything changed? He quickly grabbed an armload of wood and returned to the living room.

He banked the coals and when a warm blaze rose, hurried back to lie beside Suzan who still burned with fever and shook with chills.

## *Chapter 2*

In the summer of 1964, a camp was established for an inmate work crew designated to help with the backbreaking work of building a state recreation area five miles northwest of the small mountain community of Rifle, Colorado. The twelve inmates selected were brought from the prison in Canon City and were considered to be the least violent and most manageable within Colorado's penal system. The inmates and two staff members were housed in four trailers located by the site, which became Rifle Gap Dam. The workmanship displayed by the small crew was of exceptional quality and more projects were planned. It was good for morale, good for the State of Colorado, and good for Rifle's economy, whose small business opportunities suddenly escalated.

Kudos were in order for the originators of the idea. The camp was moved up-valley and within six years the inmate population grew to one hundred inmates and the staff increased to twelve. Soon, new fences stood proudly along highways, a water treatment plant was built, and Rifle Gap Dam was enhanced by inmate labor, complete with picnic tables, rest-room facilities, fire pits, drinking water, boat ramps, and scores of numbered camping areas, all at a nominal cost to the Department of Corrections and the State of Colorado.

As the increasing need for prisons escalated and the demand for cheap inmate labor grew, so did the facility's needs. By 1995, when Romalea Zerlich accepted the position of Senior Secretary, the minimum security prison housed one-hundred-fifty inmates, with a full staff of security officers, case management, facility coordinators, food services, special programs, secretary and warden.

Rifle Correctional Center was considered the *bastard child* of the Department of Corrections. It was never meant to become a real prison and only vaguely resembled one. There were no razor-wire electric fences or electronic lock-down doors, as in the newer, more expensively maintained prisons, and was still called *The Camp* by inmates as well as DOC personnel. When budgets were approved or denied and funds designated for the Department of Corrections were allocated, the facility at Rifle was always the last consideration for enhancements or improvements. It survived due to a willing staff more dedicated to living in the quiet town of Rifle than to the

Department of Corrections.

Roma enjoyed the fast pace at the prison. There was always some new intrigue; a new still discovered by the unmistakable reek of fermenting fruit, tattoo rigs found, or drugs confiscated on visiting day. Court would be held and inmates would be regressed from minimum to medium security, or, on fewer occasions, an inmate would escape, bringing the whole countryside to attention. Roma was good at her job and the pay exceeded what was normally available in the depressed economy of the small town. She enjoyed her fellow-workers, but hated their negative attitudes toward the inmates and their jobs. "What do you expect?" they'd counter. "This is a prison, for God's sake – not the corporate country-club you came from."

Of course, as in all institutions, mistakes were made. Several were made in the consigning of inmates to minimum security at Rifle. Some had originally been charged with murder or violent sex offenses, but due to smart lawyers, loopholes in the judicial system, or naive jurors, original charges were often reduced to mere reflections of themselves.

Roma and Dan Zerlich were living their life dream – living on the ranch. No more congested city commuting to unfulfilling jobs forty miles from home. No more fast lane for them. They tried that and it nearly destroyed them. They geared down to slow, re-established their priorities, and picked up the pieces of what was meant to be a life-long, exciting journey together. Both Roma and Dan were certain the change of pace, place, and attitude would work for them – and it was. After all, they survived the storm that tore through their lives, they would also survive the calm. Now, their marriage of thirty-seven years was enjoyably comfortable and deeply satisfying.

January 1997, Rifle Correctional Center officially expanded its capabilities to house, medicate, feed, clothe and provide for one hundred-ninety-two inmates with a staff of thirty-five.

As was the custom in most prison systems, inmates worked for the facility as clerks for Administration, cooks, servers, and dishwashers for Food Service, and mechanics, electricians, plumbers, carpenters and janitors for Facilities Management. Rafa was assigned as Roma's office clerk. He'd been convicted of paper hanging . . . forgery. On the outside he was a stockbroker and had devised a plan to methodically swindle his elite clientele. His scheme was so cleverly planned the District Attorney couldn't prove federal violations, so he was sentenced to ten years in *Big Max*, the maximum-security prison in Canon City.

National press coverage granted him instant recognition when he filtered through the various security levels within the Department of

Corrections, and by the time he ended up in Rifle, he was a legend within the system. Inmates called him Rafa, but the staff referred to him as *The Brain Storm*, and suspected him of masterminding several scams on the inside for the inmates who could afford his services. Rafa was a genius when it came to other people's finances and inmates always looked for ways to increase their limited earning capacity. Rumor was that some of the security guards at the facility also solicited his assistance, but everybody was careful not to talk about it. Privilege of freedom, Roma guessed.

After gaining permission from Warden Ivan Marsh, Roma attended the Alcoholics Anonymous meetings at the facility and knew many of the inmates on a more personal basis than her peers. It didn't create a conflict for her, but some of her peers disagreed with the Warden's decision. The inmates accepted the common bond of alcoholism, but the staff considered her admission of alcoholism a source of embarrassment. There were several staff members who Roma guessed would have benefited from the simple program and supposed that was really their cause for disdain.

Before Rafa was assigned as her clerk, Warden Marsh insisted Roma read the charming inmate's case management file:

| | |
|---|---|
| Name: | Michael Jaron Rafael |
| Gender: | Male |
| DOB: | July 23, 1970 |
| Race: | Caucasian |
| Height: | 6'2" |
| Weight: | 220 |
| Eyes: | Blue |
| Hair: | Blonde |
| Identifying Marks: | Tattoo - tribal band upper right arm |
| | Jagged scar above right eye |
| Previous Arrests: | None |
| Religion: | None |
| Birth Place: | Montmartre, a section of Paris, France |
| Education: | 1990 Graduate Oxford University |
| | Degrees in Business Finance, and |
| | International Communications |
| Family History: | Oldest of three children |
| | Father in military – Mother deceased |

It seemed incredible to her that someone so well educated would end up in any prison system, although, during her tenure at Rifle, Roma learned that money couldn't buy good judgment or moral values. But it sure bought good lawyers. Even though this was his first offense, with all the evidence against him, he should have been sentenced to forty years in the federal system.

In spite of her *Rafa education*, she liked him. He rarely attended the AA meetings, but her six-month association with him as her clerk offered her the opportunity to judge him for herself. Besides being brilliant, he was also conscientious and put in an honest day's work for the facility. Their working relationship developed into mutual respect and never crossed the boundaries of inmate and administrative staff member.

December 9, at 09:47, Rafa was working on the inmate canteen orders to be delivered later in the day. Roma and Pearl Isaac, her assistant, worked on the report for the next inmate transfers. Everyone overheard the officer describe the existing conditions to Warden Marsh: "Power to every part of the facility is out, including phones, the water supply, security's radios, and every vehicle on the grounds." It was unfathomable to imagine what could have caused such an all-encompassing power failure.

"Sabotage?"

"No sir," he stammered. "It's not sabotage. It's not just the power." The officer tried his best to gain composure. "Captain Mac is dead – another heart attack. Several inmates died from seizures, heart attacks . . . or something." Fear oozed from the officer, as he began shouting out of control. "It would be impossible for anyone to have sabotaged every single vehicle on the grounds."

When Rafa heard that Captain Mac was dead, he immediately thought of the weapons and ammunitions he knew were kept at Mac's house. He had to secure them before they fell into the wrong hands.

The cool winter morning turned into an angry hornet's nest of commotion by the time Dan Zerlich reached the facility. His pick-up truck loaded with hay quit running a couple miles up the road, so he walked to the facility to get Roma's car to jump his battery. Rafa listened intently as Dan told the warden about two cougars he witnessed kill each other while horses watched wild-eyed, and cattle collectively pushed against the fence and stampeded down the valley. Eerily spooky considering everything else that was happening.

Each passing moment brought an increased awareness that Security no longer had control over the inmate population. Hand-made contraband in the form of crude weapons came out of their hiding places and security staff members fled for their lives. Soon, there were no more cops to issue a *lawful order* or hold mid-day count.

Inmates were as panicked and confused as everyone else was and the majority of them walked away from the facility. The road to town passed Captain Mac's house, Rifle Gap Dam, wound through the narrow canyon that opened at the eighteen-hole golf course, and then continued five miles to the town of Rifle. Survival was the name of the game now. Inmates have a keen sense for opportunity and timing. Now the opportunity was present, timing was perfect, and the exodus began.

In the midst of the confusion and panic Dan literally dragged Roma and Pearl from the administration office. He told Roma to go to the top of the ridge and take cover in the cedars where she could watch the road to the ranch before heading home. He wasn't worried about Roma. She could handle herself and knew the six miles to the ranch like the back of her hand. He assured her that after he escorted Pearl past the dam and through the narrow passage of the canyon, the danger would be over, and he'd see her back at the ranch. He knew that none of the walk-away inmates would risk being apprehended as escaped convicts and would stay away from the town and its people. He was nearly right.

Roma looked down from the ridge and became vividly aware of the dangerous situation evolving. She hoped all the staff had escaped – the thought seemed ludicrous – staff needing to escape. Inmates in their required green clothing glared against winter's gray and were easily recognized. She saw Captain Mac's house, the green images converge like slime spilling over, and knew they were looking for weapons. Everyone knew the facility weapons and ammunitions were kept at Mac's house – especially the inmates. They knew all the secrets.

Rafa was one of the first inmates to reach the dead Captain's house. He entered through the basement sliding-glass doors and heard running in the upstairs rooms. He quickly scanned the floor molding and found the place behind the wet-bar that identified the false door he knew was there. Although the room was dark, he recognized the odors of metal, oil, and gunpowder. He found the racks holding the familiar AR-15, semi-automatic assault rifles, secured by a chain strung through their trigger-guards. Footsteps on the stairs warned him there was little time. Smashing a barstool, he used the heavy wooden leg to pry the bolt from the wall, and released the chain. It was oddly comforting to cradle an assault rifle in his arms again. They were somewhat outdated from the ones he'd used in Terrorist Tactical Training a couple years before.

Sounds of the crashing barstool and clanking chains brought inmates from other parts of the house to stand menacingly before him in the dim basement. Some wore Mac's civilian clothing, momentarily taking Rafa off guard. He quickly recovered and pointed the gun toward the three closest inmates and ordered them to unload the contents of the room.

"Hey, what is this, Man?" It was Willard Johnson, holding his massive black hands open in a non-threatening gesture. "You going to kill us or give us a gun, too?"

"Are you staying at the facility or headed toward town?"

"Man, I'm outta here. All I want is something to even the odds out there." Willie started to lower his hands and Rafa quickly raised the AR-15 barrel to the big inmate's head.

"I could tattoo your DOC number on your forehead with this thing before you could remember your mamma's name. All I want is some help to unload this room. I'm staying. Willie, if there are handguns, you can have one – after you help carry the guns back to the facility. That goes for the rest of you, too. Start loading." A growing crowd of angry inmates filled the room and Rafa knew he had to act quickly or he was a dead man, rifle or not. Spraying the ceiling with AR-15 shells, the deafening sound sent inmates running away or flattened against the floor. Willie was one of the latter.

"Man, you're crazy." Willie slowly rose, brushing plaster and drywall from his hair and face. He'd always liked Rafa, but was suddenly uncertain if this man carrying the rifle was sane or had lost his mind. "You're one of us, and you're willing to kill us all, to stay in that hell-hole?" He turned to look at the other seven remaining men slowly rising from the floor. "C'mon, let's haul these back to the camp, and then get the hell out of there. I want a gun."

From her hidden vantage point Roma heard the volley of rifle shots and knew they came from Mac's house. She feared for Dan, Pearl, and the unassuming townspeople of Rifle. She didn't see a single inmate travel the direction of the ranch and knew it wouldn't be much of an enticement. The six miles of winding dirt road that led to the ranch was due north – higher altitude, colder temperatures, with no access to anything but more dirt road.

Rafa was relieved as Willie rallied support from the other inmates and in less than five minutes the small room was emptied. Rafa walked behind the eight men as they headed back to the facility heavily loaded down with rifles and padlocked wooden boxes. Green-clad men hurried past them toward town, but no one interfered with Rafa. So far . . . so good. He didn't want to kill anyone to secure the weapons.

Persuaded by the AR-15, the men obediently placed the weapons on the ground in the empty yard. Rafa fired at the locks securing the boxes, spewing splintered wood and metal fragments. The volley resounded through the camp as if war were upon them. Lids flew open and revealed hand guns that Rafa recognized as .9mm Rugers and enough shells to start or finish a revolution. Other boxes contained hundreds of bullets for the AR-15's, OC Pepper Mace, tear-gas ejectors and canisters, and a couple dozen sets of handcuffs with ankle restraints. Colorado State Department of Corrections badges, and Rifle Assault Team badges, fondly referred to as *The RAT Patrol*, were neatly boxed.

Roma's body flattened to the ground when the volley of gunfire erupted from the facility. "Oh, no! They've got weapons." When she heard the gunfire earlier, she assumed they took the weapons and ran. The facility was the closest neighbor to the ranch, and the thought of them organizing and holding-up there filled her with eerie feeling of dread. She lay flat in the dirt for several minutes before mustering the courage to raise her head from behind the cedars and watch through their branches.

The remaining occupants of the camp, upon hearing the gunfire, thought the party was over and were now kicking themselves for choosing to stay. As they began to recognize their fellow inmates dressed in civilian clothes, they relaxed and with false bravado, slowly filed to the yard. Victor Grazzo, known as *Vic the Pick*, led a small group of seven men from the tower. Kim Tsu and five others came from the food services area, followed by Jeremy and a group of eight muscle-bound black men who proudly called themselves *The Brothers*. Rafa counted twenty-three as they challengingly stood before him. Willie and the remaining seven stood behind Rafa, giving an impression of four groups of men squared off.

Roma thought of Rafa as she observed the facility from the ridge. Did he leave with most of the inmates, or did his rank as camp *financier* offer him a better opportunity? She was too far away to recognize him as he stood in the middle of the open space between the administration office and the tower, surrounded by the future soldiers of Rifle Correctional Center.

Rafa was afraid Victor would still be here, but was glad to know exactly where he was. He recognized the jealousy and greed in Victor's dark eyes as he covetously examined the exposed weapons. Victor was a ruthless, cold-blooded animal, and Rafa couldn't let him reign unchallenged.

"Well, is *The Brain Storm* becoming the new Godfather of the camp?" An evil sneer twisted Victor's face and malevolent eyes glared at Rafa. He knew this would be the moment of truth, the division of power, and knew he could die. He needed a miracle. He couldn't let Victor control the weapons, but had to allow him to maintain leadership with his own followers or there would be a blood bath.

"No Godfathers, no Imperial Dragons, no Crips or Bloods, no bosses. I figure we can all benefit by this coup d'etat, if we keep our heads. This place is big enough for all of us with provisions to last for months. I'm sure you seized the moment of opportunity, like I did." Victor's expression didn't change. Glowering threats loomed behind the cold unpredictable eyes.

"Oh, I get it," started Victor. "We can each have our little corner of *The Rat's Nest* and you can become the new cop – the Man with all the guns. Is that the plan . . . Rafa?" Victor said *Rafa* with such loathing and contempt that it sounded like a slurred profanity.

Rafa's eyes never left Victor's as he knelt over the AR-15's and in one quick movement, threw the deadly assault weapon toward Victor, who deftly caught it. Victor's sneer turned to a sickening look of victory as Rafa prepared to die or kill the maggot. With the same agile movement he threw rifles to Kim Tsu, Jeremy and Willie. "There! That should make everyone happy," said Rafa, and hoped it would also place the odds in his favor. The weapons slowly became trained on Victor, and his eyes changed from deadly to cunning. Rafa felt Victor reassess his strategy and knew he relished every minute of the power-struggle. Victor had honed cruelty and intimidation to a fine art.

"What about the rest of the guns?" Victor enviously eyed the guns and Rafa knew he would kill to get them.

"I'm going to inventory them first," stalled Rafa. "Like you've done with the drugs and medical supplies. We can decide on distribution later."

"This might work out real fine," hissed Victor through tight jaws. "I've got the medications and tower secured, so you little pussies let me know if you need an aspirin for your PMS." Victor turned his gaze on Kim Tsu, who didn't back down from the evil man's glare. "I imagine you and your camp whores have got the kitchen tidy and lunch ready by now."

Kim Tsu didn't bite the bait as he retorted, "I'll let you know when you can eat, snake dung." Kim Tsu was a twenty-seven year old man of Chinese heritage and a known Master of the Martial Arts. It was rumored among the inmates that he was a respected and feared member of *The Hand* – the highly trained Chinese underworld, with US factions headquartered in the dark shadows of San Francisco's China Town, Kim Tsu's birthplace. Victor was quick to show contempt for Kim Tsu's reputation around a group of his men, but would never have tried to force his hand, man-to-man. Victor was more the ambush type, and Kim Tsu knew it. No honor. Coward to the bone.

Jeremy watched the dangerous exchange silently until now. "And I'll let you bargain for cigarettes, if you don't rough up my bro's too bad." Every muscle of Jeremy's body was dangerously alive, anxiously waiting for the least bit of provocation to blow Victor's head off, and Victor knew it. Of all the rivalries at the camp, the one that existed between Victor and Jeremy was the most dangerous. Jeremy's group was by far the strongest and fittest. Victor's group was a malignant hodgepodge of evil servants, afraid of Victor – not the proud warriors Jeremy's group envisioned themselves to be.

A mutual respect existed between Rafa, Jeremy, and Kim Tsu, the honor-among-thieves rapport that thrives in the sub-culture of prison systems. It was obvious today. Victor didn't like the odds of twenty-four to eight and grudgingly backed down.

The situation was dangerous at best, and Rafa quickly ordered the eight men behind him to haul the arms and ammunition to the administration office. Willie stayed, with his AR-15 trained on Victor, until all the boxes and rifles were secured in the telephone control room which had no window access from the outside and could be more easily guarded.

Victor Grazzo and his seven deranged followers feigned boredom with the standoff and slowly filed back to the tower. Kim Tsu, relieved that this would not be a killing time, went back to finish his inventory of the kitchen and Jeremy followed Rafa to the administration office.

Neither Willie, nor the other seven men Rafa commandeered to haul the ammunition from Mac's house, planned to stay at the facility. They just wanted to walk away like everyone else. The situation between Rafa and Victor was much more volatile and dangerous than anything they would have to face down the road. On the other hand, as Rafa pointed out, eight years, the mandatory sentence for escape, added onto their relatively short sentences did not appeal to them at all. Willie was the first to concede. Only three more months of his twenty-nine year sentence remained and he would be a free man. It was Willie who talked the majority of the group into staying. One left, but without the promised weapon and he felt lucky to leave with his life.

Roma witnessed the event taking place in the open yard between the tower and the administration building, but was too far away to understand the new chain-of-command. Her only concern was for Dan who would have to pass the facility to return to the ranch.

Satisfied that no one would notice her walking on the road, she carefully descended the rocky ridge, glad she'd worn pants and tennis shoes today. Trying to quiet her mind to sort out the day's events she recognized the fear, but also felt a strange peace, as though Earth Mother laid her hand on the land to quiet it, soothe it, hush it to sleep. When the fear rose, she quickly assured herself that if she worked at a bank or grocery store, there wouldn't have been the danger of anarchy rising, as in the prison. If this had happened on a weekend, it just would have slowed her down some, with no telephone beckoning or glaring lights to disguise the natural passage from dawn to dusk. Of course she couldn't explain why the energy seemed to drain from everything, including people. She didn't even try to understand it, but in spite of her brave thoughts, she knew that everything was different.

Roma had a deep, abiding faith in the Universe and knew that no matter what happens, there is a method to the madness of the world. A plan. Life goes on in spite of us. The God she believed in was much larger than the God of her childhood, more than the discriminating, exclusive God of the Koran, the Torah, or the Bible. Roma's God was all of them and none of them. No matter what name was given to God, she knew they were the same. She respected all of them but had found her own inner peace and spirituality, and no longer searched for the most powerful God. She knew God personally.

What adventure does life have in store for us now, she thought, as she reached Dan's pick-up? His thermos jug was full of warm coffee, so she sat on the running board and rummaged through her purse for a cigarette to smoke as she drank the sweet liquid. It tickled her that smokers always know where their cigarettes are and when Dan so adamantly hurried Pearl and her away from the facility she thought to grab her purse.

Taking the thermos and Dan's leather gloves, she proceeded up the dirt road. She passed Hilda Ranzenberger's heifers whose bleating calves would soon be old enough to wean. Hilda bred the best cattle stock and made the tastiest German sausage around and had winter-pastured her cattle here long before Dan and Roma bought the Rocking Z. Hilda and her brother, Gus, were plain country people and their little ranch was located southeast of the facility toward Rifle Falls State Park. Roma hoped they were home, peacefully taking their midday nap.

Rounding the bend which allowed full view of the ranch, she saw the Aspens she'd planted by the back porch that first spring, now tall twigs peeking over the roof of the house. Giant naked cottonwoods sprawled in their winter-gray uniforms on both sides of the creek.

Rendi and Litany stood lazily in the corral, waiting for Dan to bring home the hay. Everything looked the same. " Thank goodness," she whispered.

She didn't notice the young female wolf, the same color as dirt, stalking her from the scrub-oak on the hill above. It paralleled her for half a mile or more, reading scents on the cold winter air. Roma was lost in visual imagery of the ranch. Changing seasons fascinated her and she loved the daily evolution in the lay of the land. Winter-cold pushed life sap down, exposing rocks, rabbit holes, and Eagle's nests where they once lay hidden by vegetation. The wolf's head dropped low, as she readied for attack. An expert hunter and tracker, she could run down a rabbit and kill it with one deft snap of its neck in her powerful jaws, and never warned her prey with the snap of a twig or the crunch of loose gravel.

Without warning it lunged at Roma from the brush on the hill above. The wolf nearly scared the wits out of her as it brushed her shoulder with its nose, counting coup. She playfully braced herself in the road, daring Roma to try and tag her. It was a game the wolf could play all day, but Roma wasn't in the mood. "Trouble, you nearly scared the tar out of me." She'd used her best angry voice, but the half dog, half wolf wasn't the least bit intimidated.

Roma loved Trouble from the first time she'd laid eyes on her. She was the runt of the litter and her owners knew she wouldn't bring the high price they demanded. While Dan could barely tolerate the independent temperament of the dog, Roma reveled in her wild nature. Every hunter for miles around shared Dan's opinion; "If a dog runs game, it should be put down. Chasing a deer will kill it, just from the trauma of the chase," was Dan's argument.

"That's pretty righteous coming from you," Roma would start. "A hunter's guide who takes wealthy Easterners with high powered elephant guns out to kill where you point, and then the big courageous hunters mount them on their walls to show the world what macho men they are. Wolves have been chasing deer since God put them in the same place at the same time," was Roma's argument.

Dan knew the argument had no winners and accepted that he and Roma would always disagree on this point. But he didn't have to like the dog. A wolf breed has no place on a ranch.

Last fall Roma heard whining at the front door and when she investigated, found the beloved wolf-pup lying in a pool of blood with three bullet holes in her. Dan suspected that hunters mistook her for a coyote and shot her for the sport of it. Dan took her to old Doc Henry the next morning, and the vet was amazed that the bullet hadn't done major damage. He removed one .22 caliber slug that entered her back hip, exited the front, and lodged in the soft tissue of her stomach. Roma kept the slug as reverently as she kept her kids first lost tooth or hair from their first haircut.

"If that slug had entered even a quarter-of-an-inch in either direction, she'd have bled to death," old Doc said. So, Trouble, who would never ride in the pick-up or sleep in the house, was bandaged, drugged and sent home in the pick-up. She spent that first night stretched out by the front door. That's the only night Roma could coax her to stay in the house, but the wolf healed quickly even without Roma's watchful eyes.

The next day the local newspaper found an envelope marked: *To the Editor*. Within two days, everyone for miles around knew Roma's opinion of marking rancher's pets for target practice, hunting on private property, shooting for sport, mounting stuffed animals on walls for trophy, cowardice, and men's fragile ego's. Dan didn't go to town for coffee at Angie's Café for a couple of weeks and Roma chalked it up to his fragile ego.

Dan admitted that she was right-on, most of the time. But, as a hunter-guide, half their income came from those same wealthy Easterners and local cowards she'd so blatantly hung-out-to-dry in that damned article. But that's what he liked most about Roma; when she sunk her teeth into something, she didn't let loose until it was rendered benign or lifeless. He loved her passion. She would walk the coals for something she believed in and always saw the other guy's side of the story. Don't misunderstand. He didn't for one minute accuse her of being a fence sitter – her ability to see the other side of the coin. But she had an uncanny insight into human nature and always defended the misunderstood of any breed, be it man or wolf.

Dan was grateful for one thing; that wolf-pup loved Roma and would have died protecting her. And Roma was right – Trouble never bothered the horses or cattle, or he'd have shot the pup himself. She was always close to the ranch, but rarely visible and only Roma knew her bedding places. With Trouble around, Roma always knew when anyone approached. If it was a regular, they never knew she was around, but if it were a first-timer, they'd never forget their first meeting with Trouble.

Fond memories almost erased the dramatic assault on the day, as Roma playfully scruffed the ears of the loved animal and walked up the long driveway to the house. Even though the air was cold, she was sweating from the high sun and the brisk walk home.

Peeling off layers of clothes on the way to the bedroom she pulled on a long-sleeved T-shirt and a pair of comfortable sweat pants. The cool clothes felt good against her warm body. She ruffled her fingers through her red hair, reminding herself to put more Henna on soon, and headed for the kitchen. Out of habit, she drew water and poured it into the coffee machine to brew. She wandered from room to room, as if to verify with her own eyes that her home didn't betray her, as her work place had.

There were three bedrooms and two bathrooms upstairs, with kitchen, dining room and a large living room on the main floor. The walkout basement housed the office, another bathroom, and a large room with a fireplace – its flue extending up the entire side of the house, serving the living room fireplace as well. The house was too big for just two people, but as she noticed now, all the rooms were full, and there would always be plenty of room for the kids to stay. Furniture and treasures collected over the years graced each room with memories of growing up with Dan and their four children.

Oversized living room windows let in the morning sun and looked out onto the large concrete porch. Roma and Dan often sat in the cushioned, wrought iron chairs to watch the deer and elk come down from the dark-timber to graze in the valley at dusk. The dining room was large with sliding-glass doors that opened out to the back-porch that extended along the west side of the house. Windows framed in ivory lace curtains faced west from the country kitchen and overlooked the porch. Dan and Roma usually sat in the kitchen and drank their morning coffee at the old maple table that had once been his mother's.

Roma walked into the kitchen to get a cup of coffee, only to re-affirm the events of the day really happened, and all the power was out. As she removed the coffee from the electric pot, she began to take stock of all the other electrical appliances that would no longer work. Toaster, blender, and electric skillet sat on the counter. She opened the pantry – mixer, pasta maker, juicer, cappuccino maker, dehydrator. Closing the oak door she wondered if they'd ever be used again.

"Good gosh, the refrigerator!" She opened it, took a quick inventory, and closed it so all the cold wouldn't spill out. The clock hanging on the wall by the kitchen window said quarter-to-ten. That's funny. My watch stopped at the same time, she thought. Strange. Batteries powered them both.

She mentally scanned the basement and garage where Dan's table saw, router, drill and other electrical tools were kept. The freezer was full of garden vegetables, strawberry jam, and meat; deer, elk, rabbit and lamb, all cut off the bone and packaged into four-serving packages of steak or roasts, stew-meat, hamburger and sausage. Roma and Dan always butchered their own game. They cut it off the bone as soon as it cooled – no aging for their meat.

Packages were wrapped in large enough portions to feed unexpected company and leftovers never went to waste. Roma couldn't tolerate throwing food away. She thought of dinner now and knew there was leftover Sauerbraten that Hilda brought over last Sunday. "Whenever Dan gets home," she said out loud.

The sun disappeared behind the mountain early this time of year and the house quickly cooled with the sinking sun. She found the Coleman lantern in the mudroom, just off the kitchen, and wooden matches on the mantle.

Darkness enveloped the valley, as the waning moon rose and cast its long shadows across the silent ranch house. Roma primed the lantern and its stark brilliance soon filled the living room. She couldn't think of eating. Trying not to worry about Dan, she started a small fire in the old Franklin cook-stove that sat between the kitchen and dining room. She couldn't imagine what was keeping him. She made coffee and flipped through pages of last week's newspaper. The moon was high over the mountain when she decided to go look for him. If he was injured, he would need her. If not, he would cuss her for leaving the safety and warmth of the ranch. She could handle his swearing, but couldn't just sit and wait any longer.

Dressing in layers of thermal underwear, flannel lined jeans, cotton turtleneck and Dan's Pendleton shirt, she grabbed their sheep-skin lined long coats, banked the coals in the stove, turned off the lantern, and headed for the corral. Her work boots made clunky, dull sounds on the dry earth, bringing Trouble to her side. "Good girl. I knew you'd be close. We've got to find Dan." She talked to the dog, like she understood every word.

Grabbing the rope bridle hanging at the corral gate, she softly called to the mare standing in the moonlight. On the rare occasions she rode, Roma preferred Litany, the gelding, but Rendi was a Morgan, more powerfully built than Litany's sleek Arabian form. Rendi was Dan's work horse, and knew every nook and cranny of the ranch. The truth was, Roma was afraid of horses. Not Rendi and Litany, necessarily, but horses in general. She'd been thrown off a run-away horse when she was twelve years old, and lay unconscious for three days, slivers of fence post deeply embedded in her back. She loved to groom and feed them, but enjoyed them more visually than physically. She didn't like others to know of her fear, but Dan knew and respected it.

She easily slipped the bridle over Rendi's ears and led her to the tack-shed to saddle her, then abandoned the idea. Dan always saddled the horses and she'd never be able to cinch the saddle like Dan could. It would be a waste of precious time to try. "This will be an experience we'll both remember, Rendi. Just hang-in-there with me, girl, and let's go find Dan." She threw Dan's long coat across the large rump, and standing on a fence rung, coaxed the large mare's body close enough to climb on her back. "There, that's good. Let's go," she said, as she gratefully patted Rendi's neck, led her up the long drive and headed down the dirt road toward town.

Dan took the metal shoes off his horses every winter. He felt they were not worth risking a broken leg from slipping on the ice. Roma was grateful for the dull sound of hoof-on-dirt, as they slowly passed the dark road that turned into the prison grounds. Grateful, too, for the low-lying clouds that drifted across the moon's path. They passed Captain Mac's house as the clouds slipped past the moon, lighting her path past the dam.

Horse, rider, and trailing wolf entered the narrow canyon that would lead them to town. Another half mile and they would be at the golf course. Half way past the fifth hole, Roma reigned the bridle. She'd heard something that didn't belong to the usual night sounds. Pretty soon Trouble came running to her, whining. The wolf rarely barked. That's what made her so formidable a foe.

"What is it, Trouble?" Roma slid off Rendi and led her to the side of the road, where she heard a low groan coming from the creek.

" Thought I recognized that old side-ways gait coming down the road." Dan was trying to get up, all hunched over and holding his stomach. "Sure am glad to see you, Romalea Zerlich." He'd slumped down and Roma was at his side.

"Glad to see you too, Daniel Zerlich. Let me see what you've got there." She started to pull his hand away, but he stopped her.

"Just give me a hand up on that old nag – and let's go home."

They clumsily hobbled to Rendi's side, where she took Dan's long coat from the mare's rump and wrapped it around his shoulders. The smell of blood made Rendi skittish as Roma cupped her hands to give Dan a leg-up on the prancing mare's back. "Whoa, there, girl – give me a little help here – Rendi, girl." She calmed under Dan's touch as he clutched her mane. "That's it, girl." Roma helplessly watched as Dan struggled to adjust himself. He groaned as he pulled Roma up in front of him. "You're going to have to get us home, I'll just hang on."

"My pleasure." Roma tried to remain calm, as she knew the mare wasn't used to riding two on her back and they were nine miles from the ranch. After they passed the facility, she would get off and lead the rest of the way home.

Trouble ran ahead to scout the road. If there were any two-legged creatures out there, she'd find them. They didn't worry about the four-legged or the winged. The night was still. Only the occasional owl hoot or nighthawk disturbed the dark silence, and not a creature stirred as they passed the facility. Roma realized Dan was just barely balanced by his grip around her waist and his head rested heavily in the middle of her shoulders. She didn't dare stop. "Daniel Zerlich, don't you even think about checking-out on me now." Dan didn't respond.

The Milky Way and the waning moon lit the way as Rendi carried the precious cargo home. When the tired animal headed to the corral, Roma coaxed her to the back porch. Roma dismounted awkwardly, just in time to guide Dan's slumping body to the ground. Barely conscious, he leaned heavily against Roma as they struggled up the two stairs and into the kitchen. The braided rug was as far as they got before his body crumbled to the floor.

Roma quickly lit the Coleman lantern and gathered the first-aid supplies from the mudroom, a pan of cold water, dishrags and blankets. The lantern placed on the kitchen table shone eerily on Dan's outstretched body, revealing the large dark stain on his shirt and pants. Carefully, she unbuttoned his shirt and cut away his thermal underwear revealing a long gash under his left breast, ending a couple inches above his navel. The wound was eight inches long and gaped two inches at its deepest part. At least it was a clean cut. "This is more than a pail of water and washcloths can handle," she announced out loud. Covering the wound, she grabbed the lantern, ran out the back door and down to the tack-shed where she loaded up the box of supplies old Doc Henry gave them for emergencies.

Quickly returning to the kitchen, she knelt beside Dan and carefully washed the sticky blood away then bathed the area with Betadine. She'd helped Dan clean and stitch the wounds of cattle and horses before, but never imagined she'd have to stitch her Dan.

Scrubbing her hands with the Betadine, she stretched them into the surgical gloves found in the box of supplies, and cleaned the wound again.

"God, help me," she whispered. She knew what had to be done and carefully laid out the needle-nose pliers, the curved needle, catgut sinew, and poured alcohol over them. She repositioned the lantern to see deep into the wound. The slash was to the bone across four ribs, then continued toward the midsection. The deepest part exposed about an inch of the membrane covering the stomach. Examining it closely, there didn't appear to be any cuts to organs and there wasn't the putrid smell she remembered from gut-shot game. The raw tissue exposed didn't seem to be oozing anything but blood, so she was fairly certain there was no leakage from intestines to cause peritonitis and certain death.

Dan moaned softly when she took the first stitch, deep inside the wound. She dabbed at the bleeding with a sterile bandage, damp with alcohol. He weakly cried in pain, but she continued with focused attention, knowing the battle was now with time. She wiped at the sweat that ran into her eyes and her mouth felt full of dry cotton when the final stitch was in place. She washed the area with Betadine again and quickly bandaged it.

All through the long night she continued to wash her husband's feverish body, and when he shook with chills, she wrapped the blankets closer around him. Opening capsules of antibiotics, she dissolved the powder in water and spoon-fed him the liquid. She filled the turkey baster with cold water, placed it between his teeth, and let the water trickle down his throat. Placing wood in the wood-burning stove, she made strong coffee to keep herself awake. When he roused with pain and fever, she offered him more water and bathed the hot flesh of his face and chest. The ritual continued until the crows cawed reveille, and dawn's light forced the night to ebb.

For two days Dan feverishly wavered between life and death. Roma knew the greatest danger was from blood loss, shock, dehydration and the risk of infection. Dressing the wound twice a day, it appeared to be healing without infection. She routinely trickled water into his mouth along with antibiotics and aspirin. When he was conscious, she spoon-fed him sage tea and chicken broth heated on the stove. She dutifully fed the horses twice a day and hauled more firewood to store in the mudroom. She cleared the dining room of table and chairs and pulled the braided rug where his body lay, to rest in front of the large sliding glass doors of the dining room. When he slept, she lay beside him and succumbed to exhaustion. When he woke, she talked to him as if they were engaged in regular conversation, and hoped the sound of her voice would keep him with her. She prayed on her knees to the God of her youth; supplicated the Great Spirit and Earth Mother in the Indian Way, burning the ceremonial sage and fanning smoke across Dan's body with Hawk feather's that hung from her walking stick. She drew on the ultimate power of the Universe with every breath, honoring each God in its prescribed manner, believing in all and knowing they were one in the same. They fought fiercely and courageously; Roma willed him to live and Dan defied the spirits who came to claim him.

The morning of the third day, Roma woke to Dan's voice. "What?" she whispered, fully awake at the sound of him stirring.

"What's for breakfast?" he repeated weakly.

"Breakfast?" Tears stung her red-rimmed eyes and silent thanksgiving burned in her heart as the two battle-worn survivors smiled into each other's eyes.

"Well, the special-of-the-day is eggs, bacon, biscuits and gravy.

Or poached eggs and toast. For the more delicate palate, we have milk-toast."

"Don't you ever feed me milk-toast. I don't care how near dead I am," he ordered, in the best bossy voice he could muster. "But the poached eggs and toast sound real good."

"Sounds pretty good to me, too." She leaned over him, kissed his cool forehead, placed her cheek against his, and thanked all the powers of God – no matter what their names.

"And coffee," whispered Dan. "No more sage tea. Smells like a brush fire in here. I'll bet you even did the Indian get-well-dance over me," he teased.

"Hey," she bantered, "that dance is what kept you alive. You owe me big-time now. I might be too old to dance over you next time." She became serious, her lips close to his ear as she whispered: "God, don't ever let there be a next time."

"Amen," whispered Dan.

He winced in pain as Roma propped pillows behind his head and shoulders so he could feed himself. Poached eggs and toast never tasted so good. Coffee replaced tea and Dan lay back on pillows and almost looked like his old self again. Roma smoked a cigarette as they gazed out the sliding glass doors while he recounted what happened that first day.

He and Pearl had headed down the road after the majority of inmates left the facility. Pearl was built round and close to the ground, so she wasn't in favor of climbing over mountains. While passing Captain Mac's house the burst of semi-automatic shots erupted, spilling inmates out in panic and confusion. Fleeing inmates were dressed in varying degrees of civilian attire – the ones who could fit into Mac's clothes, Dan guessed. In their haste to get away they weren't concerned with Pearl and Dan's presence, or maybe they couldn't be seen, as he'd helped Pearl over the ditch and behind the scrub-oak about ten feet from the road. Dan heard the angry shouts coming from Mac's house and supposed the inmates were arguing over weapons. He knew Mac's personal collection of high-powered rifles and hunting knives were locked in a hidden gun-case in his bedroom closet, but didn't know where the inmates could have found semi-automatic weapons. They waited in their hiding place until the armed inmates went back to the facility

At the junction of Highway 52 they met two schoolteachers who were walking home because their car quit running while on their way to Meeker. Dan and Pearl filled them in on the events that happened at the facility. They were both heading to Parachute, the small retirement community where Pearl lived, and Dan felt comfortable leaving her with them to continue on without him. He was certain they'd meet up with others along the way.

On the way back to the ranch he stopped at the Bernard's farmhouse. He and Ben Bernard often shared tall tales over coffee at Angie's Cafe. No one answered his knock at the back door. Dan walked past the chicken coop by the garden spot where he found Ben leaning up against the back gate, emptily staring across the valley. "Ben?" The tall, thin man didn't respond. Dan knew Ben wore a hearing aide, so he drew closer and placed his hand on Ben's shoulder. "Ben," he called again.

"I was just trying to decide where Patty would want to be buried and if I want to join her." The lanky frame started to shake and Dan knew the tears were hard fought and walked toward the garden to give him privacy.

A few moments passed and Dan hollered out, "Can I do anything for you, Ben?"

Ben took a handkerchief from his shirt pocket and blew loudly as he composed himself and slowly walked toward Dan. "No, but thanks. I'll take care of things here. I thought Patty had a heart attack and tried to phone for help, then tried to start the car to take her into the hospital. Nothing worked – just didn't work. I worked on her here, CPR you know, but I couldn't bring her back. She was gone."

Dan told him what happened at the facility and that he suspected some of the inmates were still there and were armed.

"Well, I saw a bunch of them pass by, but none of them bothered us here, or if they did, I didn't hear them and wouldn't have cared if I had." He started to break down again as they both walked toward the house. "Listen Dan. I don't want to keep you from getting up to the ranch, but if you ride down soon, stop by and take Patty's hens and roosters up to Roma. I know Patty would want Roma to have them. You've always been fond of the eggs and Roma was always so good to Patty." Dan promised to stop by in a few days. Ben affectionately patted Dan on the back, thanked him for stopping by and the two men shook hands, like usual. He knew Ben wanted to be alone.

As anxious as he was to get home, Dan stopped at the neighbors he knew to make sure they were okay. He didn't know many folks in the area, but was fond of the ones he did. The sun shone at 3:00, as far as Dan could figure. It would be getting dark soon enough. He came to Tom Richardson's long drive. Another stop won't matter one way or the other, he thought.

Old Tom was retired and lived alone on the deteriorating family homestead as his wife had passed on some years earlier. Tom just let the old place go to pot after his wife died. Dan figured the old man probably lived a lot longer than he thought he would and just never bothered to make the necessary repairs. Tom liked to ride up Harris Gulch with Dan in May, to move the cattle up to the Flat Tops to summer pasture, and then down again in September to fatten them up before auction. The rangy old cowboy was good company and loved to tell stories from the old days, usually while swigging from a pint of sour-mash whiskey.

Magpie, Tom's crippled old sheep dog, looked as if she'd just laid down and died on the back porch. The back door was ajar, so Dan pushed it open and called to Tom. He heard movement in the next room and suspecting it was Tom, walked in. Dan froze when he saw old Tom lying in the worn recliner, mouth gaping and eyes staring. Just as it dawned on him the sounds he'd heard must have come from someone else, he saw the young inmate to his left, posed with a hunting knife Dan suspected was one of Mac's. He recognized Mike Morrisey from his last inmate crew and knew the boy was not the dangerous type that sometimes ended up at the facility. He'd underestimated the fear that darted from Mike's eyes as the boy lunged at Dan and burned a slash across his ribs.

Dan couldn't believe the boy actually moved on him, and from the look on Mike's face, he couldn't either. Mike darted from the room like a trapped animal, and Dan felt the warm blood ooze from his midsection. He didn't know how bad it was, just knew there was a lot of blood and he had to get back to the ranch before he bled to death. He grabbed a grungy flour sack and pressed it against his gut as he headed out the back door.

During moments of consciousness he followed the creek to the golf course and crawled along its banks toward the road. After several attempts to continue, he knew he better stay put. When he was lucid, he concentrated on applying pressure. He didn't remember much after that, and only vaguely recalled Trouble finding him.

Roma was amazed at the story. "I never would have guessed that little Mike Morrisey would do that. My gosh, I'd have said he was the gentlest soul at the camp."

"Well, he was more afraid than anything and didn't know whether to shit or go blind when he saw me. That's what made him dangerous. I was taken off guard when I saw Tom's body lying there in that old chair. If I'd been in my right mind, I'd have just gotten the hell out of his way. He took one lucky swipe at me and was just as shocked as I was when he did."

"Do you think he killed Tom?"

"No, Tom died sleeping in that chair. Mike was just going through his things. Maybe looking for money." Dan winced at the pain as he tried to shift his weight to a more comfortable position. The long conversation tired him.

"Now, don't start getting frisky or you'll be bleeding again." Roma was at his side and Dan was trying to get up. "What can I do to help?"

"Damn-it all!" The pain made him irritable. "Just help me get to the bathroom."

Roma helped him to his knees where he raised himself, holding onto a chair. His legs nearly buckled by the time they got him to the bathroom. Roma left him in the cold room and quickly brought the rollaway bed from the small bedroom, moved the braided rug back to the kitchen, and placed the bed in the dining room. Dan came back by himself and sat in the chair while Roma made the bed.

"You're not really going to make me sleep on that thing, are you?" Dan was sadly eyeing the arrangement.

"Well, you must be feeling better! If you'd rather stay upstairs in the bedroom, I guess that would be fine, but you'd have stairs to climb and it wouldn't be as warm. Or maybe you want to help me move the bedroom set down to the dining room and. . ."

"Hold on – don't get in a lather. I was just thinking – there's not enough room for you to sleep by me and I'd rather sleep on the floor like we've been doing."

"Oh, you – I just want you to be comfortable by the stove where it's warm." She was kneeling beside him and his arm went around her waist and held her to him for a long, tender moment.

"I don't ever want to miss you like when I was lying by that creek and knew I might not ever see you again." He looked into her eyes for a long time. "Take that damned thing back upstairs, please."

"I'm not a young thing anymore Daniel Zerlich and I don't want to sleep on the floor. But I do want to sleep next to you, too." She kissed him and pulled the bedding off the rollaway and hauled it back upstairs. It didn't take her long to have their mattress tumbling down the stairs, bedding and all, and soon the bulky box springs covered the braided rug.

"Please don't change the sheets," Dan protested wearily. "Just let me lie down." Seeing the look of concern in Roma's eyes, he added, "I want to smell our sheets. Don't change them."

Dan was like that. So aware of everything about her, even down to the scent of her body. She would never know what thoughts went through him lying at the creek, but she was acutely aware of her fear when she'd thought he might die.

"Deal," she said and helped him to the bed.

Lowering himself to the mattress, his hands grabbed handfuls of sheets and blankets and he held them to his face and breathed deeply of their scent. "I must look pretty silly, trying to inhale the bed, or something."

"I don't think there's anything silly about you," she said as she slid in beside him and carefully placed her arm across his chest.

The fire popping in the stove and the familiar aroma of coffee warming lulled them into peaceful sleep.

## *Chapter 3*

Laramie woke to early morning chill and was surprised and relieved to see Suzan lying encircled in Jesse's arms on the floor by the glowing fire. She wanted to rush and throw her arms around them, but sank back into the warmth of the blankets instead, content to know they were home. It seemed like she'd barely closed her eyes when Mira began to stir. Shafts of sunlight streamed through the kitchen window, and gold and red reflections danced from the hanging crystal.

"Mom!" burst from Mira before Laramie could quiet her.

"Shh," Laramie motioned for Mira to follow her to the kitchen.

"It's all right, Laramie, I'm awake." Suzan sounded weak and looked a scary sight, but Mira was already snuggling next to her under the blankets.

"Oh, Mom! You've got a big cut on your forehead. What happened?" Mira touched her mother's seared cheeks. "Your face is burned, and your hair is melted, even your eyebrows and eye-lashes."

"I'm okay, honey. I guess there was an explosion at work. I can't remember very much."

"I'm going to clean and bandage that so it doesn't get infected," said Jesse, barely awake. "I'll get soap and water. Don't try to get up. You have a concussion – I can tell by your eyes."

"There isn't any water, except what's in the toilets and tanks and we'll have to boil it first," hollered Laramie as Jesse started up the stairs.

"I'll use peroxide for now. Mira, will you gather all the first-aid supplies? It will be better to keep them all in one place. Alcohol, bandages, tape – and get all the stuff we take camping."

Mira ran upstairs as the children began to wake.

"No way to keep things quiet, now," said Laramie, as she introduced Suzan to Dominic, Jen, and Sara. "I found them on my way here. I'll tell you about it later. We can talk after they're fed and dressed." All the kids were excited to see Suzan and relieved to know that some mothers were still alive.

Laramie placed more wood on the fire and cooked oatmeal and boiled coffee. They searched through boxes of Jacinth's old clothes and all of them fit Jen and Sara. Jacinth was quite petite, and unlike Mira, rarely wore her clothes out as she grew taller. The two small sisters thought it was Christmas already. Jen sang as she danced around the room, modeling her new wardrobe, and Sara's eyes sparkled with delight, but she didn't say a word. Dominic's pillowcase was filled with sweatshirts, jeans, T-shirts, underwear, snow-boots and gloves, but even he benefited from the girl's windfall.

Black followed Laramie and the kids to the canal, a half-mile north of the house. Several people came to fill empty milk cartons and bask in their survival. Others wore the hollow mask of despair for loved ones lost, and Laramie felt an overwhelming urge to comfort and encourage them, but didn't impose on their grief.

Nothing could overshadow Laramie's high spirits. She survived! Jesse and Suzan were home, and her nieces were safe! Even though she didn't know for sure, she felt Levi and Jane were safe, too. Jane was a survivor. Watching Sara reminded her that not all families survived intact. "God bless the children," she whispered. Why did she survive with these children, and others died?

Jesse washed and bandaged Suzan's head and knew the jagged gash would leave an ugly scar. He cut the singed parts from her long curly hair and bathed her seared skin in juice from the Aloe Vera plant.

"Wow, look at your sweater," he said, helping her dress in her favorite sweats.

"It's ruined. It used to be pink." Suzan held it up for examination.

"When Laramie comes back I'll soak it in water and get the blood and soot out."

"I don't know how I got out of that building." Suzan's eyes stared into yesterday, trying to remember. A flash of Marion's limp body lying on the floor and a wall of flames and boiling smoke was all she could see.

Jesse didn't want her to remember. It was too soon to relive the trauma she'd survived, and with a concussion, she needed to remain calm over the next few days. She'd lost a lot of blood and was still in shock when he came home and found her burning with fever, shaking with chills, and talking incoherently to *Mamma*. He couldn't imagine what she had lived through.

"Here, sweetheart, eat some oatmeal. Laramie made it over the fireplace. Sure glad you Zerlich women know how to cook," he said, trying to lighten the mood.

"Marion, . . . " Suzan choked on the words and the memory.

"Shh, baby . . . don't worry. You're home. You're safe. I'll take care of you and everything will be okay." Jesse, remembering his own walk home from Golden, doubted it would be that simple. "Try not to think about it. Try to sleep. We can talk when you're feeling better."

The water-hauling troupe returned, and Laramie boiled it in big pans on the fire. Mira busied the children with coloring books, crayons, small bottles of paste, and scissors. Later, each child presented Suzan with a get-well card.

Mira read her favorite books to Dominic, Jen and Sara, who fell asleep on the over-stuffed sofa, draped over one another like children do.

Suzan looked through the colorful get-well cards and was overcome with the tender gesture. "Tell me about these kids, Laramie. You said you found them? Were they lost?"

Laramie recounted the story of Dominic, his Pappa and the statue of the Virgin Mary. "It still seems unbelievable to me, but I'm not going to try to figure it out. Dominic has faith that only children know, and such a beautiful, simple way of accepting life." She searched her memory to recall his exact words. "He says . . . *everything is the right way*. Sometimes fear is there, but he has a wonderful resource of faith to draw from. You'll have to look into those clear blue eyes and listen to him talk. He even renewed my faith that everything is the right way."

"What about the girls? Why did you bring them with you? Aren't you afraid their families will be desperately worried about them?"

"No, I don't think so. The weirdest thing happened. Tears just flowed down my face and I felt terrified. I knew it wasn't my fear. It was fear from children." She searched for words to better describe the feeling. "I only know that when I saw them, I knew it was their fear that drew me to them. I felt their fear."

Laramie read the doubt in Suzan's eyes, but continued. "I know it sounds hokey, but I can't explain it any other way. I was led to them – like something pulled me to them. It stopped as soon as I saw them. I could almost hear their fearful thoughts, it was so vivid – as if my hearing were . . . mega-acute."

"Is that a real word?" quipped Suzan, smiling for the first time since yesterday.

"I can't think of any other word to use. It's spooky, now that I put it into words."

Laramie didn't know how to approach the next subject, so just dove in, as usual. "I know it will be difficult feeding three extra children, but we stopped at the store on our way." She watched Suzan's expression. "I left your address on a piece of paper and left it under a rock in their yard. When things return to normal, I'll try to find their family, but they assured me they didn't have any family."

"Of course, they have a family. You took them from a house. Someone birthed them, for heaven's sake." Suzan was always so practical.

"Yes, I found them at a house. Their mother was lying face down in a pool of blood on the front porch."

"Oh, no! What's happened to everything? I'm so sorry, " Suzan cried.

"It's okay. Please don't cry. I didn't mean to upset you." Laramie put her arms around her. "I wasn't trying to shame you. I didn't realize you don't know what really happened yesterday. I guess, none of us do. Of course they have a family, somewhere. Or, used to have a family. When the explosions happened a lot of people died instantly, like some inner explosion happened at the same time. But it was more than that. Cars stopped right in the middle of streets and people walked home, like you did. Watches don't even work now. It's as if the life and energy were sucked out of everything."

"All I could think about yesterday was getting home to Jesse and the girls. I don't remember anything else. I thought it only happened to me." Suzan was sobbing now. "Jesse and I talked this morning, but he didn't tell me it happened everywhere and people died."

"He was trying to protect you, to give you time to heal and get better before dealing with the ugly realities. All I know is that everything is different and nothing works," Laramie said, wiping her sister's tears. "I'm just thankful you made it home."

Suzan blew her nose and lay silently for a long time. "Every child brings their own loaf of bread."

"What?" Laramie was surprised. "Mom used to say that."

"Yes, but Mom's mother is the one who originally said it. When grandma's friends questioned her sanity for having so many children, she told them – every child brings their own loaf of bread. Mom said that's why they all felt so special – they believed they brought their own loaf of bread. Mom said she always laughed trying to imagine a tiny little fist holding a loaf of bread, fresh from the oven." Suzan and Laramie belly-laughed at the image.

"I haven't heard that for years," Laramie whispered while drying her eyes.

"Well, I'm sure we'll manage, with all the little loaves of bread running around here now," said Suzan, looking at the napping children.

"Thank God you're home and safe. I think it's a miracle that you even survived."

The next three days they ate, talked, tried to stay warm, and slept, while waiting for things to return to normal. *Things* never did. Jesse dug a hole in the corner of the back yard to bury waste and each person carried the community pot to the hole, dumped it, and shoveled a scoop of dirt on the new offering. Then Jesse dug another hole.

Several tents emerged by the canal on the third night, and smoke from campfires filled the air. Laramie made two trips to the canal each day to get more water for washing hair, clothes, and bodies – there was no such thing as a bath. Cooking and cleaning up after a meal was difficult without running water and it took a lot of work to keep things clean. They were beginning to understand how disease thrives from unsanitary conditions, as there never seemed to be enough water.

On the fourth day, Suzan was up early, washed and dressed herself, and fixed breakfast of boiled eggs, bread and butter. She still couldn't remember anything from the first day except Marion's still form, the wall of fire, and the angry black smoke.

Laramie was relieved to see Suzan so easily managing the house again. Suzan was the organizer, the rational thinker, the perfectionist, the less impulsive, and the oldest of the Zerlich children. In spite of her 5'10" frame, she was small boned, and delicate – always a lady.

On lazy summer weekends past, she and Jesse donned black leather chaps and jackets and rode their Harley's through deep canyons and winding mountain roads. She braided her long, dark curly hair, put on a headband and a pair of sunglasses, and looked wildly sexy and rebellious. She was just as impressive typing in her pink lace-trimmed dress at the office, or in shorts, sandals, and camp-shirts at home. She weathered the identity crisis – the decision to work or not to work, and was finally comfortable in her own skin . . . most of the time. That damnable perfectionism could still trip her up sometimes.

Years ago, while attending a family sculpting class, Suzan was asked to describe her family members at a picnic, using the attributes of animals. She saw her dad and Jane as bears, lumbering and grumpy, but strong and courageous. Mom was a loyal cocker spaniel, happily lapping at faces, but ready to snap at anything threatening. Laramie was a beautiful butterfly, fluttering delicately, gracing all with her charm and beauty. Her brother, Judd, she saw as a bull elk, strong, strutting, courageously protecting his herd. But the most interesting was how she saw herself. She was Mother Goose, waddling around, making sure the picnic was running smoothly, organizing, organizing, organizing. Everything had to be perfect. The whole family was amused and agreed that her visualization was right on target.

Mother Goose was back and Jesse finally relaxed. He'd nursed her, fed her, bathed her and helped her dress, rarely leaving her side. The crusty, singed skin on her face and hands peeled in large hunks, revealing pink patches of tender new skin underneath. Every day she coughed up less and less soot from her lungs. She looked a fright, but felt lucky to be alive.

Jesse checked on neighbors and found that several hadn't survived. Nobody knew what happened, and everyone told a horror story. Dogs ran in packs, and Laramie and the children saw dead horses in the field by the canal.

Jesse planned to ride his mountain bike the next morning to check on his parents who lived eight miles away. He hoped the rest of his family would be there to save him from having to search the city.

## *Chapter 4*

The morning dawned cold and gray as Jane sat bundled at the cluttered kitchen table, smoking a cigarette and drinking a cold cup of coffee Ian made the day before. She knew it was time for decisions. She couldn't stay, but she hated to leave. This had been their home since the death of Levi's father, except for the times they'd stayed at the ranch with mom and dad. Red, Evee and Tad were her surrogate family. The *little house* was her safe place to grow-up without mom and dad's good intentions suffocating her and leaving her with feelings of inadequacy, failure, and again, obligation. Here, she was allowed to raise her son, make her own decisions and mistakes. Red and Evee never judged her, negated her, or offered advice, unless she asked.

She didn't disown her real family. She just resented always being expected to fill the *bad girl* role they'd assigned her. Of course, her life-style didn't offer them many other choices. But, she felt they didn't know or appreciate how hard she'd tried in the last four years to change that image and become a responsible part of society, in kind of a skeptical, defiant way. Damn – she hated that word – responsibility! She loved blaming someone else – anyone else – for all her problems. Becoming responsible for her own actions was the hardest thing she'd ever learned and the most important thing she would ever teach her son. But her family couldn't accept her life with Red and Evee; they didn't understand that it was much easier being a family with people who accepted her exactly as she was, than trying to live up to the expectations of those who didn't really know her anymore.

Part of it was her fault, and she owned that. She was the one who pulled away from them rather than try to become acceptable in their eyes – it was easier. Now, after all this time, she knew they loved her all along, exactly as she was. They just didn't know how to let her do her life by herself, to grow up in her own time. She knew their only sin had been that they loved her and wanted to mend every part of her broken life. But they couldn't alter the path she chose for herself; she had to walk through the pain to learn she didn't want it anymore.

She instantly thought of her dark past – the one she kept trying to bury. Miraculously, it seemed to have a life of its own that crept forward to shake her at the most awkward times. She knew that it can take months and even years of agony and despair to ever reach that place – the place where she was beaten down so low that she became willing to do whatever it would take to change her life. It happens one instant before the trigger is pulled, one instant before the overdose is injected, one instant before the wrist is slashed to let blood flow with warm water in the bathtub. How many times had she tried to die before she began to learn how to live?

Her ugly dependence on alcohol and drugs made her perfect company for a crazy, Indian biker who blamed the world for everything. The five years she was with him were the toughest, meanest, most dangerous and insane time of her existence. She knew she was lucky to have survived it. There were many who didn't.

If it weren't for student loans and grants, she wouldn't have been able to do it. She didn't know how she'd been so lucky to get the grants that paid for all her expenses. Someone up there must have been watching out for her. And she did it! She was actually a college graduate now! Of course, less the ceremony and piece of paper. She never stood on pomp and ceremony anyway, and what did it matter now?

Now, without water, electricity, gas, cars, and a dwindling food supply, it was obvious she must decide to stay with Red and survive the way everyone else would have to, or find her sisters and join with them to find her parents. If she could just get to the Rocking Z Ranch, she knew they would be safe. Yes, many of the same problems would exist, but she would feel safer with her family and knew the ranch had its own water supply, horses, cattle, and plenty of game to hunt. She knew Laramie would head to Suzan's, as they had always been closer and Laramie nurtured a true *auntie* relationship with her nieces, Mira and Jacinth.

That first night, when Red and Ian sat in the kitchen of the little house drinking beer, Ian convinced Red of his theory of the *energy surge*. That was the simple version, anyway – Mother Nature's redeeming energy surge to save Herself. Why did Red so easily accept this stranger into his life and his confidence – a research scientist from Sydney, Australia, for heaven's sake! She vaguely remembered hearing the words *increased awareness, survival, packing*. She'd been so exhausted, it all jumbled together making no sense, so she quit listening. But Red bought it and he was the last person she would have put money on to accept such a wild explanation. And he was definitely the last person she ever thought would try to talk her into a man!

Red approached her the next morning while Ian was sleeping-it-off. He wasn't much of a drinker – as Red pointed out to her, trying to sell her on all the wonderful qualities of this man he'd only met the day before. He actually talked her into thinking Ian would stick it out with them. What did Red and Ian discuss that first night? Did he tell him about Levi's father and *Jazz*? "Well, hell, I probably don't want to know what they talked about anyway," she said out loud.

Now, she had to decide what to do, and what Ian did was up to him. She liked Ian. The attraction had been instant. She could tell he was attracted to her, too. She had good radar when it came to reading the energy that surges between men and women. Throw in an element of danger, or anti-social behavior, and that described her kind of man in the past. Ian was respectable, educated, a good and honest man. Is that what scared her? She had never been with a man that treated her like a lady, a woman, a real person; a man who let her be strong and soft at the same time. And damn, he was so good looking; so lean and tall, at least six-foot-three. Intense, hazel-green eyes framed by hair the color of sand. She watched his bulging arms and thighs as he hauled boxes from the shop to the big house and those narrow hips didn't miss her attention either. And they talk about men sexualizing women. Ha! It had been a long time since she'd looked at a man like that and it felt good.

She stayed busy throughout the day, cutting the thawing meat from the freezer into strips to cook on the gas barbecue grill and pouring runny fruit juice concentrate onto sheets of plastic wrap to dry on the back porch. They ate all the vegetables and ice cream the second day. A lot of food had to be eaten right away and Levi shared it with kids in the neighborhood. What would they do when the food ran out? Of course, Red always knew where *stuff* was, but someday soon, even the food in warehouses would be bartered to the highest bidder, and that's what really scared them.

As she cooked the last of the meat strips, fear for her family returned and she knew she must find her sisters – live to see her brother and his wife again. "God bless you, wherever you are." Did her parents survive? She wouldn't rest until she knew! If they survived the initial impact of the energy surge, they would probably survive the winter. Mom was such a pack rat; she never threw anything away and knew how to make a meal from imagination. The Rocking Z had a gravity-fed spring on the property and a reservoir about a mile up the road that was used for irrigation and a favorite fishing hole for locals. Dad was an experienced hunter with a gun or a bow, and mom too, for that matter, so they'd have plenty of fresh meat, and mom knew everything there was to know about food preparation and preservation. *Food Storage,* the Mormon way of life – she remembered the two tons of wheat in the basement when they lived on Mariposa Street, and mom grinding wheat with the stone grinder she swore made better bread than the electric grinder. She could smell it now – that sweet yeasty smell of crusty homemade bread with honey on it, which they also stored in the basement in big five-gallon cans. Too bad she didn't have that basement now, but how safe would stored food be? How long would it have lasted when the neighborhood was finished with it?

She was proud of her work as she looked at the pans of roast, steak, chicken and pork, all stripped, roasted and dried. That would help feed them on their trip and there was enough cooked hamburger and bacon for the next three days. Evee had loved bagels and Red's freezer was full of them. Now, ten dozen lay sliced and drying on screens that they arranged for the best sun exposure. If it snowed just a few inches they could keep things frozen longer, thought Jane, even though she dreaded the thought of snow and being cold.

No, she sure as hell wouldn't freeze to death. She knew every way known to man to keep warm – she learned it from living on the street with Levi's father. She shuddered remembering the stories he told her of being raised on the reservation in the mountains of New Mexico. He did teach her some valuable lessons: if clothes won't keep you warm, wrap your feet in rags and get under newspapers, cardboard boxes, pine boughs, or anything else to keep the moisture and wind out. She learned that the more bodies in a small area, the more heat. And to do whatever has to be done for good gloves, good boots and a warm hat, even stealing them or giving up a last pack of cigarettes to get them.

Cigarettes were the best bartering item. If Ian were right, cigarettes would be worth as much as weapons in a couple of days. She had the carton she bought at 7-11 the first day and Red said she could have all of Evee's – five cartons of a generic brand she always hated, and four cartons of menthols, which she hated more, but they would taste good when the Camels ran out.

Evee had been a lot like her mom in the way she shopped – her security was in having a full pantry. She thought of her mom and the million times she had tried to quit smoking and started again. Well, someday, we may all have to quit – no more warnings from the surgeon general, she thought, as she lit up another Camel. If Mom were here, she'd know what to do with all this other stuff.

"What other stuff?"

"Ian Jayne, you've got to quit creeping into my thoughts like that."

"Well, it rarely happens," he said, as he gently massaged her neck and shoulders. "Why don't you take a break – you've been at it since dawn."

A break would be nice, but there was still too much to do. "What did you and Red find in town?" She gathered up pans of the dried meat strips and headed for the kitchen.

Ian and Red left early that morning to search for supplies. They were hoping to find lightweight camping supplies; dehydrated food, thermal solar blankets, nylon tarps, ropes, – things that Red didn't already have. If they were out there, Red would find them.

"Not what we'd hoped – everything is stripped bare, already in the hands of *those who have*, to be bartered with *those who have not*." He set down the large canvas tote-bag on the floor. "But I did find this," he said, and pulled out the most beautiful snowsuit she'd ever seen. "I figured this would keep you warm in almost any kind of weather – no matter how cold it gets."

"Purple is my favorite color, and it even has ski gloves attached to the sleeves!" She was elated – like Christmas already.

"I know you've been thinking about going over those mountains to find your parents, and you'll need to be warm . . . warmer than warm, and I found one for Levi, too, and snow boots."

In all the excitement, she missed the comment about mountains and finding her parents. She was like a gleeful child as she pulled boots, hats, metallic blankets and a couple two-man tents from the large canvas bag. Spontaneously, she threw her arms around his neck and kissed him on the mouth. Realizing her impulsive reaction, she pulled away and couldn't break the hold of his eyes, those beautiful eyes.

"I kinda liked that," he responded, licking his lips.

"I got so excited and I'm so grateful to have these things. It will make everything much easier to endure."

"I love grateful women," he said teasingly, too close for her to breathe.

She playfully pushed him away, "You men are all alike."

They were still laughing as Red came into the kitchen carrying fishing poles, bait, hooks, and an armload of camping gear – Coleman lantern, dehydrated foods and powdered drinks.

"You guys going fishing?" she asked.

"No, but I think you might need some of these things when you head over those mountains." answered Red.

"What mountains?"

Ian looked sheepishly at Red who immediately threw up his hands in that *don't-get-me-mixed-up-in-this* fashion.

Ian started to explain. "I know you've been thinking of your mom and dad on the ranch, and . . . "

"Wait a minute! Hold on just one damn minute – I'll let you know what I'm thinking – when and if it's any of your business. Besides – a person would be insane to try to cross those mountains with winter coming on. Good Lord, you know I've thought about it. It would be a madman's decision. How the hell would a woman and child survive it? We'd freeze, or worse."

"I'm going. With your sisters, your brother-in-law, and their kids – it would be a group of us – safety in numbers."

"Yea, starvation in numbers! Freezing in numbers! Insanity in numbers!"

"Then why have you been thinking so hard about it?" It was Red, who knew her so well, without hearing her thoughts *sometimes*. And he damn well knew that if she wanted to go over the Continental Divide there wouldn't be anything or anyone that could stop her. Red and Ian discussed it and Ian was up to going across the Divide with her. Red promised to outfit them.

"To hell with the both of you! You've put your heads together and got my life all figured out, haven't you?" She was fuming.

Ian was the brave soul to respond. "You can't stay here, Janie. It's really rather simple. You can't stay and Red's leaving, too. I don't want to stay here. I want to go with you and your son, if you'll have me." He had to convince her. "I'm experienced in the bush – in the outback. I can carry my own weight. I'm not all mathematical equations and calculators. The point is, I've had years to play out all the *what-ifs* and I've thought through every option. Fate, *God's Will*, or whatever put me here, so I alter the plans some, but the problems are still the same. I won't be hiking through the bush to get to my folks' old homestead in the outback. I'll be hiking over the Rocky Mountains, in the bloody winter." He had her undivided attention now. "Red has assured me that the winters here can be quite mild, in comparison to the bitter winters of the eastern part of your country. Bottom line is, you can't stay. Go to Rifle, go south all the way to Mexico, but you can't stay in the city. It will be too dangerous. The cities will die. Good Lord, the Aborigines of the never-never will survive much easier than Denver, New York, or Los Angeles. Now, Red has offered to outfit our adventure, and I'm for going anywhere away from the multitudes. You just name the spot. I'll make sure you and your son get there." He had her, and he knew it. She was a high spirited one, but she would go.

Red knew he couldn't stay in the house where he and Evee lived and loved. He planned to put anything he valued in the *vault,* then make the rounds of the city to check on friends and help out where he could. With his connections and network of friends and acquaintances, he knew he could find anything he ever needed or anyone else needed. Today was an example. The shelves were bare, but he knew exactly where to go to find the things they needed for the trip. And he knew Ian was a good man – the man for Jane, if she didn't scare the hell out of him first. Damn bull-headed woman!

"Damn, girl," it was Red's turn. "You don't have to do life by yourself! Here's a man . . . a good man, who's willing to travel the distance and offer assistance to get you to your folks and you're ready to spit in his eye!" She'd never seen Red so worked up before unless he was tearing someone's head off – literally. "You could make it, with a little help from the sun and the winter's holding off some. You know Denver – mild winters – no skiing some years unless the snowmakers create enough snow – mountain resorts crying for snow. You know you could do it!"

Hope filled her as she dared to believe them. Thinking of her mom and dad, she wouldn't have a moment's peace until she was there and saw them with her own eyes. Red would have taken her himself, but knew this was Ian's destiny, whether she believed it yet, or not. Ian was smitten and Red believed it would take a man's unwavering devotion to conquer Jane. Ian himself believed divine intervention placed him here and from the beginning, was deeply involved in Jane's life. So when Ian said, "I'll take her across the divide," Red was elated and knew that's the way it should be.

"We could pack up tonight and leave in the morning."

"Ian, are you crazy? Tomorrow? How can I decide what to take and what to leave? What part of my life should I leave behind? This place is full of me! And what about my sisters?"

"We'll go to their house first, convince them, too. They may not realize that it's not going to go away, or get any better, or be different. THIS IS HOW IT IS NOW! We have to warn them – to convince them to go with us."

"And if they don't want to go? Jesse has family in town, too. What if they've already made the decision to stay with them? You'll give it up?"

"If I can't convince them of what I know, and they choose to stay, we'll go across by ourselves. But, I know I'm right. I've thought about this a long time. Somewhere in you, you have to learn to trust."

"I do trust. I trust myself, although it seems like I've been my own worst enemy for most of my life and I'm probably the last person I should trust."

"You got that right." Red was elated.

"Okay, we'll go to Suzan's . . . and Ian, you have no sane reason to do this for us. You hardly know us, and I, . . . well, . . . I just don't know what to say – I don't know how to thank you."

"Like I said, I love a grateful woman."

"And me too," it was Red holding two bottles of his favorite brew. "You don't know how much easier this will be knowing that Jane and Levi have you with them. Thanks, Ian. I owe you, mate."

He and Ian tapped bottles as Red guzzled his down without drawing a breath.

"Oh, no, I can't do this again. I don't get along well with your mountain spring beer. Now, give me a bottle of Castlemaine Four X or Old Australian Stout, and I'll show you how to drink grog, mate."

"What's all this *mate* stuff?" intruded Jane sarcastically. "I though mate was a male-female kind of thing."

"It's the same thing as the *brothers*, only they say mate." Red was still defending Ian, siding with him.

"My woman would be my *Sheila*, my *bird*, my *good sort*, *sweetheart*, *love*, or *just deserts* in some cases, but your male friends, your brothers – those are mates. Women can never be mates," added Ian.

"So, did you two cut your thumbs and let the blood flow together to become blood brothers, too?" Might as well get all the cultures in there, thought Jane.

"I think she's a mite miffed that she can't be a mate, too." Ian was grinning from ear to ear and he and Red burst out laughing, not letting Jane's irritation at their levity get the best of them.

"You're both so immature. Speaking of boys – I thought Levi was out in the garage with you."

She saw a look of conspiracy pass between them and knew they were up to something.

"Okay, what's going on? What are you two loons up to and where is Levi?"

They shook their heads and gave each other dumb looks with outstretched palms – they really played it to the max. She flipped past them, through the back door and out to the garage.

"Aw, mom, you're supposed to be cooking dinner. This is a surprise and it's not finished yet."

"What the hell is this? Your bike! It's torn down in parts!" She didn't know exactly what she was looking at, but knew it was Levi's bike wheels and two long poles with the images of the motorcycle gas tank welded onto them. Levi looked proudly at the welding job as he pushed back the helmet to appraise his work.

"And Red let you weld it, huh?"

"Mom, I've been welding since I was six, and . . . "

"Yea, I remember the burn across your thigh, the time your shirt caught on fire, and the melted GI Joe you welded. Red promised me you wouldn't weld by yourself and now you're out here welding by yourself." She was distraught with emotion, not so much about the welding, but with everything; the decision to leave, what to take and what to leave; food to last for their journey; Ian, Ian, Ian. It was all churning in her already overloaded brain. She saw the discouraged look on Levi's face and knew she'd taken it too far. She was missing the whole point, and what did it matter anyway? Her face softened as she put her arm around his shoulders and his eyes beamed with excitement and pride as he explained what he designed to carry their stuff across the mountains.

"Oh, you made this to carry our stuff across the mountains?"

"Oh-oh. Now are you mad again? I thought Red and Ian were going to talk you into it."

"Boy, what am I going to do with the men in my life? I'm outnumbered three to one. I guess you better hurry up and finish this if we're leaving tomorrow."

A triumphant *Yes!* erupted from Levi as he wrapped his arms around her. She always smelled so good.

"I'll have Red find that hanging lantern to give you better light."

"Thanks, Mom. You won't be sorry."

Later, after dining by candlelight on ground beef, crispy bacon, canned pintos, tortillas and cheese, Ian and Jane sat at the kitchen table drinking a cup of Ian's exquisitely strong coffee. Boy, that man makes a good cup of coffee. She watched him to see if he was intruding on her mind again. The smile in those hazel-green eyes told her it didn't really matter anymore. He was part of her life and he intended to stay. She liked the feeling of comfort and security she felt from him.

"Let's make a list of the things that are absolutely necessary, and you can add whatever else we can carry. I'm going to go over to the big house and find another lantern, so we have more light."

"Where do I start?" Jane sat silently as the flickering candlelight danced on the broad shoulders disappearing out the back door. Unable to force the emotions down, the tears trickled down her sunburned cheeks as the jumble of emotions spilled out at thoughts of leaving this place . . . and Red.

Her eyes roamed the kitchen to the marble rolling pin her mom gave her. "Guess I won't need that to survive – would make a hell of a weapon though," she laughed as she wiped the tears away. The spark of inspiration led her to her bedroom dresser. In the top drawer, she counted twelve pair of worthless panty hose with runs – she kept them separate from the good ones. She put her arm in the legs until all twelve pair were strung on her arm, tied a knot in the toe where all the runs were, and dropped the body of the rolling pin into it. There! A perfect weapon! Better than the billy clubs the cops use. Ha! It really felt pretty good as she swung it around and around her head, getting the feel of it, just as Ian came into the open doorway.

"Good heck, woman. Are you going to slay all the yobs with that thing?"

"The only *yobs* are the ones putting ideas into my son's head."

"No, you're wrong about that, young lady." He was standing too close to her again. She could feel his breath on her hair, as he took her hand and led her back into the kitchen.

"When Levi went with us yesterday to fill up the milk jugs at the lake . . . oh yea, I forgot to tell you that several people were already doing their laundry and dishes in the lake, so we better start boiling it as well as adding the chlorine bleach.

"Okay, so Levi was helping you, and . . . ?"

"Yea, we were talking about how to convince you to risk the trip across the mountains and how to carry all the provisions and supplies for such an undertaking. Levi asked me if the torches would still work. I explained to him that anything that didn't operate by electricity or batteries or generators would still work. He then described a *travois* type contraption he could make using his and Tad's bike wheels and some metal tubing he knew Red kept in the garage. Oh, he also needs something leather to make a suitable harness for pulling by hand. He figured he'd make it small enough so he could pedal the loaded weight by himself. Red asked him where he got the idea and he said, . . . I remember it from when I was big."

Jane dropped the *weapon* to the floor and gave him her full attention.

"Red didn't question it, so I didn't ask, but what did he mean by – when I was big?"

She sank limply to the chair at the kitchen table as the past flooded back to her in a wave of memories. "I don't know how to explain this without sounding spooky. When Levi learned to talk he told me things that he described as, *when I was big*. They're like flashes of memory from some other time that he remembers himself *big*, or as an adult."

"What kinds of memories, specifically?"

"He remembered writing with a stick on rocks and leather, and writing with a feather. Once he described a wooden *something* made with two poles, used to pull stuff. I remember I questioned him so I could learn more or spark more of his memory. When he told me about the wooden poles I asked him if it was a wagon and he said, no, it didn't have wheels. I asked if it was a sled, and he said, no, but you could pull it over snow and he drew me a triangle looking thing and said a horse, a dog or person could pull it and it had straps to *hold you in.* He was four years old when he told me about that. I remember now. I wrote it down in my journal so I wouldn't forget.

"Does he still have these windows of memory?"

"If he does, he doesn't tell anyone. I think he became self conscious about it so I haven't heard anything for the last two or three years, until now. There were other things too. When Levi was five years old he said he saw a white eagle that told him his dad was dead and gave him a feather to tie in his hair so everyone would know who he was. The eagle told him not to forget. He showed me the feather and sure enough, it was an eagle feather. I hadn't told Levi his father was dead – he'd been dead for about a year, I guess. When he told me about the eagle, I had to tell him it was true, but he already knew. He trusts his dreams, or visions, or flashes of memory, whatever they are. I don't question it anymore. I trust it, too. And last summer when we were at the ranch there was a huge, beautiful moon and he told mom it was a *buffalo moon.* Mom asked me about it, but I couldn't think of anywhere that he would have heard it. I'd never heard of a buffalo moon. I forgot about that.

"Why didn't you tell him about his father?" It was an innocent enough question – probably deserved an answer.

"We never discuss it." The look in Jane's eyes told Ian the conversation was over.

"Well, we best get on with the list. Oh, by the way, that was great tucker – quite a supper, I don't think I've ever eaten fresh, homemade tortillas before. They were wonderful. Reminded me a bit of puftaloons from the out-back."

"Thank-you. Yes, that was quite the last supper."

## *Chapter 5*

Ian and Red helped Levi build his rendition of a bicycle-drawn travois by lantern light. They followed Levi's instructions – he was the boss. When it was finished, it looked as fine a travois as either Red or Ian could have designed.

While Red helped Levi with the welding, Ian followed Levi's instructions for making a harness from the black leather jacket that Red donated for the project. Ian cut the sleeves off, saving the leather from them to make straps to attach the harness to the travois poles. The harness was more sophisticated than originally used, as Levi incorporated the jacket pattern into the design of the harness, with breast pockets, lining, and even fringe trimming. It was definitely the latest in harnesses, and, as Levi pointed out, it would be warm and was large enough to fit over his clothes and warm jacket. The back hung lower than the front and would offer protection from the snow or rain as he bent over the bicycle to pedal and steer. It wouldn't have to be worn when the bike was pulling the travois, but would definitely be needed to pull it by hand.

When finally finished, it was about sixteen feet long, fairly lightweight, rolled on wheels, complete with patch kit, tool kit and spare-parts, and could easily be converted to be pulled by hand. Perfect!

Red laced a canvas tarp to use for the bed of the travois, and donated plenty of bungy-cords, tarps, and nylon strapping to secure its load to the frame. It was a magnificent work of art and both men beamed with pride at the small engineer who designed it.

"Go get your mom, son. This is gonna knock her socks off," shouted Red.

Jane was busy going through cupboards, drawers, medicine chests, bookshelves, and closets, selecting what to take. All the essentials were stacked in inventory piles on the living-room floor and she was in the process of choosing those special items she couldn't leave behind when Levi bolted through the back door.

"Mom, you've got to come and see what we made." He pulled on her jacket sleeve, half dragging her through the living room.

"Okay, okay. I'm coming." She hurriedly removed special photos from the albums collected over the years. She knew the ones she wanted – pictures of Levi over the years, group shots of family reunions, and the priceless photos of Evee, Tad and Red. These they would take with them, others would be left behind. If there was a safe place to store them, Red would know about it.

"Hey! It's about time you guys knocked it off for the night. You'll have to get a good night's sleep, since we plan to leave in the morning." She stretched her aching back and shoulders as she followed Levi to the garage. "I've got to get some sleep, too, or I won't be worth a damn tomorrow," she said wearily.

"Wait 'til you see it, Mom. You won't believe it!" He excitedly pushed open the garage door so she could see what all the fuss was about.

She was speechless as she walked around the travois. Her mouth gaped, but she couldn't find the words to express her amazement. "I – wow! I . . . I don't think I've ever seen anything like this. It's beautiful! It will be perfect for the trip. I can't believe you guys built this thing."

"Whoa, there. *Us guys* didn't build it. Your son here," Ian affectionately placed a hand on Levi's shoulder and proudly boasted, "designed the whole thing himself. We were just following orders."

Jane looked from Red's face to Ian's and Levi's, and they were all grinning like hyenas. She walked around it again, running her hand along the metal piping and the Harley gas tank replica's taken from the boys' bikes and welded onto the pipes. Two wheels attached to a straight piece of re-bar extended across the back, from pipe to pipe, giving the crude axle a four-foot span. It was excellent. "It's a masterpiece. A real work of art," she announced.

Levi let out a whoop and threw his baseball cap into the air as Red picked him up and placed him between his and Ian's shoulders and they carried him around the garage, out the door, and into the little house. Jane took up the rear of the parade after she turned off the lantern and closed the garage door.

"We've got to celebrate, Mom," exclaimed Levi. She looked around for something appropriate to mark the event as special and produced two cans of Diet Pepsi.

Ian found his backpack and removed a small drawstring pouch from a zippered leather case. He opened the pouch and took out a metal object. He raised his right hand and with great ceremony, presented the object to Levi. "This is to signify that the owner of this medal be recognized as the first appointee of the new generation of design engineers." They all clapped and Levi held the gold medal up for all to admire.

"My gosh, that's an African Krugerrand." Jane couldn't believe her eyes. "Ian," she started, "are you sure you want to . . . "

"It's the perfect gold medal," Ian interrupted her. "I've got a few more that I brought with me to trade for stock in ostrich farms, but I can safely say, that won't be happening." It was the grin on his face that won her over.

The presentation was much too formal for Red who took the opportunity to pop the top off a couple bottles of *bubbly*, as Ian called Red's beer, to cap-off-the-day, another saying of Ian's.

"Thanks, Mate," said Ian, as he and Red tipped bottles together.

Jane began going through the list of items with Ian, pointing out where each object was stacked on the floor.

Levi and Red watched them from the kitchen and Levi gently nudged Red's shoulder. "Red?"

"Yes, son," Red responded, as he placed a big arm around Levi's shoulders. "What can I do for you, Little Guy?"

"I was wondering what you think of those two?"

Red looked at Jane and Ian who were seriously involved in list and inventory now. "Well." Red stroked his shaggy beard, thoughtfully. "The truth?"

"Yea. The truth."

Red put his head close to Levi's. "The truth is, I think he's one hell of a decent man, and your mom deserves one hell of a decent man. I think he'd be a pretty good dad, too. I know it's kinda early to tell, but I've got a feeling about this, and I think it's just one of those things that was meant to happen – kinda like Evee and me. And that's the truth."

"Yea, but . . . " Red could see Levi's eyes fill to the rims. "You've always been like my dad."

"And I always will be like your dad. Nothing can ever change that, you know that." Red shifted his weight in the chair to see Levi's eyes better. "Look at me, son."

Tears slipped out as Levi looked at Red. "You and your mom will always be able to count on me for as long as I'm alive. But, boy, you've got to understand that your mom needs to be with a man to love her and be her sweetheart, just as much as Evee and I needed to be sweethearts together. Just like you'll want a sweetheart someday when you're a grown man. Why, your mom will be the happiest woman on earth if she finds the true love of a man." Red blew his nose and put both arms around Levi and held him close.

A few moments passed and Levi pulled his head back and looked at Red. "Will you come and see us at my grandpa's ranch?"

"Wild horses couldn't keep me away," Red assured him.

Levi looked over at his mom and Ian again. "I guess he's okay, then. I like him, too. I just wanted to know if you liked him."

"He's a real brother. A real mate, as they say in his country. I know he'd do anything for you and your mom, just like me. We've had some serious talks these four days together, and I know you can count on him."

"Okay." Levi yawned and before long, Red yawned, too. "I'm getting kinda tired."

"Me too, buddy. What do you think about coming over and sleeping at the big house with me tonight? You can have the sofa, and I'll sleep in that grand old recliner of mine. How 'bout it?"

"Great!"

They both said goodnight and left Ian and Jane to decide how to pack the treasured items for the journey. After Levi fell asleep, Red gathered up all the backpacks that Evee and Tad had used and took them over to the little house for Jane to pack.

The two worked well into the night, packing supplies. Some packs carried everyday needs like shampoo, soap, toothpaste, lotion, Jane's make-up, all the vitamins, medicines and prescription drugs, no matter how old. Clothes were packed by season; the heavy winter clothing they would need for the trip, everyday clothes, underwear, and Jane even packed some favorite summer things. Levi grew out of his clothes so fast he didn't have an assortment to choose from.

Treasured keepsakes were tightly packed and would be opened after they reached the ranch. Jane took all the items she'd kept for Levi that were once his father's; his hunting knife, the leather medicine bag he'd worn around his neck, the contents known only to him. Someday, when Levi went on his own *Vision Quest*, she would give him the treasures. She also found Levi's Eagle feather and his father's medicine pipe and the elaborately beaded leather pouch for its placement. If Levi ever wanted to follow the *Indian Way,* she would tell him of the special ceremony to cleanse the pipe and restore it to its intended purpose.

It was near dawn by the time everything was packed and properly marked for easy identification. Ian convinced Jane to get some sleep, promising to wake her after a couple hours. He took off his boots and pulled the afghan over him as he stretched out the length of the sofa. It seemed like he'd barely closed his eyes when Levi shook his shoulder and the sun was streaming in the living room window.

"Ian. . . Ian," Levi whispered. "Where's the coffee?"

"Coffee?" Ian sat up and rubbed his eyes. "Coffee's in that duffel-bag," he said, pointing to the old, worn Army-issue bag Jane used to haul their belongings in. "Who's making coffee?" Ian asked, as he tugged at his boots.

"Red's got the propane grill on to heat water for oatmeal. I wanted to surprise mom and make her some coffee." Levi was obviously well rested and raring to get started.

"Good idea." Ian tousled Levi's hair as they walked out the back door. Red and Levi wheeled the bicycle-steered travois to the back yard to load. There was already a bundle wrapped in canvas and tightly secured with bungy cords, and a smaller pack that Ian recognized as an Army issue parachute.

"What have we got, here," asked Ian, as Levi scooped coffee into the coffeepot that was already boiling over the flame of the barbecue grill. Red motioned for Ian to follow him into the garage.

"I don't want Jane to know or she'll worry the whole time, but if you ever need to start a war or end one, you'll be prepared. All you'll need is four good men or women. I didn't want to load you down too heavy, with all the other things you're taking."

"Didn't I see a parachute," Ian asked with amusement. "Are you suggesting we climb the highest mountain and wait for a good wind before we jump off?"

"Don't knock it, man. Evee and I bought that at an auction and we had some real good times under there. You never know when it will come in real handy. Hell, it would tent a small crowd if you prop it up inside. And it's waterproof, lightweight, and camouflage. Uglier than all hell, but I'll bet you'll find some way to put it to good use. I just don't want to see Evee every time I look at it, or I'd take it with me."

"I appreciate the thought, Mate, and I'm sorry I poked fun at it. I'm sure it will come in right handy, although I like your idea the best." Ian was grinning and Red knew why. He'd like to know Jane a lot more than she was willing to let a man know her at the moment. Red was counting on that changing, with time and opportunity. And there should be plenty of both between Denver and Rifle. Red believed the name-of-the-game was opportunity, and Jane just needed a little time.

Ian's grin disappeared and he became serious. "Are you sure you don't want to go with us now?" Ian knew Red had plans of his own, but he had to ask, one more time.

"Naw, I've got things to do and people to see, but I'll probably mosey over that way when the weather lets up some. Probably early summer, so be watching and listening for that old Indian motorcycle of mine."

"I'll be disappointed if you let anything stop you."

Red offered his hand to Ian and the two men slapped each other's shoulders. "You just take care of those two. They're all the family I've got left."

"You can count on me, although I don't know how much care that little lady will let me give her."

"You just let time work its magic on Jane. She just thinks she's tough. But she's scared. Why, Jane's about as sensitive and passionate a woman as I've ever known and I'm tickled to see her even being civil to a man. I haven't heard her laugh as much in the last four years as I've heard in the last four days, in spite of all the tragedy around us. And I'll tell you something else. I think you two are a good match, and Levi likes the idea, too. I can guarantee you, life will never be dull with Jane."

"I think you're right." Ian was surprised at Red's bold directness, but they both knew time was short and anything they needed to say better be said now.

"What are you two jackasses grinning about?" Jane stood with a cup of coffee, leaning in the doorway of the garage.

"Men stuff. Go on – get out of here." Red waved her out with his hands and she just stood there.

"Well, I guess I'll get a cup of java, too." Red started out the door with Ian close behind, the two of them still grinning.

"Hang onto your butts when you taste that coffee," hollered Jane to their backs.

"Now, that's coffee!" shouted Red. "Never could get Evee to make it like this." Red turned to Levi and did a high-five palm-slap in the air. "Yes, sir. Not only the best engineer around, but makes the best coffee in town, too." Red was going to miss Levi.

Ian and Jane grimaced as they drank the thick, black liquid and ate the last of the leftover tortillas and meat from the night before, as well as the oatmeal Red made. They drank another cup of the strong brew while smoking their morning cigarettes. The coffee was hot, and the morning air was cold, and they had a long way to go to get to Suzan's house.

Jane packed the kitchen things last. All the food was packed, even the canned meats; salmon, tuna, and sardines that Jane always kept stocked for quick meals. She knew they would be heavy, but they could eat them first and lighten their load. Jane packed all the spices from the kitchen, as well as Evee's, at Red's insistence. The guys packed all the rest of the items on the travois. They soon covered the large load with canvas tarps tied down with ropes, nylon straps and bungy cords. It was heavy. Now the true test would come.

They helped each other secure the packs they intended to carry on their backs and each had a container of water hooked to their belts. They were ready. Red's goodbye was short and sweet. All of them were on the edge of emotional explosion, but he quickly promised he'd see them in the summer.

Jane wore her favorite wool-felt hat with the beaded headband her mother made for her. Ian stuffed his boots in his pack and wore a pair of biker boots for the walk. They'd been Red's, so they were already broken in and felt good on his feet. Ian opted to carry his black canvas pack and Professor Neven's leather pack with all his research papers. His 30.06 was slung over his shoulder and he wore his cowboy hat. Levi wore his favorite Rockie's baseball cap – the one that Dante Bichette personally autographed three summers ago.

Red would remember every detail of this scene for the rest of his life. He watched them until they were out of sight. They headed north on Navajo Street. He knew they'd be okay. He knew they'd make it. It was a good decision.

They were a strange sight, but not unusual, and they passed several other groups – mostly traveling south. Everyone in the old neighborhood waved to them, as they recognized the Harley images welded to the sides of the travois and knew it was Red's family. Even people who didn't know Red seemed to take comfort in the familiar insignia of the brotherhood of bikers and a certain camaraderie existed.

Stopping to rest on the hill overlooking Clear Creek, just past 64th Avenue on Pecos Street, they watched the people who were now living in the many tents erected along the creek's bank. They didn't see a single lawyer, doctor, judge, policeman, plumber or waitress. Just people, all hanging onto the day like the last glow of sunset.

They heard the same stories of devastation, death, and survival. Some eyed their tightly secured belongings covetously, but then would notice the rifle slung over Ian's shoulder. Ian warned Levi to say close.

It was December 14, the fifth day since their lives changed. Many that they passed wore the empty look of despair, as if death had cheated them by leaving them here. Others looked as though they wouldn't have long to wait to join those already departed. They donned the slowly realized truth of their circumstances like invisible weights collared around their necks, stooping their backs and shoulders, and forcing heads and eyes downward. Jane witnessed the physical manifestation of depression and hopelessness en masse, and fought her panic-driven impulse to run.

She was very familiar with this part of Denver. For thirteen years her family lived in a house on Mariposa and 68th Street, just down the creek and across the field. She used to ride horses in these fields and play in the creek when she was a kid. It brought back old memories, some good, some bad. She was glad when they were ready to move on.

Levi and the travois held up well. Once he got the momentum going, he thought it was pretty fun. Except going downhill. Ian realized the brakes would be the first thing to go. He and Jane could push from the back when the hills were too steep for Levi to pedal by himself, but the first steep down-hill grade, when they turned east on 88th Avenue, scared the begeezuz out of Levi. When he realized he couldn't stop, he screamed like a wild-child, with Jane and Ian sluggishly trying to catch up with him. Finally, he quit fighting it and just let it coast, and it turned out to be quite a ride. The greatest obstacle was weaving in and out of abandoned cars and the last thing they needed was to stop and re-load. By the time it coasted to a stop, Levi could hardly wait to conquer the next downhill slope.

They continued east on the 88th Avenue bridge that crossed over I-25 and Jane immediately flashed-back to the memory of viewing a similar scene from the Speer viaduct, that first day. Now the picture was eerily quiet. Absent were the mournful wails from wounded souls and panic-stricken screams slicing the air like ripping metal. Just awesome quiet. They turned north on Washington and when they reached Webster Lake on 116th they stopped to eat hard-boiled eggs and cheese that Red had packed for them that morning. Ian figured there were only a couple more hours of daylight, so they smoked a cigarette, drank some water and were on their way again.

Most of their trek passed in silence, as the truth of the situation became vividly real to all of them, but Jane was puzzled by all the children on the streets who seemed to be alone.

"Ian."

"Yes, Janie." He'd called her *Janie* since that second day. He explained that most objects in Australia, people included, have an understood nickname. Jane became *Janie*, Mark is *Markie*, or *Marko*, TV is *tellie*, and he referred to his parents as *oldies*. In Australia, everyone he knew called him Jaynie. Jane Jayne sounded funny enough, but Janie Jaynie was just too much and always evoked hilarious laughter from her.

"Have you noticed all the children that don't seem to be attached to anyone?" she asked.

"They're not. Attached to anyone, that is. The surviving children who haven't been taken in by other families are the ones who will suffer the most. Many of their parents either died in the major thrust of the energy surge or their parents have abandoned them."

"Go on!" she exclaimed, unbelieving. "No parent would abandon their children. Most parents would die protecting their children." She dared him to refute her.

"Normally, yes. But there's nothing normal about this. Think about it, Janie. Death, fear and panic from the very first day, soon replaced by a false sense of security to have survived; the panic and security are short-lived, because the circumstances don't change. Then, reality begins to set in creating depression that totally incapacitates people. It's really just beginning now. It will get a lot worse over the next few weeks. Heck Janie, I can feel your depression as you look at the absolute despair that is so obvious on the faces we've passed today."

"Yes, but all their parents can't be dead. Surely the parents will come to their senses and survival instincts will take over. It's the human condition to survive even insurmountable obstacles."

"Human condition, yes, but, as most of them are probably sitting at their kitchen tables eating their last piece of bread or lying in their beds to stay warm, their wills become too weak to strike out, even to save their children. With depression, the spirit leaves the body long before the body gives up."

She couldn't allow herself to give credibility to what he was saying. Even she had struggled to survive and learned to live again.

"What we've got to consider here is normal struggle circumstances compared to what exists now. When people are fighting their own inner battles, everything out here in the world continues as usual. The rules are different now. Nothing is the same outside anymore, regardless of all that used to be okay on the inside. Now, not only are the inner battles still going on, but everything out here has changed," he said with a sweeping gesture.

Ian took advantage of Jane's churning thoughts and continued. "Imagine if we hadn't met and you didn't have a reasonable explanation for what happened. You see your child, full of energy and life, and you eat your last meal. You don't know where to go to get food or water. You could steal from your neighbors, and I know you would, or maybe some will even share with you for awhile, but probably not for long. You know your child will probably starve to death in the next few weeks. Would you want to live to watch your child die?"

He didn't give her time to answer as he continued to press his point. "You would abandon your child spiritually and emotionally, whether you ever left physically, or not. It wouldn't even be a choice. It's the human spirit protecting itself from intolerable pain, and what pain could possibly be worse than watching helplessly while your own child dies?"

"My child wouldn't die while I had a breath in me."

"Remember all the covers of Time Magazine of women holding the starving, skeletal forms of their children?"

"Yes – and I remember the horrible weight of guilt I felt for having food in my refrigerator."

"Well, remember the look in the mother's eyes – hollow – empty – lifeless. They abandoned hope of saving their child long before the child died."

"My gosh, Ian, it's only been five days."

"That's pretty noble, coming from someone who is privy to what happened, is connected to a man like Red – rough as guts, who could find an orchid growing in the bush, has a propane barbie in the yard, and has been able to make some kind of preparation, a plan. Yes, it's only been five days, but some mothers haven't had anything to feed their kiddies since the second day. You aren't waiting for a husband or father you don't know is dead, to walk through the door. You aren't waiting for someone to come home to take care of you."

Ian knew his words were harsh and that they both felt passionately about their different opinions. "Think about this, my sweet. Of all the people we've seen today, the only ones with life in their eyes are those who are leaving, have a goal, a destination. Those are your survivors! And, of course, the children we've seen playing along the way, whether their parents have the will to live or not. Children don't understand disaster. They live so close to the moment. If they're hungry and find a piece of moldy bread or a brown banana, they eat it anyway. And this is only the beginning. It will get worse. Much worse," he finished ominously.

The lump in her throat kept her from speaking and she knew he was probably right. She couldn't imagine herself watching her son die, but hoped she would never learn that she could.

When they reached 120th, they turned east to hopefully eliminate a couple miles from their walk by cutting through pastures. Traveling with the travois would limit what routes they could take. They sure couldn't heft it over fences. They found a couple cows with their throats cut and hunks of their flesh removed. "It's starting earlier than I guessed," Ian said, mournfully.

The thought of killing a cow to survive didn't bother him. That would be the sane thing to do and he'd seen plenty of that growing up in the outback on his parents' station in the *never-never* of Queensland. But, as he explained to Jane, "If people were thinking rationally they would group together, kill the animal, prepare the meat and divide it among themselves so nothing would be wasted and all would be fed. Instead, they cut its throat, let its blood run on the ground, steal only what they can carry and leave the rest for the buzzards. Oh well," he added, "I guess buzzards have to eat too." And they were. Five turkey buzzards stood guard over the dead animals while crows and magpies waited patiently.

They stopped to rest at Steele Street. They were only a couple miles away from Suzan's, but their muscles were beginning to visibly knot. Jane kneaded Ian's shoulder muscles with the weight of her elbows, as Ian massaged Levi's calves. Finally, after he massaged Jane's shoulders, Ian secured his packs on top of the travois and placed Levi in the middle of it all and told him to hold on while he pushed the bike. His legs were too long to pedal and he realized this could be a real drawback he hadn't thought of. Levi couldn't possibly pedal this weight all the way by himself, although he'd done well the twenty kilometers they'd already covered. Pushing and pulling worked and it was still the best method of transporting they saw as they passed others along the way.

And they had seen it all – not as sophisticated as Levi's travois, but very creative and efficient. Children on bicycles pulled wagons; fathers and mothers rode mountain bikes attached to screened-in carts originally purchased to pull their young children on family outings. Grocery carts were the most accessible means for carrying belongings, but were nearly impossible to roll on the street. Most people were on foot carrying their life's treasures on their backs and in their arms.

It was dark by the time they reached the pathway that led to the neighborhood where Suzan lived. They were greeted by the low, warning growl of a very large, black beast that stood in front of the darkened door. What would they do if no one was home? Ian saw the wavy mirage of heat and smoke escape the chimney and knew someone was inside. Jane and Levi started hollering for Suzan and soon the door burst open, revealing the soft glow of candles in the living room.

There was a family reunion, right in the middle of the driveway, as Laramie and Suzan crowded around the weary travelers. As they passed the animal and entered the house, joy and relief flowed down tense, distraught faces. Introductions were quickly made, Laramie and Suzan wary of the stranger traveling with their sister and nephew. A very good-looking stranger, thought Laramie.

"Where's Jesse?" Jane asked, afraid of the answer.

Suzan's eye's flashed with worry as she told them he left that morning to check on his parents. Both his parents were on daily insulin maintenance for diabetes, and they would die without their medicine. He'd ridden one of their four mountain bikes and should have been home by now.

When all the excitement died down, they stored the travois in the garage, unloading only the packs they needed immediately. Ian took both of his packs in the house for safe keeping, although it would be a fool who tried to pass that wild creature guarding the front door.

Suzan placed more wood on the fire to make coffee as Laramie told the story of Black, and finding Dominic, Sara and Jen.

As Suzan recounted her story of the first day, Jane intently studied her sister's grave face. She saw the ragged, purple scar healing above her eye, her peeling face and singed hair. Suzan had aged ten years since they last saw each other at the ranch for Thanksgiving. Maybe it was the dancing flames from the fireplace that severely cast her face in bronzed shadows of pain and worry. Suzan was unable to recall the details of that first day and couldn't even remember how she'd gotten home. For the first time, Jane realized how strong Suzan really was. She'd always written Suzan off as indulged, privileged, naive and weak. But looking at her now, it was obvious to Jane that she had survived a near-death experience and was lucky to be alive. Something was definitely different.

Jane explained how she met Ian, not the whole story of course, just that he'd been the scheduled guest speaker for her sociology class. She told them about Evee and Tad and that Red was not ready to leave it behind yet. Her sisters were relieved that she hadn't brought him, too, although Jane saw the empathy in their eyes for the loss of her *other* family. Ian told them of his research in Sydney and promised to explain his theory in the morning, after a good night's sleep and Jesse's return.

The weary threesome arranged their sleeping bags in the dining room, and quickly succumbed to their exhausted bodies. Jacinth pulled her sleeping bag next to Levi, whom she adored. They were first cousins of the kind that develops into the deeper love and protective feelings usually shared between brother and sister. She had been very worried about him.

Only Suzan heard Jesse open the front door in the early hours of dawn. As she poured him a cup of coffee, he slumped in the chair by the fire and fell asleep, shoes and all. She placed an afghan over him, unlaced his shoes and replaced them with his moccasin slippers and returned to the warmth of her sleeping bag. Now, she could sleep.

The sky was dark and gray with the gloomy promise of winter when Jesse awoke to hushed whispers and Laramie's transforming the bedroom into a living room again. He ached from the long bike ride and sleeping in the chair and slowly stretched his stiff muscles. The aroma of coffee rose through the smell of wood burning in the fireplace. He was barely awake and was startled by the hand thrust in front of him.

"G'day there, Jesse. I'm Ian Jayne. Very pleased to meet you, finally." Ian shifted uncomfortably, uncertain if the look he was shot was friendly, or not. He guessed – not. "Sorry, Jesse, I know this is abrupt. I'm here with Jane, your sister-in-law, and her son, Levi. I think we're the latest additions to your growing family."

Ian put his hand in his pocket. "Can I get you a cup of coffee, mate?" He was happy for an excuse to leave the whole situation and disappeared to the kitchen to find a cup. "Wyoming," he said to Laramie. "Help me out here, will you? I've got myself in a bit of a wedge. Tell him who I am. And where's Jane?"

Laramie had watched the exchange between Jesse and Ian and was thoroughly amused.

"Yea, Wyoming." Jesse had followed Ian into the kitchen and overheard his request to Laramie. "Tell me who this guy is."

"Jesse, this is Professor Ian Jayne, an innocent by-stander in Jane's morning class last Thursday, and . . . "

Jesse cut her off with, "There are no innocent by-standers in Jane's life. She takes hostages and saves them to eat for breakfast. And you've put up with her for how many days now? Five? Six? You deserve a medal, my friend." Jesse enjoyed Ian's uneasiness as much as Laramie and was grinning from ear to ear when he offered his hand to Ian. "And, by the way, this is Laramie. It's in Wyoming, but not the same."

Laramie and Jesse couldn't hold it back any longer and gut-breaking laughter rolled through the house, a welcome sound.

"Well, you really had me going there," said Ian.

"Yea, I would have been just as nervous, probably more so," Jesse said, "if the tables had been turned. But, better you than me."

"Easy for you to say. I have a knack for meeting the Zerlich women's men in the oddest fashion. Remind me to tell you about meeting Red and Levi."

"Red would scare the hell out of anybody even meeting him under the best of circumstances." Jesse was still laughing.

"Red didn't talk about Jane's family very much, but said you were a reasonable man with an open mind who loved to ride. I'd like to see your motorcycles later. If you don't mind showing them to me," he added. "Red raved about them. Said you and Suzan both have class bikes." Ian wasn't often taken so off-guard and was talking way too fast.

"Red's a good man," said Jesse. "We've met on several occasions. I don't know him well. We both ride motorcycles and I've spent a ton of money in his shop, but he's saved me just as much as I've spent. He's sure been a lifesaver for Jane and Levi, though. The girls," he said, pointing in the direction of Laramie, "have something stuck in their craw about Red and his family, but I like him okay. He's pretty imposing if you don't know him." Jesse pulled on his boots and stood to offer Ian his hand again. "Sorry I took advantage of your awkward situation. It was just too good to pass up."

Ian grasped the outstretched hand and knew for sure he had to convince them to leave. "Oh, I walked right into that one. And wide-awake. A man could get shot doing that."

"Want to go take a look at the bikes?" Jesse grabbed his coffee cup and headed for the garage with Ian close behind. Jesse gave a low whistle when he saw the travois. He walked around it, looked under it, and whistled again. "Did Red build this for you?"

"Well, Red and I followed directions and offered advice and workmanship, but Levi designed it and told us how it would work. And it does." Ian proudly bragged about Levi and his creative design. He told Jesse how Levi got the idea from memories of *when he was big*. He could tell right away that Jesse was resistant and skeptical to that line of thought, so he dropped the subject and the bragging.

Jesse admired good workmanship and design, though, as he'd been a design engineer at Coors Brewery for over twenty years. "He did a good job and so did you and Red. Looks like it's carrying quite a load. Where are you heading?"

The moment of truth was at hand. Ian sensed Jesse was neither the visionary Red was nor as trusting. He looked Jesse straight in the eye and told him, "Well, we're going over the mountains to the Rocking Z Ranch, where the parents live." He sucked in his breath, trying to read the expression on Jesse's face.

"Well, unless you know something I don't know, I'd say you were out of your mind." Jesse's gaze was steady and waiting.

Ian recognized his opportunity, and went for it. "Well, I do know something you don't know, and when you're ready, I'll go over it with you. I've got all the research of the last ten years of my life sitting in your living room, and as far as I'm concerned, it's pretty damned conclusive. I even made a believer out of Red."

Jesse would be a tough one to convince, but he was also an engineer and Ian knew his data was impressive and would appeal to Jesse's logic.

Ian grabbed both his packs and they headed upstairs to the sewing room. Ian laid his astronomical maps on Suzan's cutting table. Next to them he put Paul Neven's topographical maps. He spread computer printouts and news clippings across the floor. He continued to lay out everything that he thought might help convince Jesse of his heavily disputed mathematical theory. They spent hours pouring over the research and using a slide ruler to calculate distance and equate figures. Suzan and Jane peeked in to tell them breakfast was ready . . . oatmeal again, but they talked until they were summoned for lunch.

Jesse looked grim when he came out of the room. "Is there a simpler explanation to give Suzan and Laramie so they will be convinced?" Jesse hollered over his shoulder, as they headed downstairs to eat. Ian won him over by the same methods and measures he'd used to try to convince the other mathematicians and engineers. He'd tried and failed with them. But the promised event had happened, and he imagined they all believed now.

"Sure. You got the whole dose, but it's rather overwhelming for most laymen to understand."

"What full dose and what laymen?" Laramie demanded.

"Gather up everyone," hollered Jesse. "We're having a family counsel after lunch," he added. "Damn, I'm hungry. Haven't eaten anything since yesterday noon."

"What happened yesterday, Jesse?" Suzan asked. Suzan, Laramie and the kids were helping the next door neighbors when Jesse and Ian woke up and she forgot to ask how his parents were.

"The folks are fine. So are Natalie and Ron and the kids. John was there, too. They're all staying at my folks." Natalie and Ron were his younger sister and her husband, and John was his younger brother. "I was glad they were all together so I didn't have to ride all over town to check on them."

"What took you so long? Did you run into trouble?" Suzan had worried herself sick by the time he finally got home just before dawn.

"No. Well, some, but nothing that didn't work out okay. I checked the small drug stores in their neighborhood, but the shelves were already bare. The large stores already have neighborhood gangsters guarding the doors – *their territory,* and they've got guns. I tracked down three different bum leads for the insulin, and finally, at about midnight, I rode my bike downtown and walked the last couple miles to St. Joseph's hospital to trade dad's religious medallion collection. I was able to get enough to last for a couple of weeks. Anyway, my parents have insulin now, but I'm going to have to find a lot more if they're going to live."

"What was the trouble you ran into?" Suzan asked.

"Well, it wasn't really trouble. Just an eerie feeling. When I reached downtown, I had the strongest impression that I was being followed, or watched. I never saw anyone and didn't have any trouble at all making the trade, but someone was watching me." The hair-prickling feeling of last night swept across the back of his neck. "I could just feel it."

## *Chapter 6*

No one really knew where he came from. He was just there one day and hadn't been there the day before. Now it seemed as if he'd always been there. The other street kids loved to make up stories about him. They said Gypsies placed a powerful magic spell on him so everyone would be warned not to hurt him. They all knew that Gypsies were the real power of their culture – the wanderers – not belonging, not staying, but royalty, of course. Some said he was the unclaimed son of an Arabian sheik and his mother was a famous movie star. Only he knew the real truth – but they all knew it was better left unspoken. They liked the fantasy. It made all their lives seem more believable, less threatening. And they all protected him. He was all their children – past, present, and future.

His brokers wanted him to change his name to Lola, but he refused. After a severe beating, the brokers became aware that he was not afraid to die and, not wanting to damage their treasure, let him keep the childish name. When he said his name, it sounded like a two-year-old trying to say *yellow.* And most of the time, Lalo was like a two-year-old. It helped him survive his own life – to blank his mind and not allow himself to feel – dead in his own skin.

He rarely spoke, so most people didn't know he was a boy. He was so beautiful to look at that everyone automatically thought he was a beautiful, exotic young woman. His clients loved that he looked like a girl and they also loved his still youthful, male body. Word on the street was that clients had to take a number and wait to get Lalo. But they wanted him, waited, and paid very well. He was fifteen years old and a throw-away child, too gentle natured to fight those he perceived to be in control of his life – his brokers. Too afraid to carry a weapon to kill anyone or he would have. Too shut-down to cry and too distant to care. Just not there. Vacant eyes looking out.

Beautiful, soulful Lalo – Logan Lambert. Only Lalo knew his real name. He picked his name Lalo so he would always remember, but others wouldn't figure it out. That's why he wouldn't let them call him Lola – it was too close, someone might discover who he really was. It had nothing to do with Lola being a girl's name – he was very smart. He knew the clients liked him because he looked like a girl. It was okay with him – no one expected him to act like a man. That would have really killed him – to become a man. His survival instincts were acutely tuned and he knew that if he stayed a two-year-old girl-child, they wouldn't hurt him. He survived. His sister and mother didn't. Survival can be an ugly tool, especially when someone else is in charge of yours.

The day of the earth's rebirth – Lalo became aware of something for the first time. He wanted to live – and he knew he would. A part of him woke up and he knew he could just walk away. And he did.

Those who died the first day lay bloating. Dog packs roamed the city, sniffing out the scent of death. His home for the past five years was deserted and became more dangerous. People died daily for *things;* cigarette lighters, matches, blankets, a piece of bread, and now even a drink of water. Of course the *big things* ownership was established in the first couple of days – guns, ammunition, liquor, drugs, prescription medication, army boots, down jackets. Every time Lalo witnessed someone taking some *thing* from another, he imagined the next someone taking it from him and the next someone, and the next, and the next, until there would be one person with all the *things.* Would he be the new king? Or proclaimed God?

Anarchy! Lalo knew about anarchy! And he watched it happen every day. Some gave up their lives if they tried to keep something. Imagine – losing your life for a book of matches. He had seen it so many times before. Life was cheap. He still knew how to block out the bad parts, and he did. He climbed into a stairwell that first day and lived in the crawl space under the old deserted building on Blake Street. He peeked out during the day and watched the anarchy happen. It was quite educational and he paid attention. He crept out at night after everyone retreated to their sheltered places, and he ate anything he could find.

He knew he would survive and he wanted to. He had army boots, wool overalls, a long coat, three wool blankets, a canvas tarp, canteens of water, a hunting knife, waterproof matches, C-Rations, and best of all – a ski suit; pants and jacket. Insulated – waterproof – the ultimate in survival apparel. But he took pride in knowing he had not taken a single thing at the expense of another human being. He just happened to be at the right place at the right time. The door was open and everyone was taking out armloads of winter camping gear from the deserted Gart Brothers' warehouse down on 17th and Market. He leisurely shopped for exactly what he thought he would need.

He had never been so warm in winter. During the day or night when he did go out to the street, he rolled the long coat and ski-suit up and buried them in their plastic covers in the farthest corner of the crawl space. No one would have to kill him to get them, but he could sleep warm. That's what he was learning in his hiding place, peering out between the boards of the crawl space. He saved the C-Rations, somehow knowing he would need them later – to negotiate and trade. Half of them had already been given to the many children wandering the streets looking for a familiar face. The regular street kids immediately joined up with whoever wanted them and whoever would take care of them. They *did* know how to find people to take care of them.

Of course, everything was changed. There were hundreds, maybe thousands of hollow faced children roaming the streets with nothing but their childhood innocence to protect them. He was not unique anymore. There were no older kids left who felt obligated to protect him. There were lots of mean people, survivors also, who were beating the children for the shoes they wore or their coats. Lalo did not see many people picking up the now-alone children to feed them or keep them warm or love them. And now the children who were alone were dying. No food, no water, no heat. Lalo knew he would have to leave the dying city soon.

The decision to leave was made the night he saw a man riding a mountain bike across the lawn of the rec center on 21st and Broadway. It was an ink black night – no moon, but low cloud cover, so it was not as cold as other nights. Lalo watched him as he got off his bike and looked around the buildings, as if looking for an address. He watched him push his bike across the street to the huge oak tree in front of the old Holy Ghost building. The man took a rope from under his leather jacket, threw it over a high branch and hoisted the bike into the tree and secured it at a lower branch.

Lalo liked watching him. It was part of his education, but this was different. This man was cautious, like him, and smart too. He didn't kill people to take something from them. He traveled at night to protect himself and his *things.*

Jesse instinctively turned in the direction of Lalo. He knew someone was watching him. He could feel it. Lalo knew he hadn't made a sound and couldn't be seen, but he understood the knowing when the instincts become wide awake.

He didn't follow the man, but waited in his hiding place. The thought never crossed his mind to take the bike for himself. He could see the bike, barely visible in the tree. He wondered if he would have thought of that. He watched as two men carrying baseball bats came by, eyes darting from side to side, but not up. He knew he couldn't stop them from taking the bike. He just wanted to make sure the hiding place was good. It was. By the time the man returned, running fast and carrying a large bundle, three other night travelers had quickly hurried by, but none looked up. He watched the man look around and quickly pull the rope, loosen the knot, lower the bike and push the rope back under his jacket.

He could tell the man wasn't street-wise, but he was very good in other areas – it's all about survival. No one in their right mind would run as fast as possible into downtown unless he had precious cargo or was running from *the Man*. And there was no *Man*. Lalo heard him coming from two blocks away. There were a thousand ears in the night, all hearing the hurried footsteps, all peering from their hiding places. He lucked out – no one left the warmth of their shelter to follow him. They probably had all the *things* they wanted and chose to stay and protect them. Lalo thought this man must be a very good person to have the Gods protect him as they surely were. He didn't know if the man belonged to a family, but thought he wouldn't have taken this risk just for himself.

Again, Jesse felt a presence in addition to his own. He crouched instinctively and pivoted on his boot toe, cautious eyes peering into every corner, missing nothing, except Lalo. Seeing no one and knowing that whoever was out there obviously meant him no harm, he secured his precious cargo and quickly raced towards the Brighton Boulevard bridge. Bad move thought Lalo – dangerous neighborhood with no escape route on a bridge. He must live across the river up north. The boy fantasized about the house, the family, the love that probably lived there. It scared him to think that everyone, not just street people, had to steal away in the cover of darkness to make deals to survive. He went back to his crawl space to sleep and to make a plan.

He didn't know where he would go, but the city was dead now, and deserted except for the night people. He saw fewer people everyday and the smell of death and decay began to rise – he rose too. He rehearsed. He would travel by night, carry his booty carefully packed and strapped to his body. He felt like a large, clumsy child. It was cumbersome, but he didn't want to appear to be carrying anything or someone might have to kill him just to find out if it was something they wanted. No one needed money anymore. All the money in the world would only be tinder for the fire. If you had matches.

## *Chapter 7*

The mood grew from mild curiosity to nervous suspense and even suspicion. They wanted to know what the tall stranger said to cause Jesse to be in such a dismal mood. The very air felt heavy. Quite a change from the laughing and teasing of this morning, thought Laramie.

Cheese sandwiches were quickly eaten and washed down with the last jug of apple cider. Laramie commandeered Mira into reading to the children in the living room, as Jesse, Suzan, Ian, Jane, and Laramie crowded around the kitchen table.

"Ian has been going over some of his research with me and he has an interesting theory that seems to be right on the mark," Jesse started. "Go ahead, Ian. I wouldn't even know where to begin." Jesse placed his hands to his forehead, and added, "It's a lot to think about."

"Well, as I told Jesse, I've been working on this for ten years, collecting and researching data. There's a real short version – the earth created her own *energy shift* – to save herself, quite simply. The negative energy has been building up over several decades, but I really didn't think the event would happen this soon." Ian rose from his chair to stretch the knotting muscles in his legs.

"It has to do with the idea of *chaos time*, so simply explained in the book *Jurassic Park* – a butterfly flapping its wings in Peking effects every other atom of space and sound wave in the universe. Awesome to think about, but it's very simple really. With the sophisticated communications systems available to us today we watch wars on the tellie at the same instant they're happening. The Vietnam War was really the first to be forced on the masses through the media, and then we witnessed the Gulf War, Desert Storm and NATO troops in Kosovo, blow-by-blow. Add all the local horrors, children killing children, world terrorist activity, natural disasters, starvation, civil wars, and throw in every conceivable violent act seen at the cinema. Millions have simultaneously witnessed every atrocity the mind can conceive of. Take thirty or fifty million people watching the same horror at the same time and thirty or fifty million brains emit a tremendous amount of horror, fear, panic and unimaginable amounts of negative energy."

"I really only took my research back to the assassination of your late president, John F. Kennedy. It was churned in the brain for weeks by everyone in the world who could get near a tellie or a radio transmission of the bloody event. Princess Di's death had the same effect worldwide. The brain brews up its own stew of chemicals that can create deep depression in the collective spirit of mankind. When this happens for three decades to millions and millions of people all over the world, the collective negative energy is awesome, as witnessed by the growing numbers of depressed, incarcerated and insane in our societies."

Ian realized they just needed him to get to the facts today, and what it all meant now. "I could tell you about magnetic forces of the North and South Poles, cause and effect, global warming, sun flares, black holes, ozone layers and all the other terminology used to explain the natural phenomena in the world. I can get as technical as you want, but it won't help you survive. The earth simply shut-down. In one huge energy-surge, she cleansed herself. Blew out every single mechanism that man has ever devised to store and transmit energy. Every battery, every electrical apparatus, generator, nuclear power plant, satellite, everything powered by energy which used to transmit around the world has been rendered totally useless. That's why airplanes, trains, cars, clocks and watches, elevators, pace-makers, hydro-electric plants, water treatment plants, and satellites just quit. No power." He waited for the impact of his words to take effect.

"What are you saying?" Suzan asked the huge question lurking in everyone's mind. "When will it come back on?" All eyes were on him, and he knew this would be their moment of truth.

"The earth will not re-charge the batteries or re-start the engines. Energy storage and transmission, as we've come to know it, has changed forever. The electricity generated by the Colorado River and captured at the hydroelectric plants will never work again. That doesn't mean we won't have power again. The earth and her inhabitants are filled with energy. It just won't be harvested or stored the same. Mother Earth will show us a more efficient way to restore power. We've always had the answers really. Oil is the black gold that rules the world today. But there are other ways to..."

Laramie cut him off. "Stop, Ian," she shouted. "What does this mean to me – Laramie Zerlich, in Denver, Colorado?"

Fair enough question. Ian just didn't know how to soften the blow. "The Aborigines living in the outback of Queensland don't even know anything has happened. Some of them have died when their own brains or hearts couldn't withstand the initial energy surge, but nothing else about their lives has changed. They will survive, better than most of the inhabitants of this country and other progressive countries like it."

"Ian!" Laramie drew him back to the original question.

"Laramie, it means that the big cities will die. People can't survive if they stay in them." He waited. "It means that you have to leave here. The longer everyone waits for restoration of their previous existence, the more dangerous it will become." He waited again.

"How are you using the loo now?" They all looked at him as if he were crazy. "I mean, what are you using for the loo? The water-closet?" He tried once more. "Your bathroom? How are you disposing of human waste? Where are you getting your water? Your firewood? Are people burying their dead? Are you waiting for the grocers to open their stores so you can walk down clean aisle's with your grocery list?" He could see them mentally checking off the validity of his words.

"Many, like you, will huddle in their houses, waiting. Jesse witnessed the gangs taking over the large stores and warehouses in their own neighborhoods. My God, the tent cities are already forming at the rivers and creeks, and whole cattle are being butchered in the field for a steak, the rest of the carcass left to rot and call the vultures to dine. While we're sitting here discussing it, anarchy is rising out there." The eyes in the room bore witness to their belief. They were devastated.

"I'm sorry to be the *Grim Reaper*, but you've got to prepare now, while you've still got stores in your pantry and strength in your bodies to fight the battle. And it *will* be a battle. For years I've thought of all the consequences and, believe me, it's already happening. Some things are escalating much quicker than I originally calculated. But we have an advantage. We know what has happened."

"Janie, Levi, and I are going west, over the mountains to your parent's ranch. We want you to go with us. There will be game to hunt, cattle to raise, wood to gather, a garden to grow, and I understand they have a gravity-fed spring which pipes water directly to the house. That's a lot better than most will have. Some other enlightened folks are already starting the migration south to warmer climates. They know that to stay is to die."

The awareness of reality is often garish and vulgar. There wasn't any way to soften the truth or make it any easier to accept. It was almost as if he did it to them again; threw them back to that first day, when they thought the world was ending. Their very survivals gave them courage and hope to wait for life to return to normalcy. But this was the reality that produces insanity and suicide and murder. This is when mobs organize to kill the messenger. Ian saw it in their eyes.

How dare he make them face the truth!

Enough had been said for now. They needed to talk amongst themselves, comfort each other, encourage each other, and renew their hope. Then he could help them make a plan. He walked outside to the back porch to smoke a cigarette.

"I can't deal with this right now," said Laramie as she started to clean the lunch mess from the kitchen. "Jesse, we need more water. I used it for oatmeal this morning and there's only a half-gallon left. I'll walk up to the canal with you to help refill the containers. And, Suzan, maybe sometime tomorrow we can pack the kids up and walk over to my apartment and get some of my things. I can't keep wearing your clothes, it's too hard to wash them out every other day in the bathtub."

The group sitting at the kitchen table stared incredulously as she continued to ramble.

"Oh, Jesse, we'll have to get some more firewood, too. There's probably enough for tonight and tomorrow morning, but with all the excitement, we burned quite a bit last night because we stayed up later than usual." The horror in her eyes reflected all of their fear. Jesse calmly placed his arm around her and steered her back to the kitchen table. No one said a word.

"This is exactly what Ian's been trying to tell us," Jesse calmly explained. "How long can we haul water? How many trips to the canal will we be willing to make for everyone to bathe? To wash clothes? Will we cut down all the surrounding trees for firewood? When will we start burning the furniture to stay warm? We'll have to start with the fence for a fire tomorrow night. How long will we wait to see if Ian's wrong? How long will we ignore the truth, before we're forced to flee for our lives, or give up the fight?"

The stark truth glared with profane clarity. "Now, we have the advantage to prepare," Jesse continued. "We have choices left. We can't wait until circumstances dictate our choices. Let's make a plan now."

They listened in silence as the truth emerged and stood naked before them. "It took Ian a couple of hours to convince me, even after he laid out all the facts. He painted an ugly picture of anarchy, disease, corruption and death. You know me. I'm a 'skeptic's skeptic – the most untrusting person you know. But, I'm convinced and I'm scared. We can't wait for the weather to get better to make a plan if we want to survive this."

"But, the ranch?" Suzan questioned. "That's more than two hundred and fifty miles away! It's December and we've been lucky that the weather has been so mild since all this began. Sooner or later winter will set in and I sure don't want to be stuck on top of Vail Pass with no shelter, no food, and a snow storm on the way."

"And how in the hell can we carry enough provisions to last?" It was Laramie.

"Most people will be heading south, as Ian and Jane already noticed. As soon as we get out of the city there will be game to hunt and we can follow the river so we'll have a source of water." They could see that Jesse was convinced.

Ian came through the back door and was relieved to see reconciliation on their faces. Acceptance. He joined them as Jane produced the list of items they'd packed just yesterday morning. "Ian and I made a list of items we felt would be worth hauling across the mountains," she started. "The first thing we did was prepare all the meat that was thawing in the freezer, and prepare any food items that could be easily eaten along the way. I dried all the bagels into chips, dried juice concentrate on sheets of plastic wrap, and combined all my dried fruits and nuts together like trail mix. I have, at least, forty pounds of dried meat packed on the travois, and we can hunt fresh game along the way."

"Well, I guess we better get started," said Suzan and she took Jane's list and quickly scanned it, nodding her head approvingly. "Looks like you've thought of everything."

Laramie looked at the list and asked, "Will it be worth the trip to my apartment to get my personal items?" Then she reconsidered. "I've got to go. Half my life is in those two small rooms."

"Why don't you and Jesse ride the mountain bikes and take empty backpacks to load things into. Jane and I can start preparing the food." Suzan's mind was whirling, trying to organize the tasks ahead.

Ian offered to haul water, and Mira begged to go with him to show the way to the canal. By the time the group assembled, each child carried an empty gallon container to carry water back. The canal was only a half-mile away and Ian was sure each child could carry a full gallon the half-mile back to the house. Black followed them as they disappeared down the street.

Jesse and Laramie pedaled away on the mountain bikes as Suzan and Jane unwrapped partially thawed meat from the freezer. Jane started the gas grill and offered to tend the sizzling meat, while Suzan inventoried other food items in the pantry and cupboards.

By the time Ian returned with the children, several screens had been removed from windows, placed on the patio and filled with thin slices of potatoes treated with ascorbic acid solution, chopped onions and bell peppers.

Suzan had a crate of apples, six one-gallon jugs of powdered Tang, and boxes of whole cinnamon and clove purchased for Jacinth's Girl Scout troop to make Christmas gifts. Ian sliced apples, dipped them in the ascorbic acid solution and soon filled six more screens to dry.

When Jesse and Laramie returned, the others stopped what they were doing to take a break. Laramie was angry. Her apartment had been ransacked. The deadbolts didn't stop the looting. The door, frame and all, was pried away from the foundation boards. Suspicious eyes peered at them through cracks in doors as she and Jesse cautiously entered the rubble that had once been her safe place. She immediately went to her only bedroom to find her closet practically bare. The only things still hanging were her work dresses. Blouses and shirts in plum, sage, chocolate and taupe swam in a pool of silk color on her bedroom floor. They took all her winter clothes. The very items she needed were gone. She quickly examined the dresses still hanging, and there, tucked between them in the plastic cleaning bag from last spring, was her lime-green snowmobile suit. They'd obviously overlooked the prize in her closet, thinking it was a dress.

She remembered the boxes she'd tucked above the rafters in the garage, and Jesse helped her get them down. One of them had her felt-packed Sorrel boots, gloves, ear muffs, hats, scarves, leggings, headbands and wool socks. The box of camp clothes with hooded sweatshirts, sweat pants and long underwear was also intact. Other items, which had been packed in boxes on the concrete floor, were gone, including sleeping bag, backpack, hiking boots, and fishing gear.

They packed all the remaining bathroom items; vitamins, aspirin, alcohol, peroxide, Band-Aids, tweezers, nail clippers, and eye solutions. She returned to her bedroom and found her prescription glasses, her underwear and socks. Her fireproof lock-box of important papers was forced open and its contents lay strewn on the floor. She retrieved the papers and looked through them, taking only her birth certificate.

They'd taken all her turquoise and silver jewelry from the top of her dresser, but left the small gift boxes of treasures she kept in the shoebox under her bed. She loaded her photo albums and journals to go through later.

The kitchen was bare, but she didn't fault the looters and hoped that Maria, down the hall, had taken the food for her children. They gathered the remaining spices and packed them in the canvas shopping bag that hung on her back doorknob. Seeing Polo's empty water and food dish on the back deck reminded her that she would never see her beloved pet again.

They'd stopped at the vet's where she'd left him and there wasn't a single animal alive. The cages had all been opened, except for the one's who'd died initially. Polo's bloated form was barely recognizable among them.

Now, recounting the story to Suzan, Jane, and Ian, she didn't blame the neighbors who'd benefited from her absence. They probably thought she would never come back. She'd probably have done the same thing herself.

Although her apartment was only five miles from Suzan's house, they'd passed proof of what Ian tried to convince them would happen. Human refuse lay in piles on the ground or disposed of in bulging dumpsters, which children now rummaged through. Young men guarded the super market, where Black had protected the children that first night. The putrid stench of death and decay rose from the bloated bodies of those who had died inside the store and were now heaped in a pile at the side of the building. The dogs and buzzards were already doing their jobs. Tents and crude makeshift structures formed along the canal bank where trees were hacked apart for firewood. It was a nightmare, and Laramie reinforced Ian's insistence to leave.

The next two days were spent preparing food, gathering clothes, medical supplies, camping supplies and anything else they thought they could carry. They ate all the remaining thawed food from the freezer, broccoli, cauliflower, peas, corn, and mom's frozen strawberry jam. They saved the thawing leftover lasagna and chili, and the three dozen tamales Suzan had made for Christmas Eve for their last night.

Suzan had always used Jesse's old jeans to make backpacks for Mira and Jacinth, and set to the task of making backpacks for Dominic, Jen and Sara. She cut off the legs, using the front and back of the jeans for the main body, and cut the legs in strips and reattached them as straps and ties. She marked each bag with the child's name and packed it with two changes of clothes, a warm sweatshirt and an extra pair of shoes taken from Jacinth's assortment. In the pockets, she placed a tablet of paper with each child's name, date of birth, and Laramie's name. Also, pencils, safety pins, rubber bands, Band-Aids, dried fruit, jerky, a package of gum and one of Life Savers, and a sandwich bag filled with Tang.

If it became too difficult for Levi to pedal, Ian and Jesse both agreed it would be a simple task to convert the travois to Suzan and Jesse's larger mountain bikes. They attached carrying straps for both ends of duffel bags that could be carried between two children. The three smaller children, Dominic, Jen and Sara, with Jacinth's help, would be able to carry a pack between them, plus the backpacks which Suzan made.

Suzan selected a few pots and pans, mixing containers and their camp coffeepot, which Jesse and Ian would attach to the travois straps. They packed her large washtub with toiletries, towels, and other items that would have to be used daily for sanitation. It was quite heavy but could be carried between two adults.

They assembled all the prepared food, including the food packed on the travois, and packed it in meal sized zip-lock bags. Suzan made pemmican from dried meat, bacon fat, ground cornmeal and raisins. It actually tasted good. Beans, rice, and pasta were left in their original plastic bags. Oatmeal, flour, pancake mix, packages of cake mix and biscuit mix, sugar, salt, baking powder, soda, corn-starch, cocoa and powdered milk were packed in gallon sized zip-lock bags, as well as dates, coconut, chocolate chips, pecans, walnuts and almonds; all purchased to make cookies and breads for Christmas baskets. Honey and molasses were poured from glass bottles into plastic containers for easier transport. Twelve loaves of foil wrapped Christmas breads taken from the freezer sat on the kitchen counter for packing. Ornamental arrangements of dried red chile rista's were crushed and placed in plastic bags. The screens of drying fruit and vegetables were brought in at night to continue drying by the fire.

Laramie wondered how Suzan so intuitively knew what to take and what to leave for the journey. She would have never thought to bring iodine to disinfect water, or paraffin wax poured in empty pint cartons stuffed with lint from her dryer to form candles or poured over lint in egg cartons to form briquettes for starting fires.

Jane and Laramie helped Suzan tear a sheet into strips for bandages or slings to put with the first-aid supplies. The sisters were in the sewing room as they tore another sheet into similar strips for hygiene purposes. "Oh, no!" said Laramie, horrified. "What on earth will we do when we run out of toilet paper?"

"That's what Sears Catalogs were used for before toilet paper was made," answered Suzan, somewhat amused at Laramie's slow realizations.

"Well, we must subscribe then," she said mockingly, "just as soon as we get to the ranch and know our new delivery address."

"Find out the number to the closest Pizza Hut while you're at it and we'll have pizza delivered there, too." Jane joined in the fun as they began to name all the other conveniences they would sorely miss; Nutty Coconut ice cream, mangos, oranges, avocados. The list became more serious as they remembered all the things Mom had in the food storage room when they were kids; aspirin, iodine, alcohol, peroxide, chlorine bleach, lye, salt, yeast, vinegar, honey, rice, wheat, gluten, corn, beans, powdered milk, powdered eggs, and peanut butter. "Oh, what about the chocolate chips we used to sneak by the handfuls?" It was Jane confessing.

"So, you're the one!" Cried Suzan. "I always got in trouble for the missing chips."

"Mom only stored chocolate chips there so she'd know where they were," remembered Laramie. "Mom was the one who ate them by the handfuls. She always had chocolate hidden around the house. We used to eat it after you guys left for school." Laramie couldn't help rubbing it in. "The only time she resorted to chocolate chips was when she ran out of Hershey's with almonds."

"You've always been so spoiled!" Suzan and Jane echoed.

"Yes, I have," admitted Laramie, "and I deserved it." She squealed in delight as Suzan and Jane wrapped her in sheet strips and pushed her onto the bed.

"And stay there, so we can get some work done around here," ordered Suzan.

"Boy, you sounded just like mom when you said that," said Jane. "That's how I used to get out of cleaning our bedroom, remember Suzan?"

"How could I forget? Every time mom told us to clean our room, you'd pick a fight, I'd hit you, and you would start screaming at the top of your lungs. Mom would make you sit in a corner of the kitchen, probably eating chocolate chips, while I cleaned the bedroom by myself, as punishment for making you cry."

"Worked for me," said Jane, triumphantly.

Suzan threw more of the strips on Jane and pushed her down on the bed with Laramie. "Both of you stay there. I'll do it by myself."

"Poor Suzan. C'mon Laramie, let's help so she doesn't have to do all the work by herself anymore." They giggled as children while, together, they finished folding the torn strips of sheet.

They were quite overwhelmed as they looked at all the supplies to be carried. It would definitely be slow going for them. They tried to eliminate items, but didn't know where any short cuts could be taken. Ian even suggested taking items that they wouldn't necessarily need, but could be used for barter along the way. Suzan selected twelve pints of plum jelly she'd made in the fall. Maybe she could trade for flour along the way, as they only had about fifty pounds when it was all combined.

Jesse and Ian made one last trip to haul water and then rode the mountain bikes the eight miles to Jesse's parent's house to warn them, so they too, could prepare to leave.

Laramie watched tears run down Suzan's cheeks as she tenderly stroked the piano Jesse bought her and knew if there was a way to take it, she would. Struggling with what to take and what to leave, the sisters looked at each of the family pictures still hanging on the hallway wall, as if trying to burn the images into their memory for safe keeping.

The nostalgia was suddenly destroyed when Suzan's neighbor bolted through the door wearing the deranged look of a madman. Suzan knew his baby son and three year old daughter both died the day before so she treated him like the grief-stricken father he was and gave him food enough for a couple of days. She tied it in the beautiful Christmas basket made for the holidays, knowing it would be the last Christmas present she would ever give them.

The Turners were the first neighbors she and Jesse met when they moved into their new house five years ago - so she understood that the man who came through her door was not the man she knew. With a gentle voice she told him exactly how to prepare everything she gave him including a gallon container of the Tang she made the day before. He didn't need to know she used the water from the sump-pump that bubbled up, flooding their basement. She'd boiled the water in the basement fireplace before mixing it with the Tang and prayed it wouldn't make them sick. Her soothing voice calmed him as she told him what was in the pemmican. She included a pint of her plum jelly to give to his wife who was so distraught over the deaths of her children she couldn't help herself live any longer. Not even the will to survive could pull her back from the dreadful sorrow that claimed her.

Suzan wondered what would happen to them - they should leave too, but they couldn't bring themselves to sanity. She and Jesse offered to help bury the small bodies, but they were unable to part with their babies, so Suzan understood the deranged look of the madman in his eyes.

"It's happening. People are beginning to realize it isn't going to go away, just like Ian predicted they would," Jane said to Laramie as they sadly witnessed the exchange with the neighbor.

"Yes," Laramie agreed. "I sure wish he'd been wrong, and life would get simple again."

"Can't get much simpler than this," stated Suzan as she closed the door. "But, I have a feeling, we'll find out just how simple life can really get." Suzan didn't have to witness the devastation with her own eyes to be a believer. She knew in her heart that her whole life had prepared her to survive this. Thoughts of growing up on Mariposa Street flooded her memories; planting and harvesting gardens, canning and drying meats, fruits and vegetables with mom, butchering deer and elk in the fall. She could see her mother grinding wheat and corn in the stone grinder to make bread, and alfalfa and wheat sprouting in jars on the windowsill, spring-time walks on the river bank to find asparagus and collect salad greens. Giant, drooping sunflower heads, heavy with seeds, and large, sprawling rhubarb plants lined mom's strawberry patch. Mom believed that everything planted should be edible, right down to the roses. She pictured Moby, their cat, lying in the shaded herb garden where mint, chamomile, echinacea, basil, thyme, sage, parsley, chives and rosemary grew with the pansies and nasturtiums. Yes, all her memories led her here, to this day. She packed all her seeds she'd saved from her garden in the fall.

Their last night was spent going through photo albums, selecting special pictures, talking about their parents and reminiscing about growing up on Mariposa Street. They packed some of the pictures in plastic sandwich bags - pictures of all of them when they were kids, with aunts and uncles, grandma and grandpa, and of course, pictures of the girls and Levi, and her brother, Judd, and his wife Dani. Looking through the old photographs helped them remember the good memories as easily as the painful ones were denied.

Laramie's thoughts turned to Judd and Dani as she held their wedding picture in her hand. They'd met the day he re-enlistment in the Army. Laramie remembered how much the whole family loved Dani and knew from their first meeting that she was the one for Judd. Laramie said she was a keeper. And keep her he did. They were married six months later.

Laramie acknowledged her jealous feelings when they were married and often lamented, "We lost a brother and he found a new family." She knew their relationship would never be the same and didn't know how to grieve the change. It was hard to let go of the childhood dreams and fantasies, when real life so rudely interrupted and claimed her expectations. Accepting life as it is – that's the hard part.

Judd was four years older than Laramie and had always been her protector and hero. She remembered thinking she would marry him someday, or her dad, as all little girls do. Judd insisted his friends allow her to play football with them in the street, and by the time she was ten years old, she could out-throw, out-catch, and out-run most of his friends. Two years later, when Judd got a car, he still let her tag along with him and his friends and always let her drive the last four blocks home.

Soon things began to change. Judd became interested in girls and *cruisin,* and his friends started looking at his little sister differently. She was twelve then and starting to change from girl to woman-child. Pretty soon he quit taking her to hang-out with him and his friends. She was no longer one-of-the-boys. That was a devastating time in her life.

Judd joined the Army and was assigned to the 82nd Airborne – D Company. He finally realized at twenty years of age that his life was being swallowed up in a cocaine and alcohol induced blur, so he joined the Army to do his time, and let the government pay for his education when he got out. He didn't count on loving the military life. It disciplined his mind, his body, and honed his survival instincts to a fine science. He developed the self-confidence of a warrior. He loved it, and the Army loved him. They advanced him quickly and discovered he was a natural born leader and his men respected, and even liked him. He quickly became an expert with all the *Rambo* weapons and it wasn't long before he successfully completed Ranger Training and was persuaded to join the elite of the Army Special Forces.

After serving in the Gulf War, deeply entrenched in Iran's territory, it was only natural when Desert Storm became full-blown, that they offer him a special commission to re-enlist in active duty and go back to Saudi Arabia and Kuwait, as he was very familiar with the territory and the men loved to follow him.

Judd and Dani moved into the officer's housing at Ft. Bragg, North Carolina. They wrote frequently and the family was thrilled when the letter came telling that they were finally expecting their first baby, due in April. The last letter they'd received was very vague about when his intelligence training would be complete and when he would ship out for Saudi Arabia, or maybe Kosovo. Laramie knew time was standing still there, too, and prayed that Dani wasn't by herself in North Carolina and Judd forever lost to them halfway across the world.

Late that evening they dined on the lasagna, chili, and a loaf of cranberry nut bread with real butter. They decided the three dozen homemade tamales would be a perfect quick-meal for their first night on the road. By the looks on their faces, the unspoken question was apparent; when would a meal ever taste this good again, and when would they be dining together at a kitchen table with the fireplace glowing in the safety of a home?

By early morning, after everything was loaded into backpacks, duffel bags, and pillowcases, they began to load them onto sheets, to be tied in larger bundles to carry individually, if needed. Ian and Jesse decided each bundle should carry an assortment of all the items, in case any one bundle was stolen. Pillow cases, light enough to be carried by a child, were strung with drawstrings and packed with clothes in their size, a blanket, dried fruit and jerky, similar to their backpacks.

Jesse and Ian laid out their rifles, knives, ammunition, and Jesse's bow and arrows. There were two rifles between them – both 30.06 caliber with scopes, twelve boxes of shells, two large hunting knives and an assortment of smaller fishing knives. Jesse's hunting knife was a gift from his father on his fourteenth birthday and had mother-of-pearl inlaid in the handle and a leather sheath to carry it on his belt. The compound bow and quiver of arrows were a gift from Suzan on their fifth anniversary and they packed them on the travois, beside the mysterious canvas wrapped package that Red donated. Ian told Jesse what Red had said; "Four good men or women could start or finish a battle with what's in that package." They didn't even unwrap the canvas to see what its contents were and hoped they wouldn't have to until they unloaded the travois at the ranch. They decided to carry their rifles, considering the dangerous situation they'd witnessed evolving.

Jesse and Ian tried to design the best method to haul everything utilizing the four mountain bikes, rather than riding them individually. Numerous attempts to devise a wagon-type carrier ended in frustration. It seemed impossible to build something functional in a short amount of time, and they wanted to have at least one of the bikes available for riding. They studied Levi's travois design, searching for a similar solution or idea to evolve.

Finally, in a flash of inspiration, Ian remembered the parachute Red promised would come in handy. It just might be the answer. They removed the seats from two of the bikes, and using boards from the deck in the back yard, they wired a board to the bikes as far forward on the frames a possible, creating a five foot span between them. They repeated the process with the remaining two bikes, wiring a board as far back on the frames as they could secure it. Two ten-foot lengths of deck boards were used to separate the front bikes from the back. If a bike were needed for scouting, the whole thing could be quickly unwired and removed from the wooden frame. They attached the lightweight nylon material to create a carrying area that could be folded over to cover and secure the load. It more resembled a land-bound catamaran, than the V-shaped design of the travois and it would work just as well. It would eliminate the need to carry everything in their hands or on their backs and as they used supplies along the way, the load would become lighter. It would take a person on either side to steer and pull the thing, and sometimes they would all have to push it, as well as the travois. But they'd never have been able to carry all their supplies otherwise.

Jesse took the large nylon, roof-top carryall they used for camping trips and packed all the sheet-bundled clothes that couldn't be carried in backpacks. He placed it in the middle of the carrying area. He and Ian loaded the heavier items along the wooden framed area for better support.

When it was nearly loaded, they rolled it out of the garage and down the street for a test run. It would work great after a few minor adjustments and shifting the weight around.

Suzan and Jesse had selected cherished items they couldn't take with them and packed them in the crawl space of the basement. They worked until dawn while the children slept to finish loading and prepare the last breakfast they would have in their home. Suzan packed a lunch of peanut butter and jelly sandwiches for the first day, along with the apples they hadn't dried.

The travois was packed with the items they wouldn't immediately need including the engines and parts from the gasoline powered lawn-mower and weed-eater. The catamaran carrier was packed with everyday things; tents, sleeping bags, blankets, propane lanterns and cook-stove, Coleman fuel, food, water and first-aid items. They tied Suzan's large washtub on top and covered the whole thing with canvas tarps, securing it all with ropes and bungy cords. At Suzan's insistence, they attached the green tarnished copper sundial from Suzan's garden to the back of the travois.

By the time they were ready to go, only six more hours of traveling time remained, as well as they could judge. "Maybe that sundial will come in handy after all," Jesse granted. Nerves stretched tight, and tempers were grudgingly checked as they all felt the emotional stress of the last few days. Now it was time to leave.

She waved goodbye to the Turners. It grieved her to see the utter despair on their hollow faces, but she couldn't convince them to leave.

The children were instructed not to use anything from their backpacks. They were for emergencies only, in case they became separated from the rest of the group. They were told to stay exactly where they were if they became separated for any reason and someone would find them.

Everyone carried a backpack filled with their own items, and something else in their hands, either a stuffed pillowcase or another pack, and attached a canteen or squeeze bottle of water to their belts. Jesse and Ian both carried rifles over their shoulders and Ian condensed all his research into one large canvas carrying bag, which was packed on the travois.

Jesse and Suzan led the group, steering the catamaran. Laramie, Mira, Jacinth, Dominic, Jen, and Sara were assigned the middle, followed by Levi pedaling the travois, Jane, and Ian. Black took up sentry and followed about twenty feet behind.

## *Chapter 8*

It was December 17, only nine days after the earth's change. The weather still held to cold crisp mornings and sun filled days. They were lucky and knew it. Winter would remember its season soon enough. The bitter truth of Ian's words buffeted them every step of the way. There was no way to soften the blow of what the eyes so undeniably beheld. The banks of rivers, streams and lakes were filled with tents and makeshift shelters. Hordes of dirty, unkempt children wandered the streets and pilfered dumpsters along the way. They heard the sounds of this dying city and were glad they were only passing through. The low drone of buzzing flies and writhing maggots grated on the nerves, though they were unaware of the source of this new agitation. Suspicious eyes peered through cracks of doors and windows, and packs of dogs tried to torment and lure Black.

A trail of small children followed the group, begging for something to eat. Laramie passed out dried bagel chips and strips of dried meat until they were satisfied they had all she was willing to give. She was horrified and would gladly have taken all of them in, but knew she couldn't feed and clothe them.

Jesse and Ian would have pushed them through the night if the children could have tolerated the pace. None of the group was used to walking distances carrying their own weight on their backs and in their arms. The children tired and Laramie alternately carried Sara or Dominic in her arms. Rivulets of perspiration trickled between breasts and along spines as the concrete and blacktop streets magnified the pale winter sun. They stopped to eat peanut butter and jelly sandwiches and apples, and cried out in pain as they massaged each other's backs and shoulders.

Jesse continued to push them onward. He wanted to get as far through the city as possible. Their possessions were covetously eyed, but between the exposed rifles he and Ian carried over their shoulders, and Black following behind, no one bothered their group.

As the last whispers of sunlight faded behind Lookout Mountain, the exhausted group stopped to set up camp. Levi and Jacinth had alternated pedaling the travois and their young muscles were like rubber bands by the time they stopped for the night. Two tents, butted up against a ten-foot cliff, faced east and slightly toward each other with the travois and catamaran in the center. A black and red billboard loomed on the cliff above them, espousing the amber hued smoothness of Black Velvet Whiskey.

They drank the rest of the water from their containers and ate the three dozen tamales saved for this meal. Black posted himself on top of the cliff underneath the billboard to watch in the night, gnawing bones Suzan brought for him.

They fell into sleeping bags without washing or changing clothes. There would be time tomorrow to replenish water and boil it for drinking and washing. They knew they weren't far from Clear Creek, and decided to follow through its narrow canyon to Idaho Springs, instead of walking west on I-70. There would be fewer towns and, Jesse hoped, fewer people.

Black growled threateningly in the night and both Jesse and Ian bolted from tents fully dressed with rifles ready as shadows quickly disappeared. The night passed too quickly and they woke tired from restless sleep but their minds were keen to the danger present.

Ian and Jane agreed to watch the children and guard the supplies, as Jesse, Suzan, Laramie, Mira and Levi followed Jesse east toward the South Platte River to find more insulin for his parents. Suzan needed to say goodbye to Jesse's parents who dearly loved her and treated her as their own daughter. It was against Jesse's better judgment for anyone else to go with him, but they all agreed it would not be wise for him to travel alone. Ian convinced Jesse to leave his rifle so he wouldn't be a target for thieves or appear threatening himself.

Watching the small group disappear among the others heading east toward I-25 and the South Platte River, Ian placed his arm around Jane's shoulder. "Oh, they'll be fine, Janie, girl. Don't worry." The simple gesture brought instant relief to her fears and worries.

"I know you're right. I just get nervous watching them go to that place everyone has warned us about. And I can't believe I let my son go with them."

"You let him go because he wanted to go. That's good practice for mothers," he said teasingly, as he squeezed her shoulder tighter. "Besides," he continued, "they'll look more like a family instead of a search party."

"I'm going to go find the creek and fill up these containers," Ian said as he untied the straps securing the plastic gallon containers to the catamaran. "Do you know how to shoot a rifle?" He looked at Jane as a slow smile formed on her lips.

"Why, Ian Jayne." She was going to love this. "Didn't anyone tell you I could shoot a tick off a dog's ear at fifty paces?"

"I'm not talking about a scatter-gun. All I want to know is, can shoot this rifle?" he said, as he pushed his rifle in her hands. Ian was getting as much pleasure out of this as Jane.

"Well, I don't know," she teased, as she looked it over. "Don't you have to put the bullets down this little hole and poke them through with a broom handle or something?" she said, fingering the rifle barrel. "Would you like to place your bets now, or later?" Her eyes sparkled with the challenge.

His mouth opened and out fell his ego. "I'd be willing to give it a go. In fact, I'll wager a months stipend that I can better you at fifty paces."

"You're on, Ian Jayne. You just name the time and place. I'll use Jesse's rifle."

"What?" He said in mock amazement. "Not right here in the middle of town?"

She rubbed her chin, as if seriously considering his suggestion. "Naw. Don't want to excite the natives. My daddy taught me not to waste a single shot. Besides, I'll enjoy watching you stew in your own juices for awhile, thinking about it."

"My *juices* will love stewing while looking forward to the event." He waved his hat to her in a grandiose gesture as he headed toward the river.

"Oh my, my, my. What a man!" exclaimed Jane as she watched him walk through the buildings toward the creek and over the chain link fence that was torn down for easier passage to the creek. The few cattle that grazed along this stretch of I-70 had disappeared. They had covered far more distance than she would have imagined possible for the novice trekkers. Thank goodness they were all physically healthy. She was in pretty good shape herself, in spite of her smoking.

Jane had always measured herself against her sister Suzan, as if Suzan were the yardstick of perfection. She viewed Suzan with awe and admiration half the time and with guarded suspicion and envy the rest of the time. They were both the same height, but Suzan's 5'10" willowy frame seemed to float graciously over space, where Jane felt like a runaway bulldozer in comparison. That's how she compared their lives, as well; Suzan rising majestically triumphant over life's travails, while she plowed her way blindly through every rut and obstacle in her path. She could never quite vocalize the electric filled sparks that lay just beneath the surface between them. She'd just accepted it as, *that's how it is*.

Jane and the kids were busy collecting trash and tinder to burn when Ian returned with the rope of eight jugs laced across the bare limb of a cottonwood tree.

"The creek is only a half kilometer south. Lots of tents, lots of people hauling water. Not a pretty sight. Trees have been hacked away and they've started tearing down the wooden fences on the south side of the creek."

Deep rivulets carved by countless rainstorms etched the cliff side where Jacinth, Dominic, Jen and Sara played pioneer, a new game they *made up.* Jane was amazed as she watched the children's society evolve. There was no prejudice in them, only remnants of what they'd learned from their own cultures. Sara and Jen were as proud of their black skin as Dominic was of his brown skin and Jacinth was of her white skin, but they played with no differences of color, race, or gender. I know a couple thousand politicians who could take lessons from these kids. Why can't adults be so civil about their *civil rights*, she wondered.

When the water boiled and cooled, Jane re-filled the canteens and squirt bottles for carrying. She washed the kids and herself while Ian scouted for more firewood for the evening meal. Then they took a long afternoon nap knowing that Black would warn them of danger.

Jane woke to the aroma of coffee brewing. Her stiff muscles groaned as she joined Ian to wait for a cup of the strong, dark liquid. "Where did you learn to make such great coffee?" she asked as she stretched her arms skyward and then touched her toes to stretch her spine. "I thought Australians drank tea."

"Oh, yes. We Australians love our tea." When Ian said Australia, it sounded like *orsTRY-ya.* Jane loved to listen to him talk. "But we really consume twice the amount of coffee. I was raised in the never-never of Queensland. The Aborigines my father employed on the station drank a dark liquid called Billy Tea. Poppy said it was tea, but it was strong enough to dye yarn or stain boots. They'd boil water in an old can over the fire and put their pounded barks and dried leaves and roots in the toe of a sock and throw it in the can to boil. It was about the best use they ever found for a pair of socks. The *ol oman* of the group would throw in a handful of roasted seeds and it was the best tasting brew I ever drank. So, I've never been fond of the weaker teas. The closest I can come to duplicating the taste is strong coffee with a bit of chicory added, when I can find it. It's not the same, but I keep trying."

"We all love your coffee. We look forward to it." It was ready and Ian poured them both a cup. "What ever will we do when the coffee is gone?"

"We'll always find something strong and dark to brew," he assured her.

"If I know Mom, she's got at least fifty pounds stored somewhere."

"Fifty pounds can be stretched to a hundred pounds if you mix the right barks and seeds with it."

"My mother is going to love you," Jane warned.

"Mother's always love me. It's their daughters I have a problem with."

Ian was trying to lead her down a path she couldn't take, yet. "I imagine you have a string of broken hearts of daughters as well."

"The only broken heart on my string is my own," he admitted. "Speaking of running out of coffee, have you given any thought to quitting smoking?"

"Hush your mouth, you traitor," she spat. "I'll quit when the last cigarette is gone, and probably sell my soul to the devil to get another." She was as relieved for the change of subject as Ian was.

"It does appear much like the devil's handy-work, being so bloody dependent on nicotine."

"It feels like the lesser of all the evils, to me," she replied.

"I'll make a pact with you," he offered. "We'll smoke three cigarettes a day, one after each meal. "Maybe a fourth with the last cup to top-off-the-day," he added.

Jane agreed. "Once we start over those mountains, the air will be thinner and we'll be begging for more air to breathe anyway. It will be character building. Don't even mention the *D* word to me, or the deal is off."

"Janie, girl, you are the perfect example of the *D* word. Your very survival is a study in *D*," he insisted.

"You're wrong, Ian. Discipline has nothing to do with overcoming life's little dramas. It's the *S* word that applies. Surrender is the only way to find peace, no matter how disciplined a person is. Discipline sounds like tight-fisted control to me – surrender is freedom from having to."

"Maybe you've hit on something. I'll have to think about that. I've a lot to learn from you, Janie. Right now I'd like to strike a bargain." There was a gleam of the imp in his eyes.

"What kind of bargain?"

"We'll smoke one more cigarette with another cup of coffee and our pact will start tonight, after supper."

"You're on."

Jane enjoyed their relaxed and playful conversation over a second cup of coffee. She felt comfortable with Ian and realized she'd never taken time to nurture a friendship with a man that also held the promise of passion and love. The promise was electric between them and she loved the patient path they were walking together. Probably from years of discipline, she thought, laughing to herself.

The sun's path marked only an hour of daylight remaining as the children woke from their needed naps and Jane began organizing the evening meal from cans of stew, beans, and spinach. The sooner the canned foods were eaten, the lighter their load would be.

Smoke plumes from campfires trailed the air mingling the smells of burning wood and trash with the odor of cooking fish and the stench of rotting flesh. How long will it be before the fish are gone from this already depleted creek, she thought as she viewed the smoke filled horizon. And will they ever think to bury or burn the dead before disease thrives and kills them all? Ian painted a picture thick with the feverish marsh greens of typhoid, the bruised purples of cholera, and the blood-reds of bubonic plague. The city forgot this century's hard-won lesson that filth breeds disease and death, and its deathblow was ominously eminent.

"I think when Jesse and Suzan return we should make another water run before morning. Maybe you'd like to walk to the creek with me." Ian was whittling a stick for Dominic to dig with. The four children played well together and created quite a display of carvings in the already deeply etched cliff behind the tents.

"I'd like that. Maybe we will be able to get an early start in the morning. I hope everything went okay at the river. I sure don't want to spend anymore time here than absolutely necessary."

Soon Ian had sharpened sticks for Jacinth, Jen, and Sara who went happily back to their digging. "We'll have to stay until Jesse finds more insulin, which could take days, so don't get in too big a hurry to leave."

"I imagine they should be showing up soon." Jane disregarded his statement. "I'm going to go ahead and feed the kids now, before it gets dark."

Ian searched the horizon for familiar forms as the sun slowly sank behind the mountain. He finally left his watch-post, lit a Coleman lantern for Jesse to identify their spot under the Black Velvet billboard, and joined the children and Jane to eat.

The weary travelers returned as Jane was getting the children settled in the tents. Even with the long nap they'd taken, they were ready for sleep. Everyone was relieved when they heard the news that Jesse was able to find the life-giving insulin for his parent's trip.

Suzan was full of heart-felt love and tear-filled good-byes with her in-laws. She knew she would never see them again and would dearly miss them. Laramie brought another loaf of bread to the group and her name was Kate. Ian declared her *Katie* and the small girl seemed to fit right in, even though her name had been changed from Kathleen, to Kate, to Katie, all in one day.

Ian noticed Jesse's sullen mood and chalked it up to saying goodbye to his parents, so he didn't pry. The grim picture painted by Laramie of the scene at the River City was explanation enough. Suzan found an extra ten pounds of flour and was thrilled that Ian had suggested she bring her plum jelly to barter.

After dinner was over and the children were settled and sleeping, Ian and Jane gathered the empty gallon jugs to make their final trip to the river before leaving Denver.

Laramie was unusually quiet after settling Katie to sleep between Dominic and Jen. The flaxen haired girl was unusually outgoing considering the terrified, crying child of this afternoon. She listened as Jesse described her as an outraged wild woman who wrestled the girl away from two dangerous men, Laramie still ranting and raving from the top of her lungs as she carried the child away. As she listened, she thought hearing Jesse tell the story triggered the tears streaming down her face and the fear she felt. The longer she sat on the cold ground, the stronger the fear became.

"Jesse," whispered Suzan, pointing to Laramie. She knew Jesse was still upset by the scene at the river – the other story that no one talked about. She'd never heard such hostile accusations erupt from this man she thought she knew so well, but she didn't question him about it. Nobody did. "Jesse, it's Laramie."

Jesse recognized the same intense look on Laramie's face that he'd seen earlier, before she found Katie. He was exhausted from the day's events and couldn't imagine leaving again to find another child. "Good Lord, what will we do with another child?"

Laramie rose the same time Ian and Jane headed for the creek. "Where are you going?" Laramie directed the question to Jane who was trying to read the desperate look in Laramie's eyes and the trail of moon glistened tears.

"C'mon, let's go Laramie." Ian put his arm around her shoulders as Jane looped her panty-hose encased, marble rolling pin around her belt, her *yob knocker,* as Ian called it, and they walked toward the creek.

A raging necklace of bonfires hung on the banks of Clear Creek and Ian was outraged at the waste of resources. "They should be conserving and preparing. It only takes a small amount of fuel to boil a pot of water or heat a can of beans. They don't have to create forest fires to stay warm." He knew Denver would become a desert, once again.

"It makes darkness and danger seem less threatening," said Jane, familiar with the comfort, light, and warmth of fires burning in trash barrels along the Blake Street train yards; memories from a younger, more reckless time.

Laramie began to visibly shake as they neared the creek. They didn't want to intrude or seem threatening to any of its new inhabitants and chose a dark place on the creek bank to refill the containers with water.

"You follow Laramie," instructed Ian. "Stay close to her. Don't leave her. I'll fill up the jugs and keep my eye on you. Don't worry – I'll be close. Just stay with Laramie."

The moon slipped behind the low forming clouds and the stars seemed to have abandoned them as well, as Jane and Laramie walked arm-in-arm from one bonfire to the next.

They came to a place under a large cottonwood tree and Laramie pulled away from Jane and stopped. Her eyes were transfixed on the ragga-muffin child who huddled next to a ghost of a woman. The woman's empty eyes stared at the raging flames and the charring carcass hanging above the fire.

Three men sat close to the fire eating hunks of the charred flesh, the juices running down their chins and grinning at the two women as if they were new found chattel.

The leaping flames instantly brought the threatening dream to Jane's conscious memory. She'd tried to bury it that first day, the warning dream to protect Levi and now she recognized the broader meaning – to protect all the children. The flames told the dream – the remains of the sizzling carcass hanging over the fire was a vivid flashback. She felt at her waist where she'd looped the end of the *yob knocker* around her belt and, with one hand, slowly released the knot that held it.

Laramie's presence drew the mother's stare from the leaping flames to Laramie's eyes. In unspoken desperation the woman's entreating eyes flashed from her daughter and back to Laramie, begging for her help.

The three men stood simultaneously, still wearing shit-eating grins and ogling them through leering eyes. Jane knew the evil these men were capable of. They stood about ten feet away, she judged. C'mon, you sorry bastards, just a couple more steps, she silently challenged them.

"You pretty girls hungry? Lookin' for somewhere to light?" The big one loomed over her, but not close enough yet. Jane didn't respond. She kept her hand on the taut nylon knots of the weapon. "We could use two more women joining up with us. Ain't much life left in that one," he motioned toward the woman. "We only got that split-tail she brung with her."

"Two more steps, you son-of-a-bitch," Jane hissed in whispered contempt.

The vile man obeyed and took a threatening step toward Jane. "That's it. Come on now, one more step." At the same time the mother lifted her daughter and pushed her toward Laramie's open arms.

The man again directed his words to Jane as he took the last step toward her. "C'mon, bitch. You could do a lot worse, and" . . . a loud TWACK! rang through the air as his skull was split open by the marble cylinder and his body hurled backwards across the raging bonfire. The other men froze in disbelief, horror written on their faces and fear in their eyes, as the deadly weapon continued to viciously whirl past their vision. As the body began to burn, they finally came to their senses and grabbed his boots and dragged him away from the fire as Jane disappeared into the darkened night.

Ian watched in amazement at the fierceness of the warrior in his Janie. He'd watched the moon accommodate the sisters as it ducked behind the low clouds, offering the protective blanket of darkness for escape. He thrilled at the strategy and expert reactions of the woman he grew to love more each day. An odd excitement grew in his gut and he eagerly anticipated the future.

After keeping vigil for over an hour, to make sure neither of the men followed the sisters, he quietly trailed back to the Black Velvet billboard. There was no question in his mind that he was exactly where he was supposed to be. Jesse and Suzan greeted him with open hugs and relief after listening to the story that Jane and Laramie related when they returned. Jane could hardly remember swinging the *yob knocker* over her head and striking the man squarely in the temple. Ian filled in the blanks where her memory was pale.

Laramie had already washed the eight-year-old girl, dressed her in a long T-shirt, and tucked her into her own sleeping bag. Thank God she'd been wearing warm boots and a heavy wool coat. The girl was naked under the filthy coat that had obviously belonged to her mother, but it would be warm and large enough to dress in layers underneath.

"She was abused by all three of those men from day one." Laramie said disgustedly. "I can't even guess what she's lived through. She is practically comatose from trauma and hasn't uttered a word. She finally cried herself to sleep in my arms."

"I know what she has lived through." Jane covered her eyes, unable to block out the horror of her dream. The group waited, but she couldn't get control of herself as her body was wracked in sobs. Ian pulled her close and encircled his arms around her.

"It's cannibalism!" she gasped. "They're eating the children." Her words visibly shook them.

"No. It can't be. It can't be true," cried Laramie as the ugly scene revived itself of the charred carcass sizzling over the bonfire and the men tearing great hunks of flesh from the bones they held.

"Believe it," Ian said flatly. "I didn't think it would happen so soon, but I noted it as a definite occurrence in the large cities. I noted it as happening in about the third week after the initial change. It's not even been two weeks, but – believe it. People in remote areas will know how to live off the new land, but those in the cities have lost their ability to forage for food."

Ian turned to Jesse. "I think we should leave before daybreak."

"I agree," said Jesse as he wiped the horror from his eyes. "In fact, I think we should begin right now, and wake the kids to pack up the tents and leave as soon as possible."

"Good! I'll lace these water containers to the travois. We could probably be safely away from the city proper and into the mountains by morning if we leave soon."

Within an hour they finished packing and roused and dressed the children. Laramie and Suzan were amazed at the kids. They accepted the whole rushed ordeal as a daring adventure and were excited to be finally leaving the dangerous city. Especially Katie and Tara, the latest additions to the group, their daring rescues still vivid in their child minds.

As the group moved away from the Black Velvet billboard, the moon caught the shadows of the cliff where the children had carved in the afternoon. The children's carvings were enshadowed, as well as the deeply carved rivulets formed by years of rainwater and snowmelt washing down the hill.

There, low on the cliff where the children had played pioneer, were the crudely carved words . . . THE RITE WAY.

"No one on earth will ever see this message again. It's unquestionably for us," said Ian. "The moon in its lunar path, shining on this specific spot, at this exact moment in time, will never happen again. It will be changed by the next rainfall."

They stood in silence for two full minutes until the moon's passage slowly erased the message from the cliff forever. Laramie moved to the cliff wall and touched the deep natural rivulets and the newly carved places. She could no longer see the words, only traces of childish carvings. But none of them would ever deny their existence and the message so clearly shown them – Dominic's innocently spoken words . . . *everything is the right way.*

## *Chapter 9*

Roma woke with a start. “Dan!” Her hand found the empty space in the bed, and she sniffed the air. “What’s burning,” she hollered as she jumped up and grabbed her robe from the chair.

“What is it? What’s the matter?” Dan came running from the back porch into the hazy dining room carrying two potholders and an empty pan.

“What’s burning?” Roma was wild eyed.

“Damn, girl! Nearly gave me a heart attack screaming like that.” Dan looked at the empty pan in his hand. “I made biscuits for breakfast! The fire was too hot and burned them to near coals, so I tossed the rest to the birds before the house filled up with smoke.”

“What time is it?” she said, running her fingers through her hair.

“Time? Well, the sun’s been up for awhile. Is that close enough?”

“Well, why did you let me sleep so long?” she fussed.

It’s going to be one of those days, thought Dan. “Probably because you didn’t sleep at all last night.” Dan marched to the cupboard and reached for the box of Bisquick and poured some in the bowl, threw in a couple pats of butter, and added water to make a soft dough. “Guess now that you’re up, you can help me figure this stove out.” He pressed the dough into flour on the counter and cut biscuits with a glass. Roma smeared butter in a pan then placed the rounds evenly inside.

“The trick is to wait until the fire has quit raging,” she put her arm through Dan’s, “put them way in the back, so the draft of the door doesn’t create a hot-spot,” she kissed him on the cheek, “and leave them in long enough to rise and brown.” Her voice was low and soft. “Takes about ten minutes, sometimes less.”

“Guess I was thinking about bread loaves,” he grinned. “Must have been in there half an hour or more.”

“Well, Dan Zerlich – I’m happy you’re fixing breakfast. You’ve been so antsy since we took the stitches out and I’ve been thinking we should take a ride to the Bernard’s and see if Ben and Patty want to part with a couple of hens and a rooster. It would be nice to eat real eggs again instead of that powder I keep for baking.”

She noticed his face light up at the idea of getting out for a ride. It was about the only thing she'd adamantly insisted on – no riding until the slash across his gut was completely healed. She couldn't keep him from doing everything else he'd insisted on, but she'd held firm about getting on a horse too soon. He'd begun to feel housebound, even though he walked the length of the ranch a couple times, checked on cattle, walked the creek, cleared the spring, and stocked the woodpile.

"Where are we going to put chickens?"

"Well, they'll be safe from critters in the strawberry patch, until we can get a hen-house and coop built. We've got all that chicken wire in the barn."

"Yea, chicken wire and just about everything else. I guess that would work for awhile. Nothing can get to your strawberries, that's for sure."

Roma put a fence around the strawberry patch that first summer to keep the deer out. And then strung chicken wire over the top to keep the raccoons out. Then she hung netting over the chicken wire to keep the birds out. Never did get a full bowl of strawberries that first summer.

She ran to the stove when the smell hit her and opened the oven door and removed the perfectly browned biscuits. "Yea, just about ten minutes," she beamed proudly. She poured them both a cup of strong coffee and scooped the rest of the strawberry jam onto plates.

"This the last of the jam?" asked Dan.

"There's more in the freezer, but I've got it all insulated so things won't thaw out for awhile – at least until the kids get here." Her eyes grew distant and Dan knew she was off somewhere along the trail looking for the kids. She was certain they were on their way to the ranch. He'd tried to convince her they would probably wait until spring to make the trip, but she insisted they were coming now, and she nearly had him converted to the idea, too. Strange ideas filled Roma lately, but he couldn't talk her out of this one. She said she felt them getting closer. Some days she'd be in a blue funk and tell him the kids were stalled, or in some kind of trouble or danger. Damn! Half the time she had him praying and worrying, too.

"If you'll help me throw the saddles on, I think I'm healed enough to get the horses ready. We should take a few pillow cases to carry the chickens in so they don't raise a ruckus."

"I'll take a couple of back-packs, too, and throw in those grain sacks so we can fill them up with Ben's chicken feed and strap them to the horses."

"How long you been planning this little outing?" Dan teased.

"You're not exactly fun to live with when you're like a caged animal, you know. I've been waiting for this day. I've just been worried about you . . . and I've been worried about passing by the facility." There! She'd said it!

"Now, Roma, you know how I feel about that. I don't care how many guns they have. They're in the same situation as everyone else. They can only hold up there until the food runs out, and then they're going to starve to death or leave, unless they learn some skills and become part of the community. They're our closest neighbors. I'll be damned if I'll cut clear around the mountain to avoid them."

"Dan, you didn't see them that day. There are probably thirty or more and they're armed with machine guns, or automatics, or whatever-in-the-hell they were."

"It's not a prison anymore, Roma. No one is guarding them or making them stay. If anything, it's a warehouse with men guarding it. They don't have a strong enough commitment to anything to start a war. Can you think of any thirty inmates who could decide on one leader and unite in a common cause they're willing to die for? They're just men with guns. I've got guns, too."

"You're not a cruel man, or a dishonest man, looking for ways to con the world." She was still trying to convince him, and they'd already had this conversation. "You don't think the world owes you a living. You haven't lived off the weak, you've always worked hard and been concerned with your neighbors and taken care of people with less than you."

"Okay, Roma." Dan threw up his hands. "We have a couple of choices here. If our kids are coming across those mountains, like you think they are, and I'm not saying they're not, or that you're crazy, or anything." He wore a smile on his face and fought hard to soften the fight that sparked from her eyes – and the way her mouth tightened when her back was up against the wall – defensive like. "Do you think the kids will go clear around the mountain, and up that old mountain road, and double back to get here? Don't you think it would be better to try to make peace with the men at the facility? Form some kind of truce before our kids get here?"

"Oh sure! You make it sound like you're dealing with rational men. Honorable men."

"You've always been the one to champion those men. Always defending their *spirit within*." It was a contradiction to him – inmates with gentle spirits. "Now, why the change? Aren't they regular guys anymore, with soft hearts and heartbreaking stories?"

"I guess it was different in the AA meetings. A sincerity comes out in people when a common problem holds them together." She sighed in resignation. "I know you're right. I know I'm just afraid of the ones that I considered ruthless and cold-hearted. They're probably not even there."

Dan grabbed his coat and headed toward the corral. "I'll saddle up."

"Maybe only the nice ones stayed," she shouted after him. "Armed to the teeth."

Why can't I shake this fear, she thought while dressing. She ran a brush through her bright red hair and put her favorite wool hat on. "Left the henna on too long. Everyone will see me coming for miles."

What am I really afraid of? She searched her mind and knew the fear centered around the kids and she was bouncing off it. Trying to place it somewhere near her and it was really with them and she couldn't do a thing about it. What she really wanted to do was load up the horses and go search for them. "God bless my children," she said aloud. I have to be here when they come, she thought. I have to prepare. I can only wait. There's nothing I can do. Just leave it to God. She felt an urge to run, to get away from the fear. "God bless them," she repeated.

Roma filled Dan's thermos with coffee, put the rest of the biscuits in a sack for Ben, grabbed her hat, gloves and coat from the mud-room and headed to the corral.

The day was dry and cold. That Colorado-winter-cold that chaps and weathers the skin. Coloradoans swear that the sun shines everyday. There wasn't a cloud in the sky today, no chance of moisture. Just dry and cold.

A couple storms blew by to the north and south, but they were still dry on the ranch and Dan was beginning to worry about the cattle. The hay was still on the trailer, hitched to the truck about four miles down the road. He'd have to find a way to get the hay in before snow fell. He knew he could hitch Rendy and Litany to sled type carriers. Not together. Lord, that would be something – trying to get those two horses to work together. But, between the two of them they could haul it back to the ranch. Would be a couple days work, but that's the best idea he could think of.

Sitting on Rendi's large back felt good to Dan, although he doubted if he was fit for a good run yet. Roma rode silently beside him, always watching him for signs of pain or discomfort. Trouble followed somewhere behind. He couldn't see the wolf breed, but knew she was close to Roma. Probably off chasing game somewhere, thought Dan.

He knew Roma was brooding over something – probably about the kids. He didn't know what had come over her, but she always was closer to the spirits than he'd ever felt. He had to trust her instincts. Somehow, he had to make it safe for his family to cross the road by the facility and make it safely to the ranch. He knew the chances of violence erupting from that powder keg were real. But he didn't think they would hurt Roma. She was a woman, and a damned beautiful woman at that. Always had been, and he'd known plenty of men who would have loved to have her. But she wasn't up for grabs and was personally known to many of the inmates. They admired and respected her. Dan felt it when they were around Roma. How much of that was rules and regulations? He hoped Trouble was close.

The cool air and warm sun felt good. Roma watched for the pair of eagles she knew hunted the valley in winter, but there was no sighting them today. The road to the old Puma Paw Ranch turned sharply to the north as it passed the facility and they didn't notice any movement on the road or at the prison. Maybe they deserted the place, Roma thought hopefully. Halfway around the lake Dan motioned to the far shore where four men fished its banks. Damn! Had to be inmates. Guess they were getting bored, too. The men seemed to be looking right at them and Roma waved. "Why the hell did I do that? I don't even know who I'm waving at." They didn't wave back, but she was sure they'd been seen.

The ride to Bernard's small farm was just what they needed. The cold air felt invigorating. Both Rendi and Litany strained against their bridles to run. By the time they'd traveled the ten miles, Dan was ready to sit and visit with his good friend. His incision ached and he realized there was still some mending to do.

They tethered the horses by the garden gate and Dan called out to Ben. Probably inside. Dan hoped he had some coffee on. Loud knocking on the back door went unanswered and Dan noticed the packed two wheeled trailer by the chicken coop. Surely he wasn't planning to leave the farm? He and Patty had lived here for years – long before Dan and Roma moved to the ranch. Dan called out again and Roma knocked louder.

Investigating the wagon, Dan found a sealed envelope tucked under the rope that bound the load. It was addressed to him.

*Dear Dan and Roma,*

*Don't have the will to find out what has happened to this old world. Life's been good and I've seen plenty. Packed a few things that Patty would want Roma to have. Load got heavier than I'd planned. Hope you can get it to the ranch without much trouble. Help yourself to anything in the house that you want. You know where the key is. Don't know why I locked it. Never locked it unless we were taking a trip. Just know, since Patty's gone, staying here has been the longest trip I ever took without her.*

*Hope you and Roma understand. I'm not a coward, just tired and lonesome. There's leftovers in the refrigerator. If you come in bad weather, you may have to stay awhile. Make yourself at home. Always have coffee.*

*Just going to sleep now. I know Patty's waiting for me. Come to the garden by the peach trees and cover us up.*

*My love to Roma.*

*Ben and Patty*

Dan looked through the garden to the peach trees and saw the large mound of earth with the shovel sticking out. A turkey buzzard clung precariously from the slender limbs of the small tree. Oh, Lordy! He took the key from under the large rock by the woodpile and opened the back door. "Will you make us some coffee?" he asked Roma.

"Well, what does the note say?"

"I'll tell you over coffee."

His ashen face told her plenty. She knew it was serious and that he'd tell her about it in his own time. She knew when pain came hard, Dan took his time to get through it.

She soon had a small fire going in the fireplace and the coffeepot on the grate. Patty's African Violets were dead and their leaves hung limply over porcelain planters. Patty's joy had been picking through antique shops for porcelain planters. On closer inspection, Roma saw that all the plants had died back. Even the hardy philodendron lay in limp lines across the piano and the cane plant was brown and brittle. Guess Ben was too grieved to care much about plants.

She watched through the cold kitchen window and saw the buzzards flap their great wings skyward and heard the warning caw of crows. The sound of crows seemed to disturb most folks. Edgar Allen Poe probably started it all. Roma liked crows – shape-shifters of the Indian Way. But the sight of buzzards told her there was more than shape-shifting going on. "Oh, Ben! No!"

Dan couldn't believe his eyes when he came to the deep hole. The buzzards and night predators had done their jobs well. Two half eaten skeletons lay entwined, the bigger one with its arms around the smaller one. Ben's Sunday best suit and Patty's blue satin dress were covered in droppings, dried blood and other stuff Dan was afraid to identify. They'd been dead and lying here for days, waiting for Dan to bury them. Dan began shoveling dirt across the remains of those two dear people and tears stung his eyes at the tragedies of life.

Dan and Roma didn't know what happened the day the energy was taken away. Roma said Mother Earth just had enough. Dan knew it surely had to have some scientific explanation, but without the television to tell them about it, they'd probably never know. Who decided who would live through it and who would die? Or did their own physical bodies and energy impulses determine that? Was mankind thrown back two hundred years? How many survived and how many died? Who was tracking history now? Who was taking the new census? What day and time was it, or did it even matter anymore?

Roma took a hot mug of coffee out to Dan as he finished filling and packing down the fertile soil. Together, they piled rocks on top to mark the grave – the same rocks that Ben had dug from the hole and laid to the side.

"I should have never left him that day. I knew he was in pain and I thought he just wanted to be alone. I should have helped him bury Patty and brought him back to the ranch to stay with us for a few days. He was distraught, and I knew it, but I thought it would pass."

"Everything was in such turmoil that day, everyone was distraught. Ben made his choice to be with Patty."

Dan pulled the letter from his jacket pocket. "Guess you better read this. If there's anything you want from the house, you may as well take it now. The house will probably be claimed by someone, sooner or later."

"Well, this has always been a beautiful place, and with its own well, I'm sure you're right. I can't imagine people from town migrating further into the hills though. With winter coming, people who decide to leave will probably go south to warmer climates." She opened the letter and read Ben's last words.

"He just didn't want to live here alone, without her. Don't know that I wouldn't have felt the same way if you'd have died that night." Roma wiped her tears and headed toward the chicken coop. "He just laid out a sack of feed and let them pick what they wanted." She looked in the coop. "If we'd have waited much longer to come, these chickens would have died too. Some of them are probably sick now."

"I told Ben I'd be back in a couple days. He probably took care of things here and laid down in that grave with Patty the day after I saw him. It's already been a couple of weeks. I'm surprised any of those birds are alive."

They counted ten hens, two roosters, six chuckers, and three pheasant. Six birds lay dead in the coop. Roma brought water and laid out more feed for the remaining birds and they perked right up.

She and Dan went through the house, discarded all the rotting food from the refrigerator, and drank the rest of the coffee. Roma picked up doilies she'd watched Patty crochet while smoking cigarettes and drinking coffee in the old country kitchen. Dan looked for weapons while Roma looked through cupboards. Food and guns were not to be found and were assumed packed on the trailer. Patty's hand stitched quilt was missing from her bed and Roma knew Ben had packed everything he knew was dear to Patty. "I'll be proud to have them, Ben," she whispered.

"Guess I'll try to get Rendi to pull that wagon up to the ranch. It will be a nice little wagon to have around. Can use it to haul the hay with, too.

"Do you want to wait until after dark?" Fear found its way to Roma's thoughts again.

"No, I don't want to wait. Why should we wait? If they're going to give us trouble, I'd rather it be in good light, so I can see where it's coming from." Roma helped Dan hoist sacks of chicken feed into the backpacks strapped on either side of Litany's rump. "Besides, maybe we can reach some kind of understanding with them." He read the expression on Roma's wary face. "At least we'll know who's there and who we're dealing with."

"That's what I'm afraid of." Roma couldn't shake the foreboding worry nagging at her. She cringed every time she thought of who would choose to stay and take advantage of the stores of food, drugs, clothes, warm bedding, and commissary inventory. And who controlled the weapons?

By the time Dan rigged the trailer to Rendi and had the chickens, chuckers and pheasants in pillowcases and perched on the trailer, he knew it would be dark before they reached the ranch. He wasn't looking forward to running into the inmates. Maybe he was borrowing trouble, and there wouldn't be a soul in sight when they passed the facility. He could hope, anyway.

The going was slow. Rendi wasn't used to pulling and balked at the heavy load following so close. "Come on, Rendi. You can do it, girl." The big mare calmed at Dan's voice. "That's it, girl. Let's go home."

Shadows grew long across the valley and by the time they passed the golf course and entered the narrow canyon leading to Rifle Gap Dam, there were only a couple hours of daylight left. The dirt road that followed the south side of the large reservoir was cold and deserted and no one fished the north banks, as before.

Dan felt the tension mount as they neared the road that turned into the facility. The dull clump of horse's hooves echoed hollowly against the valley walls. He knew they were being watched and prayed for safe passage. No sooner had the prayer escaped his heart than two men emerged from the side road. One carried a weapon that Dan recognized as an automatic rifle. No match for his .270 hunting rifle – not in combat, anyway.

"Hold up there," ordered the man with the rifle. "Hey, Miss Roma."

"Thank God! Willie, is that you?" Roma gasped.

Willie lowered the rifle and removed his hat. "Yes, ma'am."

"What in hell are you still doing here, Willie?" she braved. "Why didn't you leave like everyone else?" She didn't know the other man and barely recognized Willie dressed in civilian clothes and hair growing on his face.

"Well, ma'am. I ask myself that same question all the time. Seemed like staying was the best thing to do. Didn't want eight years tacked onto the three months I had left," he laughed. "Doesn't make no sense at all, now. Everything's changed and isn't anyone who cares if I'm here or gone – not even the law. Ain't no law, now." Roma felt the sadness in Willie's words and in his voice, but it was Dan who spoke.

"Then why are you still here, and why the automatic rifle?"

"Rafa sent me out here to warn you. I'm still here to help keep the peace, if you can believe that." He laughed again. "Don't that beat all?"

"Rafa is here, too?" Roma was surprised. "Why did anyone in their right mind stay here? Why protect this place? Sooner or later the food and supplies would all be gone here, too."

"Ma'am, Victor has a group of men here who would have ridden rough-shod over the town, if Rafa hadn't stayed to keep him in line. I asked him why he didn't just kill the son-of-a-bitch . . . sorry Miss Roma – no offense."

"Victor Grazzo is here? Oh, no! What grandiose plans could Victor possibly have for this place, or the town's people?"

"Victor don't need a plan or a reason to hurt people. It's just his nature."

"Why doesn't Rafa just kill him or let you? Hell – let me. Heaven knows I've killed plenty of game or cattle that was hurt or crazed, to put them out of their misery. From what I've heard about this man, he's as dangerous as a wounded animal." Dan had a point.

"Putting a wounded animal down is one thing, sir. This is how Rafa explains it, anyway. Lining eight men up and gunning them down is something different."

"But . . ." Dan started.

"And I agree with you, Mr. Zerlich. The whole community would be better off without any of those men. But that's what they used to say about me, too." Willie scratched his head and put his hat back on. "I don't claim to understand Rafa's logic, but it could have been me siding with Victor, if this had happened a few years ago. Me and Victor was tight in days past, so I have to stop and think when Rafa says maybe those men will soften and turn their backs on Victor." The big black man laughed again. "There's been more rehabilitating happen in the past two weeks than happened in the past thirty years. Don't ask me how, but now that everything's different, some of us are liking the idea of settling down in a community ourselves – kinda like starting over."

"Well, can we come and go in peace on this road, then?" asked Dan. It sounded like they may be able to become neighbors, after all.

"Sir, I hope so. In time. We were fishing and saw you passing by this morning. Rafa swore us all to secrecy so the rest of the men wouldn't know. There are thirty of us here. Used to be thirty-one, but one turned up dead – prison style, a couple days ago. One of Kim Tsu's men. We don't know why, and didn't ask. Kim Tsu probably killed the man himself. Traitors can't be tolerated." Willie was silent for awhile. "I guess if you wait long enough, we'll probably all kill each other off, if we don't get away from here."

"Then leave, man. Go find yourself a good woman and settle somewhere. Help rebuild the town. When planting needs to be done and gardens are ready to harvest, everybody will have to pull together, or mankind probably won't survive another generation. We'll die off like the dinosaurs did." Dan was adamant and reminded himself of Roma on one of her soapboxes.

"Yes sir, in time. Like I said, I'm here to help Rafa keep the peace and when the time comes, I'll know the next thing I got to do." Willie drew a deep breath and let it out slow. "Right now I have to warn you that things are pretty explosive here. Rafa don't think it will last more than a month or so, but until then, we can't guarantee your safety across this road. It all depends on who sees you passing. This time it was me and Rafa, Doug here, and Manny. Next time it could be Victor. Rafa just wanted us to warn you."

"Willie," Roma felt the fear envelop her again. "Our family is on their way here." Her voice broke. "I don't know when they'll be here or how many are with them, but they're coming. I know they're coming."

"Miss Roma. Rafa's down entertaining Victor so I could come down here to warn you. You got to believe he'll do everything he can to keep his eyes on Victor and make sure no one is harmed. Just pray they come when Rafa's around. You got to go now."

Dan shook Willie's hand. "Sure appreciate your position here. Thanks for the warning. Watch for our kids."

"Yes sir."

"God bless," said Roma as they coaxed the horses past the road and left the men who'd come to warn them.

"Thank goodness it was Willie instead of Victor Grazzo," said Roma. "Victor is one of those inmates assigned to Rifle by mistake. He should have never been released from maximum security."

"I don't think I've ever had him on a work crew," said Dan. I don't know if I've ever met the man."

"Believe me, if you had ever met him, you'd remember." Roma thought of the rare times he'd come to the office. "He usually had someone else do his running around for him, but I notarized his signature on appeals a couple of times, so he had to come to the office in person." She remembered him from disciplinary hearings, too. "One time he even got another inmate to take the rap for something we were sure he'd done. The other inmate was regressed and twenty days he'd earned off his sentence were added back on."

"A real sweetheart!" Dan mumbled. "Well, if we're lucky, we may never see him again. Let's not borrow trouble. You'd have had me galloping open throttle down the road with twenty rifles all firing at the same time, just in case there were still outlaws there."

"There are still outlaws there. I just wanted you to be aware we could run into trouble." Roma was more afraid now knowing Victor was there than she'd been before. He was one she thought sure would have left at the first opportunity.

"Look, honey. Willie Johnson sounded pretty reasonable to me. Your friend Rafa is there. You've always considered him a cut-above, as if you could judge who was worthy of trust and who wasn't." Dan thought of his argument against Trouble, Roma's pet wolf, and decided against bringing that subject up. "You've always trusted your intuition about people – trust it now. Willie will tell Rafa the kids are coming. Hopefully, Victor will no longer be a problem."

"Yea."

The hay was still loaded on the trailer behind Dan's beat up old pick-up truck. Poor old thing looked a light pink now instead of the bright red of its youth. Checking the cab, nothing appeared to have been disturbed.

"We need to start hauling this hay back home soon," said Roma. "It will be easier with this smaller trailer."

"Sure am glad the snow has missed us, so far. We need the moisture, but we need to get it home and into the old barn. Maybe we should start tomorrow."

"Let's see how today's excitement settles with you tomorrow. You might feel like one more day of recuperation wouldn't hurt."

"I am a bit sore, but Rendi's been a real trooper. She's the smartest horse I ever saw. Almost like she knew to be gentle today." He reached down and affectionately patted the mare's neck.

They passed Hilda and Gus's heifers and Roma noticed the white-faced cow bellowing across the field. The sound was forlorn and wailing – almost mourning.

"Are these cows hungry?" She asked Dan.

"No. They've still got plenty of natural fodder. Doesn't look like Gus and Hilda have been around for awhile though. Maybe we'll have to plan another trip to check on those two after we get the hay hauled back to the ranch."

"You heard Willie just say it would be dangerous to pass the road now. Why do you insist on thinking everything will be okay and a killer will be passive?" Roma was riled.

"That's why I'll take you with me. I have a hunch about those men. I saw you wave at them when we passed them fishing. That's just you. That set the feel for our encounter. Willie acted real pleased to see you. He was respectful – *Miss Roma* and *Mr. Zerlich*. I'll bet most of those men up there would love to put a bullet into Victor if he dared even suggest anyone try and hurt you, or any woman. Those men are sitting up there – a community of men. Now, what do you think will be their next move?"

"You're pretty smart Dan, and I see where your head's going. But, I don't think there will be many women willing to join them up there. They'd be treated like chattel."

"Roma, what's the one thing you think you know about men?"

"They're mostly pig-headed and spend too much time peeing on trees! They're too damned territorial."

"Besides that. Everyone knows that! I mean, what are you always trying to convince me of when you come home from those meetings?"

"That they're gentle, wounded spirits. Hurt children. Underneath all the bravado and macho attitudes, we're all alike – men, women, and children. No matter what our color, race or religion."

"That's right! I rest my case."

"You never believed that anyway, Dan Zerlich. You're just using my own words to win an argument."

"No, I've already won this argument. I'm beginning to believe you're right. I haven't ever heard an inmate, or any man, talk to me on the level that Willie Johnson was talking. You're a woman, you expect it. I'm a man and I'm telling you, something has changed."

"I'll have to think on that awhile," said Roma, daring for hope to believe him.

Soft scrunching sounds of rubber tires and the slow plodding of horse's hooves on the dirt road were the only sounds in the growing darkness. Low clouds blocked the stars and the moon formed a faded glow in the dark sky. Roma knew the ranch was right beneath them when Litany quickened his pace, anxious to get back to the corral and a sack of grain.

"I'm going to unhook this trailer by the house. It'll be okay until we unpack it in the morning." Dan was glad to be home. He was even happy the bedroom was still downstairs by the wood-burning stove in the dining room. "Boy, am I tired."

"I'll take these birds and let them loose in the strawberry patch." She groaned under the weight of the backpacks of feed. "Guess I'll bring up that five-gallon water trough down by the corral. We'll just have to keep our ears open for critters and the .22 close by."

The chickens didn't much like their new home with nothing to shield them from predators except opened mesh wires. They clucked and made such a fuss that Roma shoved the old wooden cart that sat in the yard for summer plants into their temporary coop. She broke a bale of straw in the bottom and underneath it, and threw a blanket over the netting that roofed the cart. It would keep hawks and eagles from spotting them from above and make the chickens feel more secure. The pheasants and chuckers scurried under the cart and as soon as she secured the gate, the chickens took their places inside the bed of straw, like they knew it was for them. "Yes, you're going to like it here."

She was already on the porch when she noticed Trouble whining and sniffing at the strawberry patch gate. "Trouble!"

The wolf breed perked her ears then hung her head and slowly approached Roma. "These birds are not for you." Roma scratched the pup's ears and scruffed the thick fur of her winter coat. "I'll give you an egg sometimes, but you'll have to help me keep the critters away from them."

Roma knew it wouldn't be long before the snow was flying on the Rocking Z. She and Dan had to haul the hay, build a coop and hen house, and prepare a new way to heat water from the spring so the pipes wouldn't burst. Guess we won't get bored this winter, thought Roma. Ranching was always a full-time job. No reason that would change now.

Dan lay across the bed after adding wood to the stove, relieved to be lying prone. The day had worn him out. He wasn't fully mended and resented that his body didn't spring back like in his youth. "It's hell to get old."

"Hey, speak for yourself. I intend to get a lot younger in the next few years. I want to live to be a wise old woman. I don't want to miss a minute of it. Life has been so exciting and I'm just dying to know what's coming next."

"Well, I wish it would come a little slower, or in smaller doses." Dan yawned and Roma knew he'd be snoring soon.

"I'll fix something quick for dinner. I still have those biscuits I was taking to Ben. I'll put some cheese and sausage on them. Sure will be nice to have an egg in the house again."

The soft rhythm of deep snores filled the house as Roma cleaned up the kitchen. She poured herself the last of the coffee and reached into the two-gallon jar and pulled out a menthol cigarette. She liked them all sitting on the counter in the glass jar where she could see them. She'd emptied two cartons into the jar, one menthol and one regular. Maybe she was a little insane in those first days when Dan struggled between life and death. White filters were menthol and brown were regulars. There were still two cartons in the kitchen cupboard. Someday, the jar would be empty. She had to ration them and she'd never been a disciplined person and knew she wouldn't be now, although she had cut down miserably.

She often studied her relationship to smoking. It fascinated her. Dan didn't like her smoking. He'd quit several years back. Roma knew he'd never experienced the same relationship to nicotine that she did, if addiction could be measured. She must have quit at least a hundred times in the forty years she'd smoked since she was fourteen. She'd given up alcohol and drugs and knew it was done on a daily basis. *A Day at a Time*, as they say in AA. But cigarettes felt like . . . *the rest of your life*, and she just couldn't face the rest of her life without her first and last drug. It was definitely a love-hate relationship.

Her father once told her that she'd go to hell for smoking cigarettes. Roma believed she'd always created her own hell, but sometimes had to admit that cigarettes opened a lot of doors that led to the hells she'd created. Like the hell that would probably take her body away from her someday. If she'd never broken that one rule from her youth and the church she was raised in, she'd probably never have broken all the other rules. Funny how breaking the rules works. The next one is always easier. And the hell always became blacker.

Every winter Roma fought the day bronchitis would strike her weakened lungs. Sometimes it turned into pneumonia. She didn't dare take antibiotics for anything else because she didn't want to build up an immunity to them. So far, the rest of her body obeyed and she was healthy. Except for winters. Something about that below-freezing air hitting her lungs that ushered in the viruses. She'd quit for three months every winter for the last four years. Each time, she'd sworn off and rejoiced in her freedom from the deadly drug. It was always so easy to start again.

Tobacco is strong, sacred medicine. It was never meant to be inhaled by humans on a regular basis that became addiction. Even the Indians acknowledged its poisons, and warned their people of its killing power, but still used it in their pipes and ceremonies and honored it as it was meant to be used – its pure form for pure reasons.

"Well, I may as well enjoy another one, since I'll be quitting again soon." Damned irrational rationalization! This time she chose a regular. She hated the battle!

## *Chapter 10*

Highway 58 wound its way through the narrow canyon and crossed the river nine times before finally emerging on I-70 at Idaho Springs. They passed cars, trucks, buses and vans that would forever remain metal tombs and the stench of rotting corpses became etched in their memories forever. Naked currant bushes grew close to the road, and skunk cabbage stalks stood four feet tall, predicting the coming winter's snowfall.

Jagged granite jutting from steep formidable cliffs enclosed them and narrow patches of sky where the sun crossed quickly left the canyon cold and bitter. The winding road allowed only limited sight and each new turn was met with caution. The children took turns pedaling the travois while Ian and Jane pushed, and the steady uphill climb seemed steeper and steeper with each mile. Decay and death hung eerily in dark, rock-lined tunnels where the drone of glistening, green flies was maddening. They stopped to rest and eat only when well away from other travelers. They pushed too hard, and knew it, but felt winter threatening as days grew shorter and nights became colder in the narrow canyon.

Pine beetles of winters past laced the evergreens with their deadly eggs, carving great patches of rust on the rugged mountainside. Cottonwoods lined the creek and creeping cedar glowed green against red earth.

Suzan and Jesse pushed and pulled the catamaran between the obstacle course of cars and trucks. Blisters formed on tender feet and hands, and muscles cramped at night. They camped where the air smelled free from death and other travelers were out of sight. Each night they warmed water over a small fire to wash dirt and grime from faces and hands, massaged sore calves and shoulders, and redistributed food supplies for the next day. Owls hooted and coyotes worked the night, yipping their signals from ridge to ridge. Soon, the night sounds became welcome and calming, and no longer scared the children.

At dawn they dressed in layers of their cleanest dirty clothes and tried to stick old Band-Aids over new blisters. Coffee was finished, oatmeal eaten, and sore muscles forced tired bodies onward. Blue spruce paled between the ancient stands of lodge-pole pines whose barren trunks rose forty feet before their sparse boughs opened skyward.

They passed Idaho Springs where groups camped along the banks of the creek by the city park. Armed men guarded families and belongings all along the way and travelers passed without speaking. Fear hung close behind the eyes that met and everyone seemed suspicious.

The day grew dark and cold as the wind filled the valley with heavy low lying clouds. Scarves, hats and gloves came out of backpacks to block the biting wind. The resident mountain goats that usually clung to the slopes of Georgetown disappeared in bedding places under scrub oak.

The children were weary and Jesse would have stopped, but with a couple more hours of daylight he encouraged them onward. Silver Plume was so close. Soon, the low clouds became alive with blowing ice.

"Jesse!" Ian shouted to be heard over the roaring wind. "Jesse. We can't go any further. We have to find cover!" The storm had moved into the canyon quickly, and snow was creating white air, burning their eyes and lungs.

"I know. I've been watching for a cross street. I know we're near Silver Plume." Jesse gasped as the icy wind sucked his breath away. "Watch for a side road, anywhere to pull off and find shelter."

They traveled blindly, holding the straps of the catamaran to stay together. Sara clung precariously to Laramie's back and Dominic gripped her hand while Jen, Katie and Tara held onto her coat-tail. Ian pulled the travois as Levi and Jane pushed. Jesse and Suzan awkwardly maneuvered the catamaran, and Mira and Jacinth's fingers froze in fists as they pushed. They pressed into the wind with faces downward and eyes closed, and didn't know if they were being driven backward or were slowly moving forward, but their feet kept shuffling to the bumping movement of the person ahead. It seemed the march would never end before they felt the cliff-side and followed it blindly to the entrance of an abandoned mineshaft. Ian and Jesse pulled the crossed boards away from the dark space and they left the travois and catamaran outside and all filed into the small hole in the mountain. It was dark inside, and smelled of ancient earth and rotting things, but it was dry, and the wind was blowing away from the opening.

Laramie brushed snow off the children and stripped their gloves to rub warmth back into icy hands.

"Laramie, don't go out there," Jesse hollered. She tried to leave, but was forced back by the driving wind and ice.

"I need a pan to heat water to warm the children," Laramie cried over the howling wind. "We don't even have a dry blanket to warm them."

"We'll get the sleeping bags after we thaw out," said Ian. "The blankets and sleeping bags will be dry. They're under the parachute on the catamaran." He blew into his cupped hands to warm them. "We'll be snug and warm in awhile," he tried to assure her. "The kiddies will be fine – just keep them moving."

"Are we going to die now?" sobbed Katie.

Huddling close to keep warm, the muffled sobs from the children broke Laramie's heart. "No, Katie, we're not going to die. Not now."

Surely they wouldn't die now! Should they have stayed in Denver? Were they really going the *right way*, as Dominic always said?

"Dominic, are you okay?" He'd been so quiet.

"There's a light coming, Mamma." Dominic was excited and the word *Mamma* sang out to Laramie.

"No, Dominic, there's no light, just the white from the snow, honey."

"There's a light coming. I see a light."

"Dominic, there is no light, it's . . . "

The light was blinding and filled the small opening to the abandoned mineshaft. Arms shielded eyes from the light as a crackling voice barked, "Good God, a'mighty!" The voice howled on the blowing wind, "Follow the light," and left as quickly as it came.

In a dazed stupor the group looked at each other to verify that they saw the light and heard a voice. No one spoke. The light filled the space again and the voice shrieked, "C'mon! It's damn cold out here!"

The lantern swung high and two eyes peered from woolen casings and bare fingers shot through tattered gloves clutching a snow covered furry thing. "C'mon!"

The snow was already drifting, filling holes and hiding rocks. "Hold to the rope!" boomed command, as frozen hands searched and found the rope that steadied numb legs.

They marched a couple hundred yards when the line stopped at the end of the rope. A large house blocked the blowing snow revealing wide stairs leading to tall doors where pink doves winged through purple Columbines on the stained glass windows illuminated by the light from within. Flames fanned by the wind rose from a large fireplace as the group quietly filed into a large living room.

"I've never seen so many candles burning at one time." Suzan's eyes glowed in the soft candlelight. "Only in pictures of rooms like this at Christmas time." The group gawked shyly around the room like they'd been plucked from hell and placed in a warm fairy-tale. The aroma of ham, baking bread and sweet potatoes nearly drove them wild. "This can't be real." Suzan rubbed her hands and stomped her feet again. She would probably wake up any minute.

The old woman took her woolens off and draped them over the staircase banister. "Get those snow flocked coats off and get near the fire. This ole house is too darned big to heat good. The kitchen's better though." She plucked ice balls from the fur of a large white cat. "Missy here, told me you were out there." She vigorously rubbed the long white fur with a doily from the mantle. "I had to follow her – no tellin' what kind of creature she was huntin'." The cat squirmed away, pawing at the door to go out. "No ma'am, you can't have that big ole dog in here." The woman opened the front door a crack and the white cat squirmed through. "Found yer dog out there. That's who she was after." Her tongue clucked loudly. "A German Shepherd raised her from a kitten, and she'll take up with any ole mutt now."

Suzan wiped a windowpane, and sure enough, the white cat was curled next to Black in the corner of the front porch. "I'd forgotten all about Black, and we were rescued because of him. By a cat!"

"Well now, I don't know if I'd give the cat all the credit." The old woman sank down in the velvet recliner and proceeded to roll a cigarette.

"Here. Have one of these." Ian handed her his pack of Marlboro's.

"Nope. Those things'll kill ya," she said, licking the paper and rolling it between stained fingers.

"Well then, let me light it for you." Ian struck a flame on his lighter and the old woman's eyes twinkled with the attention.

"Hasn't been a man offer me a cigarette or a light in – I don't know how long." She eyed him appreciatively and the lines in her face softened, revealing a once-handsome woman.

"God a'mighty, where's my manners. Get up close to the fire! Pull them chairs up! Sit!" Laramie and Suzan obediently arranged elegant wing-backed chairs and matching footstools crescent shaped around the fire. "Don't know what kinda fools'd be out in this kinda weather."

"The storm came up so quick. I thought we could make it to Silver Plume," admitted Jesse, embarrassed to be the fool that had pushed them so dangerously.

"Well, you did. In fact you nearly passed the town completely. I don't know how in heck you ever found that ole mineshaft. I thought I was the only one who would ever find it again. Guess God remembered, too." She cackled as she reached into a pocket on the recliner, drew a large swig from the narrow necked bottle and handed it to Ian. "Have some young fella, and pass it around. It'll warm ya up some before we eat."

Ian took a big swallow, sucked in his breath, and didn't dare pass it around before handing it back to the woman who placed it in the pocket, chuckling again. "Make it myself. Pretty good, yea?"

"Oh . . . ," Ian gulped to catch his breath. "Yes. What do you make it from?" he whispered.

"Spring pine – so the sap's running, honey on the comb, if I can get it – molasses if I can't. I let it ripen 'til honey-suckle blooms and strawberries are red. Throw some of them in too, with other stuff growin along the way. Mix it in five gallon crocks, then strain it into old vinegar bottles," she held up her bottle, "like this here." After tossing down another swig, she handed it to Ian who graciously declined. "Blows the corks off sometimes so I drink those first. Gets me through the winter. Best medicine I ever had. Not a bit of arthritis and rheumatism that gets other folks."

"Yes Ma'am." Ian was amazed she was still alive. He could have sworn he'd tasted kerosene that went down easier.

"Well, now that we're all toasty, let me show you the kitchen." She was halfway to the door, "Well, are you comin?" she hollered back.

Suzan was the first to follow. The old house fascinated her and the old woman living in such genteel surroundings was a mystery.

"Guess you're wonderin how I came to live here?" She talked as she walked from candle to candle with a long wooden match. "Well, I don't. Not normally."

Suzan admired the copper-bottomed pots and pans that hung from hooks at a central island – all the latest gadgets for the true gourmet, definitely not the old woman's style. She opened cupboards where blue crystal goblets and Dutch Windmill china stood in neat rows – service for twenty-four. Silver flatware in velvet lined drawers; finely honed carving knives in wooden cabinets; stainless steel cookware in the walk-in pantry; and every staple a cook would ever need, neatly organized on shelves. She was in a dream kitchen and wished they could stay for the winter.

"Rod and Gussie Harris ran a bed and breakfast outfit here. Old family home. Knew Gussie's parents when they were kids. Gussie always used to feed me from her back door. I'd come down the mountain 'bout once a week and Gussie would have a picnic basket all ready – always had a pie on top – or homemade cinnamon rolls. We swapped baskets all year. I'd hunt herbs and berries for her, load up the basket and bring it back." The old woman's eyes watered and she wiped them with her flannel sleeve. "I brought Rod a bottle of medicine down once in awhile. Said his old truck didn't run right without it." She cackled loudly at the joke between them. "Gonna miss them two. Never did tell 'em goodbye. Figure I don't need to, long as I'm here."

Suzan followed her to the old cook stove where potholders hung on hooks. "Got some water warming on the side and there's a big ole tub on the back porch for bathin', next to a wood-burning stove for warmin'. Help yourself after dinner – looks like you and your group could use it."

Suzan was embarrassed by the inference. "No harm meant, honey. Just know what a warm bath means to weary bones. Never got to take one much after snow fall except down here once in awhile if no visitors were stayin' over. Sure did like a warm bath though. I've already had two since I been here."

Laramie came in as the old woman grabbed potholders and opened the stove door. Crusty ham and a big pan of sweet potatoes soon steamed on the wooden counter. She reached back in and took out two loaves of brown bread, and pulled a bucket of butter from the pantry, and lined them up beside the ham and potatoes.

"Guess it's ready. Ain't much of a cook, but do know how to read directions. Everything comes in big bags of mix anymore. No such thing as buying a sack of flour – just a sack of bread mix." Her crackling laughter rang through the kitchen and soon the others followed the delicious aroma and stood around the counter.

"Don't do dishes, but help yourself to anything you're willing to wash up afterwards." She picked up a pie pan lying upside down on the table and cut off a big piece of ham, and heaped on scoops of soft sweet potatoes. Laramie sliced the warm bread and lathered two pieces with butter for the old woman. "Gotta have honey on mine. Since there is some – there – on the counter." She looked closely at Suzan, Jane and Laramie. "You girls better take two helpings of everything. Put some meat on them bones. Heh, heh." Soon they were seated around the table where great chunks of ham lay on fine china plates next to real silver forks, spoons and knives.

"Guess I'll say thanks." Heads bowed and hands clutched together. "God, I don't know where they come from, and sure don't know how I found them. Thanks for sending them. We'll have a fine birthday celebration. Amen."

The group of weary travelers looked around the table like they should be remembering something. "Is it your birthday?" asked Jane.

"No. It's Christmas Eve."

A hush fell and tears slipped from startled eyes as they looked from face to face, thankful to be alive. Time had quietly slipped away, one day turning into the next. They hadn't marked the days and didn't even have a calendar. Even Mother Goose was caught unawares and her mind rushed to think of simple gifts to leave from Santa.

"Everything's the right way." Dominic's smile caught the old woman and his blue eyes held her there.

"He's got it."

"Ma'am," said Ian, with tears in his eyes, "I think this is the best meal I've ever eaten." He sopped up ham drippings. "And I'm washing the dishes."

"I'll help, and if you'll point the direction of the wood-pile, I'll bring in enough to warm this place for the next few days." Jesse beamed as he popped the last bite of bread and honey in his mouth.

"I'll start bathing the kids and get them ready for bed. "Oh," said Suzan, "all the clothes are outside."

"Now, not to worry. There's enough ole clothes in the bedroom closets to outfit the town. Rod and Gussie kept what they called *period* clothes in all the closets, and welcomed the guests to wear them while they were here. Gussie was so proud of them. I'll bet she even has kids clothes somewhere – she had a whole slew of grandkids in Nebraska who used to come visit each summer. Let's go lookin'."

The old woman licked her pie plate and turned it upside down on the table, grabbed a candle and a long match and headed up the stairs. "There's candles in every room, just don't forget to snuff 'em." The wide walnut staircase smelled of wood soap and the banister was worn smooth from many hands caressing it over the years. The large hallway led the length of the house with four doors opening on each side.

"Now, all the rooms are fixed up ole-timey like, with bed commodes and all. I just go outside, but you may want to use them with the kids and all." She opened the first door on the right. "I sleep downstairs in that ole recliner by the fireplace. In fact, I haven't even been upstairs since I buried Rod and Gussie. Had to come up and get some clothes for burial, you know. She crossed the floor and lit the candle over the fireplace. "There's a fireplace in two rooms and they both open up to the next room, big like, so take your pick."

Suzan, Jane and Laramie stood with mouths gaping. Two four-poster beds with feather mattresses and comforters stood along the wall. Battenberg lace curtains adorned French doors that opened to a small deck with chairs. A carved oak armoire stood from floor to ceiling. Suzan opened the doors and was astonished at the long lace-adorned dresses and gowns that hung elegantly from satin covered hangers. Two mirrors caught her and she gasped to see herself. The old woman cackled.

"Don't ya just hate those things?" She laughed until her sides hurt and she wiped tears from her eyes. "I knew a mirror would give you a start. I could tell you were city girls. You still got polish on them long nails . . . kinda." She laughed again.

Suzan looked at her long ragged nails, snagged, dirty, half red and half bare. She looked at the mirror. Dirty face and matted hair. Wind burned foreheads revealed white strips where headbands had been and brown weathered hands met white arms. Pretty soon the whole house shook with laughter and long lace nightdresses lay on beds. The second bedroom opened to the first revealing three queen sized beds. Long underwear and jogging suits hung in Gussie's closet and stacks of kid's clothes were neatly folded in one of the dressers.

It didn't take long for Jesse to have a fire roaring, the kids to be bathed and dressed and playing dominoes on the living room floor in front of the fireplace. The sisters took turns pouring warm water over each other and soon joined the others dressed in long, flannel, lace-trimmed gowns. Ian and Jesse didn't have near as much fun and came down the stairs dressed in the same clothes they started with.

The old woman cackled between swigs of medicine. "Guess Rod was a mite shorter and rounder than the two of you. But you smell better."

"We can get our things tomorrow and change into cleaner clothes. Ma'am, I would love to make you some coffee – Australian style, dark and strong like our tea." The clear twinkling eyes told him she would love it, too.

The fireplace popped and flickered as they told the story of the first Christmas while drinking coffee and smoking cigarettes. Soon, the woman snored softly and Ian covered her with the woolen afghan lying by her side.

Jesse and Ian carried the children up the stairs to feather beds while the sisters snuffed the candles and took the bones and scraps from dinner to Black and the cat. Such an odd sight – to see the black wolf so gentle with the white cat. The wind had stopped and snow fell silently now.

"It's so peaceful. Why can't we stay here?" asked Suzan.

"I guess we can," answered Laramie, "but we would end up on the same journey – heading to the ranch to find Mom and Dad. And what would we do here when the food runs out?"

"The same thing we'll have to do at the ranch."

"Yes, but we'll be settled there. We could never feel like this was home. It's beautiful and I'm so grateful she found us, but it's not our home. It's not even her home. She won't even sleep in a bedroom. It was someone else's home, offered to us this night."

"I know you're right. It's just so good to be clean again and wearing clean clothes."

"Well, I'm sure going to enjoy it tonight," said Jane. "I'm really tired, and those feather beds are calling."

"I can hardly wait for morning to see where we are," said Suzan, "and see what this looks like in the daylight."

The sisters snuffed the last candle and climbed the stairs as the old woman snored loudly.

Suzan was the first awake and grabbed a long velvet robe from the armoire and crept to the window. It was cold in the old house and the sun was just cresting the mountain. A white wonderland shone below and the spruce boughs hung heavy with thick snow.

The old woman's afghan was neatly folded on the floor and boxes of Christmas decorations were stacked around the recliner. All the window shades were open and soft light lay on blue velvet sofas and chairs arranged in a cozy conversation corner on a wine and pewter oriental rug. Family pictures framed Blue Boy and Pinky, and gentlemen on horseback chased hounds and a red fox over the bookcase.

Suzan started a fire in the fireplace and stoked the coals in the cook stove, where water was already simmering in the coffeepot. A library off the living room revealed an old high-back Stein player piano with sheet music opened to "The Carols of Christmas Day."

She'd already forgotten. "It's Christmas Day!" She rushed to the kitchen pantry and pulled out the bag of bread mix, and before long, was kneading a batch large enough to make cinnamon rolls, too – "If I can figure out the cook stove."

The front door opened and cold air rushed in. The white cat ran to the kitchen and curled around Suzan's legs. The old woman drug a large blue spruce into the living room floor and pulled the tree holder from its box.

"Let me help you," called Suzan, as she grabbed the end of the tree and together they stood it in the middle of the large living room.

"Thought you'd still be sleeping. Just wanted to surprise the kiddies. Found some honey on the comb in Gussie's pantry, some cinnamon sticks, dried apples and all sorts of stuff to make wassail with. Course, it would sure make good medicine, too." The large tree nearly filled the empty space in the center of the room and after several attempts, it finally stood straight and tall.

"How did you ever get that big tree here all by yourself?" It had taken both of them to wrestle it to its final resting place.

"Well, dragging it is some different than trying to right it again. Took a saw to cut it and a rope to drag it with. Couldn't have done it by myself. Heh, heh."

Suzan looked closely at the old woman and noticed for the first time that she had been truly beautiful in her day. Large, deep-set dark eyes that snapped when she laughed, high cheekbones and a square jaw. Long gray hair was knotted on top and held in place by two polished rib bones and a leather lacing. Leathery skin the color of brass revealed many years of wind and sun. Hard years.

"Well, what do you see, Missy?"

"I'm sorry. I didn't mean to stare. I was wondering how you live. Where you live. You're very beautiful. I was wondering how you'd look in one of those long lace gowns upstairs."

"Oh, pshaw! They used to say I was beautiful. Now they just think I'm the crazy ole woman who is always walking the river. I collect herbs and roots, you know. Some's best gathered at night or in the full moon. Scares the folks who don't know it." Her eyes grew distant in memories. "Frank D didn't think I was so crazy though." She cackled her funny laugh and brushed dirt and snow off the tree. "Didn't mean to drag the dirt on this fine polished floor."

"Don't worry about the floor. Tell me more about where you've lived, and who was Frank D?"

Suzan followed the woman into the kitchen where she busied herself making coffee, embarrassed with talk about herself.

"I guess I've lived everywhere on these mountains from Denver, in the ole days, to the Grand Mesa. Sometimes in a cabin up on the Blue, sometimes in a cave up above Glenwood. Haven't lived in a town since Frank D died. He used to come huntin' or fishin' in the seasons." The dark eyes faded away momentarily. "Most recent I've been living at an old cattle camp, just over the hill a days hike. There's an ole trailer up there. Guess the owners just let it go to the critters, so the critters and me been sharin' it for a couple years. I been walkin across that mountain every week for two years to see Gussie. Never had a daughter – only Gussie. She'd let me mom her sometimes. Kinda liked that. Gonna miss Gussie – Rod, too – good man." Dark, memory-filled eyes began to twinkle – "Hasn't been a man flirt with me like that since . . ." She checked the coffee and sniffed the bread rising under the dishcloth. "Guess you found the sack of bread mix. Do you know how to make cinnamon rolls?"

"If you'll help me with the cook stove, we'll have a whole batch by lunch time."

"I can work that stove!" She slapped her thigh and Suzan poured coffee as Laramie came down the stairs.

"Are we the only ones up?" Laramie yawned and stretched.

"No," hollered Ian from the stair landing. The old woman poured him a cup of coffee and offered him an *eye opener,* which he declined. Soon, Jane, Ian, and the old woman were sitting in the living room by the fire, smoking a morning cigarette and admiring the tree.

Before long, the children were up and clamoring around the tree, excited to start decorating. Suzan and Laramie made hot chocolate, pancakes, and opened cans of peaches. Breakfast was finished, the old woman licked her pie pan and turned it upside down on the table, and bread dough was punched down and formed into cinnamon rolls.

After everyone dressed in new clothes gifted by the old woman, she led them to the travois and catamaran. They couldn't imagine how they ever found the abandoned mineshaft. They'd blindly trudged as far north and west as possible after completely bypassing the town. The entrance, practically hidden from view, was almost in a neighbor's backyard. Jesse noticed odd footprints and tried to remember if he'd seen them before. The hair pricked on his neck and old haunting fears nagged at his memory.

He and Ian dug the travois and catamaran out of the snow and pushed and pulled them to the house. "I'm curious about the ropes," said Ian.

"Oh, I've strung ropes halfway across these mountains, just to keep my way during such storms as last. I can tell by the knots which rope I've found and where it will take me. Used to get me to that ole mineshaft you found, on days when I took too much medicine. Heh, heh."

Ian placed his arm around the old woman's shoulders to help her navigate the snow, which she obviously didn't need help navigating, but was sure pleased to have his arm around her.

Bed and Breakfast Brewery Inn, written in bold purple letters on a turquoise sign, dangled by chains from a post standing by the front door. The house was painted turquoise with the same purple trim as the sign. Most of the neighboring frame houses, painted in bright fuchsia, mauve, plumb, blue, and aqua, were built in the 1800's, when the town and mining were booming. Just down the road was an old church with a bell steeple and across from it was a large three-story brick building – The George Rail Museum. "We've lived here all our lives and never really looked at this town," said Jesse.

"That's the way life was taking us," said Ian. "Always hurrying somewhere, never seeing."

Jesse stacked enough wood by the back door to keep the house warm for a month or more. Ian and Jane went for a walk where the old woman showed him, and came back with two wild turkeys. The old woman built a fire outside, gutted and singed the birds and plucked the pinfeathers. She insisted on cooking them outside, over the coals, so nothing would interfere with her cinnamon rolls.

Yeasty bread smells mingled with spices from brewing wassail as they all joined in to decorate the tree. Years of collected ornaments, from the angel topper, to the tiniest bell, were hung with care. "Each one carries a memory," said the old woman, who happily doctored herself all day. "Never been down a day with rheumatism," she bragged. "Had a few days drunk, though! Heh, heh." Her cackling was contagious and laughter soon filled the house. "Grandest tree I ever did see," she said, stepping away and admiring their work.

Pale winter sun dropped behind the mountain as roast turkey was placed on the lace-covered table. Large blue porcelain bowls filled with mashed potatoes, carrots, green beans, and cranberry gelatin, crowded the china plates and fine silver. Suzan insisted the old woman eat on china this one meal. She agreed.

Lively Christmas carols rang from the antique piano while the children sang and the old woman ate cinnamon rolls. Wassail and coffee warmed their bodies as love filled the house and warmed their hearts. After the children went to bed, Suzan continued to play quiet lullabies by Brahms, and Steven Foster's lonely love songs until soft candlelight flickered and embers glowed.

"I don't think I've ever enjoyed a Christmas more," Jesse said as he snuggled closer to Suzan in the feather bed. "And to think – we didn't stand in long lines, spend a thousand dollars, or stay up late wrapping expensive paper around expensive gifts."

Plumes of smoke rose from chimneys as the morning sun glistened in crystals from crusty snow. Jesse and Ian shifted loads, tightened straps and soon they were packed and ready to go.

The old woman and the white cat were gone, along with the leftover cinnamon rolls. The afghan was neatly folded by the recliner, the pie pan was upside down on the table. A note showed from one corner of the pan and Suzan read it out loud.

*"Don't think I've ever had a real Christmas before*

*Thanks*

*Just hold to the rope – Someone's always been there before*

*Help yourself to anything you want*

*Safe Journey"*

"We didn't even know her name. I can't believe she didn't wait so we could say goodbye and thank her for everything." Tears fell from Suzan's eyes as she folded the note and tucked it into her shirt pocket.

"She didn't need our thanks and she never says goodbye, remember?" Laramie wrapped her arms around Suzan.

Suzan shuffled around the kitchen, found paper and a pencil and quickly wrote:

*If you have a rope to Rifle, come to Dan and Roma Zerlich's Rocking Z Ranch.*

*Lots of pines and wild berries. Just follow the smell of cinnamon rolls.*

*We'll lead the rest of the way.*

*Thanks for showing us a real Christmas.*

*With Love,*

*Jesse, Suzan, Ian, Jane, Laramie, and the kids*

Suzan took the barrette out of her hair and laid it with the note on the kitchen table. She'd seen the old woman admire it, as she admired the bones and leather in the old woman's hair.

The day remained cold but sunny as the group continued up I-70. The gradual climb and slick snow made the going slow, but their jubilant spirits eased their loads. The kids walked in front most of the way, singing Christmas carols. No one ever heard Sara's voice until Christmas day, when they sang. The clarity and strength of her sweet voice bounced from the valley walls and echoed back like an angel was serenading them. Dominic held Sara's hand most of the day and said, "Everything's the right way."

They camped at a *billabong,* as Ian called the small lake, and even caught fish for dinner. Suzan made biscuits from a sack of mix and lathered them in butter, taken from the pantry. The old woman's cackling was heard in their hearts and they slept under pines to the sound of her snores.

Eisenhower Tunnel, built in 1973, is 1.6 miles long with a separate tunnel for each direction, each two lanes wide. Silent cars could be seen and odors of death and decay hung heavy on the air. The group edged forward, trying to get a better look. Was it only a month ago during Thanksgiving holiday that they'd passed through the large caverns? Who'd have thought they'd be walking them now?

As they stood staring at the great gaping mouth, its repulsive breath churning the stomach and raising the bile, two men emerged from the eastbound tunnel, retching and gasping at the side of the road. Ian and Jesse crossed the lanes and were horrified by their physical appearance and putrid stench. Both had urinated and defecated in their clothes and smelled like they'd soaked in a bucket of musk. They gasped and struggled to catch their breath.

"We left our families on the other side. They'll never make it through." The man doubled over, retching and coughing. He fell to his knees and his friend lay outstretched in the clean air, sun glistening on the slime that covered him. He smelled gut-shot and Ian covered his mouth to keep from upchucking.

"Get out of those clothes or you'll never get away from the smell." Ian stood away from them as they stripped to their underwear and began rubbing snow on their bodies to remove the foul odor. Jesse ran to the catamaran, loosened the straps and pulled the parachute cover back. One of the men was too heavy to properly fit in their clothes, but baggy long sleeved T-shirts, flannel shirts and sweat pants would be better than freezing to death – too small or not.

"Tell us what happened." Ian coaxed the men away from the foul smelling clothes. "Maybe the side you came through is the worst of it. If we can get through, we can help your family."

"Man, there's no way anyone could get through there and come out sane." The large man broke down in sobs. "I've never been so scared in my entire life." His body shook with the memory. "And you must be out of your minds to be heading that direction. There's no food, and the people who have some, won't share. My kids are sick and my wife's expecting our third child any day now." He grabbed Ian's jacket and screamed, "What the hell has happened?"

Ian forcefully loosened the man's grip. "Settle down man. You've got to keep your head or you'll all die." The man calmed and Ian saw his terror-induced insanity. "Gather wood kiddies, anything that will burn."

He led the men to sit while Jesse started a fire and Suzan mixed Tang and water in a pan. The men breathed easier as they warmed by the fire. “How many are waiting on the other side?” Ian spoke with authority, and the men calmed.

“There’s three women, one man, and five children,” the large man said, wiping his eyes. And there’s no way I can go back through and get them.” His shoulders shook and he dropped his head at the ugly admission of fear.

“What happened in there?” Ian asked softly. “Tell us, so we can help and be prepared ourselves.”

“It wasn’t so bad at first,” started the smaller man. “The smell was bad, but we covered our mouths. We had a lantern.” He nodded at his friend, “Mike hollered and when I turned to help him, I dropped it and it exploded into flames.” The man fought to continue. “It was a body. Mike tripped on the bloated mass and when he fell on it, the body exploded and we were both covered with rotting guts. We continued, clinging to the rail, but the smell got to us. We tried to run, but ran into more corpses and cars.” He hung his head and sobbed. “We crawled when our legs got too weak to walk. I shit in my pants when the second body exploded.”

Ian looked at the tunnels, quickly scanned the mountain and asked Jesse, “How feasible would it be to go over the top.”

“The other side is rocky cliffs. Loveland Pass goes to the south and would be a five-day trip even in good weather. If a snow storm caught us up there, we could be trapped for days or weeks.”

Ian and Jesse walked into the tunnel holding bandannas over their mouths. They continued until it grew dark and the stench raised their bile.

“We’d never make it! The fumes in there are toxic. Their lantern probably would have exploded whether it was dropped, or not.” Ian placed a hand on Jesse’s shoulder. “There’s got to be another way.”

Ian tried to open the doors that led through the center of the tunnels, where all the controls were. The electronically controlled security doors wouldn’t budge. Jesse scanned the abandoned cars, picked up a large rock and smashed it against the trunk lock. The trunk flew opened, revealing a tire iron, jack, and spare tire. He repeated smashing trunks open until he found what he was looking for – a crow bar. The men grabbed blankets from the open trunks and wrapped them around their shoulders.

It took twenty minutes for Jesse to pry the center control doors open. The stale air rushed out and three bodies lay close to the entrance. They were trapped in there – couldn’t open the doors. Two of the bodies were bloated, one missing a leg from the knee down where maggots writhed from the dark stump, and the third looked like he’d died recently.

The central core was wide enough to drive trucks through. Control stations lined both sides. Ian and Jesse walked a couple hundred yards into the core. It was bad, but not as bad as the tunnels. It was colder inside the core and the bloated, rotting bodies weren't as deteriorated as those in the outer tunnels. It was possible.

"Is the central door open on the other side?" Ian asked the two men.

"No, just the tunnels, " answered Mike.

"I've got a plan that might work. If we go through the core, we can send your family through the same way. There's a big old turquoise house a good days travel downhill, just on the west end of Silver Plume. It's comfortable. Would be a great place to have a baby. If you're lucky, an old woman will be there, and I'll bet she knows about birthing and such."

"Treat her kindly and make her some cinnamon rolls," added Jesse.

Ian shared his information with the men and told them what to expect in Denver, if they still chose to go there. Mike and the smaller man had come from Frisco and told Jesse and Ian of the vigilante groups along the way. Neither man was armed, and it would be hard going, unless they found a way to hunt game. The old woman would help them.

"All right. I guess it's time to do this," said Jesse.

"We'll string a rope between us. Don't let go of the rope," said Suzan. "Remember what the note said."

Ian tied the crowbar around his waist, and he and Jane led the group, pushing the catamaran around the bodies. They could see a truck on the right side and steered to the left. Laramie and the children held the rope in the middle and Suzan and Jesse pulled the travois in the rear. Black was hesitant to enter the death chamber, but reluctantly followed behind.

"Keep your bandannas pulled up over your noses and mouths. I'll keep talking along the way, so you can always hear me. I'll tell you what's ahead, so there won't be any surprises." God, he hoped he was right! "If you get scared, just remember you've got a hold on the rope and that someone has been there before you."

The two men disappeared in the light as the tunnel turned left, leaving them in total darkness.

"Everyone holding the rope?" hollered Ian.

"Yes," bounced off walls and echoed dully.

"Okay. We're off! Shouldn't take more than an hour, if we're lucky. And from what I've seen so far – we're pretty darned lucky."

"Yea," the children cheered.

"Sara," Dominic whispered, "we're going the right way."

Levi and Jacinth held hands, and Mira, Tara, Jen and Katie followed Laramie. They held the rope as dilated eyes strained to see, and halting hesitant feet shuffled to the drumbeat of their hearts. Bicycle tires scrunched along the concrete floor, as "obstacle left," sounded from the front, or "obstacle right," and the group moved as directed.

"Damn! . . . Bloody . . . Rotten! . . . " exploded from Ian and the stench of putrid entrails penetrated every ounce of air, and every cell of their bodies responded. Ian choked while vomiting, "Far right!" Sara and Jacinth vomited too, as the group hurried to pass the rotting corpse and escape to better air. Metal clanged against metal, and "a truck – go left," gasped from Ian's mouth. The putrid vapors from the truck reeked of death and bloat.

They hadn't gone fifty paces when Ian called out, "Hold up." Ian stripped from his vile smelling jacket and shirt. Buttons bounced on the floor as cackling laughter rang through the core of the tunnel. "Did you hear that?"

"Hear what?" answered Jesse.

"I heard it," said Laramie. "Sounded like she's right in front of us."

"Okay! Okay . . ." Ian breathed a deep sigh, "Let's go slowly. Hold on to the rope."

"I'm swinging the crow-bar in front of me. If it hits something, I'll tell you what direction to go – like before. We'll make it – but it may take longer than I expected. Just hang on – we'll be out before we know it."

They hung to the left wall for a long while before, "Ian!" shrieked through the tunnel.

"Janie – Janie?"

"Wait, Ian! Stay there. I'm walking in something slimy. I'll try to walk out of it. Oh God – It's moving, and I can smell it."

"Let's keep going as far left as we can. Whatever it is, we don't want the whole group to walk through it."

"Ian, I think we should back up and go right. The smell is getting stronger, it's right ahead of us."

"I smell so wretched, I can't smell anything else. Back up! That's it. Hard right to the other wall. Oh God, yes, you were right."

"Heh, heh," crackled through the long chamber again.

"Yea – she's ahead of us!" Ian and Laramie said in unison. "Just hold the rope. She'll get us out of here."

"Kids – kids," hollered Laramie. "Take off your jackets and I'll secure them under the straps of the catamaran. That way they'll still be clean when we get to the other side. You'll only be cold for awhile."

The group crept forward, changing directions seven more times as Jane directed them around corpses in varying degrees of rot. They stopped as churning bile dictated, and clothing was stripped before continuing. Fear rose and it seemed they would never find the end, and the cackling laughter rang to lead them forward.

"Ian!" Jane hollered. There's definitely something big ahead of us." She sniffed the air. "I can't tell what direction it's coming from. It's bad!"

"Everyone hold up." Ian sucked in his breath. "I'll investigate." Cautious footsteps bounced off the walls and Ian slowly made his way forward. "Talk softly, Janie, so I can judge how far I've gone."

"Ian Jayne, you need a bath. I don't know if the stink will ever come out of your jacket. Suzan brought some lye soap, and if that doesn't work, nothing will, but . . ."

"Damn! . . . Bloody . . . Rotten!

Ian hit the floor hard and struggled to get his balance. The slime oozed under his feet, and maggots writhed over his hands. He retched and retched, his stomach convulsing in dry heaves as he knelt on all fours. "Oh God," came in whispers. "I think we've found the end." He coughed and spit until the taste of blood left his mouth. "Jesse, I'm going to need your help with the crow-bar. I don't think I've got the strength to do it myself."

Jesse followed the rope forward. "Come right to me," gasped Ian. "The worst of it is on the left. If you can find the center of the door, it should be close."

Jesse barely kept his heaving stomach from emptying the rest of its contents. "I've got it. It's about ten feet ahead of you."

They heard the crowbar slip from the metal door several times. It wasn't working. "Jesse, work in right above and below the locks."

"I can't feel the locks. Wait, maybe this is it." The crow bar popped again, clanging on the concrete floor. "Once more," Jesse bellowed, pushing with all his might. "Arrggghhhhhh!" burst from his throat as the door groaned open and the muted light of dusk glared through the gaping door, blinding them.

A ghoulish cluster of dead bodies lay just inside the door. Ian crawled the fifteen feet to daylight while Jesse helped push and pull the travois and catamaran onto the snowy ground. Freedom! Cold mountain air! Life! They would remain forever synonymous to Ian.

They lay exhausted on the snow-covered ground as the sun cast long shadows on the west face of the mountain. Tents soon stood on the small spot of remaining sunlight and Jesse started a fire.

Wafting smoke drew a man and two frantic women to the camp. Ian, ashen and weak, described the horrifying experience in the core, and assured them it was better than what their husbands had experienced in the tunnels. Mike's wife clutched her stomach full of child and Suzan could see the baby was low – ready for birth. She calmed the hysterical woman and told her of the turquoise house with purple trim and the old woman who loved cinnamon rolls and slept in a velvet recliner by the fire.

"Why don't you get a good night's sleep and head out in the morning?" Suzan recognized the haggard look of despair in the woman's eyes. "You'll be rested, stronger. Mike will meet you on the other side."

"I don't think the baby will wait, and I don't want to be stuck here without him." She grabbed her stomach and doubled over. "I've got two sick girls down the hill and this baby isn't going to wait. I've got to go now."

Suzan placed her hand on the woman's stomach and felt the hard muscles contracting. "How far apart are your pains." The woman looked at her like she must be crazy. "As far as you can judge – five minutes, twenty minutes?"

"About fifteen, maybe only ten. I have to go. Now."

"It would be insane. The fear and stench could incapacitate you – you'd be forced to have the baby inside all that filth and rot. I don't know how you'd continue – and it would be pitch black. We're not conditioned to squat, birth, and get back to work. It doesn't work that way for us." Suzan knew anything could go wrong with childbirth.

"Jesse!" Suzan called. "There's a problem." Ian and Jesse both came, along with the man and the other woman.

"Hopefully, if you're set on going now, your labor will stop."

"Oh, no! Don't tell me you're in labor now?" The man was frantic. "We can't go through with you in labor. Have the baby here and then we'll all go through tomorrow, or the next day."

"No. I don't want this baby born in a snow bank without Mike. I'm going through now." She was adamant. "Got to."

"Well, let's get our gear up here then. Guess it doesn't matter if we go through a dark tunnel after dark." He put his arm around her. "It'll be okay, hon. We'll get that baby born on the other side."

The small bedraggled group stood at the entrance of the foul smelling core. They held belongings in sheets and pillowcases. The children were thin and pale with dark circles under their eyes.

"Maybe with both entrances open now, the gaseous odors will have dissipated," said Ian. "Remember to keep your bandannas handy. It helps some. Wait a minute." Hurrying back to the travois, he cut off a length of rope and gave it to the man. "Have everyone hold onto the rope." Ian tied the rope to the man's back belt loop." He noticed the man's walking stick. "Feel with the stick in front of you and go around all obstacles."

The men slapped each other on the back and Suzan embraced the women. "Just keep talking to each other. Hearing voices is calming. Keeps you grounded. You can do it. Just hold to the rope." She hugged them again. "Good luck and God bless."

Suzan wiped tears from her eyes as the group disappeared into the core of the tunnel. "God help them," she whispered. Jesse's arm slipped around her shoulder and held her tight against him. "They'll never make it." Her tears were bitter reminders of the awful smells and sounds – their own sounds of retching and gagging.

"They'll make it." He looked at her and smiled. "We made it."

"Yes," she smiled back. "We did, didn't we."

"You're quite a woman, Suzan Gant." The statement surprised her. "I don't say it often enough – how much I love you." Jesse pulled her close and she smelled his maleness in the circle of his arms.

"Don't ever quit loving me. Don't ever quit holding me. I need to hear you tell me you love me." Her tears fell silently down his shirt. "I keep you so far away sometimes. Please forgive me. I need you, Jesse. Don't let me push you away."

"Maybe we'll both learn how to love each other better. You're so strong, and I've tried to weaken you so I would feel stronger – as if I could keep your strength below mine. I always had to be the boss. The *man* of the house." A deep sigh escaped his throat. "I'm sure thankful for your strength now." Tears fell in Suzan's hair. "Funny. Life becomes more precious when death is so close." They held each other until the stars shone brightly and the cold prickled their skin.

"You okay, now?" Jesse smoothed her hair away from her face and kissed her full on the mouth.

"I'm okay, now."

They walked arm in arm to the warmth of the fire where Ian, Jane, and Laramie sat with coffee mugs warming cold fingers. Ian soon held two steaming cups of the strong, black liquid, and handed them to Suzan and Jesse.

"Do we need to go over maps again?" Asked Ian.

"No. It's pretty cut and dried from here on. I can't think of a shortcut. I think our best bet is to stay to the road. Every other option would be too treacherous to travel this time of year, but from what Mike said back there, we might run into trouble with vigilante-type groups."

"I think if we stick to ourselves, we won't be seen as a threat to anyone. No sense borrowing trouble anyway."

"Sure hope you're right." Jesse felt uneasy. So far, since they'd carried their rifles exposed, nobody had bothered them. "Sure hope you're right," he repeated, as the hair on his neck prickled.

Sounds of night predators gave way to sunshine and day predators. Turkey buzzards circled overhead and crows stood in formation around the newly revealed opening to the core of the tunnels. No one interrupted their destined duty.

Traveling downhill toward Dillon and Silverthorne was precarious. Muscles strained against their heavy loads and boots slipped on the snowy road. Twice, the momentum of the steep downhill slope pulled the catamaran and travois out of control, across six lanes of highway, almost claiming their belongings over the edge of the steep cliff. Sun shining on the four-day-old snow added to the melt and the ice that formed. They were high above the creek and tips of tall mountain pines were barely visible. If their supplies went over the edge, it would take days to retrieve them from the bottom of the canyon, but it was nearly impossible to slow their carriers.

Other groups passed them going east and warned them of armed vigilante groups below. They, in turn, told the travelers about the tunnels.

Golden arches of McDonald's glared against the white snow at the foot of the mountain pass, along with Texaco, Village Inn, and the Best Western Hotel. One armed man stood at the foot of the exit and they quickly by-passed Silverthorne and Dillon. The air was tense as armed men and women guarded their homes that dotted the lake. The steep mountain that led to Frisco appeared too great an obstacle for their tired bodies, but they crested the ridge after nightfall and camped next to others heading east.

Days were short and nights seemed shorter as the weary group passed the exits leading to Frisco. Jesse felt uneasy, as if they were being followed, and realized everyone felt the same.

A northern wind picked up and thick cumulous clouds covered the mountaintops, their gray underbellies setting dark shadows on the valley floor. Frisco loomed to the south and the group groaned under their loads as they forced themselves up the highway toward Copper Mountain.

They camped on the shoulders of the road and rose early to bitter cold and biting wind, but still, they continued past the summit of Vail Pass. The downhill descent was steep and the blowing wind was blinding. They stopped more frequently to warm the children and eat light meals of dried fruit, nuts and pemmican. Their supplies were dwindling and they needed to hunt, but they had to get off the mountain.

The storm hit late in the afternoon. Steep cliffs rose to the north and Gore Creek carved a deep crevice to the south. The wind was freezing and Jesse knew there would be no kind-hearted old woman looking for her cat this night.

The game trail was barely visible on the north side of the mountain. Jesse stopped the group and told them to wait under the pines while he and Ian investigated the high cliff above them. They had to find somewhere soon, before it started snowing. Zigzagging across the face of the mountain the game-trail took them higher until they viewed the group between treetops and the road seemed a trail itself. Jesse continued and came to a clearing. It was a good wide spot, but offered little cover. Ian waited while Jesse continued to search – for what? What was he expecting to find? He walked a few feet to where the trail dipped and formed a sharp U-turn from the clearing where Ian waited.

"Ian," Jesse called out from the edge of the mountain. Ian followed the trail and came to the small opening of a cave where Jesse waited.

"After you, Sir Jesse," Ian said bravely.

"What do you think?" Jesse hesitated.

"Well, if it's big enough for all of us, I think it's great. It'll get us out of this cold for the night, anyway."

It was musky and dark inside and the smell of cat pee hung heavy in the air. "Could you stand the smell?" asked Jesse.

"It's more a matter of whether we can stand to smell each other in closed quarters."

"Boy, isn't that the truth."

They stooped over, entered the cave and felt along its walls. It seemed large enough and they didn't hear anything inside but their own heavy breathing.

"It's warmer than outside, by a long shot, and out of the biting wind. I say, since a mountain lion or a bear hasn't attacked us yet, we give it a go."

"Well, let's do it before we freeze. Sure wish we had the lantern to check this out better."

Wind carried the promised snow and made it difficult to drag and push the travois up the narrow trail. Jesse and Ian collapsed the catamaran and drug the parachute-enclosed supplies up the mountain while Suzan gathered snow to melt for coffee and hot Tang. By the time they returned to the road for the bicycles, the snow fell heavily and covered their tracks as quickly as they were made. Good, thought Jesse. Maybe the eerie feeling he'd felt for the past few days would leave. No one could possibly see them from the road, and their tracks disappeared in the falling snow.

The lantern blazed brightly inside the mountain revealing a large cavern with a low sloping ceiling. Jesse and Ian stooped to enter, and Suzan and Jane did automatically, envisioning bats tangled in their long hair. It was creepy at first, but everyone was amazed that Jesse found it.

"You mean, you've never been here before? You didn't know it was here?" Ian was amazed. He'd followed Jesse right to it. He was sure he'd known about it before walking up the mountain.

"No, I just knew we had to get out of the weather or we'd be trapped like before. There was nowhere to go, but up." Jesse took it in stride, but Ian knew there was more to it than that – like finding the mineshaft. It was too much of a coincidence to brush it off as logical choice.

"I saw deer head up the mountain. Maybe, since we'll probably stay for a day or two, I'll start out early and see if I can bag some fresh game." Ian dug through the supplies for extra shells for his rifle.

"Would you like some company? I'm pretty good at spotting game."

"Ah, Janie, girl. I believe we have a wager to settle, as well." He tried to recall her exact words. "What was it. Oh yes! I believe it was *shoot the tick off a dog's ear*. Yes, I believe that was it exactly. Oh – at fifty paces."

"Well, yes. It was fifty paces, but fifty – sixty. Heh – if you miss a tick on a dogs ear, it doesn't really matter how far off you are. Let's go seventy paces."

Ian's laughter filled the cave, and everyone joined in as they crowded around with pemmican and dried meat. "And what would you like to wager?"

"Well, let's just see who gets the shot tomorrow."

Jesse and Ian hid all signs of the fire they'd built at the mouth of the cave, then pulled a loose-rooted buck brush plant in front of the cave entrance and placed a rock on the roots to hold it in place. From the inside, they threw a blanket to block the blowing snow. No one would ever be able to spot them now.

Laramie arranged the children's' sleeping bags along one side of the cave walls and Suzan organized the supplies on the other side. Jane, Ian and Jesse drank coffee and poured over topographical maps to try and pinpoint where they were. Tired and weary, they decided it didn't really matter where they were. They were safe. And warm. And sleepy.

Jane was tormented by nightmares in the night. Warning dreams to protect the children. Children dressed in white – screaming. Silent screams. An old crone rising from murky water carrying a sacrificial child above her head turned into a wolf lying in red snow. The smell of sage – the healing herb of the Indian Way. She woke restless and grouchy and was happy to leave with Ian before the others woke.

It was good to be out in the cold, brisk air – away from her stifling dream. The wind blew fiercely as they started up the path that led over the top of the hill. Visibility was limited at best. The elements didn't bother Jane near as much as the lingering dream. Maybe she should have awakened Suzan and told her about it. I'm making too much out of this, she thought. Jesse's there and Suzan and Laramie are like she-bears when it comes to their kids. She tried to rationalize her fears – to shake the warning.

They crossed an open clearing on top of the mountain and Ian led her to a spot under close growing pines that offered protection from the blowing snow and bitter cold. They hadn't gone more than a mile and Jane was surprised to be settling in so close to the cave. She was used to walking across mountain ranges when she'd gone hunting with her dad. This would be good. A chance to get to know each other better and close enough to the others to return quickly, and surely a big old buck would walk right past the clearing at the edge of the stand of pines. They brought a two-man tent, a small coffeepot, sleeping bags and a change of clothes. Jane unpacked trail-mix, coffee, jerky, pemmican, cigarettes, matches and water. With any luck, they'd be eating venison tenderloin for lunch.

## *Chapter 11*

Laramie grew uneasy and restless as she listened to the sounds the wind carried as it whipped through the branches of the trees. It reminded her of some forlorn melody she couldn't quite remember – like a memory hidden deep within the generational stamp of time.

They were lucky to have found shelter from the cold wind and the snow that had fallen steadily since twilight. It was cramped inside the cave, but Jesse read the storm clouds correctly yesterday when he made the decision to find somewhere dry to stay for a couple of days. They slept hard last night, and today they were trying to dry out their wet shoes and clothes and stay warm. The children snuggled under the covers for a long time before getting up – it felt so good. Breakfast was delicious –peanut butter and crackers never tasted so good. There was plenty of snow to melt that Suzan mixed with the powdered Tang.

Now, as exhaustion claimed the group in a mid-morning nap, Laramie's eyes filled with the un-summoned tears and the fear of the child as the forlorn sound of the wind brought her back to the haunting melody she couldn't quite remember. The sounds of tinkling brass – like wind chimes. No . . . more like the sounds of the old player piano in the basement on Mariposa Street. She strained against the wind to hear the melody. How long was she lost in thought while listening to the wind bring the melody to her? The tears of the child silently fell from her eyes and she honored them. She knew. The tears came before the child. There was a child out there somewhere and she must find it. Lurching forward, she was suddenly reminded of the soreness in her legs and the ache in her back from carrying the heavy pack the day before. She'd been sitting too long, and yet she knew she must go out in the snow and find the child whose fear was calling her. As she neared the mouth of the cave, the cold air assaulted her lungs. How could a child survive in this weather? Could a child possibly be alive out there? But the melody became more distinct and the quiet tears still beckoned her. She looked back at Jesse, deep in the sleep that exhaustion brings. She didn't want to wake him, but they had all agreed not to go anywhere alone. She knew she must go soon, as mountain daylight can quickly succumb to night and she had to obey the call of the child's fear.

Jesse was in the dream place and was hard to awaken. He was being pursued in sleep, just as he felt watched and followed by day, even before they left Denver. He couldn't remember when he first noticed it; his awareness that something was very close and watching him – sensing it, feeling it – almost feeling its breath on his neck. He hadn't slept well for several nights and his nerves were stretched tight. Waking, he was startled and felt the presence even closer. He tried to mentally describe the feeling; danger, warning, evil?

His eyes met Laramie's and he realized the glint of madness she saw there must have frightened her. "I'm sorry to wake you, Jesse, but I have to leave and I wanted you to know that I was going."

"Going? Going where? Where do you have to go?"

"Well," she felt embarrassed to explain her feelings, "I'll know when I get there. I have to follow the music. Can you hear it, Jesse?" He saw the desperation on her face – the look that hoped he wouldn't think she was crazy. He listened intently, trying to hear what she heard, knowing that he wouldn't. Maybe he could – or was that the wind blowing through the treetops?

No, he couldn't hear the music, although he would much rather have heard the music than felt the demons of the last few days. He was learning to trust instincts – the intuition. And to honor the sensitivities in the rest of the group. Something happened that first day at 9:47am. He didn't understand it, but now he believed it. The senses were heightened, increased somehow. Awareness was acute, hearing and sight were finely honed, inner urgings were honored, all directed by an unknown power that came from within. Each of them experienced something different from anyone else. Were they gifted? Or had the veil of past lives been removed? Usually a skeptic, he came to respect the *gifts* he witnessed – the knowing, or the memory – he couldn't quite describe it. He could almost accept his own gifts. He could feel the closeness, but his only resource was fear. He couldn't read the feeling – he only felt the danger.

Knowing he couldn't let Laramie go out in the weather by herself, he pulled his boots on and zipped his hooded sweatshirt. Over that he put on his trench coat, the one lined with sheepskin, the warm one. The main force of the blizzard had moved on, but wind gusts still whipped through the pines and it was bitterly cold. Thank God for this cave. They would have frozen to death out there, for sure. How *did* he know there was a good cave up here? It was absolute guidance – very clear – very precise, almost as if he had always known it was there. Like a memory. He knew exactly where to walk - the precise direction. And the timing was perfect. Jesse worried that they would leave footprints and be followed, but it started snowing heavily just a few minutes before they came to the small entrance of the opening in the rocks. The cave was about five hundred feet up the game trail that twisted up the steepest part of the mountain. It would appear impossible to ascend from below. The years of wear by the deer and elk left a deep, narrow path, invisible from the road below. Jesse walked right to it, guided by . . . what? The blizzard left a blanket of snow with three-foot drifts that re-designed the terrain of the night before. But they were warm and safe. Even though they were unable to build a fire inside the cave, they stayed warm in the arms of Mother Nature. It was as if She led him there. She gave him the memory of her safe haven, and although he was far from understanding it, he didn't question or deny it.

Jesse and Laramie agreed not to wake Suzan and the children sleeping so heavily, and moved quietly in the cave as they prepared to find the child tugging at Laramie's emotions. As close as Jesse could guess, only about six more hours of daylight remained. He still looked at his wrist where he'd always worn the watch that Suzan gave him on their tenth wedding anniversary. Now, it was in his pocket in the leather pouch Roma made for him.

He'd never called Roma *mom*, as he did his mother, but there was a bond between them and a love that had always been there, even before he knew he loved her daughter. Roma said they had traveled another time together and she knew him well. She had strange beliefs about a previous existence and how certain souls seek each other out in this one.

Now, as he watched her daughter, asleep with exhaustion, he realized how much of her mother was in her – that was scary! He'd watched her deciding what to pack and what to leave, preparing food, backpacks and survival kits, as she called them. Each child had one and knew they would survive if they were separated. Each child knew their job, and each knew they were part of this family now. The memories became tender and filled with emotion as he watched her sleep, and he didn't have the heart to wake her. He should leave a note, but Laramie was ready to go and so was he. They left the peaceful scene and entered the cold, outside world of reality. It was still there.

"Take care of them, Black," hollered Laramie, as they headed down the narrow game trail. She knew he was close and could hear them – he never went far from the children, not only Sara and Jen, but all the children. He was truly their guardian.

"I'll let you lead, just watch for anything out of place – I've been thinking that someone is following us, although I don't know how the heck anyone would survive out here alone," warned Jesse, watching their back-trail. Noticing Jesse's caution of the last few days, she immediately forced herself to be more aware of their surroundings, as she trusted Jesse and his instincts. She became so focused when she heard the music or the voices and felt the child's fear, that it was difficult to hear anything else. Jesse whispered for her to stop as his eyes scanned their back-trail.

"You're really getting spooky, Jesse. If someone really is following us, they must not want to hurt us, or they would have tried by now, don't you think?" Of course she was right, but he just couldn't shake the feeling.

"Don't you hear anything? Besides the music, I mean?"

Listening, forcing herself to try to hear what Jesse heard, she shook her head. The wind was blowing, making it difficult to hear anything but the music, and it was something she not only heard with her ears, but also felt in her bones. *The knowing* – she couldn't explain it when she heard it, but now she never questioned it. She accepted it and didn't argue with her rational mind. She only knew she had to honor it.

There! He knew he was right! He heard a sound coming from behind them. Twigs breaking underfoot! Someone was following them. He crouched and scanned their back-trail but the blowing snow and bitter cold prevented him from seeing more than a hundred feet. It wasn't only what he heard, but what he sensed. As Laramie pointed out, whoever was following them must not want to harm them or they would have, but that didn't make it less threatening. He sensed someone watching them even before they left Denver. It made him uneasy. Why didn't they just reveal themselves? How were they surviving out there? How many were there and what did they want? It was unnerving. He made a decision to track whoever it was after he and Laramie returned to their temporary home. Two could play this game.

The major part of the storm moved by them during the night, but the biting wind froze his face and the snow blowing off the tree branches made it difficult to see. He followed Laramie and hoped she knew where she was leading them. Part of him chided himself for being so foolish as to agree to go out in this weather just because Laramie was determined there was a child out there who needed her. The other part of him reminded himself of the other times she felt this same feeling and had been right. Damn-it! Every child needs a Laramie in their lives – someone to love them like she can, but he hoped she wouldn't pick up every fearful kid because of this inner feeling. That's the part that scared Jesse. What kind of reasoning would drive her to ignore all other logical, rational thought and take risks that jeopardized her very life? He loved her like she was his own sister, but she was so damned stubborn! She would have gone without him and he knew it. He didn't understand the overwhelming, heart-rending force that pushed her to obey. He hoped that whatever it was would soon pass so they could focus on the real problems. And there were plenty. They'd be lucky to get to the Rocking Z alive, without taking all these risks in the meantime.

He didn't dare let anyone know his real fears. They looked to him to guide them to the ranch and to get them there safely. But would it be safe there? Jesse knew the easiest way to the ranch would lead them past the minimum security prison. What happened there that first day? Had convicts gone to the ranch? It would be the perfect place to live undetected. Would Dan and Roma be there? Were they still alive? These were the fears he kept inside. The same fears they all tried to bury.

As they peaked the ridge, Laramie stopped and put out her arm to stop Jesse as she cocked her head in the wind to pick up the sound again. The tears were frozen on her face as her eyes scanned the area below. She looked north – up the ridge, and started walking again, this time with urgency in her stride.

A couple of times Jesse thought he could faintly hear the music. He judged that they'd walked for over an hour and were probably no more than two miles from where they started. The minute they changed direction, Jesse heard the music too. It was real. It was *Für Elise*. It was the first song Suzan learned to play on the piano – her favorite song. He felt the absolute victory-joy of a child as he hurried through the deep snow towards the sound. Music? Was the electricity back on? Was it all a bad dream after all? Was it over? A rush of hope entered his mind to explain the sounds of the music. He visualized a genteel home with a grand piano and women in flowing gowns sipping tea, with gentlemen standing in small groups by the fireplace, drinking brandy and smoking the after-dinner cigar.

When they approached the run-down cabin, his hope vanished. At the back door was a mound of drifted snow with a boot sticking out. They didn't even stop to see who it was. They'd seen too much death. Without knocking, they entered the kitchen with its cast iron skillets hanging from hooks beside the wood-burning stove. It felt like they'd stepped back in time.

The chill inside belied the warmth of the scene, but at least the wind and snow weren't blowing. As they stomped the snow from their boots they heard the cranking of the Victrola, the needle being placed on the record, and *Für Elise* began again. Laramie followed the sound to the front of the house where the little boy stood with tears streaming down his face, half hiding behind the Victrola.

"Grand-mom told me to play it loud so everyone could hear. She said we would have a dance when she gets back. Did you come for the dance?" Laramie was kneeling in front of the boy holding both of his hands in hers. He wasn't even afraid of her. Jesse was amazed that she knew exactly what to do in these situations and he was grateful, because he felt inadequate to comfort the boy.

"When did your grand-mom leave?"

"I think it was yesterday morning. Grand-pop didn't feel too good, but he went to find her anyway. He's not back yet. Grand-mom said if any company came to give them a piece of cake. She made it just for the dance."

Leading them back to the kitchen he lifted the dishtowel that lay over the delicious looking cake. It was chocolate, Jesse's favorite. Laramie glanced at Jesse looking at the cake and she could almost see his saliva preparing for the taste. Hat in hand and shifting his weight from one foot to the other, he was like a kid trying to decide which part to eat first. She must have had the same look on her face because they looked at each other and burst out laughing. It felt so good to laugh, like a dam bursting and the flood waters washing everything clean. They wiped tears from their eyes when suddenly the wind burst through the front door bringing a gust of bitter air and blowing snow. Hurrying to shut the door they caught a glimpse of a lone figure disappearing into the timber.

Jesse chased him until he thought his lungs would burst and realized that whoever it was must be in a lot better shape. Gasping for air, he turned back to the cabin and followed the odd footprints that circled the cabin where he entered the front door. They were small. The thought occurred to Jesse that maybe the intruder was a woman. He remembered seeing the footprints before and how unusual they were and was now convinced that someone was following them.

Laramie gently explained to the boy that since his grandparents were not there, he would have to go with them. At first he absolutely refused. He was adamant they would be back for him anytime, but reluctantly agreed after she promised to leave them a note telling them where they were going. She didn't tell him what Jesse whispered to her when he returned from chasing the intruder. She didn't tell him about the one-armed man lying under the drifted snow by the back door. When Jesse returned, he'd taken enough of the snow off the body to determine there was nothing they could do for him. The earth was too frozen to bury him and daylight was quickly fading. They had to hurry and get back to the cave to the rest of their family.

They decided to gather any provisions they could carry. Jesse took the old 30.06 deer rifle lying on the fireplace mantle. There were a couple boxes of shells for it on the closet shelf. There were many things they could use, but they could only take the things they were able to carry. They gathered up medicine, coffee, flour, honey, salt, soda and soap and stuffed them into a hand-sewn leather backpack they found by the back door. While in the pantry, Laramie discovered a big brown envelope with a variety of seeds the old woman saved to plant in the spring and threw it in the leather bag too. The boy rolled up the sleeping bag he slept in the night before.

Laramie went to the bedroom to gather some clothes and was in awe of the beautiful blues, pinks and lavender that flowed through the room like a graceful waltz. She felt herself step back in time – to another era. I could stay here forever, she thought. The walls were filled with old, well preserved family photos in beautifully quilted frames that matched the exquisite handmade quilt on the bed and the curtains on the windows. Dainty crocheted doilies laced the edges of flowering African violets and Wedgwood china figures that adorned the Victorian bed tables and dresser. A worn gold mirror, brush and comb confirmed many years of use and care as it rested on the beautiful antique dressing table. The woman who lived in this house had loved this room. Laramie reverently ran her hands over the fine hand stitched quilt and knew it represented years of quiet nights by the fireplace in the living room. She noticed the wood carving of a bear on the chest of drawers and crossed the braided rag rug to admire the fine workmanship. Life and love happened in this old cabin and now it was over. She hoped those who knew these rooms would be able to return someday.

The boy stood in the open doorway while she admired the carving. "My grand-pop made that bear with his carving knife," he said as he opened the top drawer. He lifted up the stack of ironed handkerchiefs and pulled out the knife. "He made this leather sheath for it, too." Laramie held it in her hands and knew it was important to the boy. "He said I could have it when I get big."

She noticed the stitching of the leather sheath was as expert and precise as the stitching of the quilt. "They could have lived here forever and would have survived," she said out-loud.

"What?"

"Oh, I was just thinking how much your grand-mom and grand-pop knew about living. I think your grand-pop would want you to have this now." She extended the knife in its leather sheath towards the boy. He shrank from it and looked at her. Sensing her meaning, tears welled in his large blue eyes.

"But it's grand-pop's and he'll give it to me when I'm big."

"You can take it now, and when you come back, you can put it right back in its place under the handkerchiefs." Laramie couldn't remember seeing a cloth handkerchief since she'd watched her own grandpa wipe his eyes at Uncle Bud's wedding. Had they survived? Or was one of her nephews now carrying her own grandpa's knife? She reached down and swept up the boy in her arms and held him to her.

As he clutched the beloved sheath and knife, he reached over her shoulder and grabbed the bear off the dresser. "Big Moe's got to go, too."

"Oh, you know this bear?"

"Sure I do. We all know Big Moe – he ate my grand-pop's arm off. After that, he whittled with his knees holding the wood. He put his knife away after he carved Big Moe. Said he couldn't do it anymore and I would have to do the whittlin' from now on." With that he took out a small Swiss Army knife and held it up for Laramie's inspection. "This is what I whittle with, but no one whittled like my grand-pop."

How do I get in these situations, thought Laramie. But she knew that it was not mere coincidence. An inner power was guiding her – all she had to do was follow. "I guess I should know your name since you're coming with us."

Proudly he proclaimed, "My name is Cody Martin Clancey – but everyone just calls me Cody. I heard that man call you Laramie. Are you from Wyoming, too?"

"No, I'm not from Wyoming, but my daddy always wanted a ranch in Wyoming, and my mamma and daddy went to Laramie on their honeymoon, and mamma loved it so much, she named me Laramie."

"Well, we both got Wyoming names, so that means we're alike." The boy looked at the knife and looked at Laramie and the tears came as he said, "My mamma calls me Cody, Wyoming." The moment turned long and tender as the tears finally came and Cody cried into her shoulder, clutching Big Moe and his grand-pop's knife.

"And how old are you Cody?"

"I'm six years old and I was born on December 9$^{th}$."

"Oh, my gosh" said Laramie as the date flashed in her mind. "You had quite a birthday this year."

"No, not really," he said. "I thought they forgot my birthday, but at night Grand-mom surprised me with a chocolate cake and home-made ice cream 'cuz it's my favorite. And we all danced to the Victor - Ola." Laramie threw back her head and laughed.

"But didn't you go to school on your birthday?"

"I don't have to go to school yet. Grand-mom teaches me

numbers and words. She said I can go to school when my mom and dad get the ranch going and can come and get me. We have a real ranch in Cody, Wyoming." His eyes were wide with excitement. "With horses and everything. I've been here with grand-pop and grand-mom for two Christmases. Mamma said they need me here to take care of them – they're getting kinda old, ya' know."

"When are your mom and dad supposed to come back to get you?"

"Their airplane was s'pposed to get in Denver the morning of my birthday and they were going to be here for my party, but I think they had to stay at the ranch. Sometimes when cows have calves, they can't go anywhere. We don't have a phone here, so they can't call us, but grand-mom says we don't worry, 'cause *no news is good news*."

Laramie realized his grandparents probably didn't know the world had changed at 9:47am, December 9$^{th}$. How weird to even think about it. They had no telephone, no electricity and a well on their property. They probably didn't know anything happened until they tried to start up that old Jeep she saw by the barn.

She decided not to question Cody about the events that happened since his birthday. Where could his grand-mom be, she thought. His grand-pop's journey ended a few feet from the back door. The storm covered his body during the night. If the wind hadn't blown so hard, they may have never known he was there, but the drifting snow exposed one lone boot as evidence of his existence. They survived the initial impact, but something else drove them out into the bitter cold. Why did she leave by herself? Why did he try to follow? Was she just going a short distance and coming right back?

The questions haunted Laramie as they followed their own footprints back the way they'd come. Obsessed with tracking the intruder, Jesse insisted Laramie and Cody wait by a dead pine clearly visible on the ridge while he searched farther north for tracks. He found only his own. How could he have eluded them? Jesse followed the path he'd taken when he gave chase, even to the tree he leaned against to catch his breath, but from there the odd prints went only a few hundred feet further and just faded away on the rocky ledge. As he searched for sign, he felt that same feeling he'd felt so many times in the last week. That feeling of being watched – that uneasy sense that someone he couldn't see was breathing his same breath. It made the hairs on the back of his neck rigid – an eerie feeling.

Reluctantly, Jesse gave up the search and returned to rejoin Laramie and the boy waiting on the ridge. Laramie looked like a real mountain woman, wrapped up in the cape of coyote pelts. She couldn't resist taking it from the woman's closet. She found it while looking for warm clothes for Cody, convincing herself it wouldn't really be another thing to carry if she wore it. It was the most exquisite thing she'd ever seen. Now she was glad she had it, as the sinking sun no longer offered respite from the bitter wind.

It would soon be dark and as tired from the day's events as they were, they quickened their pace. If it got dark on them, Jesse doubted they would find their way back without Laramie hearing the music to guide them. He wouldn't question her hearing, her silent tears or her overwhelming feelings of fear from a child again. He heard the music, too. It was real all right. She just heard it a couple of miles sooner. He couldn't even allow himself to start questioning why or how. He just knew that's the way it was.

Lalo barely escaped Jesse's examination of the rocky ledge. He was wedged in the crevice of the two rocks that formed the drop-off into the canyon below. The only thing that saved him was Jesse's fear of coming closer to the edge. He heard Jesse's breaths coming in short, deep gulps and prayed that Jesse couldn't hear his own. Lalo had crossed to the ledge on the fallen tree, knocking the snow off the limbs as he fell into the crevice. He was sure Jesse would see the signs of passage, although he wasn't sure how he would ever get out of the crevice again. He was torn between screaming for help and holding his breath so he wouldn't be found.

How many times had he been in a similar situation – that place between life and death? Only now it was different. He wanted to live. When he was sure Jesse was gone, he examined his situation more carefully. It was a wonder he was still alive. The crevice was so small and narrow, he was barely held there. The muscles in his arms were cramped and pains shot through his shoulders and neck as he tried to relax them to concentrate on a plan of escape, not from man, but from nature. Using his back and feet to brace himself in the crevice, he hacked his way through the ice above him, releasing huge chunks that cascaded over him into the chasm below. Finally, after inching his way up the narrow crevice, his shoulders and elbows held him on the top of the ledge. There, just inches from his face were Jesse's boot prints. If Jesse had walked just two feet closer, he would have fallen through the ice. Melting and re-freezing snow from many storms on the north side of this ridge had formed a false ledge – the ice that Lalo had to chip away to escape. Maybe it wasn't fear after all that kept Jesse from taking the last step. Something was watching over them.

After resting safely away from the ledge to regain his strength, Lalo decided it was time to return to the lean-to he had so hurriedly erected the night before. He found refuge in the boulders about two hundred feet above and to the north of the entrance to the cave. He chose a spot higher than the cave, so he could be safe, but unseen, while watching for them to leave so he could follow. He definitely had a vantage point because he could see them, but unless they looked up at exactly the right spot, they would not be able to see him. It was a difficult way to travel, as he had to be ready to go on a moment's notice. Most of the time he could get close enough to overhear their conversations, but when the storm came, he had to find somewhere safe and dry and far enough away from them so they wouldn't cross his tracks in the new fallen snow. Last night was miserable and cold. He realized he might die. Mother Nature could be very unforgiving, but somehow he knew She wanted him to survive.

He saw the body with the boot sticking out, lying by the back door. He also found the woman's body just a few feet from where Jesse and Laramie passed when they were hurrying toward the music. When Laramie and Jesse suddenly turned north on the ridge, he panicked, and searching for anywhere to hide, he stumbled into the open hatch of an old root cellar. Once inside, after his eyes adjusted to the darkness, he found himself not in a root cellar at all, but in an earthen room that once served as a home. It was furnished very comfortably and he was tempted to stay. It was a palace compared to the makeshift lean-to he hurriedly formed just the day before. Lalo was startled to see the old woman lying in the corner with papers in her hands. She looked as if she just nodded off while reading and his first impulse was to be quiet so he wouldn't wake her. Then, as his eyes focused more clearly, he noticed the old tin box beside her filled with letters and the gray waxen face and the body with no breath. He covered her with the quilt she had pulled around her and left her in her chosen grave. He knew the signs of death and guessed she chose this place for final rest. He pried the papers from her stiff hands and placed them with the letters in the tin box. He didn't know why they were important to take with him. He just knew they were.

Emerging from the death place, he carefully closed the wooden hatch and covered it with fallen snow, trying to conceal its existence. He feared he would not be able to find Jesse and Laramie without following their tracks and exposing himself. Looking north, in the direction he knew they were headed when he last saw them, he too heard the music. Like Jesse, it filled him with false hope of everything returning to normal.

When he reached the cabin, he circled to the front so his tracks wouldn't be found. He didn't want them to discover him and now he questioned why he followed them in the first place. He sure didn't want them to know it was him following them – not yet. They wouldn't want him with them – they would make him leave. He *had* to follow them – was driven to follow them and he wanted to live. He knew this when he saw Jesse again at the River City.

And there was Mira. Just remembering her eyes looking into his made his heart ache with longing. In her eyes he saw a memory – not from this life, but of time past. He saw her spirit – her true light, and knew she could see his, too. They were related – they were spirits who crossed the same path at the same time and they honored each other. Never before had he felt so much love. He wanted to look into her soul again and find the depths of his own. Would anyone understand his feelings? He hardly understood them himself. His very survival and existence had depended on his physical body. This was different – it wasn't connected to the physical and that's what was so foreign to him. Never before had he experienced feeling with the heart. He learned to numb most feelings just to survive. Now he knew he had a soul and the memory of the feelings would be enough, even if he died today, but he wanted to live.

Approaching the cabin from the front, he tried to inch close enough to windows to overhear conversation coming from inside, but the heavy growth of snow covered bushes made it impossible so he chanced trying to hear at the front door. Surely, they would leave by the same way they came and would never see his footprints leading to the door. Pressing his ear to the door, he clutched the handle and tried to open it just a bit. That's when the gust of wind practically dragged him into the room. He felt duped and betrayed by Mother Nature and ran from the cabin like a trapped animal. He ran blindly and carelessly, not thinking about tracks anymore, just trying to escape. Any sensible intruder would have known to run the opposite direction, not lead the follower toward his house. He knew Jesse would give chase and he couldn't risk being caught.

With Jesse just a few hundred feet behind him, adrenaline carried him up the hill without even realizing where he was going – primitive instincts guided him. He barely caught himself at the edge of the cliff – there was no time to decide. He saw the fallen tree and tried to cross to the other side of the ledge. The blowing wind and snow masked the sounds of his falling through the limbs to the crevice below.

Now, with daylight fading, he must beat them back up the hill to his hiding place or risk being discovered. He must be careful to keep a wide distance between them, or Jesse would sense his presence again. Gulping the frozen air he realized for the first time how much his lungs hurt and his body ached, but he couldn't slow down now. Stumbling over a dead branch, the sharp snap of it breaking shot through the frozen air. He lay prone and still in the snow, fearing that Jesse heard it and would be back to investigate. No one came. He had to hurry. He picked up the broken limb to use as a walking stick. Knowing that darkness would soon surround him and the thought of another freezing night alone left him drained.

He hoped there would soon be a chance to prove himself to Jesse. He knew Jesse didn't trust him – that he didn't like him and somehow hoped he could change his mind. It all started that day by the South Platte River, the first day he saw Mira. Jesse felt the need to protect Mira from him. Maybe that's the way fathers feel towards their children. Maybe.

Using the broken limb as a walking stick made it easier to navigate the deep snow. He hurt his ribs and back when he fell in the crevice and knew that his muscles would be painfully sore in the morning, but he couldn't let it slow him down. Lalo knew he would reach his lean-to in time to hide before Laramie and Jesse reached the entrance of the cave. Traveling with a child would slow them down, and they were weighed down with the extra supplies taken from the cabin. The only thing he carried was the tin box full of letters. While running from Jesse he had dropped it in the snow, but after freeing himself, there it lay – just feet from Jesse's boot prints.

Following his own tracks back up the mountain he tried to put the pieces together. Why did Jesse and Laramie leave the safety of their cave on this bitter, windy day? They obviously went to get the little boy. They didn't seem to know the people who lived there, but Laramie led Jesse right to the cabin, so she must have known it was there. And there was the music. When he first heard it, he couldn't believe it – he thought the blowing wind was playing tricks on his ears. He knew there was no electricity – anywhere – so how could he be hearing music? He'd heard the song so many times before but never knew the name of it – one of those haunting, nostalgic melodies that probes the memory for a forgotten time. The sight of the Victrola jolted him back to reality. Today had been quite an adventure, but there were so many questions without answers.

The more he thought about them, the more he laughed at the odd band of travelers. They were obviously family and cared about each other. But all those kids! And it seemed to be Laramie who took care of them – well, they all did, but it seemed like she was the mom – some of them even called her *mamma*. But she was too young and too white to have mommed all those kids. They were a bizarre bunch, but he wanted to belong to this family – this odd mingling of humanity. He laughed when he compared his *street family* to this new family – some things weren't so different, but on the street, the families come and go and there were no loyalties, no parents, and no love. Usually the oldest or the meanest designated himself as the boss. If the *brokers* treated him well and he made a lot of money, everyone wanted to be his friend and treated him like he was really somebody. If the *brokers* threw him out, there were no friends. They just banded together with the other throw-aways to survive. He remembered some nice women over the past years. Of course they were throw-aways themselves, but something inside of them yearned to be good mothers – they had tender hearts. Those were the best memories.

Now he wanted to be part of a real family. This family had a mother and father, aunts and uncles, brothers, sisters, cousins and an odd assortment of throw-away kids – like him. How did they decide which kids to take and which kids to leave? Lalo remembered the incident at the river when Laramie claimed one of the street kids was hers. The two men fighting over the little girl didn't dare deny her the child. There were hundreds of kids without homes now. Not just the street-kids, but regular kids who were not of the streets, who had parents until a few weeks ago. Those were the kids that would pay the price for innocence.

Lalo was no longer unique – he was just one among thousands of kids without parents to care for them. He heard at the river that the gangs were using kids for barter; trading a kid for food or a pack of cigarettes. He even heard what happened to some of them, things that were too harrowing to think about. But he believed it – he knew it was true. Something ugly happens to people when their survival is threatened. And it was about survival.

Breathing more easily now, he knew he must be well ahead of Jesse, Laramie and the boy. He felt a little guilty that he couldn't offer to help them carry some of the provisions from the cabin. Even though his ribs and back hurt, he felt jubilant, lighter somehow. He was uplifted with every bit of new information he could find about this real family. He even began to fantasize that they would someday ask him to join them because he would prove himself so valuable. Today was a close call and he couldn't risk being caught before he could prove himself. He was certain Jesse sensed being watched and followed, but he also had to know that he meant them no harm.

Jesse didn't see or feel what happened between Mira and him at the river that day. He didn't understand. Jesse only saw the look on his face when he found them together, and he mistook it for lust or evil intentions toward his daughter. In Mira, Lalo sensed the most tender and pure spirit he had ever felt from a human being. It was the closest feeling to love he could remember. He would never hurt her. It didn't feel sexual, it felt soulful – as if he finally found something precious that he'd lost – a part of himself. He loved to say her name. "Miranda – Mira." He closed his eyes and saw her almond shaped eyes looking into his soul and he could hear the music of her child voice.

Suddenly, he stopped in his tracks and cocked his head to hear the muffled sounds carried by the wind – barely audible sounds of an ugly memory. As he moved closer, he heard a frantic, guttural, tearing voice, screaming and pleading into the growing darkness. He raced blindly through the deep snow towards the screams and knew he was getting closer. The child's voice was terrified and pleading for mercy. He recognized the brutal sound of fist against flesh! The pleading stopped – he had to hurry! The only sound now was from the cursing man, swearing and threatening; the cocky, arrogant, braggart voice of the child abuser; the bully hurting the younger, weaker, smaller; the man forcing the woman child, a painful memory. When he came to the clearing, the child's screams and pleading were silent, but the man's cruel threats and premature victory sounds jogged the ugly nightmare. The bitter bile rose to his throat as he recognized the act that was assaulting his memory. Lalo automatically lifted the broken tree limb high over his head as he approached the man's back side over the child. The brutal threats coming from the man were too painfully familiar to Lalo. This animal was the worst breed of human filth – there was not enough pain in the world for his kind.

Lalo, for the first time in his life, attacked. He fought for himself and all the children that were forced by the ugliness of humanity to endure the abuse of the vile, the perverted, the mean, the crazed, the ignorant, the evil. Hearing something approach from behind him, the man turned his head, his eyes staring at Lalo in disbelief and fear. The tree limb came down with such force onto the man's head that Lalo himself was amazed at the strength unleashed by pure rage. The blow was well placed. The man's body slumped, giving Lalo the chance to deliver the final, lethal blow, directly across the bridge of his nose. The force of the blow threw the man several feet from the exposed body of the child.

It was almost dark. The tinge of gray remaining in the sky lent a shadowy iron cast, fitting for the death scene. There, in the icy snow lay his beloved Mira, legs forced, revealing the white of skin, red of blood. Her eyes were blankly staring into the cold, frozen air, and he knew she was dead.

The wretched, agonized scream of the animal tore from his throat in a sound that warned all who heard it to beware of his anguish. The dead form of the man lay five feet away. Still clenched in Lalo's hand was the broken limb from the tree. All the anguish and rage were unleashed as he attacked the malevolent beast, killing him over and over again. All the years of buried rage at humanity, at God, mother and church exploded from him onto the lifeless form. The dead body became the object of revenge for every evil, treacherous, perverted act done to every man, woman, and child. Lalo didn't stop beating the man, and the animal sounds didn't quit ripping from his throat until every ounce of rage drained from him.

Tenderly he gathered Mira to him to warm her still body. He thought she was dead, but ragged, shallow breaths escaped her lips. She was in shock and traumatized, but she was alive. Oh God, sometimes that felt worse – to still be alive. He pulled his coat open and enclosed them both inside as he rocked and sobbed, sobbed and rocked. He knew her life would be different from this moment on. His righteous rage and bitter tears were for her innocence robbed – her childhood desecrated – defiled.

"Oh God," he sobbed. "Why did you let this happen? Please take my life and take this memory from her." He rocked her and warmed her and his tears washed over her – a bitter baptism. She was limp and seemed lifeless – her spirit somewhere else. Her breaths came in shallow attempts to sustain her draining life. Lalo whispered close to her ear, the tender, soothing voice of a mother he could barely remember, the strong, protecting voice of a father he never knew, and the pure love of souls remembered poured from his heart. He begged her to come back – pleaded with her not to leave him – he promised to take care of her, and never to let anyone hurt her again, as long as he lived. In broken sobs he told her all his secrets, his dreams, his fantasies and all the childhood lies that had kept him alive – given him hope – helped him survive the ugliness and pain. He desperately tried to bring her back from the black abyss she had so willingly given herself to.

Sobbing in whispers, "Come back, Mira," washing her in tears and tender pleas, "Don't leave me, Mira, please God, send her back," he begged for her life. He pleaded with God. He wrestled with the angel of death, fighting for her soul. The battle was also for his own sanity, his very survival. Breathing in short, wracked sobs, he felt her breath against his cheek, her body trembling, and her spirit slowly return. There were now two hearts beating, two children sobbing together, breathing each other's breath. Alive! He knew she would live – they would live. "Oh, God, thank you, God, thank you, God."

The ravaged, reckless years of the street-child were over for Lalo and his fantasies shattered. He would never hide in the dream place again. He would gladly have given his own life to have kept this from happening to Mira – the purest vision of innocence he had ever seen. He would spend the rest of his days helping her to survive the reality of her life. And she would survive – he willed her to survive.

Laramie heard the voices, felt the fear of the child and recognized Mira's screams of terror. She knew they were too far away to help and the foreboding tears streamed down her face and when Jesse saw the anguish in her tear-filled eyes, he knew. Cody was used to traveling in the snow, but the wind and blowing snow slowed them and Laramie knew that time was running out for Mira. "We've got to hurry, Jesse. There's trouble."

"What kind of trouble – which direction, Laramie?" He knew to trust Laramie's intuition for children in danger.

"Back up the hill – close to the cave. The wind is carrying the voices. Hurry, Jesse – hurry! I'll follow with Cody. We'll be okay. Just listen for the voices. You'll hear it, Jesse – just hurry! It's Mira, Jesse! Someone is hurting Mira."

When Jesse heard Mira's name, fear tore through his heart. He dropped the leather pack and other things he'd been carrying. While running up the hill he began to put shells in the 30.06 rifle taken from the cabin. That's when he heard the mournful cry echoing down the mountain – the anguished death-cry of the breaking heart. It was the most foreboding sound Jesse had ever heard. Fear gripped him and stopped him in his tracks. He looked down the hill at Laramie and Cody – they heard it, too. He was paralyzed by fear. What animal could have made that spine-chilling sound? It couldn't possibly be human.

"Hurry Jesse! Just follow the sound," Laramie shouted from below.

“Please, God, help me.” What would he find? What kind of creature made that anguished sound? He turned back up the hill hoping he would never hear that sound again. The blowing snow made it impossible to see. Earlier, while chasing the person following them, he almost ran right over a cliff. He didn’t see it until he was just feet from the edge. He assumed the person fell over the edge and that would be the end of it. Damn! He knew someone was following them and he should have tracked him before. He was so sure that whoever was tracking them meant no harm. The coward waited for him to leave so the women and children would be unprotected. "Damn!" Hadn't he seen enough horror and insanity in the last couple of weeks to know that no one could be considered harmless – that everyone was out for their own survival? What a fool he was – and he almost had him earlier. He should have kept tracking. He shouldn't have taken anything for granted. The son-of-a-bitch didn’t go over the ledge! It was a ploy to get the children. Mira! "God, help me get there in time,” he prayed. “Help Mira, God, please help Mira."

Jesse stopped to catch his breath and listened for any sound. Laramie said to follow the sound. How far away was he from the cave entrance? It couldn't be more than half a mile. "God, let me get there in time." He listened, but it was eerie –almost peaceful. The wind quit blowing as if time were waiting for him to catch up. He hurried in the direction of the cave. When he reached the game trail at the foot of the hill he saw a different set of boot prints – a new track, not the same ones he saw earlier – the odd ones. These were bigger – heavier, and there was only one set going up toward the cave, none returning. Only a quarter mile left!

Too much time passed since Laramie first felt the child's fear and heard the voices. And then, the blood-chilling scream. “My God – what was that?” A million fears ran through Jesse's mind as he struggled to reach the cave. "Please, God, let me get there in time." The cold air bursting in his lungs made him light headed and he knew he should stop and rest, but he had to hurry – time was running out. The awful silence terrified him. Where was Mira? Which direction?

At that instant, Jesse found the cross trail with two sets of prints, one was the same as he'd been following – the larger, heavier boot print, one was smaller, lighter – Mira's, being dragged and pulled, resisting, falling. The predator came out in Jesse. He knew he found the right trail. The terrifying thoughts that went through Jesse's mind allowed him to become the killer – the deranged. He cocked the rifle and crouched low as he hurriedly followed the heavy boot prints north on the ledge. He knew he was getting close. He could smell the danger and knew that whoever it was that had his Mira was evil. He prepared for the worst. He knew he could die or kill to save his child. It was too quiet. Why wasn't there any sound? Was he too late? “Please, God, let her be alive. Let me find her in time.”

Jesse found them sobbing, rocking together, Lalo whispering softly in her ear and stroking her face. He didn't notice the lifeless, mutilated form laying a few feet away, as his only concern was for his daughter.

In the cave, Levi finally cut through the cord around Suzan's bloodied wrists. She didn't know how long she'd been unconscious, but she knew the man had Mira and that she had to save her. Thank God for Levi’s pocket knife!

The man had found the entrance of the cave and entered as Suzan was showing the kids how to make tea from pine bark. Why hadn't Black warned them of a stranger's presence? He was a large man, and had to bend down, his face coming so close to Suzan that she choked on his foul breath. He feigned friendliness, claiming to be lost when he stumbled on the entrance of the cave. He scanned the contents of their safe-haven. Suzan watched him and knew he was looking for signs of a man's presence. No one would just be out strolling in this weather and so close to dark.

Shocked at seeing all the children, he asked, “Are all these kids here yours?”

She ignored the question and knew he was buying time. “My husband and the other men will be back soon. They’ve gone to trap rabbit,” she replied. She knew it was a weak threat and her mind whirled furiously searching for a way to discourage the evil intent she saw in his eyes.

“Your men were crazy to leave you here all alone with all these kids.” He knew there were no men – not close anyway. He'd been very careful to notice tracks, but when he saw a hint of a trail with the prints going downhill, he knew there was something up there. His only problem was the wolf – it was not a family pet. The mean looking animal guarded the cave about fifty feet from the entrance. He cut him pretty good and knew that wolf would have killed him. He would deal with what was left of him later – it would be fine eating tonight.

His intention was to rob whatever he could find to take – maybe a cache of guns or something worth bartering with down in the valley. But when he saw Suzan and all those kids, the lust came out in him and he decided to satisfy his physical cravings first. He could come back for their supplies later. Then he saw Mira.

"Why hell, Mama," he said, roughly grabbing Mira's wrist. "You got a whole slew of them kids here and I'd treat this one real good, like she was my own."

Suzan recoiled from the evil sneer on his face and her eyes darted, frantically searching for anything she could use as a weapon. Mira struggled and the man laughed and said, "This is exactly how I like my girls. Wild and scared." Suzan knew she had to kill him, but how? Jesse kept the guns hidden. She wouldn't be able to get to one quickly, and she would also lead him right to them. Her rage was too close to try to bargain with him. She couldn't keep it down to think clearly. She tore at him with her fingernails and kicked at him to free Mira. He anticipated her move and back-handed her, reeling her backward into the rocky wall of the cave. That's all she remembered.

She put her hand to her head and felt the sticky blood there. How long had he been gone – did he take anything else – anyone else? She quickly scanned the corner where they kept their backpacks of supplies. There were the children, huddled together, watching her through terror filled eyes. She knew she must have looked like a mad-woman and shouldn't leave them by themselves, but she couldn't wait for Jesse to get back. The man would be long gone, and Mira, too.

Why did Jesse and Laramie leave them alone and unprotected?

When she woke up they were gone and she had no idea where they were. Enraged tears coursed down her cheeks. "Oh God – the children. How can I leave them by themselves? I would be doing the same thing – leaving them unprotected." She was talking out loud – she had to regroup, to think more clearly, but all she could focus on was finding Mira. Where was Black? He would protect the children! He always protected the children!

She desperately searched for the guns. She knew Jesse put them under the shelf of rock in the farthest corner of the cave. She didn't like this part of the cave. It was too small and too dark. Ah! Feeling the cold handle of the .357 revolver gave her confidence that she could rescue Mira from the man. She knew she would kill him.

Not knowing how much of a head start they had, she prepared for the worst and quickly told the children what to do while pulling on her boots and long coat. "Jacinth – you're the oldest, so you're in charge. Black is probably outside hunting somewhere, but when you see him, bring him inside with you. He'll protect you."

Pain tore through her head and she fought the darkness threatening to overpower her. Desperation and fear for Mira pushed her to hurry. "Levi, you and Tara fix something to snack on while I'm gone. I hope I won't be long, but stay warm, under the blankets." The children nodded their heads in understanding, but she saw the terror in their eyes. "I would go out to find any one of you if anyone tried to take you from us. Right now I need to find Mira." Hugging the children, she silently prayed for their safety. She didn't really know when she would be back. She knew she would track the man who took her daughter until she found them and killed him.

It was almost dark when she started down the narrow game trail. She could still see the footprints of the man with Mira's smaller prints being dragged along. It was suddenly very quiet. The wind quit blowing – it was eerie. She went only a short ways when she found Black, lying in the red-stained snow. She could see his breaths blowing in the cold air and when he heard her coming, he tried to get up, but was crippled by the deep gash in his front shoulder. "There, Black, stay – I'll come back for you soon." She hurried to follow the boot prints. When she found where his trail veered off to the north she heard someone shouting from below. She automatically crouched low and leveled the gun in the direction of the hollering. She waited. She was ready. Soon, she was able to discern Laramie's voice, and someone else – a child's voice. Standing upright, she was able to see Laramie and Cody coming up the trail loaded down and shouting something she couldn't understand, but it was about Jesse and Mira. Racing down the hill to meet them, she quickly retold the details of what happened in the cave. When they all reached the place where Black was lying, Laramie told Cody to stay with the dog until they returned. She knew they weren't far from Mira now.

They ran, following the boot prints in the snow. Now there was only one set of prints – the large boot prints – deeper prints, he was carrying Mira. There was a place in the trail where the boot prints stopped, revealing signs of a scuffle . . . and Mira's sweatshirt. "Oh, God, noooooooooo." Suzan knelt in the snow bank with Mira's shirt pressed to her face and screamed at God. Laramie pulled her up by the arms, assuring her that Jesse had probably already found Mira . . . and the man. Suzan still had the revolver in her hand and killing in her heart, as she followed Laramie and the boot prints.

They got to the clearing only moments after Jesse. Suzan raised the revolver at eye level, ready to pull the trigger. All she could see was the man's back, beating the rag-doll form she believed to be Mira. She had a clear shot. Even though he was moving around, she could do it. She could kill him – he had her daughter. Her finger slowly squeezed the trigger when Laramie realized the horrible mistake that rage was allowing and lunged for the gun at the same time it exploded, throwing Suzan back into the trees.

Jesse reeled from the sound, dropping Lalo's limp form onto the snow. Laramie went to Mira, her nearly nude body trembling in the red snow. My God, there was so much blood. Laramie checked Mira for any cuts, but found none she could see and knew the vacant look in her eyes kept the secret of much deeper wounds. Laramie held Mira's shivering body close to her, covering her as much as she could with the cape of coyote pelts she brought from the cabin – it would be warm.

Suzan, shaken by the horrible mistake she almost made, weakly crawled to Laramie who was propped up against a pine tree holding Mira. Barely audible sobs came from Mira's throat. "Thank God! She's alive," gasped Suzan, and she gently took her from Laramie. Jesse picked up the gun from the snow and fully intended to finish the killing.

"That's the man who took Mira," whispered Suzan, pointing at the bloody form of the man with the big boots. That's when Jesse first noticed the form lying so eerily in the snow. Limbs twisted in unnatural abstract angles and red snow surrounded the unrecognizable face.

"Where did *he* come from?" asked Jesse, looking in disbelief at the man. He turned the gun toward Lalo lying unconscious in the snow. "Then who . . . ?" That's when he recognized him – the boy who looked like a girl. They didn't know his name, but Jesse knew immediately that he was the same street kid – the hooker he'd found with Mira that day at the river. Emotions exploded inside him at the memory. His gaze instinctively went to the boy's shoes that were wrapped in ragged pieces of leather – the odd footprints that had been following them.

"I don't believe it!" Jesse was astounded. "I don't know how he's survived! This is who has been following us all the way from Denver, and the same person I chased today from the cabin. He must have found Mira before I did and killed the man." Suddenly, Jesse realized the terrible error. "My God, I almost killed the boy." They were overcome by horror at the brutal loss of innocence and childhood, as shafts of moonlight broke through the pines.

Reminding Suzan and Jesse of Cody, who was waiting with Black, Laramie agreed to stay with Lalo while they took Mira back to the cave. Laramie went to Lalo and gently placed his head in her lap. She knew the animal sound they'd heard earlier came from him, and knowing he saved Mira's life she felt the universal shame. Though badly beaten, she knew he would live and hoped he would forgive them.

Later, as Lalo lay under the sleeping bag where Jesse carried him, he remembered Laramie and Suzan washing off the dried blood and dirt. They dressed him in a pair of Mira's long underwear, as he and Mira were about the same size. Quiet tears filled his eyes as he looked over at Mira, sleeping as though nothing happened that day. And her innocence filled him, as he remembered the covenant he made with her. Although his body hurt everywhere, he had never felt happier.

## *Chapter 12*

In the silence of night, after emotions calmed and every child was sleeping, Suzan and Jesse lay quietly talking in the darkness. Jesse couldn't forget the killing rage he'd felt and Suzan could still feel the cold metal of the deadly gun in her hands.

"Jesse, I could have killed you," Suzan whispered. "It's horrifying to think that it could have ended in your death and the death of that boy."

"What happened to Mira was a ruthless, cold-blooded brutality. I could have killed that boy thinking he was the one who'd hurt her, and you could have killed me thinking I was the one who'd taken her. We were trying to save our daughter. We're not to blame. We did what anyone would have done. It was getting dark and we could barely see. Emotions were explosive and it all happened so fast. I'm just glad you're such a lousy shot."

"Jesse, I had you in my sights. You were a dead man, as far as I was concerned. Laramie's the one who realized it was you and the terrible mistake I was about to make. She knocked the gun out of my hands at the same time it fired."

"Well, thank goodness one of us could see." He reached over and tenderly kissed her goodnight, hoping to calm her fears. "This will all be an ugly memory someday. We're going to survive. Even Mira." He realized his words were trite and inadequate, but he felt unable to deal with his own jumbled emotions; the violation of his daughter, the dead man laying in the red snow, and his memories of the River City.

"You're right. We will survive this," Suzan answered, welcoming the end of this day and praying for the peace of sleep.

Only when he heard her breathing slow with the sleep that exhaustion brings, did Jesse allow himself to think the thoughts that he would never be able to share. He could hardly stand to think them in the privacy of his own mind they were so appalling and confusing to him. Lalo . . . what kind of name was that? Obviously a street name. He was enraged when he saw Lalo at the river with Mira, and he didn't want him traveling with them now. Why the hell didn't he stay on the street where he belonged? Why did he have to follow them and remind him of that day by the river? He sure as hell didn't like feeling obligated to him and he didn't want him near Mira. How could he feel that way towards the person who had saved her life? Shame and embarrassment nagged at his conscience, but it didn't change how he felt. The memory of that day at the river and the first time he saw Lalo rushed back to him – it wouldn't let him forget.

Remembering, it seemed so long ago – December 17th. They had walked all day to find a place to set up tents, well away from the hundreds who migrated to the river for water. Jesse needed to find more insulin for his parents who were planning to go south to Pueblo. The small amount he was able to bargain for on that desperate bicycle ride through downtown wouldn't last them long enough for their trip. Jesse agreed to meet his parents, sister, brother, and their families by the Denver Post building at I-70 and I-25 the next day. That group would then continue south to Pueblo. He was relieved they all would be traveling as a group. Insulin would be harder and harder to find, and his parents would eventually die without it.

Every doctor's office, medical clinic and grocery pharmacy they passed was deserted and stripped clean of all equipment and supplies, especially drugs of any kind. They passed Humana Hospital off of 92nd and I-25, only to find it deserted and ransacked – there was no insulin. Everyone they asked along the way told them they would have to go to the river to find things like prescription drugs.

The next morning, Suzan talked Jesse into letting her go with him so she could hopefully barter for more flour while he found a connection for insulin. The sun was shining. Events of the last week didn't matter to its existence and unconsciously brought a ray of hope to all who felt its warmth. Suzan, Laramie, Mira and Levi went along for the outing, hopefully to find some flour and enjoy the peacefulness that mocked the day. Ian stayed with Jane and the remaining children, to guard their temporary home and supplies, happy for the time alone to talk about the future.

As the small group crested the hill overlooking the South Platte, they couldn't believe their eyes. The river was boiling with life – as if the city had moved to the river, and indeed it had.

There were tents and makeshift shelters erected all along its banks for miles, and every tree had been cut down for firewood. But the more desperate ended up along the four miles of the South Platte River between I-70 and the 6th Avenue Freeway, where they intersected I-25. It was a dangerous place. It reeked of evil, fear and desperation. This was where survival supplies could be found. It didn't take long for those who had *things* to set up their temporary places like a huge flea market. The desperate took their most valuable possessions to trade for what they needed to survive.

Communication networks evolved quickly at this dangerous place. Throw-away kids came from the streets to become runners who carried messages or looked for family members for the weary survivors. They made it their business to know who the newcomers were, and thousands came daily. Signs and messages written on cardboard boxes or paper sacks were erected everywhere identifying families by name. In one day, a good runner could make the circle through the crowds and know who was new, what they had, and what they needed. It saved the weary travelers the effort of making the trip to the core of the ominous River City to find family or supplies they needed to continue on. The runners were rewarded with food or something they could barter for food.

The average stay at the river was two or three days to find the needed items and group together with others headed in the same direction – to make a plan. Those who stayed longer were lulled into complacency by fear or the hope that it would all be different in the morning, and when their food supplies ran out, they bartered what was left just to survive or stole from the newcomers who still had food. That part of the river became the inner core, the dark underground, the black-market. It was dying before it ever became alive. There was no way to replenish the food that was eaten. No one buried the hundreds who died daily, adding to the already mounting sanitation problems, allowing disease to thrive. The stench that rose from this place warned all who entered of the death, disease, and decay, but they came anyway.

Unfortunately, most of the survivors who came to that part of the river were hungry, depressed, and morally depleted, wearing the unmistakable mantle of hopelessness on their faces, their children hungry and dehydrated. The desperate – they were the most vulnerable and would have been better off bartering on the road or joining forces with others going away from the River City. But they came to the river. They were easy prey. Many never left.

People in need of medications to survive, didn't, unless they found a source at the river and bartered their treasures for their lives. If a new commodity was needed, runners were sent into the abandoned downtown area or guarded hospitals to find the new item requested. It was efficient and dangerous.

Looking down at the hundreds of tent tops and makeshift shelters, Jesse sensed the danger, and Suzan gladly agreed they should wait up river, while Jesse went to the River City alone. Others had gathered with their children to wash clothes, barter, or just to visit – and maybe she would find some flour.

Laramie begged Jesse to let her go with him. When he saw her face, wet with tears, and the determination in her eyes, he knew she would go there, with or without him. Suzan couldn't imagine adding another child to their group, but knew the fear for the child that Laramie felt, demanded she follow, as they were all learning to trust the gifts of knowing. Hugging her sister tenderly, Suzan tucked the loose curls of Laramie's hair under her hat and smudged dirt on her cheeks, to disguise her youth and femaleness, and assured her they would have room for one more child.

As the two walked along the river path, they didn't see Lalo following them, as he stayed well behind. He couldn't believe his good luck to see Jesse again. The first time he'd seen him was that night downtown, when he watched from his hiding place as Jesse hoisted his bike high up in the tree branches. He was sure he was very smart, but why would he be at the river? Lalo himself avoided the river, only talking to the runners as they made their rounds in search of supplies to barter with the survivors. He knew a lot of the runners, the throw-away street kids, but he never went into the market place of the River City. He knew it was too dangerous. This day he would go, just to watch Jesse. What did he need that he would take a woman with him into the River City and who was the woman – his wife? He could tell that she had tried to disguise herself, with dirt all over her tear streaked face and hair tumbling out from under her hat, but she was definitely a woman and very beautiful. He saw that she was anxious and distracted, as if she were searching for someone, as most people were.

Following them into the market area, he got closer and could overhear their conversation. It didn't take him long to discover they needed insulin and it didn't matter what strength it was – just insulin. Lalo knew it would be difficult to find without having to give up everything you owned, unless you had connections. Surely this man wasn't going to barter for the beautiful woman? The woman was becoming very distraught. Tears streamed down her face, eyes frantically searched the crowd . . . for what? Or who?

Signaling to one of the runners that he recognized, a tall kid with dirty, stringy, blond hair and bad complexion – the one they called *Pock* because his face was so pitted, Lalo pointed Jesse and Laramie out of the crowd. Lalo bargained for the insulin, assuring Pock that he would be well rewarded. Pock, anticipating the coveted Lalo, agreed to find the insulin, the promised reward worth whatever price he would have to pay.

Approaching Jesse and feigning to have overheard his request for insulin, he agreed to find it, but insisted the exchange take place away from the bartering of the River City. Jesse, fearful of wasting precious time, reluctantly agreed to wait for him by Paglaicci's

Restaurant, up on the hill and away from the river. He hated having to put his trust in the dirty street boy, but he didn't have a choice. He couldn't let his parents leave without the medicine to keep them alive – hopefully long enough to reach Pueblo.

Suddenly, he'd become aware of the angry exchange taking place between two men, each tugging an arm of a small, terrified little girl, arguing over her, both claiming ownership. Before Jesse could stop her, Laramie swiftly moved into the middle of them, hollering and cussing at the top of her lungs, startling the two men. A crowd gathered and Jesse couldn't believe the words coming from Laramie's mouth as she grabbed the girl, cussing and shaking her for *leaving the tent*, and *wandering off,* and *not minding,* and *boy, are you going to get a good whipping*, and on and on like a woman possessed. The two men haggling over the girl were dumb-founded and didn't dare step between the wrath of a mad-woman and her child. Laramie, still ranting and raving, stomped away from the crowd, the terrified child under her arm, totally ignoring Jesse as she left the way they'd come, away from the River City.

Unbelievable, thought Lalo, as he watched, speechless, like the rest of the crowd. But, unlike the others, he and Jesse knew she rescued the child from the men, saving her from an ugly fate. Lalo heard what they were doing with abandoned or alone-now children at the river and he stayed as far away as possible, until today. He followed Jesse and Laramie knowing his connections with the street could help in bartering, but also to be another set of eyes for this man who showed he was not street-wise by bringing a woman here. Women especially were not safe at the River City, but this woman, whoever she was, could sure hold her own.

Laramie carried the limp, crying child under her arm for a good two blocks, yelling and screaming at her all the way, and no one dared interfere. When she felt she was far enough away, she slowed her gait, hoping Jesse was following. Unable to continue the charade, she left the trail and dropped to her weak, buckling knees and hugged the child to her until Jesse's hand gently touched her shoulder as he knelt beside them. Lalo stopped off the trail as well, as he wiped the tears from his face, remembering memories of tenderness between another woman and child.

Relieved that Laramie chose that direction to leave the River City, Jesse encouraged them to continue on so they wouldn't miss their connection for the insulin. He prayed it would be enough to get his parents to Pueblo. They reached Paglaicci's Restaurant at the agreed upon hour, as far as Jesse could figure, but Pock wasn't there yet and they welcomed the chance to rest and wait. Thankful to be away from the river and the smell of death and decay, he hoped he'd never have to go back. What if the wretched looking runner didn't show up or couldn't find any insulin? He would have to go back and keep looking until he found some. That's when he saw Lalo.

He'd been careless in watching them and didn't notice Jesse and Laramie leave the trail or realize they were sitting on the hill, right above him. He'd stopped to seek a place with some privacy to relieve himself. Jesse, watching absentmindedly from above, saw the young woman, and wondering why she was there by herself, was hypnotized by her striking beauty. She was tall for a girl, Jesse guessed eighteen years old, with tawny skin that matched her honey-gold hair and she moved with the grace and agility of a dancer. She was searching for something, a hiding place maybe. Jesse was lost in fantasy as he watched the exotic, lithesome creature that had captured his attention.

Suddenly aware that Laramie was intently watching him, he became embarrassed that he could look at a young woman and allow himself to become so distracted. Straining to see what Jesse was looking at, she caught a glimpse of Lalo at the same time she saw the homely, pock-faced runner coming towards them, carrying something in a brown paper bag. Getting to their feet, Laramie still holding the little girl clutching her neck, they eagerly anticipated the success of this dangerous business and their return to the others farther up the river. The bargain was made. There was enough insulin, hypodermic needles and all, to last his parents for at least a couple of months, maybe more. Relief and even gratitude washed over Jesse as he reached under his jacket to produce the knife he brought to barter for the life-giving liquid. It was the hunting knife with the inlaid mother-of-pearl handle he'd treasured and cared for all these years – the one his father gave him on his fourteenth birthday – a fitting trade. Pock was pleased with the exchange and departed as quickly as he came, much to Jesse and Laramie's relief.

As Laramie and the child started down the trail, Jesse looked back, hoping to catch a glimpse of the beautiful woman again, totally unprepared for what he saw. There, facing directly towards him, the beautiful girl was taking a leak. From a penis! Pock approached the urinating boy who shook the last droplets off as he looked approvingly at the knife. Handing the knife to Lalo, he cupped the boys exposed genitals, moving closer to him, blocking Jesse's view.

By the time they reached the river where Suzan, Levi and Mira were waiting, Jesse was so angry that Laramie thought it was with her. She didn't know what happened, but knew something had dramatically changed and wondered if he was angry with her for bringing another child to their group. Suzan rejoiced in the cache of insulin and the hope of life for her beloved in-laws. With so much to celebrate, she couldn't understand Jesse's foul mood and his insistence that they hurry.

There was still plenty of daylight, and she had a promise of flour, just a quarter mile away. She'd carted her plum jelly all this way and waited for Jesse and Laramie to return so Laramie could watch the children while they went to barter. Now she insisted they go. Reluctantly, he agreed, willing the image of that boy and the vivid memory of deceit to leave his enraged mind.

Lalo had hurried his business dealings with Pock, knowing that Jesse and Laramie would be eager to take the insulin to a safe place for hiding. He was afraid he would lose them if they were traveling with a group, although he sensed Jesse was more a loner. Hurrying along the river, he almost missed Laramie sitting on a rock, holding the rescued girl, with Mira and Levi crowding around to see the newest addition to their group.

"What's her name, aunt?" Mira was hovering over the child like a new toy.

"Well, I don't know yet," answered Laramie, brushing the child's long hair from her dirty face.

"Kathleen," answered the girl, loving the attention.

"Well, Kathleen, has anyone ever called you Kate?" Laramie was impressed by the girl's friendliness, unusual for such a youngster, especially considering what she'd just been through.

"Kate is my grand-ma."

"Well, you're Kate now, if that's okay with you."

"I guess so," replied the girl, grimacing as Laramie wiped her face with a bandanna, wet from the river.

Laramie didn't notice Lalo sitting just down the trail, straining to listen to their conversation. She didn't see Mira walk down the river trail to collect rocks along its banks or see the young boy follow. Her thoughts were consumed with food, shoes and clothes for another child as she sat on the rock washing the River City grime from the small, delicate body.

It amazed her that most of the children she was led to were all about the same age, between five and eight, and they'd been able to bring enough clothing on their trip to at least to keep them warm. Hopefully there would be enough clothes to keep Kate warm, too. Sanitation, keeping bodies and clothes clean, was definitely going to be a problem. She mentally sized up the child, guessing her to be about five years old and the same size as Sara and Jen, the two little black girls she'd found that first day.

Mira intently searched the bank of the river for the perfect rock and would have been happy to haul nothing but rocks across the mountains, but she was willing herself to be selective and find one special rock. Her grandmother in Rifle started her collecting rocks years ago, and she had packed just a few to take on the journey, each one special to her. Granny always said she would know the perfect rock, that if she listened real close, she would hear it call her. That's when she saw it – the perfect rock, laying in the palm of the outstretched hand, calling to her, offering itself to her. She didn't hear Lalo behind her and was startled, but the momentary fear left her as soon as she looked in his eyes. They stood facing each other for a long time, two children lost in the forgotten memory of spirits found. It was a solemn moment, a communion of souls, memory from worlds since passed. Neither of them looked away or felt embarrassed. They knew and remembered each other. They didn't let the memory drift away. They kept it close and honored it. There was no need for explanation even though they didn't understand, and the soul was allowed to remember.

"Who are you?" was spoken almost simultaneously. They both laughed with embarrassment and the moment passed. Exchanging names, Mira told Lalo of their plans to cross the mountains to get to the ranch where her grandparents lived, and he feared he would never see her again. At that very moment he vowed to follow them. He would rather die going over the mountains to be near her, than live here to be an old man, without ever seeing her again. The intense feelings passing between them would live in his heart forever. As they sat on the bank of the river, quietly talking, he delighted in her innocence, held her hand in his and dropped the forgotten special rock into her palm as their eyes again glimpsed the soul, remembering.

It didn't take long for Suzan and Jesse to barter for the flour, both parties elated with their found treasures. Jesse was anxious to get back to the others at the river, get the insulin to his parents, return to their tent and forget about the horrors of River City and the betrayal of the day. Gathering the children to head back, he scanned the river for Mira. That's when he saw them – the faggot-street-whore from the River City with his own daughter, Mira. He was holding her hand, giving her something. What did he give her, what were they talking about, what was he telling her? The shock and deceit he'd felt earlier turned to rage as he ran down the path to rescue his daughter.

Laramie and Suzan watched in horror as Jesse grabbed Lalo by his collar and viciously threw him away from Mira, angrily accusing him of trying to *steal his daughter* and turn her into a *street animal* like himself. The injured soul, seeking refuge, protected itself and crept away as Mira's hand closed over the special rock, still remembering.

Now, as he lay in the warmth of the cave, not a soul was awake to witness the anger mounting in him all over again. How could he have been so deceived? How could a boy look so beautiful? Tears stung his eyes as the embarrassment became confused with shame. Being attracted to what he thought was a young woman was bad enough, but it horrified him to discover he was a boy. Of course he didn't know, few did. And now the homosexual-faggot-whore had saved his daughter, was in his space, his cave, and he was supposed to feel indebted to him. How had he survived the trip? He must have followed them all the way from Denver. Jesse remembered all the times he'd felt someone following them, so close, yet he could never find him. Damn! How could he have been so fooled!

Reliving the memory of that day conflicted with the gratitude he felt toward Lalo for saving Mira's life and killing the man who had so savagely brutalized her. Opposing forces whirled and melted into black confusion as dreams of self-inflicted demons filled his tormented sleep.

At dawn's light his eyes opened to the knife with the inlaid mother-of-pearl on the handle that his father gave him on his fourteenth birthday. The significance of the gift was lost on Jesse. All he felt was anger that the injured street-whore could get so close to him in the night, without his knowing. He should have killed him last night when he thought he was the one hurting Mira – God knows he tried. Why didn't Lalo just stay in Denver so he could let the emotions of that day by the river be forgotten?

Jesse didn't let himself remember that there's a plan. Lalo needed them and Mira needed him to survive, but Jesse wouldn't let himself hear the inner voice telling him to trust the plan. Trust was the farthest thought from his mind, crowded out by the conflicting emotions so heavy in his heart.

When Lalo awoke he remembered his dream – sawdust sifting in slow motion through the shaft of sunlight. He knew the dream was important and what he would do. He made a plan. Lying there, willing the dream to stay so he could see more, he heard Jesse leave the cave and knew from the sound of his movements that he was angry.

Lalo knew what the anger was about. He saw it in Jesse's eyes as he'd seen it so many times before – in the eyes of other men. The anger that erupts when they think they've been tricked, and the mean rage they feel for being attracted to him. Would it be better if he'd been a woman? Yes, he thought so. Men can live with their feelings of lust better than being betrayed by their own eyes.

He understood it and had learned to live with it. Looking like a woman had kept him alive. He didn't try to look like a woman, and many times, trying to make himself look more like a boy, he'd chopped off his hair or shaved his head, but he still attracted the men. Now at least he was close to Mira and maybe he would be able to help Jesse understand. Maybe someday Jesse would forgive him for surviving.

Lalo knew what he felt for Mira wasn't about lust, sex, or anything about being male or female . . . it was about something inside that recognizes the soul and is allowed to remember. Women understood it so much better, but women were always more spiritually minded, as far as Lalo could tell.

Trying to turn over, he stifled a scream as the pain in his head exploded and searing flames shot through his chest. He'd been beaten before and knew it could take weeks for his ribs to heal. How would he travel? Would they leave him here?

Jesse stood outside the cave, searching for any excuse to leave Lalo here and get on with their journey, leave this pain filled place. He knew he couldn't explain his anger to the rest of them and his mind churned, trying to think of a way to leave him . . . be off the hook . . . not feel obligated. Standing outside the mouth of the cave in the twilight of morning, everything looked different somehow – clean – not like it was just last night – dirty and defiled.

As the first glimmer of sun peeked on the horizon, he angered at the promise of hope and warmth given to man so indiscriminately since time began. A new day. How dare the sun shine on so much pain? The day should be marked with darkness to hide the atrocities they witnessed and the cruel thoughts dominating his mind. Jesse thought of all the days the sun shone; on the living and dying, the fearful, the grieving, the old and young, the dark-hearted and depraved, the abandoned kids, the loved kids and even the street kids. Why does it shine on all, not judging whether they deserve to be warmed by its presence? Lord knows he would have had a lot of dark days if the sun judged who was deserving.

Jesse knew in his heart that it was Lalo who saved Mira's life. That stupid, street-kid for whatever reason, followed them all the way from Denver, because of that day at the river.

Finding the knife this morning shocked him, rudely reminding him again, bringing back the scene of Lalo and the ugly pock-faced runner fondling him. Did Lalo know about the insulin buy? He obviously managed to get the knife back.

He knew he would have to talk to Lalo, no matter how he felt. Jesse was a fair man, even though trusting anyone was difficult for him, especially when it concerned his family. He had very definite opinions about what was right and wrong, and homosexuality was wrong, unnatural, foreign and repulsive. Lalo was of the street and Jesse admitted he had no idea what that kind of life demanded. And what made him a son of the streets? He wanted to know all the details of Lalo's life, but knew it wasn't any of his business.

As hard as he tried, Jesse couldn't justify or rationalize the hate and disgust he felt for Lalo. He knew his own feelings created the turmoil inside him. Thank God he figured that out! It took some of the power away from the rage at Lalo. It surely wasn't his fault that he looked like a girl. It probably helped him to survive on the street. "This street person was put in our lives and we don't have to know why, all we have to do is trust." Remembering Suzan's words from last night stung his memory. Why couldn't he trust?

The sun was up full, shining on his face as he stood outside in the cold morning air, allowing the fog and blackness of last night to be cleansed, and the hope and promise of a new day relieved his tormented spirit. And his heart softened . . . some.

Black let out a painful bark to alert Jesse that someone was coming. "Good dog," he stroked the wolf's head in appreciation. Jesse had used fishing line and large eyed needles to put a couple of stitches in the wolf's shoulder to close the wound. Black wouldn't stay in the cave and was wagging his tail this morning when Jesse came out. He was glad he would be all right. Black was a good watchdog, although he'd worried that the smell of the wolf's blood would bring mountain lions out of their dens, but there was plenty of blood and dead meat just a quarter mile up the ridge, thought Jesse, remembering.

Looking down the hill, towards the road, he strained against the sun to see, but the road was clear. "Yo, mate." It was Ian's voice. He and Jane were coming over the top of the mountain carrying a big buck. Boy, if they weren't a welcome sight, all loaded down with back-packs, sleeping bags, guns, and now a big buck . . . he could almost taste it. Jesse crossed the ridge and started up the hill towards them to help carry the heavy load. He was startled when he came to the primitive lean-to and realized this was where Lalo stayed that first night, the night the blizzard raged so fiercely. "How the heck did he survive here?"

"What?" asked Ian as Jesse stared in amazement, brushing his hair back from his forehead, as if trying to clear a path for answers.

"Will you look at this. This kid followed us all the way from Denver and he actually stayed here the night of the blizzard. God, I don't think I would have survived here . . . not during that storm." Ian and Jane were confused as they looked for the kid Jesse was talking about and seeing the questions on their faces, began gathering up Lalo's things to take back to the cave. "It's a long story," started Jesse as he recounted the details of yesterday, as best he could.

Shocked at hearing her dream described, Jane and Ian just stared at each other, knowing they made a bad decision when they left to hunt. Ian placed a finger to his lips, warning Jane not to disclose her warning dream. No good purpose would be served by telling Jesse she'd been warned in a dream to protect Mira. She knew she would never discount her dreams again, as the unquestioned tears fell from her eyes. But if she had told him yesterday, maybe he could have stopped it from happening. If she'd believed it herself, she and Ian would never have left the cave to hunt. "Black?"

Jesse looked at her quizzically, as he hadn't mention Black when telling them about yesterday. "Black was slashed pretty bad in his right front shoulder, but I took a couple of stitches last night and I think he'll be okay."

Avoiding his questioning eyes, she offered to bring Lalo's belongings to the cave if he would help Ian carry the buck down the hill. Agreeing, he wondered when he'd made the decision for Lalo to stay with them. He knew he owed him that much for saving Mira's life, and he sure couldn't just leave him, although, looking back at the crude shelter, he knew Lalo would have survived, one way or the other.

Looking at Mira lying so close, Lalo watched her eyes glisten with tears and saw the painful awareness of last night return. "Mira," he whispered, "I had a dream. I saw the sawdust fly," he whispered softly, as her tears fell and her eyes lost their memory in his. He knew his physical pain would heal faster than the pain so brutally carved in Mira's memory. "You'll see the sawdust fly, Mira. I saw it in my dream."

Lalo didn't look much like a girl today, his right eye completely closed and purple, his lips swollen and split. He hurt everywhere except his legs. Thank goodness he could still walk. Suzan brought him pine tea sweetened with Tang that she and the children made the day before. Everyone was so nice to him. Even the children came one by one and thanked him for saving Mira. Something changed in the way Jesse treated him too – maybe he wouldn't make him leave.

When Jesse left so angry this morning Lalo was afraid he'd be left behind and they would take Mira away. When Ian and Jane returned and everyone went outside to see the deer, Jesse knelt beside him and thanked him for saving Mira. Holding the knife with the mother-of-pearl inlaid in the handle, Jesse said, "I think this belongs to you now. You've earned it." Involuntary tears welled and Lalo couldn't believe his ears.

"If you want to we'll talk when you feel up to it, but I am very grateful that you were there to save Mira. We may never have seen her again. I'm sorry I hurt you so bad, but you'll be safe with us until you get stronger. Then you can decide what to do." Unable to speak, the tears slipped down Lalo's swollen face, and Jesse accepted the tears as gratitude and left him with the knife his father gave him on his fourteenth birthday. Mira felt her father's tears on her cheek as he bent down to kiss her. It was good.

Much of the day was spent skinning the deer and preparing the meat for later meals. Ian and Jane were glad to be back to the shelter and warmth of the cave, although their time together was good for talking, making plans and getting to know each other. They shared about their lives before they met and their concerns for the future. Right now, all they wanted to do was make it to the Rocking Z – the future would happen soon enough.

Jane shared the details of her dream with Ian, the night of the blizzard, before they decided to leave to hunt the deer they'd seen on the next mountain. They convinced each other the dream was triggered by all the horror they'd seen in the last two weeks, that to share it would place the ominous weight of danger and worry on the rest of the group. They dismissed it as fear and worry that brought the dream to her restless sleep, as all of them suffered terrible nightmares. She would never discount her dreams again. They were sent to her as a warning, to prepare them.

The dream she had in Denver, the night before everything changed, crept back into her memory. The dream about Levi . . . she'd kept it to herself for so long, until the night before they left Denver and she knew what would happen to the children. She knew because she'd dreamed it, but it was so horrible she couldn't tell anyone. Still, it was sent to her as a warning, and when she saw the scene around the campfire with Laramie and the child, she knew the truth, and thank God they left that night. From now on, her dreams would be heeded as warnings. That's when she overheard Laramie talking about Lalo's dream.

"He wants one of the hides I brought back from the cabin because he dreamed about it," Laramie was telling Suzan, as they carefully cut the choicest cuts of meat away from the backbone.

"What did he dream?" asked Jane as she tossed one of the meaty bones to the patiently waiting Black, who eagerly accepted it after the ritual sniffing.

"Something about *when the sawdust flies* and he and Mira making something out of the hide. He says it will help her heal." They searched each other's faces.

"Give him the hide," was said in unison.

Mira was listless and remote, choosing to lay in her sleeping bag most of the day, acknowledging no one, not speaking, just staring or sleeping. Suzan periodically asked if she was hungry or thirsty, but there was no response. Sometimes she just lay by her and held her close and rocked her, brushed her hair back from her eyes or softly sang to her, deciding not to pressure her to talk about it, just to let it fade a little. Each of the children went to Mira with hopes she would feel better or an offer to get something for her, or just touch her. The children didn't know what happened, but knew it was something bad. Laramie and Jane each sat with her, held her, talked to her. Lalo whispered to her and their eyes got lost in each other's souls before drifting off to sleep again.

Cutting the deer meat from the carcass took most of the day as the three women discussed the children, the hunt, and of course Mira and Lalo. The conversation turned to their brother Judd and his wife Dani. Where were they? Would they ever see them again? One thing was certain; if they were alive, they would know where to find them. And mom and dad on the Rocking Z; what would they find when they got there? Now they were sure they would get there, they just hoped the road ahead would be brighter than the devastation they left behind.

They laughed at the memories of growing up on Mariposa Street, the old piano they forced down the basement that would never see daylight again. They remembered Gypsy, Judd's German Shepherd, and how he'd shared his ice-cream cones. "He'd take a lick, and Gypsy would take a lick. Yuk!" They laughed at memories of Laramie trying to saddle Lightening, the pony with a mean streak; crashing the neighbor's swimming pool when no one was home; tubing down the river; playing at the gravel pit; eating peas, radishes and strawberries while weeding the garden. There were so many good memories – they forgot about the bad ones.

When Lalo awoke, Laramie gave him the tin box she found in the snow where he'd dropped it the night before. He told her about finding the old woman in the earthen room and taking the box with the papers. He said the box and papers were important to someone. Laramie thought it would probably be important to Cody someday. She was sad to hear the woman was dead. She imagined her coming back to her cabin someday – the place she obviously loved so much. She guessed she wouldn't be quite as happy there now, with her husband gone, and now Laramie understood why she had to find Cody and why she could hear the music. Cody would have died there without his grandparents, and now that both of them were gone, he would want the tin box someday.

She went through the supplies they'd brought from the cabin and took the largest hide to Lalo who immediately took out the knife Jesse gave him and began carefully measuring and cutting, even though it hurt him to breathe. He knew exactly what he wanted to do with it and although she wanted to stay, watch, and ask questions, Laramie left him alone to his work and his dream. But what did he want with the hide and why was he cutting it up? What had he dreamed? And how could it help Mira get better?

The sun was bright and in spite of the cold air, it was invigorating for them to be outside. The children put on jackets and played on the mountain in the crude, makeshift lean-to, pretending they were Lalo who was now their hero. Every once in awhile their laughter would drift down and Laramie would remind them to be quiet so no one would discover them there. They didn't notice much activity on the road below, just a few small groups taking advantage of the good traveling weather. No one noticed them.

Whatever happened that first day verified Ian's theory and research of energy responding to energy; negatives and positives being out of balance. It was good for them to talk, and laugh, and acknowledge all they had overcome, instead of dwelling on all the negative events of the past three weeks – creating even more negative energy.

Jesse and Ian returned with armloads of firewood. "I don't know how we lucked out," said Ian, "but someone's been up there with a caterpillar and pushed all the dead fall into a big pile – probably for fire prevention."

"Yea," agreed Jesse, "and I want to get back to that stream before night fall to replenish the water supply." He and Ian carried empty jugs for water about a half mile up the side of the mountain and over the top. He also wanted to check out the terrain, now that he had a good vantage point. He didn't know how long they could risk staying in the cave, although they would have to stay a few more days for Mira and Black to heal. Lalo, too.

The sun was going down as they stopped to rest, taking in the breathtaking view below them, signs of the blizzard still visible even though the snow had already melted from the pine tops. Jesse couldn't believe his eyes when he first saw it – smoke curling from the top of the mountain. It couldn't be! He sniffed the air, and sure enough, it was smoke.

"Smells like dinner to me," said Ian good naturedly, recognizing Jesse's agitation.

"Everyone in the world will know where we are. Where in the hell is it coming from? We must be standing right over the cave. It's got to be 300 feet beneath us."

Forgetting the water, Ian followed Jesse down the mountain and into the cave. There, in the very back where the walls sloped down, Suzan was cooking deer meat in the pan Laramie brought back from the cabin. The children's smiling faces were aglow with the dancing flames from the fire, as they anticipated the savory dish.

"Have you lost your mind?" It was quite obvious Jesse was upset, but the wonderful aroma of the meat captured all their attention. "Do you want everyone in the world to know we're here?" He still couldn't compete with the thought of the hot meat. "How did you know the smoke would vent outside, anyway?"

Suzan shoved a piece of the sautéing meat in Jesse's mouth to shut him up and he immediately fell to the floor in exaggerated praise, moaning loudly as he devoured the succulent treat. He almost forgot how good hot food tasted. They were so afraid to start a fire for fear that passersby would detect the smoke. The meat was delicious, and all the children laughed at Jesse as they stuffed the delicious deer meat in their mouths. Mira and Lalo were even enticed by the delicious aroma as they crowded around the pan with the children. It was good to see Mira respond and Lalo move around some, even though it was obvious he was in a lot of pain.

Jesse grabbed more from the pan as Suzan explained that she remembered feeling the draft last night when she was in the back of the cave and realized there must be a vent going out. Before she started the fire, she lit a twig and watched the smoke trail up through the walls somehow. She didn't question it, she just built a fire.

"Well, what if someone sees the smoke?" asked Jesse as he devoured another hunk of meat from the pan . . . it was soooooooo delicious.

"Then, we'll be having company for dinner." They all rolled on the floor of the cave like children, as their knees became weak from laughter. "How many people do you think are standing on top of these mountains, looking for smoke?" asked Suzan, as Jesse began to grin too. It was about trust!

It was a good night. Laramie surprised everyone, especially Cody, with the chocolate cake she'd brought from the cabin – the one his grandmother made for the dance. They even splurged and made coffee, the aroma reminding them of gentler times, and as they talked around the fire, the laughter of the day renewed their spirits, energized them, gave them hope.

The children settled down quickly, bellies full, tired from the sunny day and thin air. Mira let Suzan bathe her and comb her hair behind the blanket thrown over the rope for privacy. Mira didn't talk, and Suzan didn't press her, just watched as she scrubbed her body until it was red. She understood the dirty feeling would take a lot more than soap and water to disappear. It would take time, and there was plenty of time for healing. She helped her dress and held her quietly for a long time. "You'll never know dear, how much I love you, please don't take my sunshine away," softly drifted through the cave, as Mira and the children were lulled to sleep and the fire died down to glowing embers.

Jesse was awake before dawn. He lit the lantern, started the fire in the back of the cave and re-warmed the half pot of coffee from the night before. He was concerned, and Ian, being unfamiliar with the terrain, retrieved his maps and joined him over coffee so they could make a plan. The Coleman lantern flickered as they poured over the maps. Ian indulged in a cigarette and Jane, smelling the smoke, immediately crawled to the back of the cave to join them. "Oh, the good old days!" sighed Jane. "Sitting around a campfire, smoking a cigarette, drinking a strong cup of coffee with my man," she said as she playfully cuffed him.

"Well, you must know something I don't know!" hissed Ian, trying unsuccessfully to whisper. Embarrassed, he looked at Jesse who was poking the fire and trying not to smile.

"I mean," Ian continued, "you're so damned pig-headed, how would a man know if he's your man? Jesse, I don't know how you've tolerated these Zerlich women for so long – they're a headstrong lot – all three of them!" Ian was embarrassed and Jesse, not wanting to lend more attention to it, sat back down to the maps, Jane secretly taking pleasure in Ian's outward show of emotion and embarrassment. He was usually so cool and controlled.

Both Laramie and Suzan lay smiling in their sleeping bags, straining to hear every word. Jane had been so secretive when she and Ian returned from the hunting trip, not a moment of small pleasure would she give them, not one single detail. Well, the cat's out of the bag now, sister dear! In a matter of moments, Laramie and Suzan were snuggled close to the fire, drinking coffee and sharing sly smiles with each other. Now Jane would have to tell them all the details, which still weren't any of their business, as she'd so rudely pointed out yesterday, but Ian was wearing the truth on the tip of his tongue and apparently carrying a hot flame somewhere else too.

"Okay, okay" laughed Jane as Ian stomped out of the cave to

check out the weather with Jesse close on his heels. On their way out, Jesse said something about a family council after breakfast, so they could all agree on the plan he and Ian were making. It would depend on all their approval, as it would take more time and miles than originally planned.

Suzan and Laramie scooted closer to Jane, so the children wouldn't hear all the details. "Nothing happened," started Jane.

"Well, something pretty heavy must have happened for Ian to react the way he is. I mean, it's the most I've heard out of him, unless he's talking about his research."

"Oh, Laramie, you've always considered yourself the family expert in matters of the heart, even though you're the youngest and haven't been involved with anyone for the last two years. And what the hell would you know about romance?" she barked at Suzan. "You and Jesse have been married for seventeen years."

With that, they hooted and cackled together like old times. "All right Jane, why didn't you *claim your man* during the hunting trip? Ian is obviously mad about you, and frustrated as a bull in November."

"Suzan, you have such a way with words." Jane was getting irritated because serious feelings were surfacing, and the memory of Ian and their conversations while hunting returned. "Ian is married to a woman in Sydney, Australia." That shut them up, thought Jane, as she watched their mouths gape. "They haven't lived together for five years, but he's still married and that's not even the issue, since the love they once shared is obviously gone."

Laramie and Suzan sat in silence and listened as Jane told them all the details...after all, they were sisters. "He caught her with another man! Can you imagine? Ian's woman cheated on him!" Jane's eyes grew large in mock astonishment. "How can I be with a man who has such a lily-white, idealistic, illusory view of real life? Damn! I've been with more men than I care to remember, some that I can't remember, some I hope I never remember, and some I can't forget. Where does that put me, if he bailed out of a marriage because his wife committed adultery?"

"I mean," Jane said angrily, "he didn't even look back, wouldn't even talk to her, not one word. No forgiveness, no *I hope you find happiness*, nothing, not even a good fight, just wrote her off, and wouldn't sign the damned divorce papers either, just to spite her, I guess."

As her frustration and fears spilled out, Jane became more solemn. "I could tell when he was talking about her that he had loved her madly, was totally committed and living his life as if it would go on blissfully forever without a ripple. Can you imagine what that must have done to him? He was devastated! Where the hell did he come from anyway, to have such an idealistic view of life, people, and love? What? This couldn't happen to him? He just moved out and buried himself in his work. And he wants to be *my* man? Hah! He'd chew me up and spit me out every time he looked at me if he knew the details of my past, and I'll be damned if I'll ever tell him about it. Now, you tell me, how can two people have a relationship without being completely honest about where they've been and what happened to make them who they are today? Tell me that!"

It was the expert who spoke first. "Well, it sounds to me like he was honest with you. He told you who he was and what happened to make him who he is. I think he's a pretty decent guy and you're scared to death."

"And besides," said Suzan, "how do you know how he would react to your past? You obviously haven't told him about it, but he's not dumb or blind. Surely, he got a good idea that night with Red at the big-house when he said they stayed up and talked that first night."

"I just don't want to get all tangled up with love and all that crap again, and then he'd be gone, off researching somewhere, out of my life. I won't give myself away. I can't go through that again, and I won't put Levi through it again either." The tears were streaming now, the sarcasm quiet, the deep emotions obvious to the expert and the one with no memory of romance.

"Maybe it's too late to keep love from happening, and you're scared to let him know how you feel about him. You're the one who isn't being honest here."

The words stung Jane and she knew Laramie was right. Her sisters knew her too well.

"Talk to him, be honest, open, and willing to let him see you. The real you, minus the sarcasm, the humor, the bullshit you usually hide behind." Suzan moved closer and put her arm around Jane's trembling shoulders. "You're a good, decent, honest woman, Jane, and your past shaped you and molded you into the woman you are. You deserve to be happy. Don't you think it's time you opened up your heart and allowed yourself to be loved by a man again?"

Laramie moved to the other side of her and the three sisters drank the last of the coffee while Jane smoked another treasured cigarette.

"You're right as usual," she said, as she inhaled deeply and blew out slowly, trying to savor every tar-and-nicotine-filled-drag. "Damn, it's miserable trying to spread these out, and save some for later. Discipline was never my thing."

"So, quit changing the subject and go talk to him."

"We'll talk, but not right now. I need to sort out the truth in me, somehow. I know I have to be honest with him. He is a good man and I guess I'm just afraid he won't want me, if he knows the truth."

Ian and Jesse came back in with the water they meant to get last night; the children were waking; it was time for washing, combing, dressing in their cleanest dirty clothes and eating breakfast. The intimate moment between the three women was claimed by the demands of the day, but lingered in Jane's heart, as she contemplated making peace with her past, and talking to Ian, the research scientist from Australia. The man she was falling in love with.

## *Chapter 13*

Lalo was overcome with emotion at the gifting of the knife from Jesse. He'd hoped by some miracle that Jesse would accept him into their group, their family, but never imagined he would actually be staying with them and so close to Mira. When Jesse carried him up the hill and Laramie and Suzan dressed him and put him in a sleeping bag next to Mira, it was like a dream come true. He was afraid he would waken to the lonely solitude and cruel existence of the day before, but the pain reminded him it was real. The pain, a small price to pay for the dream.

He watched Mira sleep as he silently prayed for her withdrawn spirit, and knew she could hear his fervent whispers supplicating the powers that be to release her from the wretched agony of the soul so violated. He knew the place where wounded souls go to hide and he didn't want her to stay there forever. Occasionally her eyes would open as if to make sure he was still there, watching guard for her return. And he was.

Using the knife, he cut the hide Laramie gave him, telling Mira everything he was doing, knowing that she would hear him. The more he cut, the easier it became to hold the knife at the right angle to the leather to cut the narrow lacing needed. It was more difficult than it looked when he'd watched the old woman that used to sit at the corner of 16th and Larimer Street, cutting the leather strips. He'd watched her take the small scraps of leather, sometimes only two inches square, and starting with a hole in the center, she cut around and around until there was a long lace. It always fascinated Lalo how she could make a long lace out of such a small scrap. She never objected to Lalo watching as she took the lacing and braided a pattern with eight strands to make the trinkets which passersby took as they dropped dollar bills in the woven basket. He often placed dollar bills there himself or brought her more scraps of leather. Now he wished he'd taken one of the braided strands, but he knew he'd remember the pattern from the dream.

In whispers he shared all the details of the dream with Mira; the cutting, soaking, stretching, braiding and the two pieces of wood placed exactly together to make a handle. He knew what he had to do as he continued to cut the hide, the lace growing longer as the hole in the middle grew larger.

As the children came to see what he was doing and to look at Mira, he encouraged them to stay and talk so Mira could hear - to tell their stories, share their secrets and giggles. Soon they were crowded around Lalo and Mira and talked comfortably about the people they missed. If they mentioned their mother or grandpa, Lalo asked them to tell him about them, what they looked like or smelled like. It became a game as the children giggled about garlic or beer and cigarette breath, big funny noses, and fat, hangy-down arms. Some of the younger children fell asleep as the memories spilled out, relieving their spirits of bottled up emotions.

Luck was with them, as the weather was mild the next two days and the children were able to play outside, even though it was cold in the shade. Laramie showed them how the sun moves across the sky, and as the shadows move, so do the sunny places. They made a game of playing in the sun streams.

The smell of wet clothes and sweaty boots inside the cave was more than Jane could handle so she devised a clothes line between two trees and hoped they would dry in the too few hours of sunlight that searched for earth through the tree tops. Suzan and Laramie began sorting through the dirty clothes and soggy socks to rinse in the water Ian and Jesse brought from the stream. They couldn't help overhearing the laughter and memories flow from the children as they gathered around Lalo and Mira.

"Remember how Mom always said when she wasn't feeling good, if she could just sit in the sun, she'd get better?" Laramie scraped the last bit of mud off Dominic's boots and set them with the other clean ones.

"Yes, I remember. Mom believed the sun's energy could heal just about anything."

"Should we take Mira outside, in the sunlight, maybe tomorrow? I worry about her just lying there." Laramie tossed socks and underwear in one pile and shirts and pants in another.

"Haven't you watched Lalo and what he's doing with the children? It's the best medicine there is. She doesn't respond to Jesse or me, but Lalo just keeps talking to her as if she were awake and listening. I think it's healing her just to hear all of them talking and laughing. I just wish she'd talk to me."

"It's good for all the kids to talk about the memories, the families they'll never see again. I've learned more about them today, by eavesdropping, than I've learned the whole time we've been together. Seems like runny noses, dirty bodies and hungry belly's is all we've had time to deal with. They haven't really had a chance to become individual yet, but Lalo's pulling it out of them." Laramie twisted the water out of the last of the socks and heaped them on the pile. "They trust him. He's really like a child himself – he's one of them, no parents, no family but us now. He's good for them. Jesse doesn't like it. I can tell he's agitated when he comes in and sees Lalo talking to Mira or touching her hair, or anything."

"I know, we've talked about it. He'll get over it. He fluctuates between gratitude and mistrust, or fear – I don't know exactly what it is. Maybe it's a father thing. Lalo's a boy, a street kid at that. Jesse's afraid Lalo is taking his daughter away from him, but Lalo's the only person she'll respond to at all, so he'll have to learn to live with it. It's almost as if she left the rest of us."

"Do you hear how tenderly and lovingly he talks to her, the beautiful words of encouragement and the stories of hope he tells her?"

"I can never hear the exact words," said Suzan. "Only the soft, calming effect of his voice. It's almost like a melody. It even soothes me. I've been so tempted to move closer or go sit with them on the floor so I can hear better, but I don't want to break the magic I see happening. Know what I mean?"

"Yes, I feel the same way. We're all healing, sunshine or not."

Jane came in for another load of wet clothes to hang and was nearly run over by nine cowboys and Indians who stole all the clean shoes. When she joined Suzan and Laramie, she asked, "Have you heard those kids? I can't believe that Dominic just explained that a medicine wheel has twelve stones around it. Did you know that?"

"No, but we'll probably learn a lot from these kids!" Laramie was convinced the children were extraordinary and she never passed up the opportunity to rave about *her kids*. But it wasn't just her kids. They were beginning to feel a sense of extraordinary awareness in all of them.

"How's Mira doing today?" Jane's reaction to the news when they returned from hunting yesterday was about what everyone expected. If Lalo hadn't killed the man, she would have. "Have you talked to her about it yet?"

Suzan was miffed by the question, like an accusation that she was neglecting her responsibilities, and responsibility was her middle name. "Not in detail, only to assure her she's safe now and the man who took her is dead and he can never hurt anyone again." She tried to keep the anger from her voice. "I think it's a good idea to take her outside." Why hadn't she thought of that? "The fresh air and sunshine may help bring her back to this world again. Tomorrow, if the weather holds, I'll take her to the stream and we'll make a small fire and make more tortillas. She always loved to help me make tortillas."

"Speaking of tortillas, where are the rest and I'll start rolling up some of that deer meat in them for tonight," said Laramie, anxious to be busy and not a witness to the sparks she knew would fly.

Suzan handed the soggy clothes to Jane who eagerly accepted her assignment to return outside to hang them on the rope. Jane knew she was being dismissed, and felt as if she'd intruded on her sisters' conversation.

The chores of living were automatically determined by the ones most willing to do them, as usually happens. They all helped with the cooking, but the majority of the food preparation and preservation fell to Suzan, as Laramie claimed the primary portion of responsibility for the children. Jane loved to be outside with the men, so she gathered firewood, helped hunt, hauled water and replenished the pine boughs which were used for bedding and making tea.

Suzan remembered that's how it was when they were growing up on Mariposa Street, too. Since she was the oldest, she helped her mother with the gardening, cooking, canning and cleaning. Jane and her brother, Judd, were usually outside with the horses, as Laramie played house with her dolls, or that's how she remembered it, anyway. She was eight years old when Laramie was born, so it was natural that she had most of the responsibility in helping Mom.

She missed her mother and especially now, wished she were here when she needed help with Mira. What do you say to a daughter who has been so violated? Mom would know. How often Suzan had cried out to her in the past years, asking her to help sort out emotions, or just to hear her reassuring voice on the telephone, convincing her that everything would work out and time was her best friend. Even without telephones, she felt her mother's presence so strongly sometimes, like that first night, when she lay helpless on the sidewalk, so close to home, yet unable to continue on her own strength. Maybe that's the gift mothers give their daughters, the courage and ability to persevere, as they've watched their mothers live through so many hells of their own.

Now it was her turn to be the strong mother and help Mira have the courage to persevere, to endure, to live. She hoped the right words would come to her when she talked to her tomorrow.

Suzan resented Jane asking if she'd talked to Mira yet. Jane thought she'd seen it all and lived through so much more than she, just because she'd lived the life of a junkie on the streets. So, should she be rewarded for being a drug addict? It just didn't seem fair that every time Jane got in trouble, or needed money or someone to watch Levi, everyone ran to her rescue. No one ever rewarded Suzan for paying her bills on time, making sure they ate properly, keeping her house clean, caring for her children, and always being home for them. Yes! She was responsible!

Mom and Dad sent Jane to a treatment center to detox her and help her get straight, and then they all lived at Mom's house, even Levi's father. Suzan predicted she wouldn't stay clean, and sure enough, she didn't. Then they helped her get an apartment and brought her home again when things got so dangerous between her and that crazy Indian that they all tried to help because he was Levi's father. As far as Suzan was concerned, Jane's last act of rebellion was living with that biker, Red, and his live-in biker-bitch, claiming them as her family who *accepted her exactly as she was*. Well, bully for her! She wrote her real family off like so much dog crap! Was she really mad because Jane found someone to love her as she was, or that she didn't need her real family anymore? Damn! Why couldn't she just let it go? Why did it always make her so angry?

It was a fierce sibling rivalry, probably from the first day Jane so rudely interrupted their perfect little family with just Mom, Dad and her. She'd always been the one to help Mom, and Jane was the one who got out of work and was always in trouble. With her adult mind, she knew she loved her sister, but her childhood memories always inflamed jealousy and resentment. Jane never had to do anything special to get her mom and dad's love, and Suzan always tried so hard to be perfect, so they would love her more.

Mira looked exactly like the pictures of Suzan when she was growing up, and everyone always commented how much she was like her. And that was the part of the problem between Mira and her. Suzan was a perfectionist and wanted her children to be perfect. Mira brought her face-to-face with herself. She was so much like her, not only in looks, but also in mannerisms and attitudes, and Suzan spent a lot of time trying to change the things in Mira that she didn't like about herself. She didn't like the power struggle that existed between them. She couldn't remember it existing between her and her mother, so it must be wrong. She was very careful to encourage Mira and Jacinth's relationship so the same sister pattern wouldn't be repeated, but she was doing it to them just the same. She didn't know how she was doing it or what to do to change it.

She was ashamed for the way she treated Jane in the past and the way she resented Mom and Dad invariably rescuing her. Why couldn't they just be sisters like she and Laramie were? When Jane asked her if she'd talked to Mira yet, it brought back all the resentment. What right did Jane have questioning her about her nurturing her daughter? Or was it that she just felt so inadequate to do so?

"Where are you?" Laramie was deftly rolling up the meat filled tortillas and placing them on the flat rocks by the fire ring Suzan built last night. "I've been watching your face and I feel so much pain from you. What are you thinking about?"

"Oh, I was rehashing all the anger I have towards Jane and her inference that I should talk to Mira. I know I need to have a talk with Mira, and I plan to. Why does she always make my inadequacies seem so blatant?"

"Maybe, you need to have a talk with Jane, too."

"No, I've said all the ugly things to Jane that I will ever say to her."

"Then maybe it's time to say all the beautiful things you've never said to her."

Suzan smarted at what seemed like a reprimand from her little sister. It was right on the mark and she knew it, but she wasn't ready to hear it yet. "What do you know about my anger and what's happened between Jane and me?" she retorted sharply.

"Hey, you can have all the anger you want, and you're right, this is between you and Jane. I don't know anything about it except that it's old stuff. Don't you think you've hung on to it long enough? It doesn't hurt Jane anymore, but it's still hurting you. You're the one still paying the price for anger or resentment, but you can keep it for as long as you want to."

Suzan's eyes looked far away, through the stone walls of the cave, through the years that clouded her heart and left her with glaring imperfection. "I guess she really is quite a woman to have experienced all she has and survived, with or without our help. I know that deep down I really admire her and cringe because I know that I couldn't have done it myself."

"That's why you didn't have to do it. And thank God, I didn't have to do it either. I'd probably still be out there, dying. Jane and I can't do what you do either, and you and Jane can't do what I do. That's why we're all together now – we need each other. We've been prepared for this, you know."

Those wise blue eyes held Suzan's for a long time as the two women drank in the strength of the other. Suzan's determination to have the anger melted as Laramie's tolerance for her imperfections filled her. "I really hate it when you're right."

"I know, I hate it when anyone else is right and I have to admit it."

The children's voices became all but whispers, as Suzan looked lovingly at Mira watching Lalo cut the leather. Dominic, Sara, Kate and Cody were asleep, all draped across one another, and the older kids drifted out, one by one, to help Jane.

"Maybe we should all have an outing tomorrow, up at the stream Jesse found. We can make tortillas while the kids play and Mira and I can go downstream to talk." Suzan's eyes pleaded for support and Laramie knew she needed help to get through this.

"That's a great idea, I'll make a couple dozen extra burrito's for supper, and we'll take the leftovers with us tomorrow. Oh, I put the last of your dried green chile in some of these, but I separated them because the kids don't like them hot. Maybe we could even make up some more of the Tang you brought. The kids love it and think it's such a treat."

"We're almost out of Tang, too, but I'll bet there's enough for another week if I mix it with the powdered Gatorade Lalo had." They'd combined the cache found in Lalo's shelter to help supplement their own dwindling supplies. She was beginning to worry about running out of food before they reached the ranch, although there was plenty of game and Jesse, Ian and Jane were all good marksmen.

She remembered hearing Ian and Jesse talking about finding a way to by-pass Vail and then discarding the idea because of the altitude. The risk of getting caught in a snowstorm at eleven or twelve thousand feet in the wild was one they couldn't take. Suzan was relieved. She'd hated the thought of traveling over the mountains instead of just walking down the highway. Surely the city of Vail couldn't be as dangerous as Jesse and Ian feared. She agreed that the Vail residents who were sticking out the winter would view them as the danger, and the ones who were already out of food, would want theirs. But what kind of threat could they pose if they just walked through the town? Once Vail was behind them the trip would be much easier, as the elevation dropped dramatically and there would be less chance of their freezing to death. She had to go through their supply inventory and pack up again. They would probably stay here in the cave for another few days until Mira, Lalo and Black were stronger.

Loaded down with a canvas tarp full of wood, Jane joined in the burrito making and agreed a picnic by the stream tomorrow would be fun. She started the fire so Ian could make his exquisitely strong coffee that they all looked forward to drinking at the end of the day. "Boy, this flint striker doo-dad of Lalo's is really great for starting fires. Tomorrow, when we go out for the picnic, let's take the flint along so we can all get a good look at it in the sunlight and be on the lookout for more while we walk. I don't know if there's any flint up here, but maybe somewhere between here and the ranch we'll run into some. It's in pockets of rock, and if we can find even a little, there will be more close by."

The kids came in cold and exhilarated by the fresh air and Laramie groaned as she looked at all the boots, caked with mud, again. "Where do they find all the mud?"

"Yea, you kids go outside and wipe your boots off on the door mat, and next time, walk on the sidewalk, not the mud puddles." They all hee-hawed at Jane's sarcasm as Laramie vowed to let the mud build up on their boots until they were all six inches taller. She grudgingly joined in the good-natured teasing, and agreed that even if there were sidewalks, the children would have gone out of their way to walk through the mud. She had a lot to learn about being a mother.

As the evening passed with good strong coffee and spicy deer meat wrapped in tortillas, Suzan's thoughts turned again to the words she would say to Mira. How would any mother know the right words? Her heart broke for her daughter and the abrupt thrust from light-hearted childhood to such a violent deprivation of coming to her own natural peace with her body and sexuality. Last night when she was helping Mira bathe, Suzan felt the shame that consumed her daughter. It made Suzan angry that women, even in childhood, were given the message that if something like this happened, somehow, it was their fault and they were dirty, less desirable, less worthy. Where did the message come from? She couldn't ever remember discussing such issues with Mira, but somehow, Mira got the message. Suzan couldn't make it go away or pretend it never happened, but it was clear that her own reaction to Mira was critical to how her daughter would perceive herself now. She was determined to get past her personal power struggle with Mira and find the right words.

In her quest, she sought out the privacy of the cold, dark night, the moon dancing in and out of the breeze blown pines gifting the air with their fragrance. She knew Black would be the only witness of her pleas to the unknown *higher power* she never before trusted to tell her the truth. Somehow even the stars seemed to intrude, close enough to hear the ugly beliefs in her heart.

Her soul searching brought the despicable truths of her inner-most soul blatantly to her awareness; since Mira was so much like her, how could Mira be perfect; how could she be deemed worthy of love and happiness? Of course she had to control Mira, mold her, make her into an acceptable, worthy person!

She punished Mira her whole life for being like her. She was the one who gave it to Mira – all the messages of unworthiness, not lovable, unclean, at fault. It was her own shame at being human, imperfect. And Mira became the sacrificial lamb to pay for the sins of the mother. Shame and remorse at the bitter truth burst from her heart, as she looked skyward and unabashedly cried out to the universe; "God, if you're there, let me see it differently. Let me know the truth. Please help me to help Mira!"

No sooner had she spoken the words than the familiar phrase in any language and religion, the very moral fiber of every civilization, the simple words she'd heard repeated so often as a child, came to her memory; "Love thy neighbor as thyself."

"This is my daughter, not my neighbor. My daughter, for God's sake," tore from her throat as if to prove she was always misunderstood by this unseen *God*, and her prayers were never really heard, much less answered.

Again, clearly, as if the wind was speaking to her, she heard, "Love thy neighbor as thyself."

"Damn you, damn you, damn you! You don't understand! She's my daughter, she's a part of me, my soul, myself." She screamed the desperate words as she fell to her knees, pounding her fists into the cold, unforgiving rocks, as if to force the earth to accept her soul-wrenching confession of every mother's agony; her daughter is a part of her, and she is a part of her mother, and her mother before her, and before her.

"Love thy neighbor as thyself," mocked her over and over as the message chanted through the tree tops, until the wind died down and the provoking calm allowed her to listen to the repeated pleas from the depths of her being; "Love thyself, love thyself, love thy neighbor as thyself, as thyself, as thyself, as thyself."

The clarity and simplicity of the message numbed and shocked her, and her hibernating soul was released from the confines of space and time, revealing the ancient memories of a forgotten spirit-bound past.

Once again she experienced the feelings of abandonment of being separated from her origin, her Creator, the casting away of spirit existence to accept the physical being, shame for not being perfect, somehow not worthy to be in the Creator's presence – a debilitating lie perpetuated by religions since life's most primitive existence, passed on by generations of fear at not being special – chosen. Man's timeless struggle.

It was the agreement, witnessed: the agreement with her creator in thinly veiled spiritual existence, to accept a physical body and experience life here on earth, with all memory of previous awareness eclipsed.

She knew it was her choice to be on earth at this time, birthed by her particular parents who were chosen to help her learn exactly what she needed to complete her journey, her life. She had always struggled to be more special – the favorite – the most loved, as countless generations before her – the birthmark of humanity. Now she saw why she couldn't love Mira unconditionally. She didn't love herself. And now she knew that Mira too, chose the perfect parents to learn and experience this life, as she'd agreed.

Now, the struggle could end and surrender could take its place in her heart. Instead of the painful memories, she was lovingly held in the lap of the Goddess, the Great Mother in Heaven, and delivered to the silent rhythm of soul renewal, the cycle of renewal that every woman knows; change, renewal – the natural rhythm of life.

She knew she would have the words to tell Mira, and felt her mother smiling in approval and love at her newly found reality. "Does every person have to discover this by themselves?"

Yes! The answer came to her heart like something she had always known down deep in the very fiber of her being – like a memory. Affirmation that she was not alone in this infinite universe, but was part of everything. She had to come to this awareness for herself, and now she knew the truth.

She didn't feel the cold of the night as she sat on the rocks, hugging her knees, allowing the divine intuition to envelope her, warm her, heal her. The truth became so obvious – like a veil lifted from her consciousness; she knew she was part of the plan; she didn't have to be perfect as there is no right or wrong way to do life; there only is, and she felt deeply loved just for being. And this is how it is now, her journey, her truth, her part in the plan.

Every star bore testimony to her awareness, and she felt an abiding peace and comfort as she returned to the welcome darkness of the cave. Quickly, she removed her outer clothes, slipped into the sleeping bag, and entered the deep sleep of the child, secure in the knowledge that its parents were close.

Morning came quickly, and the clear memory of the night before danced lightly in her heart. She was energized, anxious to embrace the day, a new day, a new life.

Her gaze fell on Mira, and for a long moment she allowed herself to feel the love, the honor of being her mother. "She is perfect exactly as she is. How could I have ever felt otherwise?" she thought, as her heart was filled with revelation, renewed hope and healing.

There was something different about Mira, and as she came closer, kneeling over her daughter, she was overcome with passionate tenderness. Sometime in the night, Mira performed the symbolic gesture – the most primitive act of grieving, of shame, of dishonor. She used the knife that Lalo had cut the lacing with and cut off all her long hair. Oh, the pain that replaced the lightness of her heart began to swell for her daughter, as she gathered her in her arms and the dormant tears of compassion and understanding flowed through her into her daughter.

How could this child know the ancient ritual of grief? Had all the earth's secrets been unlocked for discovery by those who survived that first day? Or was this part of the cycle of renewal, change – the rhythm of life? Whatever the reasoning, Suzan would be able to trust the process. She silently vowed to be there to help Mira, in any way she was allowed to transition the span from child to woman so abruptly forced upon her daughter.

She placed the leather moccasins her mom made them on their feet, and helping Mira up, wrapped her in the coyote cape of furs and led her daughter out of the cave and up the hill to the spring Jesse found. They sat viewing the sunrise and even though the morning breeze was cold, her heart was warmed by the understanding gift of the night before.

The chiseled beauty of her daughter struck her, as the last remnants of childlike features seemed to have vanished with the cutting of her long hair. Yes, they were women together. She hadn't noticed Mira mature so rapidly. Had she just refused to see the truth or was it part of the change, the renewal from that first day?

They sat by the stream until the sun was full above the horizon. At first Mira couldn't meet her mother's gaze and hung her head low. She wouldn't allow herself to face what she might see in her mother's eyes and Suzan understood. As she voiced what was in her heart and made amends to her daughter, assuring her of the love and compassion and esteem she felt for her, she recognized the love in her daughter's eyes. Their shame, unworthiness, blame and ignorance were washed away by soul cleansing tears, replaced by the acceptance, love and respect each saw in the other's eyes; a benediction to human suffering, a promise of hope.

This was all Mira ever wanted – to know she was loved and accepted by her mother. With swollen eyes and full hearts, they walked arm in arm down the hill and back to the others, who were just beginning their day.

Mira entered the cave first and the absence of her long hair was noticed immediately. She always used to brush the hair from her face to see, but now her features were in full view for everyone to witness. They saw the over-night transformation from child to woman, like the sleeping larvae crawled out of the cocoon just this morning, and returned as the butterfly. One by one the surprised voices turned to admiration and praise of her physical beauty. Mira was embarrassed by so much attention, but sat by the fire instead of returning to her sleeping bag where she'd been most of the time.

Jane and Ian offered to fix Mira a cup of coffee, which surprised her. She usually had to plead with her mother for a cup of the strong brew.

Jesse didn't say a word about his daughter's new look and didn't know if he liked it or not – but she hadn't asked his permission. Suzan's eyes told him something happened between mother and daughter that he couldn't even try to understand. Whatever it was – it was long overdue, and he knew it was good. Suzan's eyes held a wisdom he remembered from her mother's. Acceptance. Peace.

Jane knew something wonderful happened to Suzan and Mira the instant she saw them. "Sooner or later, it had to happen," she said, as she and Suzan hugged each other. Suzan sobbed into her shoulder and begged her sister to forgive her for the years of judgment and jealousy.

"There's nothing to forgive. I've loved you and wished I was like you all my life, but I'm not you, I'm Jane. The unearthing of awareness comes from within, happens to the best of us, if we're lucky. Mira's one lucky girl to have you for a mother, just like we are to have Mom."

Suzan was filled with new appreciation for her sister's journey and was again reminded that she was part of a bigger whole. The spirit of the earth, the stars and sun in the sky filled her again, as she became more aware that there is a plan, and if she stayed out of the way, it would be better than anything she could plan.

Laramie poured herself another cup of coffee and cuddled up next to Mira by the fireplace, as she witnessed the healing. Life was good. She watched Lalo gather up hunks of Mira's hair and cut a piece of his leather lacing to tie around them. She knew he would keep them forever – they were a part of Mira.

## *Chapter 14*

Early morning emotions became tranquil as the sisters and children headed up the hill to eat lunch by the stream. Hearts were light, spirits high, reverence for life and hope for the future incredibly increased.

The pale-yellow, winter sun shone indiscriminately, somehow forgetting the miracle of forgiveness witnessed only moments ago, allowing the details of light-giving to continue as if nothing had happened to interrupt its destined labor.

Suzan built a small fire to cook tortillas from the dough she'd made earlier, and the children were content to gather kindling and fill empty water jugs with Jane. Black gingerly trotted along to exercise his healing muscles, his sniffing nose raised skyward, then earthbound, to read the informing scents. They all relaxed when he curled up to rest under a pine, a short distance above them on the hill.

Laramie and Mira helped Lalo walk downstream, carrying the leather lacing wrapped around an Aspen limb, until they found a place deep enough to submerge the bundled limb, anchoring it with big rocks under the cold water. Laramie didn't know Lalo's plan for the lacing, but was touched by the tenderness between the two children. Or were they children? Mira glowed when Lalo whispered words of healing close to her ear. Laramie hoped she would live long enough to see the same love-filled adoration for her, in a man's eyes.

She'd tried to find the *right* man for her. She'd become disillusioned and discouraged after two separate attempts to build relationships. They both ended in heartbreak and painful loss, but also relief. For the last two years she'd kept pretty much to herself. Dating occasionally, always disappointed. The previous experiences taught her exactly what she would or wouldn't tolerate in a relationship. She'd learned she couldn't make a man become her dream and if she couldn't accept him exactly as he was, then she needed to get the hell out before falling into the pit of complacency, settling for less than the dream. She'd developed strong boundaries and knew her expectations were high but she was still young enough to believe her life-mate would be revealed at exactly the right time. She longed for the deep love that exists between two souls found, and the satisfying physical relationship that develops with the passionate living of life together. Oh, what a romantic she was. Were her expectations of the dream too much to hope for?

Mira offered her hand to help Laramie up from the comfortable rock where she'd been daydreaming – she and Lalo stood above her, with mirrored grins on their faces, as if they read her thoughts.

"Ah yes, I'm here again," she said, and dismissed the daydream. They identified the fresh tracks of deer, raccoon and rabbit as they walked upstream to return to the others.

Mira helped her mother make round tortillas as Lalo watched and eventually joined in. He couldn't remember ever feeling anything so soft as the pliant, white dough in his hands and played with it for so long, Suzan proclaimed it his. Soon, all the children squeezed their own piece of dough, turning them brown from the dirt on their hands; the pleasure well worth the sacrificed dough.

The day passed in quiet communion with each other. No one rushed the moments, disciplined the children, or discussed their fears. Even the children absorbed the tranquility, revealing the heightened level of bonding that transpired only yesterday while they watched Lalo cut the leather lacing. They felt like a family now, linked by newly revealed emotions and deep-felt compassion for each other.

“Jacinth?” Whispered Jen.

“What?”

Jen’s dark eyes glowed with secrecy. “We want to cut our hair short, too. Like Mira.”

“Why?” Jacinth searched the faces of Jen, Tara and Katie. “Mira thinks she looks funny, now.”

“But, that’s the point,” said Tara.

“Oh, I get it.” Jacinth whispered. “We’ll all look the same, so Mira won’t look funny?”

“No, silly, so she won’t feel different from everyone else. She’ll still look funny, but so will all the rest of us. It’ll be a way to show Mira we think she’s just fine like she is, because we’ll all look alike.”

“I don’t think my mom will let me cut my hair,” said Jacinth.

“That’s why it’s a secret.” Tara put her finger to her lips and disappeared. Soon, Levi’s knife lay on the ground in the center of the four girls.

“Hey,” whispered Jacinth. “Where did you get Levi’s knife? He never lets anyone use it, but me!”

“I told him you needed it for something special,” whispered Tara.

"Here, you go first," she said, handing the knife to Jacinth.

"No – I'm not going first. My mom will kill me. You go first."

"Okay, but, you'll have to go next, because you're the oldest."

It didn't take long for blonde, brown, red and black hair to lay in clumps on the ground. When Levi, Cody, Dominic, and Sara found them, Sara's hair was added to the pile. Next, Jacinth cut Levi's tail and the pile of hair soon grew to include Dominic's and Cody's. Now, they would all look like Mira.

"Where did the kids disappear to?" Suzan asked, taking the last tortilla off the griddle.

"I'll round them up, if you're ready to leave. They're down the hill by the stream." Laramie stretched and every muscle in her body screamed, reminding her of the frantic race up the mountain a few days ago to rescue Mira. Lalo and Mira followed her down the hill and found the giggling children huddled behind an outcrop of granite boulders. She gasped as the children tried to hide the pile of hair. Mira touched each of the shorn heads. Tears fell from her eyes as she sat on the ground in front of Jacinth and picked up handfuls of the honey colored hair that was her father's pride and joy. Jacinth's fearful stare slowly turned to a grin and Mira's arms encircled her sister's shoulders as a loud cheer erupted from the children. Lalo retrieved the knife and cut off his long hair, too. Laramie laughed while wiping tears from her face as the children ran up the hill to Suzan and Jane.

Jane was shocked, but recovered well. "I see the kids have solved the tangled hair problem."

"It was a little more than that. They . . ." started Laramie.

"They did it to support Mira," finished Suzan.

"You should have seen them. They were so scared." Laramie dumped the pile of hair on the ground and examined it closely. "Yes, I'd say this is ready to bury."

Suzan and Jane bent closer and saw the white specks on the dark strands. "Lice!"

"Yes, lice, body crabs, whatever we name them, they're with us now." Jane automatically scratched her head. "I don't know of a way to control it until we get to the ranch and can wash clothes and bedding frequently. It was bound to happen, sooner or later. Some of the kids may have had them before they joined us."

"Ugh!" Suzan picked up the pile of hair with a stick and examined it closely. "I can't stand the thought of crabs crawling all over my body. I don't care what they're called. Crabs, lice, I don't care." Suzan's high-pitched voice was laced with panic and Laramie began scratching her head.

"Do you think we have them, too?" Laramie asked while searching the hair on her arms.

"Well, if we don't now, we probably will before this is over," answered Jane casually. "And, believe me, you'll know it by the time they've settled in good."

"Check my hair," said Suzan. "Do you see anything?"

"Not yet," said Jane, "but every time you brush your hair with the same brush you've used on the kids, you'll be transporting them. And every time you wash the kids, you'll be stirring them up." Jane laughed. "Relax. We'll get rid of them when we get to the ranch. There's not a helluva-lot you can do about it now."

"What do you mean – relax?" Suzan was distraught. "What do people do to get rid of them?"

"There's medicine. Or you can use kerosene, like they used to before the medicine was discovered."

"My God. Why didn't I think of this? What can we do? I can't live with lice crawling all over me and everybody else."

"Can they make us sick?" asked Laramie.

"I never got sick from lice. They're a nuisance. A pest. I've seen sores on horses in stables from lice, but they go away as soon as the horses spend time outside and are kept groomed. I don't know if the birds pick them, or what, but, they're not visible anymore."

Suzan cringed. "I can't do this. I'm not going to get lice. I can't get lice!"

"Well, kids get lice!" Laramie meticulously picked through Jane's long blonde hair trying to detect anything white and crawly.

"Don't see anything in your hair either. Maybe we won't get them. The kids wallow all over Black and play in the dirt. We can't keep them as clean as we used to."

"We can't keep anything clean!" Suzan screamed hysterically. "I can't keep things clean without running water! There's never enough water!"

"Suzan, Suzan." Laramie put her arm around Suzan's shoulder and Suzan immediately pulled away.

"Don't touch me! And don't let those kids near me. I'm sick of having dirty hands all the time. And look at these fingernails!" She held dirty, ragged fingernails out for inspection. "I'm sick of trying to cook food and keep it clean before it gets eaten." She wrapped her arms tightly around herself and began crying and rocking. Laramie and Jane searched for the kids and were glad to see them playing down stream and away from earshot.

"We'll haul more water and start washing hair everyday, if that's what it takes." Laramie was beside herself and would do anything to comfort her sister.

"At least the hair is shorter now, and won't be as hard to care for," said Jane. We'll just wash it more often.

"Oh, God," cried Suzan, covering her face with her hands. "This is too hard. I don't want to do this anymore," she choked between sobs. "I can't stand wearing dirty clothes all the time. I want it to be like it was before."

"Well, it's not!" Laramie put her arm around Suzan and this time she didn't pull away. "This is how it is now. But we can do this. We have to do this. We want to live and we want the kids to live. It won't always be like this." Laramie's soft voice calmed Suzan. "When we get to the ranch, we'll find a new way to live." She brushed Suzan's hair back from her face. "You'll see. It will get better."

"Should we chop our hair off, too?" Laramie looked at Jane.

"No, I don't think it's necessary, yet. If we keep it braided and try to wash it more often, we should be okay. If we get them, we'll deal with it then."

"Let's check the kids. Maybe they don't all have them." Suzan's thinking began to clear and she was determined to keep them from spreading to everyone.

The kids were gathered and Laramie used Lalo's knife to try to even up the crude haircuts. She searched all ten heads and soon, every head was cropped close and only four of the kids had the white parasites in their hair. Jane explained what they were looking for and that it was not something to be afraid of. It would all be better soon. She showed them how to check each other and they were satisfied to learn that all their favorite animals got them, too. Jacinth was horrified to learn her head harbored the crawly critters and was glad her hair was short now. Suzan hugged her daughters and was glad that for whatever reason, the kids thought of cutting their hair.

On inspection, they all looked adorable with their short haircuts. The sisters wondered why they hadn't thought of it themselves. Clear faces shone below dark or light hair, allowing full view of innocent eyes and proud smiles.

"I guess I should be thankful they're all so healthy. I can't imagine what we'd do if any of them got sick."

"I'm glad you're feeling better." Laramie buried the infested hair while Suzan started gathering the supplies they'd hauled up the hill.

"I still don't like being dirty." She laughed. "But, I'll try not to become a basket-case in the meantime."

By the time they were ready to leave, each person carried a bundle of wood, water or tortillas. Suzan watched admiringly as Mira's tall, slender form walked ahead of her, helping Lalo down the hill. When did she become so beautiful?

"She's a picture of royalty," said Jane.

"Yes, what treasures we have, and we don't really even realize it. Something has happened, Jane, more than I experienced on the rock last night. Something magical is happening to all of us. I feel it."

"I think we all feel it, a kind of knowing, an awareness, something. I can't quite put a word to it, but it's getting stronger in all of us, every day. Almost as if we're being allowed to work through our deepest fears and emotions in a matter of days, rather than the lifetime it would have taken before, to untangle the jumbled mess of the baggage of our lives."

"I know – I sense it in the children, too. It's happening more naturally and subtly with them, probably because they don't have so much *excess baggage* to untangle."

"They accept the power they feel." Jane became thoughtful. "They don't question their intuition. They haven't lived long enough to become cynical, like the rest of us untrusting, adult, *experts* on life," Jane added. "They're on automatic pilot, listening to a different drummer, not filtering from heart to head like the rest of us have learned to do, denying our own intuition."

"That's it exactly. I've been thinking about it all day, and you've said it perfectly. When did you get so smart?" she joked, as they entered the cave, laughing together.

Ah, the smell of coffee, thought Jane as she succumbed to the scent of Ian's aromatic brew. Every time she smelled it, the rich essence sliced wide swaths for sweet, new memories in her heart, graciously replacing the old worn-out pain she'd hung onto long past its usefulness. Ian had a gourmet distinction when it came to coffee and made the best she'd ever tasted. But it wasn't about coffee. It was about Ian. Her feelings for him intensified with each passing day and it was going way too fast for her to hold onto. Time seemed to have no connection to the awareness of the spirit – time was either standing still or going full speed ahead, not waiting for earth to turn, moon to draw, or sun to mark the day.

Ian watched her through the diminishing light of dusk, and he knew her struggle with time going too fast. He never had the, *eat, drink, and be merry, for tomorrow we may die,* attitude toward life. He was much too pragmatic and organized for that. Every detail of his life was thoughtfully planned and placed in its proper place for his determination later – usually much later. Everything was different now, not neatly predictable as his black on white life of before. Now there was no need. Time was no longer dictating when to sleep, wake, eat, play and sleep, again – or when to love. There were no deadlines, or rush to discover, no urgencies pushing his mind's clock.

The one event he'd tried to predict happened without his permission and it wouldn't allow him the satisfaction of knowing its time. Time – the puppet-master. He'd spent ten years of his life buried in research and the recording of facts, and when he'd least expected it, all the facts and research didn't help a mite to prevent it or prepare for it. The only advantage for the sacrificed years was knowledge of what really happened, and it didn't change a thing. In fact, if truth be known, it was a bloody let down, not having to worry about it anymore; the after-shock, depression of its loss left an empty space where his work had been, but filled him with respect for the art of real living.

After all the years of research he'd learned with a certainty that all the scientists in the world couldn't alter the earth's course. Her spiritual energy was much more significant than could be proven by scientific fact-finding. His research left him with a great respect for the earth's spirit and survival capabilities. He watched her react to the collective negative energy and knew she felt a heartbeat of her own – life's natural rhythm. She would save herself, as she had so many times before.

He was shocked to discover that he felt much more alive when faced with the reality of death than when lost in the mundane routine of life. "There's so much freedom when listening to the natural rhythm of life – all you have to do is honor it, follow it, obey your heart." He spoke to Jane's soul, hoping she would somehow feel his heart-felt plea. He knew her struggle, lacking trust when it came to following her own heart. She did a good job of turning it off, that's for sure, he thought, remembering all that Red shared with him, much more than he'd cared to know then. Her past was none of his business, but now he was glad he knew the details. It helped him understand her caution.

Jane was so strong a woman, not in the bellicose, brutal sort of way he'd come to loath in so many women of the outback – something to prove – manless, but womanless, too. No, Jane was much too passionate and full of life to have to prove she could do it better than a man, even though she preferred to appear that way sometimes – wearing the attitude like armor. She'd overcome so many obstacles in her life that would have finished off most women or beaten them into submission. But not his Janie – not by a long-shot. He felt her passion rise with his own, the longing of her desire and the love in her heart. He hoped and prayed she could let go, trust the rhythm.

He would wait. He'd vowed he wouldn't push her. He was certain they were destined to do this together, whatever *this* was. Why did she hinder herself with time? For him, he'd decided; no more marching to the drum of the clock tick-tocking. It's not about time, Janie. Now it's about life. He willed her to feel his thoughts as he could hers.

She watched his eyes watching her. Life is happening, it's not about time anymore. The thought was sweet. Her gaze still held his hazel-green eyes.

Yes Janie girl! Trust your intuition! Trust life! Trust your heart! She was responding to his thoughts, her heart yielding to inner truth like a forgotten memory found.

I trust him with all my heart, she thought. All I have to do is let the fear go, feel his heart beat with my own, trust life. He grasped her outstretched hand in his as they both arose and walked hand-in-hand from the cave, greeted by the cooling air as the sun's last glimmer sank behind the mountain. They walked the short distance up the hill and Ian wrapped the sleeping bag he'd grabbed around their shoulders as they sat on the very rock where Suzan sat the night before. Moments of silence passed between them, as they quietly absorbed the silent communication, allowing the presence of deep-felt love to fill their longing hearts. His arm around her shoulder felt right – it really belonged there, and she allowed the emotion to warm her heart and body.

Ian stood, and holding both of her hands, lifted her to her feet, pulling her into his arms. He held her to him, relishing the feel of this woman so close against him. The softness and warmth of her body quickened the rush of his blood. He buried his face in her flowing hair and drank in her scent. He breathed in the perfume of her desire, and it filled his veins with the ancient rhythm of yearning.

Her body responded with arousal of urgent passion so long denied, liberating her from all restraint and inhibition as she sought the taste of his hungry mouth and exquisitely salty skin. They breathed each other's breaths as intoxicated desire surrendered.

The long-controlled demands of body and heart were explosively obeyed as the crescent moon stood watch in the night sky, and low-lying clouds offered their blanket of protection as the emotion filled rocks warmed the fervent flesh of lovers, drunk with sensuous satisfaction.

When hunger abated and urgency calmed, heart and body reached out again in slow, tender, rhythmic waves of passion, releasing affirmation of completeness as their sweet lovemaking surrendered to serene fulfillment.

They lay entangled in each other's arms while body calmed and blood cooled, allowing the intensity of the night to abate and stars to reclaim their brilliance. Clouds departed and winter cold replaced the moon as the most prominent guest, as Jane snuggled closer and laid her head on Ian's chest to listen to the promise of his heartbeat. Never before had she so totally belonged anywhere as she felt at this moment, here on this rock, with this man. All of her was present. Every molecule of her body was alive, every color of her soul created a kaleidoscope of vivid awareness.

She didn't have words to tell him, but he felt the poetry of her heart and foreign tears crept down his cheeks in quiet gratitude that he trusted life long enough to be placed here and now with this woman – his Janie. Life or death, no longer a threat or promise; but now, he didn't want to miss a single second of his future with her. "Thank you, God, and I know you're there," the scientist from Sydney, Australia, whispered softly in the dark.

"Yes, thank you, God, and I know you're there," Jane whispered back. As reluctant as they were to leave this magical place in the night, they were forced to concede to the sharp night air and return to the warmth of the cave. "I hate to leave here. I wish the night would never end, but I can't stand to be cold," she said in whispers, hoping she wouldn't wake the others, as they stood at the entrance of the cave.

Holding her shoulders, he searched her face intently, their declaration of love reflecting in each other's eyes, as he vowed, "Janie girl, from this night forward, you are my wife, and I hope you'll have me as your mate, forever." His voice broke with emotion. "The promise of this night is just beginning, and you won't ever have to be cold again."

On tiptoe, she placed her lips on his and softly said, "You are my husband and I will be your mate forever."

Quietly, they entered the cave and tried not to disturb the sleeping group as they zipped their sleeping bags together and shared what remained of the night, in satisfied, peaceful sleep in the comfort of each other's arms.

Night was too short and dreams too quickly played themselves through Jesse's mind. He stood outside the cave as early morning dawn turned darkness to light. He knew they must leave the safety and warmth of the cave. A lot of healing happened here. He couldn't explain it, but was happy he felt it. The air seemed cleaner now, and somehow, the future seemed brighter. His heart was changing, too.

Mistrust turned to faith that they made the right decision, in spite of the tragedies.

Being found in the snowstorm by the old woman and her cat, going through the center of the tunnels, finding the cave, Lalo rescuing Mira from probable death, the children, cutting their hair – everything. It made him believe that they were being guided and watched over. He felt it in even the smallest decisions, like whether to stay another day. He knew they had to leave. Winter would trap them here if they didn't move on and he felt the next few days would be good for traveling. They would pack up today, and leave early in the morning. He knew it was time.

His decision was met with mixed emotion. Of course they wanted to stay a few more days. All of them, for different reasons, would take their own special memories of the cave. It was a place of miracle healing and revelation. Mira's brutal attack definitely traumatized all of them, but Mother Earth offered her protected warm belly for their healing. He hated to admit that Lalo was the one who saved Mira's life and the only person she responded to. Lord knows he tried to comfort his daughter, but he felt so inadequate. He couldn't imagine her nightmares and memories, but he saw the life in her eyes when Lalo was near her. Thank God he'd been there that night.

While the sisters gathered and packed supplies, Lalo and Mira walked up the hill to retrieve the submerged log with the leather lacing. It was heavy with the weight of the water, but they carried it between them down the hill until they found the perfect group of pine trees. Lalo carefully stretched the lacing around the four trunks, careful to allow for good air circulation. The lacing would be exposed to the sun most of the day and with only one day left, it would have to dry in a hurry. That would be enough time to stretch the narrow laces, and hopefully dry enough to carry out his plan.

Cody worked hard to whittle the piece of Ash branch to Lalo's specifications. By the end of the day the whittled parts were complete. The children were curious to learn about the project, but Lalo was secretive, assuring them they would all know about his plan in a couple of days.

Mira never left Lalo's side and hovered over him like the mother he'd lost so young. He rarely thought about his life before the streets of Denver, but nightmares still brought vivid reality to the faces of his sister and mother, even though they'd been dead for seven years. If he'd been older, he could have killed the man and saved his mother and sister. His mother forced him to leave them in the dimly lit warehouse basement. Sitting back-to-back she had untied his hands and then his ankles. His fingers were not strong enough to pry the knots from around his mother's wrists. She made him tear the long chain from around her neck where she kept her wedding rings – the ones Lalo now wore around his neck on a new chain. She told him to sell them to buy food to stay alive. He never did. She squatted down and made him climb up on her shoulders and then she stood tall so he could reach the locked window while the man was in the other room hurting his sister. She made him promise to run far away and not tell anyone his name, or the bad man would find him and take him back to the room. He knew they were dead because he saw pictures in the newspaper and the story that they were hunting for him. They didn't find him and soon assumed him dead, as well. Mira touched his shoulder and jolted him from the ugly memory.

Would she ever speak again? Would he ever hear her say his name? He looked into her innocent, questioning eyes and again saw the reflection of his own soul. "I'm okay. Just bad memories." He traced a smile on her face. He loved to touch her. "Don't worry," he said. "Everything is okay."

He put his arm around her shoulder and headed back to the cave. His ribs felt better today. Maybe they weren't broken after all. Probably just bruised. It was easier to walk. Tomorrow, before they left, they would come back and get the lacing.

Suzan sat on the rock and knew she would survive the dirt, the critters and the weather. She vowed to help her daughter work through the brutal attack that stole her childhood. She said a prayer of gratitude for Lalo and thanked the Gods that his attraction to Mira was honorable and spiritual, and knew he was sent to save her daughter and help her recover. She prayed for her and Jesse and an end to their years of strife and struggle for control and respect. Now, the struggle to survive became the goal and each person's strength was respected and necessary to win the battle.

After dinner of tortillas and meat, and all the coffee was gone, Ian and Jane retreated to the rock to rejoice in two hearts found. Her passion matched his in every way. Had love ever been so beautiful?

"I wish we could stay here forever," Jane said, as she snuggled closer to him.

"Wherever we are together will be fine with me, Janie, girl. I can't get enough of you. Even though I know it's so much more than physical, it feels electric – filled with energy." He searched for the words. "I've never experienced anything like this before. Our electrical impulses and energies are talking to each other. It's phenomenal."

"That's why I don't ever want to leave. Maybe it's the place. The rock."

"The nights are getting colder, that's why we have to leave."

"Does that mean the honeymoon will be over when we have to leave?" she teased.

"As far as I'm concerned, the honeymoon hasn't even begun yet and will never be over."

"Do you really think it's related to the earth's energy field?" Jane traced his lips with her finger.

"I definitely believe people's energy is relating to the earth's energy in a brand new way, and," he whispered, "I personally like it very much. I can't imagine my life without you now. I knew it from the first moment I laid eyes on you – you were a woman I would love to know. Now, you are my woman for as long as you'll have me. I've never felt more alive."

"I'll miss this rock. We'll have to come back again, someday, just to tune-up our energy." Jane shivered. "Oh, it's much colder tonight than I remember last night being."

"Yes, Jesse's probably right to suggest we move off this mountain in the morning. But I'm with you – I'll miss this rock, too. I've felt its heartbeat. It's made a believer out of me." Ian got serious, with a far-off look in his eyes. "I've searched for you my whole life, and now that I've found you, I don't ever want to lose you."

"I'm not going anywhere, Mister Jayne. Like I said, I'd be happy if we could stay here forever. I don't want this to ever end."

"The stars are beautiful here, but a little cloud cover would warm us right up."

"Well, we can't have everything," she teased. "I'm satisfied with stars." She knelt down and picked up a small stone from a crack in the rock, "I'm taking my own piece of the rock so we can have it with us wherever we go."

"Oh Janie, I wish I could show you the world. I wish I could lavish you with diamonds, and jewels, and fur coats, and spoil you extravagantly. I've never felt so much love from one human being, as I feel from you!"

"Thank you, Ian . . . for loving me. I haven't said the words *I love you* to a man for so long, they sound foreign, but the feelings are wonderful. I never thought I would ever feel like this." She reached her arms around his neck. "I do love you. I didn't think I could love a man like this. I'm glad to know I can. Thank you for loving me."

Tears fell from Ian's eyes as he held her. He'd never felt happier or more alive.

Lalo and Mira reached the stand of pines just as the sun rose over the mountain. Leather lacing stretched around the pines felt cold but not wet. They carefully unwound the lacing and cut it exactly in half and cut it again until eight strips of equal length lie side by side. Lalo took the two pieces of Ash limb Cody had so gladly whittled and carefully wove back and forth around one of them while Mira kept the strips from tangling, until the wood piece was completely encased in woven lacing. He explained to Mira what he was doing as he worked. Then, he carefully butted the two pieces of limb together and completed the lacing until a sturdy handle was crafted with long leather strips dangling.

"There." He rolled the dangling strips around a small limb. "While it continues to dry, it will become tight around the wood. That's what the old woman in my dream told me." He admired the weaving. "It will make a perfect handle." He took Mira's hand and led her back down the hill to the cave. "We can work on this while we travel. Each morning and night, we'll weave until it's finished. I'll teach you how to do it." Mira glowed with excitement at the chance to learn the weaving.

Black met them as they neared the cave. He felt the excitement of departure and anxiously paced back and forth on the trail, ready to get going again. The group silently looked around, feeling the protective serenity and the great healing that had happened while there. Suzan sat on the rock as Jesse and Ian tightened the travois and catamaran. Jane soon joined her and together they silently relived the comfort and love they had both found.

It was much easier traveling downhill. Spirits were high and no one complained. Muscles developed where soft parts had been which made their loads seem lighter. Black's injuries were nearly healed and Lalo didn't let his painful ribs take away from the joy he felt at being allowed by destiny to be a part of Mira's life. Their love for each other was apparent to everyone as they walked hand in hand down the road.

Jesse knew they were close to Vail and hoped there wouldn't be any trouble along the way. Lack of food and supplies would be the problem, as it was everywhere. The few grocery stores in the mountain towns had been emptied long ago. He understood their fear – he felt it, too – the need to protect what few provisions and belongings they still had left.

They camped just east of the wealthy ski resort. Jesse could see the town below and felt the uneasy fear that belied the peaceful looking valley. Snow capped mountains dropped fingers of snow into gullies and motionless ski lifts now marked lifeless trails.

Lalo and Mira huddled in a blanket and wove the long strips of leather lacing. Lalo sat behind Mira and encircled her in his arms as he guided her fingers to learn the weaving. He whispered healing words and softly sang a song that he remembered his mother singing to him as a child. Mira learned the song and as the children joined in the circle around them, they too, joined in the singing.

*I am with you in the dark of night and in the light of day.*

*The light of love will show the way and fear of night will fade away.*

*Don't be afraid. Don't be afraid.*

*The light of love will show the way.*

Suzan was sure she knew the song. It filled the heart and haunted the memory, searching for a forgotten time. The melody was the last thing she heard before drifting to sleep and reached her ears before morning light – Mira and Lalo were at their weaving early.

As Vail grew closer, Jesse's fear grew stronger. They met no travelers heading east and saw very little movement from houses as they silently pushed their carriers down the highway.

Suddenly, four armed men emerged from an underpass where a small fire burned and a coffeepot with mugs sat on the rocks. They sure didn't look like a community welcoming committee.

"Hold up there," hollered one of the men as he opened his jacket and displayed what appeared to be a sheriff's badge. "I'm the local sheriff here, and you'll need to pull off the road under here and let us search your belongings."

"Why the search?" Ian eyed the man warily as he held his rifle ready.

"Several break-ins have happened and we're trying to recover the stolen goods," said a yellow-haired man.

"But we haven't even stopped in the town. We're just passing through." Jesse eyed the other two men as they poked at the parachute-covered catamaran with the barrels of their rifles.

"Don't matter." The man with the badge spat chewing tobacco at Jesse's feet. "Start unloading."

"We're not unloading anything and the first one of you who touches any of our possessions will get a bullet in his head." Jesse pointed his rifle at the man with the badge and Ian aimed towards the two inspecting their supplies.

"Hey, Jed. They've got a parachute." The two men eyed the sisters. "That ain't all they've got."

"We're just passing through – on our way to California where it's warm. We don't want to have to kill anyone to get there." Ian's eyes penetrated the younger man until he backed away from the supplies.

"All we've got are the few belongings we were able to carry with us. We've been hunting along the way for food and don't have anything you'd be interested in enough to die for."

"Now, look here mister. You talk funny and I don't like you, but I'm the law here and ain't no one going to die." As he stepped forward, Jesse raised his rifle to the man's chest.

"I don't know who you are to be calling yourself sheriff, but I'll blow a hole through your heart if you take one more step." Jesse's insides shook, but his rifle didn't waver.

"Looks like we're going to have to do this the hard way, then." He waved at the yellow haired man. "Start unloading Lendle."

The man looked at the barrel of Ian's rifle pointing at his chest. "Let them pass. They got kids with them." He stared at the kids huddled close to the women.

"Jerry!" The man yelled. "Shoot him."

The sullen man standing close to Lendle took a step forward and Ian's rifle exploded as he shoved another bullet into the chamber. "Who's next?"

The man fell and grabbed his foot, writhing and screaming in pain.

"Damn! You didn't have to shoot him. We need your supplies." The *sheriff* rushed to the bleeding man. "Take him down the hill and pull that boot off him before his foot swells and we have to cut it off." The other two men helped the injured man down the hill

"I told you we had to hunt to eat." Ian eyed the big man. "You've got weapons and there's plenty of game."

"Yea, we've got weapons, but we don't have ammunition." He cocked his gun and revealed an empty chamber. "Been out of ammunition for nearly two weeks. Was hoping you were just bluffing."

"Why in bloody-hell are you pointing empty guns at people?" Ian shouted. "I could have killed that man." He pushed the big man wearing the badge. "I would have shot you next."

Jesse couldn't believe his ears. It was ludicrous. They were in fear for their lives and were ready to kill or die to protect their belongings and the women and children.

"Jerry and I had a reloading set-up, but looters took everything," the man started. "By the time I figured out that whatever happened wasn't going away, there wasn't a bullet in this town, or anyone willing to part with the ones they had."

Jesse untied the travois. "Anyone got a 30.06?"

"Two of us do." The big man couldn't believe these strangers were going to part with ammunition.

Jesse handed him a box of bullets taken from the cabin. "Here. I hope there's a good shot among the four of you. It's all we can spare."

"I'm sorry we scared you," he said, placing the box in his jacket pocket. "There's plenty of scared folks all down this valley. Seems like everyone who's come through has been hungry, cold, and scared to death of what's going to happen next."

"I guess the whole world is pretty scared, but the only thing that's going to happen next is we're going to re-build and learn to live off the land again." Ian walked down the embankment to check on the injured man. The two outside toes on his left foot were missing and a few bones looked shattered. "It could have been worse," said Ian. "I obviously didn't want to hurt you too bad, or you'd be dead. It'll take a couple weeks to heal, but you'll be okay if you clean it good and watch for infection." Ian looked at the pain filled face. Do you have alcohol and bandages?"

"Yea," he sputtered. "Back at the cabin."

"Well, you better wrap something around that so you don't bleed to death."

"Come on!" Ian shouted. "Let's get going."

"Will he be okay?" Asked Jesse.

"Oh, he'll live. Won't win any foot races though. The bones are pretty shot up. No telling how far they'll have to dig to get out all the fragments. Can't believe my shot was so far off at such close range though. I aimed for his ankle."

"Come on. It's safe. We can go now," Jesse told the kids. "The man will be okay." He walked ahead and Ian took up the rear, rifles ready. "I can't believe it," whispered Jesse.

Light snow started falling late that afternoon and continued for the next four days. The going was slow and dangerous. Vail Valley was dotted with small mountain communities and everyone viewed them as a threat or prey, and many did have ammunition for the guns they carried. No one really wanted to kill or die and bartering was refined to a pure science.

By the time they reached Glenwood Canyon, Suzan's plum jelly was gone, Jane's stash of flint rock was diminishing, and cigarettes were hard fought to part with, but were as precious as ammunition when it came to bartering.

## *Chapter 15*

It took a week for Dan and Roma to build the new chicken house. It was slow going at first. They used one side of the tack shed as the back and Dan created a large roving cage that could be moved to new pecking grounds and re-attach to the main coop at night. The chickens especially liked being over the garden spot to peck the seeds and remnants of last summer's harvest.

Roma was distracted. She knew their family was coming. At night she fought recurring dreams of lights and shadows that left her puzzled during the day. She struggled to reach the light and never quite recognized the shadows. She knew they were trying to reach the light, too, but couldn't see their faces and longed to know who they were. Sometimes she felt she was traveling with her children, every step of the way. It seemed she knew when they were in danger and when they struggled. When she felt her own spirit sag, she prayed to all the powers that be to protect her children. When she felt their spirits give up, she rushed her energy and encouragement to them. Sometimes the feelings were so strong she just wanted to get on a horse and go find them – help them get home safely.

Dan felt helpless to comfort her. He knew she felt things and understood things of the spirit that he didn't even try to comprehend. She'd eventually work it out, but was a strange one in the meantime. He often watched her moving through the rooms, touching things, moving plants, taking inventory of spices, soaps, medical supplies and he didn't even ask about the two gallon jar of cigarettes on the kitchen counter. He quit trying to figure her out a long time ago. He was just grateful they were still sharing their lives together. Their struggle had been hard and long, but they'd survived each other. He couldn't deny that life with Roma was exciting, and she could still walk across the room and stir his blood. Damnedest thing! He could be mad as hell at her and leave the house and miss her terribly. Any time he saw the sun rise or set, or game crossing the valley, he wanted to share it with Roma, like her presence somehow made it real or more beautiful.

In spring they would walk the ranch to find new shoots of wildflowers or a new family of fox kits and listen to the forlorn mating call of nighthawks diving through the sky. Elk bugle in the fall, rabbits screeching under eagle's shadow, puma's mournful cry in heat – all the sounds and colors and scents of life delighted Roma, and Dan's delight was living close to her. At night Roma slept as close as she could possibly get to Dan. When he rolled over, she rolled next to him, when she turned, Dan rolled next to her – a constant loving, touching ritual in the night that healed the past and blessed their days.

And where was she off to, now? "Where you going?"

"Well, I don't know. Guess I'll just walk down the valley a ways. Don't you hear anything, like a low, mournful wail?"

Dan listened for sounds on the wind. "No, only the crows and those screws rolling around in your head," Dan teased.

"Wish I could hear the screws instead of some of the things I hear."

"Do you want me to go with you?"

"No, Trouble will find me. I won't be alone."

"Well, don't go getting yourself into something you can't get out of. My hip feels a storm coming. Next day or two we'll see snow fly, I'm sure."

"I'm just going down the valley. Be gone a couple hours maybe – not overnight. Now that the chickens are happy, I can think of other things and I just want to find what that sound is."

"I'll skin that rabbit I shot and start the fire for supper. Feels like it's been a long day already."

"I'll be home by dark. Don't worry."

Dan watched her jump the creek and saw Trouble parallel her from the scrub oak. That wolf-breed always knew where Roma was. Guess that pup was a good thing, after all, thought Dan. "No one around to complain about her chasing game since we're all chasing game, now," he said out loud.

Roma listened for the sounds on the wind. She couldn't remember where she'd heard it before, but now it haunted her. Mournful sounds, like grieving. Soft grieving. Copper reeds lined the ice-fringed creek, contrasting with the gray remnants of sagebrush. Roma prayed the kids would make it before bitter cold enclosed the valley in hibernation.

She was getting closer, and could see Trouble perk up her ears. The sound was definitely coming from an animal – a low moaning.

Hilda Ranzenberger's heifers grew larger as the sound became more distinct. Maybe one of the calves was in trouble. Turkey buzzards and magpies circled overhead and spotted the ground. The large red cow with the white face and legs, pushed against the fence and whined her mournful cry over the dead calf now bloating with decay. "Oh dear." Roma saw the engorged udder and huge teats dripping their milk on the ground.

"Well, mamma. You're in a fine mess." Roma circled the cow and knew she had to do something to relieve her.

"C'mon, girl. Walk away from that baby. I can help you if you'll let me." Roma almost lost her lunch when the foul smell reached her. The buzzards were bold and didn't want to leave their feast. She stood twenty feet from the cow and continued to talk softly. "God knows I'm crazy and I haven't ever milked a cow, but I'll sure try. Just come. I can't help you while you're pushing against that fence and standing over that carcass with all them buzzards around." Roma tried to make the clicking sounds she'd heard Hilda make. "C'mon, girl. That's not your baby anymore. It belongs to the earth now." She found a long willow branch and swatted the cow's rump to get it to move.

"Come on. That's it. Come away from the fence so I can help you. That's it, girl."

The large cow seemed too big a challenge for Roma, but she couldn't just leave her in the shape she was in. "Now, God help me, I'm going to try to relieve your milk. I do know that's what has to be done to make you feel better." Trouble lay twenty feet away, apprehensively watching from the brush. Roma told her to stay and hoped she wouldn't try to eat any of that carcass. She patted the cow's rump trying to decide which side was correct. "I hope it doesn't matter. Hang in there with me girl." She grabbed the soft engorged teat and squeezed as she pulled down slightly, as she'd watched Hilda do. A painful bellow loudly erupted and the cow pulled her back leg up. "Now, don't go kicking me. We've got to cooperate here. I don't know what I'm doing, and you obviously know now, too, but we'll try again." She firmly clenched two of the teats in her hands and squeezed and pulled and squeezed and pulled. Finally, steady streams of the white liquid splattered the ground and formed a steamy puddle. Trouble ventured closer and began lapping at the rich milk until she had her fill. Roma pulled and squeezed all the teats until she couldn't coax any more milk out. "Good grief, girl, you must have had a gallon or more all packed up there." She brushed her hands together and felt pretty pleased with herself. "I did it." She laughed and patted the cow's rump. "I mean, we did it."

The red heifer mooed contentedly as Roma walked from one side to the other. "Well, Bessie, I see you'll have to make a decision here. You can stay and get in the same shape again, or you can come home with me and I'll just keep milking you everyday." She petted the cow's large shoulders. "I sure would like having fresh milk, cream and butter, but as you can see, I'm not used to this and you're not really my cow." Roma walked a few feet down the valley. "C'mon, Bessie. I know Hilda won't mind you coming to my house. I'll take good care of you. You can have a covered stall all to yourself and share the corral with Litany and Rendi. You'll still be grazing the same valley."

The large animal didn't move. "C'mon, Bessie. Oh, you don't like the name Bessie?" Roma thought of all the names she would call a cow. "How about Alice?" The cow didn't move. "What about Maggie?" She slowly started forward. "All right, Maggie. C'mon home!"

Trouble raced ahead to scout the trail beside the creek that wound down the middle of the valley. Roma walked a slow pace clicking like Hilda, with Maggie close behind.

Dan couldn't believe his eyes. Dan thought cattle were the dumbest animals alive, but Roma hadn't taken a rope with her so that cow must be following. "Milk cows must be a lot smarter than range cows," he speculated.

"What have you got here?" Dan flipped back his hat and whistled.

"She lost her calf and we'll be able to use the milk. Wouldn't it be great to have butter and cream year round?"

"And who's going to milk her everyday?" Dan was grinning from ear to ear. He knew Roma was afraid of horses and cows.

"I just milked her in the field and she let go with a gallon or more."

"You milked her? In the field?" Dan could hardly believe it.

"Yes, I milked her." Now Roma wore the grin.

"Well, she's probably on her way to drying up if her calf died."

"If I milk her morning and night it should build her back up. Even if we have to throw it out, she should be producing pretty good by the time the kids get here."

"Well, I'll be damned." Dan slapped the cow's rump. "I don't believe she just followed you home."

"Her name's Maggie." Roma walked to the corral and opened the gate to the stall and brought in hay. "Can we hay her for a couple days?"

"Maggie?"

"Yes, Maggie. I figure if we hay her here, after a few days, she'll know where to go to be milked and she'll come on her own – won't she?"

"I'll bet she will if you tell her to." Dan just shook his head. Roma never ceased to amaze and surprise him.

"That rabbit's nearly done and there's coffee on the stove." Dan put his arm around Roma's shoulders and they walked back to the house. "I still don't believe it."

"I'm going to the camp tomorrow," Dan said, in between bites of rabbit and biscuits. "Do you want to come with me?"

"Why?"

"I thought you might enjoy the ride, if the weather holds."

"No, I mean, why are you going?"

"Now don't start in, Roma. I want to make some kind of peace with that outfit. I don't like feeling worried about my neighbors. I want to ride into town to get seed, if there's any left. I want to check on Gus and Hilda and some other folks around. I don't want to be a prisoner on my own ranch."

"Well, did you want to invite them to dinner, or what?" She had that smirk on her face.

"That might not be a bad idea," Dan said triumphantly. "Now that you brought it up, that's a hell of an idea."

"No way. I'm not inviting any of them to come snoop around here and decide what they want or think they need." Dinner was over, as far as Roma was concerned. She grabbed a cigarette and poured another cup of coffee.

"I was thinking more of cooking them dinner at their place. Maybe take some eggs and butter, and a pail of fresh milk." Dan saw her eyes soften. "Barter with them. Make them see the outside can be of value to them. Maybe they can become a working part of the community, now that all has been forgiven and no one knows what the score is anymore."

"Well, it's a long-shot, but it might work. I'd like to tell Hilda about her calf and see if she minds if we keep the cow. I didn't see any sign they'd been in the pasture, but their other heifers and calves are doing fine." She barely whispered, "I'm worried about Gus and Hilda – not hearing anything from them or seeing any sign they'd been to check their herd." It wasn't like them. "If those men at the camp have kept them from passing on the road or hurt those two old folks, heaven help them – the whole town will be down on them."

"That's exactly what we have to avoid," said Dan, relieved that Roma didn't put up a battle.

"Okay, then. I guess I would like to go." Roma hoped Victor wouldn't be interested in stopping their coming and going and that Rafa was still there.

Fog hung low in the valley and the cold, biting air reminded Dan and Roma that sub-freezing temperatures would soon be on them. Litany and Rendi's breath steamed from their nostrils as they broke into a soft gallop down the dirt road. Trouble crossed in front of them and Roma was glad she was close.

Roma said a Maggie prayer while remembering their milking time this morning. There wasn't nearly as much milk as before. How long had her calf been dead? Surely she wouldn't be drying up already? Well, prayer can heal anything or anyone – even cows, thought Roma. "God bless Maggie. And I'll just keep milking her."

"Hilda's herd looks good. That calf has only been dead five or six days so her milk should be okay. If you talk real nice to her." Dan frequently teased Roma about her conversations with the wildlife, but inside him he knew there was something special and kinda weird about the way animals responded to her – like they really could understand what she said. And she just talked to them like they understood every word.

He remembered one day, last summer. It was late in the day when Roma watered the strawberries. He was sitting on the porch, reading the paper when the doe and fawn approached to within fifty feet of Roma. He heard her talk to that doe like they were sitting at the kitchen table over a cup of coffee. "Now, I know what you're here for, and I don't blame you one bit. They're the best crop I've ever had." He watched her slowly put the hose down, stoop through the gate and slowly go from one plant to another until her shirt was full of the ripe berries. "I don't mind sharing, but you can't have them all. I imagine you've been bringing your fawns here for dessert every summer." She dumped the strawberries in a pile twenty feet from the fenced plants and slowly backed away, all the while talking to the doe and its fawn, who hadn't moved a muscle. "These are for you and your baby." She picked up the hose and continued her watering. "When I pick berries, I'll share, but you can't have them all." The sight mesmerized Dan. Roma just kept watering and the doe and her fawn inched forward in halted steps like two street mimes. The doe ate a few and then called her fawn to eat. Dan had never heard the bleating language of deer before, but he couldn't deny he heard it then – it was similar to a sheep's bleating. The fawn joined right in the feast and when the berries were gone they pranced back into the cedars. Damnedest thing he'd ever seen or heard.

The road leading to the facility loomed ahead and they reigned the horses right up to the fence outside the administration office. Willie couldn't believe his eyes.

"Now, what are you doing here, Miss Roma?" The semi-automatic rifle slid off his shoulder and into his hands, expecting

Victor's crew to show up any second. "You know it's dangerous here. Probably more now than before." He could see Dan was armed and hoped there wouldn't be a need to use their weapons.

"Willie, we need to pass by here to check on friends, get seed to plant in the spring, maybe do some bartering with you. Surely there's something you need, even though you're probably better supplied than anyone around here. Is Rafa still here?" Roma peered behind Willie just as Rafa came through the door.

"Yes, I'm still here, but sometimes I wonder why."

Rafa looked tired and ten years older. She looked from Rafa to Willie and wondered when they had last changed clothes or taken a bath.

"You look terrible. You men can't keep living like this." Roma was almost in tears looking at the haggard face of the handsome young man she had enjoyed so much.

"They came to be neighborly – to barter and such." Willie's eyes searched from Dan to Roma. "They want to come and go on the road to check on friends in town and try to find seed for planting."

"Roma, I wish more than anything that I could tell you this place is safe. We're housing a crazy, power-hungry criminal here. I've come close to killing him a dozen times, myself." Rafa glanced around the edge of the building. "I imagine he'll be up here soon."

"What stopped you from killing him?" Dan asked.

"If I kill him, or any of the leaders who are armed, it will turn into a war zone. I keep hoping there will be a peaceful solution to this. We're all getting tired of the stand-off." Rafa brushed his hand through his hair and Roma could see the exhaustion on his face. "I know you're hoping your kids are on their way, and I only hope I'm awake when they come by and Victor's sleeping. About the only time we get any peace around here is when he's asleep. Damned, miserable son-of-a . . ."

"I'll put him out of his misery. Sounds to me like it would be doing everyone a favor." Dan said, matter-of-factly.

"One of his men died last week. He only has six other men behind him. They're weakening. The fight's leaving them. We're hoping to outlast him. The rest of us have talked, and we all agree – we'll let his own men deal with him – and they will. Eventually."

"In the meantime, you're not eating right, sleeping regular, or keeping yourself clean, from the looks of you." Roma hoped she could talk some sense into him.

"Yea, you're right about that. We're a sorry looking bunch, but so far, we're keeping the weapons away from him. That's my only reason for staying. He wants the weapons, and I know he'd go into town and terrorize those people."

"Hell, those town people are tougher than you think. They'd kill him." Dan was sure of it.

"Maybe. But how many wives or children would be raped and tortured right in front of their husband's or father's eyes, and how many cows butchered for a steak?"

"We've been talking and we think your idea about joining the town people and living with the community is good, but we've got to make it safe here, first." Willie was convinced they were doing the right thing.

"I don't know how you convinced everyone here to let that man live, if he's the only thing stopping the idea of living a productive life again," said Dan.

"I made that decision on the first day," answered Rafa. "I brought the ammunition here and gave the leaders rifles. It was either that, or kill all thirty-some men. I really thought they could be reasoned with, after a few days. But I feel the end is close now."

"You're right about that." Victor stood ten feet away, his men behind him. "I keep telling the little weasel to give my men rifles and a few clips and we'll be out of here."

Dan nearly buckled when he saw Victor for the first time. He'd never seen another human being that reeked of evil like this man did.

"You didn't tell me we had visitors, Rafa. I see you're surviving just fine, *Miss Roma*. But I guess I don't have to call you that anymore, now, do I. You see, the rules have all changed. Now," he paused and fondled his rifle, "it's the one with the most guns, and I've only got one so that makes Rafa the boss now. I keep telling him I'd like to go to California where winters are warm, but he's afraid I'll hurt someone on the way. No trust in humankind, that Rafa."

"Victor, would you really hurt women and children? What about your mother? Don't you want to.find your family? You finally have an opportunity to live in the community and rebuild what's left – become a productive part of the world." Roma saw the sickening smile spread across Victor's grimy face.

"I love women and children, Miss Roma." He licked the barrel of his rifle as his men laughed behind him. "I wish I had one to eat for breakfast every morning, after a good nights sleep." His men mocked her.

"Your mother would be ashamed of you, Victor Grazzo." Roma made no attempt to hide her contempt, but his expression never changed.

"Miss Roma, I killed my mamma when I was twelve years old. She always was ashamed of me." The evil eyes never left her stare. "You're a fine looking woman, Miss Roma. You can stay." Victor raised his rifle to Dan's chest. "You can go."

"I'll gladly go, but I'll put a bullet in your head or that wolf will have your throat for lunch, if you even twitch like you're going to lay a hand on Roma."

Victor's evil grin disappeared as his eyes shifted to Trouble and back to Roma. He didn't see the wolf crouched on the rock above him. Trouble's teeth were bared in a vicious sneer and the low rumbling from her throat grew louder.

"If you lay a hand on Roma, that wolf will have you. If you try to shoot it first, you'll have two bullets in you." Dan said evenly. "Your choice."

"Oh, see what I mean." Victor lowered the rifle and the grin returned. "The man with the most guns wins." Victor and his men turned to leave. "Hope we see you again, soon, Miss Roma. We'll do lunch." The cunning grin reappeared and carnivorous laughter erupted from the group of men as they spread into the yard. "Don't go to sleep Rafa or I'll be the one with the most guns."

Dan let out a breath of relief. "I should kill every one of those sons-of-bitches! I could shoot them in the back, right now, with no remorse!"

"And we can do that any time we want. We can just line them up, and gun them down. But that makes us just like them. Killing is killing. I know that his men are wearing down. They're not as willing to back him when it comes to a showdown. It will be over soon." Rafa's weary face pleaded with Dan. "Just go home and give it a little more time."

"We came to tell you we've got chickens and a milk cow, if anything changes here, and you want to barter. I imagine you're getting pretty tired of powdered eggs, by now."

"I'd love to have any kind of eggs," said Willie. "What I'm getting tired of are peanut-butter crackers, potato chips and candy bars. Everyone's afraid to be out in the open to cook anything. All the food comes in institutional size containers." Willie broke out in a grin. "I'd love an egg. Or a glass of milk."

"Well, we sure could bring some down, if you can get us into town once in awhile." Roma was hopeful they could still work a deal.

"You tell us when, and we'll make sure you come and go in peace," Rafa offered.

"If it's not snowing tomorrow morning, we'll go over to Gus and Hilda's ranch. It's just a half mile past the dam, toward Silt. We'll go the back way into Silt to check out the feed store for seed. We would be ready to head back about midday."

"Sounds good to me. We'll be watching for you," said Rafa.

"That should do it." Dan offered his hand to Rafa. "You're a better man than I am, Rafa. I'd have shot the bastard and the rest of them if they'd wanted any. I don't know what's happened to this world, but if all men think like you, there won't be any problem rebuilding our civilization."

"I don't know about that, but several of us here seem to have had a tremendous softening of character since that first day, and we just don't try to figure it out anymore." He looked at Roma as they started to leave. "I've missed your company. Maybe we'll be able to see more of you soon – act like real neighbors."

Dan and Roma headed toward the ranch with Trouble scouting the ridge where Roma hid only weeks ago.

"Meeting Rafa really surprised me. He's a born leader. Hope it turns out like he thinks and he doesn't get killed in the meantime." Dan was sincere and Roma was impressed.

"It's what I've been trying to tell you all along. If you just look into their true spirits, you'll see the good in them."

"Well, I looked into the true spirit of Victor and didn't see anything good there." Dan shuddered at the memory of his first glimpse of the evil remnant of humanity.

"What was Rafa in there for?"

"His case management file said forgery." Roma tried to remember the details. "He shuffled over sixty million dollars of wealthy client's money on paper until he had a sizable nest-egg tucked away somewhere. By the paper trail they put together, they were never able to prove he actually profited or spent any of the money, or he'd have been in a federal penitentiary somewhere. I can't remember the details, just that they couldn't prove anything concrete and had to drastically reduce the charges."

"Sounds like a pretty smart man," Dan said. "But, if he was so smart, why the hell did he stay?"

"To get the weapons and keep Victor from getting them."

"That's what he says, but something doesn't fit. Guess I'll just have to think about it awhile."

"Well, don't work it too hard. I think a lot more happened that day than electrical – whatever. Something we may never be able to explain. The brain's electrical, too. Something happened."

"You may be right. You just may be right." Dan fidgeted a bit. "You were right about that pup of yours, too."

"Oh?"

"I'm sure glad she was with us today. I don't know if Trouble would have really taken him, but I'm sure glad Victor believed it. I'd have died today trying to save you from him."

"I know."

There eyes met and reaffirmed, again, that there really are people meant to share their lives together. Call it fate, or God's will, the grace of God, or universal energy – they both knew it was true. And they both knew they were pretty lucky to have it.

## *Chapter 16*

Thick clouds hung low in Glenwood Canyon. Bitter cold whipped through its narrow chasm sucking the breath away. Noses ran, eyes watered, fingers froze through mittens and feet became numb from the cold.

Jesse desperately sought a sheltered place to set-up camp. The strong west wind had battered them for over an hour, chilling them to the bone. He chose the lower path that followed the river hoping it would offer more protection when the storm reached them.

"Finally!" A large area far enough from the river to escape its freezing moisture, close enough to get water, and right in a triangle formed by the concrete walls holding the elevated highway above them. "I knew it was here," he hollered at Ian above the roar of the wind. "Let's get everything under the parachute. We may be here for a couple days."

"I'm going to try to find some wood before it's covered with snow. This storm system that's coming is immense and slow moving. It's been moving over us for hours and is slowly getting worse." Ian was ripping the straps from the catamaran and pulled the parachute from around the supplies.

The children quietly huddled under the parachute while Suzan, Jane and Laramie secured it over them and their supplies. "We've got to get these kids warm," said Laramie. "Jen and Sara have been coughing and crying for the last couple hours. They're cold and hungry. It's not fair to expect them to push as hard as we can. Their bodies burn their meals quicker than we do." Worry spat out angrily.

"Jesse has been watching for a couple miles for somewhere sheltered and safe to camp."

"Suzan, you don't have to defend Jesse. I'm not saying it's Jesse's fault, I'm just worried. Their coughs came on so suddenly and they're running fevers. Unless you know of a doctor close by, I don't have any idea what to do for them if it's something serious."

"I know. Jacinth's got it, too."

"Levi and Cody have been coughing, too," said Jane. "There's no way to isolate them from the rest of the kids. They probably picked it up a couple days ago. It's been so cold the last few days."

"Where's Mira?" Suzan said anxiously. "Did she go with Ian and Jesse to find fire wood?"

"I know Lalo took off with them, but I didn't notice Mira leave," said Laramie. "She's probably with them. It's pretty hard to find Lalo and her apart."

"That worries me." Suzan looked at Laramie hoping she would dissuade her fears.

"He's a boy, and Mira's a girl," said Laramie. "But they're so much alike."

"I'm not sure he's very much of a boy," answered Suzan. Both Jane and Laramie looked at her in surprise.

"What do you mean," they asked in unison.

"He lived on the street," she whispered in a low voice. "How do you suppose he kept alive on the streets? There's only one way I know of that young boys stay alive for very long on the streets of any city."

"I've thought of that," said Jane. "But using sex to survive and sexual urges are two different things, but equally used to survive."

"Are they?" Suzan looked at her naively.

"I don't know where you've been living, but where I lived, we all used sex, survival or not," answered Jane.

"Like how?" asked Suzan.

"Sex, to me, is survival. Simple," answered Jane. "Survival of the species, survival of the feminine mystique, or the power women seem to think they have over men, and survival of our spirits." They looked at her like she was crazy. "Creativity, for heaven's sake."

"Sounds like you think sexual energy is some kind of trade off for being alive," said Laramie.

"Not for being alive – but sometimes for staying alive – physically, mentally, emotionally, spiritually." Jane waited. "Well, tell me of another type of energy that is more powerful from the time we're about two years old and find out we want our daddies to approve of us."

"That's some kind of twisted thinking – that's not sexual energy. That's a little girl creating romantic feelings about life. You know, the princess and the prince. The castle and the wicked witch." Suzan was such a romantic.

"It's sexual energy in its purest form. Innocent. Before hormones come along and mix it up with bodily functions and everything else that feels good." Jane looked at Laramie who'd been pretty quiet.

"I disagree. What you said about sexual energy being the same as creative energy. I think that's right – but – only in the purest sense. I mean – come on! I would never compare my feelings about dad when I was two years old with sexual energy. It seems warped to even say the two subjects in the same sentence. Little girl feelings are romantic, teasing, pleasing, possessive, demanding . . . " Laramie's eyes grew big and she whispered, "Wow." Almost the same stereotype I would apply to a sexy eighteen-year-old."

"Well, don't kid yourself – a sexy eighteen-year-old has had years of practice – starting with her daddy."

"Jane – you're a sick woman." Laramie couldn't let it go. "A little girl adores her father and equates him with everything that is good, honorable, sweet, soft, all those wonderful feelings that we had for dad."

"I agree with you." Jane was enjoying the lively conversation. "The operative word here would be *purest* – in its *purest* form. That's the little girl world of creative energy. Sexual energy leads to creation in a very real, physical way – and that was *our creator's* plan. We sure get them confused and complicated though."

"That's for sure. Just for the sake of argument – try painting a picture the next time you feel sexual." Suzan laughed and patted Jane's back.

"Have you thought about your own creative energy?" asked Laramie, when the laughter died down. "I mean – having another baby." Laramie was glad to shift the conversation. She'd have to give the whole idea a lot more thought.

"I was told after Levi was born that it was a miracle I'd ever been able to conceive in the first place. I guess my female parts are all messed up. Scar tissue everywhere." The admission startled Suzan and Laramie. "Guess his father was very strong medicine and one of those wiggling little tadpoles just found the target at exactly the right moment in time. But I doubt I'll ever have another exact moment in time, and I'm lucky to have Levi." The silence became thick between them.

"Speaking of having babies," said Suzan, "I've got to find Mira. They should all be back by now."

"I think it's too dangerous out there to find anybody." They listened to the wind howling and pulled back the flap of the parachute. The overhang from the highway above them sheltered them from the blowing snow, but six feet away, a whiteout was in progress.

"My God! It came so fast. I've got to find Mira!" Suzan began frantically pulling on her boots and looking for her hat and gloves.

"You can't go out there, Suzan. She's probably with the guys. She'll be safe with them. They'll protect her. If you leave, we'll be sending out a search party for you." Laramie pleaded with her.

"I don't think she went with them. She was here after we'd secured everything, then she just disappeared." Suzan crawled out into the bitter cold.

"Suzan, don't go out there." Laramie and Jane begged. "We'll never be able to find you."

A white figure appeared as if a curtain had parted. Covered with a crust of snow and eyes barely visible, Suzan brushed her off and they slipped under the protection of the parachute.

"Mira!" Suzan shouted. "Mira." Suzan's voice cried with relief. "I was so worried. We didn't know if you'd gone to help find wood, or what."

Mira opened her bulging coat and a collection of dried twigs, bark and round hard pods dropped onto her sleeping bag. Suzan saw the coiled leather whip hanging from Mira's belt. She didn't know it was finished. The craftsmanship was beautiful. There is so much about her that I don't know anymore, thought Suzan painfully. She looked quizzically at the pile of dried twigs, barks and pods. "That may be good for kindling, but it won't build a fire, honey."

Jesse and Ian returned with armloads of wood as soon as the words were spoken. They crawled under the sheltered area rubbing hands and pulling off frozen boots. Jesse took one look and Suzan and saw the worry on her face.

"What's wrong?"

"I didn't know that Mira went with you."

"Mira wasn't with us," said Jesse.

"Then where . . .?"

Lalo inspected the twigs and pods Mira had collected. "She was at the river," he said. "I saw these growing by the river." He handed a prickly twig with pods on it to Suzan.

"These are rose hips." She rummaged through the twigs and bark. "Pine boughs, sage brush twigs, pine bark." She smelled the other twigs. "I don't know what these are. These look like thistle pods." Suddenly she knew. "It's to make tea with."

She turned to Mira, but Mira was sound asleep, boots, wet jacket, and all. Suzan felt her forehead. "She's not running a fever. God, I wish she'd talk to me." She undressed her daughter and helped her into a sleeping bag. By the time Ian was able to coax a small fire and boil water, the coughing under the dome of the parachute was identifiable. It came on so quickly and was undeniably pertussis. Whooping cough!

"I've got children's Tylenol and children's aspirin," said Jane. "I don't think antibiotics will touch it unless it turns into something bacterial, heaven forbid. I think it just has to run its course." Jane tried to remember what she heard about whooping cough outbreaks on the reservation. "It's so uncommon now. It's hard to tell what to do for it."

"Boil the medicine that Mira gathered." Lalo said matter-of-factly.

"What?" Both Suzan and Laramie though they'd misunderstood him.

"Boil what Mira collected. It's probably a remedy. It's exactly what they need."

"Mira wouldn't know what's in those things." Suzan looked incredulously at Lalo. "How would she?"

"How does anybody? All medicines come from natural sources. How did anyone know how to use them until they tried?" He looked at Mira sleeping. "I wouldn't know what to pick – but I didn't pick them. No one led me to them, but someone led Mira to pick them."

Suzan looked from Laramie to Jane. Jane just opened her hand to Lalo. "From the mouths of babes."

Lalo shot her a look that she instantly recognized. "Sorry, Lalo. It's just an expression." She could tell she'd touched a spark of something, but the look left as quickly as it appeared. "No offense."

"None taken. Guess there are different kind's of babes, huh?" He grinned when he realized his identification with the word *babe*.

"Yea," Jane circled her arms around Lalo and rubbed his back. "And sometimes the street is hard to leave behind. I never liked being called *babe* either – not the way most men meant it, anyway."

"Pretty demeaning, sometimes."

"Yea. Sometimes."

Suzan broke the dried twigs, bark and pods and disappeared into the whiteness to give the natural herbs to Ian to boil on the fire. When she returned in a few short moments, she was already covered in snow. "How on earth will we keep a fire going in this storm?" Suzan searched Jesse's face, but there wasn't a good answer.

Jesse knew it would be difficult. All the fallen trees and limbs they were able to find were wet. "He'll find a way – don't worry."

Jane determined that Cody, Dominic, Jen and Sara were the only ones with the real whoop that identified whooping cough. Jacinth,

Tara, Katie and Levi had colds and a cough, but not the distinct cough of pertussis. "They probably never had DPT shots when they were babies," said Jane. "The rest of the kids should be protected."

Thirty minutes passed before Ian returned with the pan of barks, twigs and pods, all boiled down to a strong tea. Suzan didn't know how he'd managed to keep a fire going, but she took the pan and poured each of the kids a dose of the dark, steamy liquid.

"It's medicine. It will make you feel better," she promised when Sara made a face at the bitter taste. Jane gave them Tylenol and bundled them up in warm clothes and sleeping bags.

Each day Suzan followed Mira to gather bark, pine needles, twigs, thistles and rose hips by the river. By the third day the snow was so deep they had to dig through it to find the healing herbs. Lalo was right. Mira knew where to dig and what to add to their daily collection.

Several times in the night Laramie completely changed the children's clothes. Their coughs were violent and they often vomited whatever she'd been able to get down them prior to their coughing spasms. Jane and Suzan helped sponge-bathe the feverish bodies and made the herb tea several times a day. Dirty, mucous covered clothing piled in one corner for burning grew until their cleanest dirty clothes were filthy. Jesse and Ian felt helpless as they watched the limp bodies grow pitifully weak. Sara, Dominic and Cody were severely dehydrated and Jen began coughing blood. Laramie concentrated on spoon-feeding the strong herbal tea day and night, whenever they were awake. It seemed to be the only thing that would stay down.

Ian and Jane tried to hunt, but couldn't find any game. It quit snowing, but it was already so deep that hunting herbs or game was impossible. Low clouds hung in the canyon, blocking the sun and keeping everything cold and wet. Their supply of food was drastically low and if another storm came, they could be trapped for weeks. Laramie boiled pemmican with water and the few remaining dried apples to make soup, which warmed the children and stayed in their stomachs.

On the fifth day, they attempted to walk out of the canyon. They knew it would be hard, because the weakened children didn't have the strength to walk. They only made a couple of miles with Suzan, Jane and Laramie dragging the travois and catamaran through paths that Ian and Jesse cleared in the snow. They finally stopped in a sheltered area, exhausted. Frozen feet hurt when wet boots were pulled off, and Ian knew they could die here.

"God won't let us die here." Jane looked at Ian's nearly frozen feet and started a fire to melt snow. "She hasn't brought us all this way to die."

"She?" Ian said.

"She's taken us this far, and she has a lot more to do with us before we're through."

"All I want her to do is give me back my feet." Jane's concept of God always tickled him, but whatever God was watching over them now was okay with Ian.

Jane rubbed Ian's feet and Suzan rubbed Jesse's while snow melted over the fire and Laramie bundled the kids in sleeping bags. It took hours for their feet and hands to warm. After drinking a weak tea to warm their empty bellies, they fell exhausted into their haphazardly arranged beds and woke late the next morning.

Laramie didn't have the strength to get out of her sleeping bag when Dominic shook her. "Mother," Dominique whispered in her ear. "I dreamed you were riding on an Eagle's back pointing the way for us to go."

Laramie rolled over and felt Dominique's forehead. "You're feeling better, aren't you sweetheart?

"Yes. You turned into the eagle and fed us the rest of the tea with your big beak." Dominic looked at her with absolute belief in his clear blue eyes. They still intrigued her – a blue eyed Indian. She managed to pull herself up on one elbow and stared at the dry twigs and pods in the bottom of the pot.

"Well, someone fed you the rest of the tea." She looked at Sara, Jen and Cody. They were sound asleep. Their makeshift tent was empty except for her and the sleeping children.

Suzan entered carrying a steaming pot. "We need to get up and break camp." She looked worried. "Ian and Jesse left at daybreak to try to find game. They don't want us to wait for them – they said to start moving before the next storm hits and they'll catch up with us on the road – probably at Rifle, by the river." She dished up a watery brown porridge and woke the sleeping children while Laramie dressed. "You must be exhausted, but feeding the kids the last of the tea must have been exactly what they needed, because they're much better this morning and their fevers are gone." Handing Laramie a bowl of the watery mush she drew in her breath. "Laramie – you look terrible. Damn girl – you need to sleep, too, you know. Can't stay up all night and pull carts all day." She sounded half-mad. "Can't be nursing the nurse. You need your strength if we're going to make it out of this canyon today."

"But, I didn't . . ." started Laramie.

"No buts." She shoved the bowl of mush into Laramie's hands and motioned for her to eat. "Come on kids – hurry up and eat so we can pack it up." Suzan grabbed up cloths and backpacks and shoved them into pillowcases.

"Suzan – stop." Laramie looked at her incredulously. "What's up? Why are you so angry?"

She was on the verge of tears. "I don't know. I didn't want Jesse to go hunting with Ian." The tears sprang from her eyes. "I think we should have a man with us." Laramie was giving her one of those defiant woman looks. "I mean – what if someone tries to mess with us?"

"What's your point?" Laramie was definitely not getting it.

"Well, Jane always went with Ian and that was fine. I didn't mind keeping an eye on Levi while she was gone. Jesse was here and it felt safe."

Laramie finally understood. "Suzan, nothing will happen. What happened back on the mountain was terrible, but it's over and nothing like that will happen again."

"It's the only time he left us alone and that's when women appear vulnerable – when there's no man around to protect them." The words came out in choking sobs. The children watched silently as they continued to eat.

"Jesse and Ian were both reluctant to leave, but knew we could starve to death if we get caught in another storm like the last one." Her heart went out to her sister. "We'll be fine. I don't think most men would mess with this group of women." Laramie stroked Suzan's shoulder and brushed her wet cheek. "You were by yourself then. You *were* vulnerable and he was an evil man." Suzan wasn't comforted. "It wasn't your fault Suzan."

Sobs broke from Suzan's throat as the weeks of guilt for not protecting her own daughter were released. Mira must have overheard from outside the tent because she came in and quietly leaned against her mother and put her arm around her waist. It was ironic to see the daughter comfort the mother. We're all women together, bottom line, thought Laramie. Suzan just came before Mira. Maybe they can heal together now. Laramie quickly finished her bowl of mush and began helping the children gather their things in their backpacks. The empty pot with remnants of herb tea was a mystery – she didn't remember feeding them the rest of the tea – but someone did.

It wasn't long before they were trudging through the snow. The storm broke and the sun began to shine through the mist creating a mystical landscape. The children were able to walk and help push, so the loads seemed much lighter.

They came to the clearing of the entrance to Hanging Lake and knew they didn't have much farther to go before they reached Glenwood Springs. As they rounded the steep canyon wall an eagle dove and held Laramie in its shadow as it hovered just inches from her head. Her whole body shifted inside and her heart skipped a beat as the giant bird swooped up the wall of the rocky ledge and shrieked its scream, echoing off the granite cliffs.

"Good heavens, we'll never see that again as long as we live," hollered Jane. "What did she tell you?"

"Tell me?" Laramie was transfixed. Remembering the words that Dominic spoke to her in his sleepy voice, and still seeing the granite cliffs through the eyes of the eagle, she felt the awesome responsibility of the children press down on her. Its message was to protect the children . . . to lead them . . . to get them to safety.

"Yes – what did she tell you? Eagles are the messengers of the Gods. They carry great messages when they come. And that one definitely came to you."

Jane stopped the group and walked back to where the children were gathered around Laramie who was unmistakably shaken by the closeness of the great Eagle. "It's a good place to stop and have something to eat." She looked deeply into Laramie's crystal blue eyes and saw the terror there.

"The children. Something is going to happen. I have to protect the children." Laramie was on the verge of shock.

"Come on – let's fix something to eat. Suzan" Jane hollered for Suzan who was still watching the eagle screech through the canyon – it flew higher and higher until it disappeared into the mist of the sun. "What can we scrape together in a hurry," hollered Jane.

"About the only thing we can scrape together in a hurry or otherwise is cornmeal mixed with the rest of the flour and some snow. Unless we can stop and build a fire so I can cook it."

"No, lets mix it stiff and eat it." Her face grimaced. "It won't taste good, and we'll have to keep walking to keep from freezing if we mix it with snow, but I hate to take the time to build a fire. We're almost out of the canyon. I think we can make it before nightfall if we don't make any more stops."

Laramie quickly unloaded the travois. They all knew about the guns packed by Red – in case of an emergency, and when an eagle is the messanger, you better pay attention. Jane was surprised at the guns – automatic assault rifles, and thousands of rounds of ammunition. She gave a quick lesson on how to load them and they hung the heavy weapons over their shoulders.

"I'll never be able to carry this thing and help push or pull the travois," said Suzan.

"Let's keep them just under the parachute cover so they'll be handy, but out of sight," suggested Laramie.

"What kind of trouble are you expecting?"

"I don't know, but now we'll be ready." Laramie surveyed their back-trail and knew that no one would have been crazy enough to try to get through the canyon in this weather. "Hopefully, we won't ever have to use them."

## *Chapter 17*

"Rafa, you got to come quick, man!" Willie was wild-eyed. "There's a bunch of women and kids coming down the road and Vic's men have already spotted them. There's going to be a mess of trouble."

"They're probably Dan and Roma's family. Dan told me they'd probably head this way." Rafa knew this was the showdown he'd dreaded. He grabbed a rifle and followed Willie.

The wind was blowing bitter cold as the sun sank behind the hogback. "Good God, where did all those kids come from," whispered Rafa. A bunch of women and kids! Vic looked ragged from the weeks of cold and poor diet, as Rafa knew they all did, but not near as bad as this ragged group before him now. His eyes searched from face to face – Roma's daughters for sure. Where were their men? His quick scrutiny halted as his eyes rested on the exotic young woman. Something so familiar. Photographs flashed through his memory to place the striking features.

"No one passes this road unless I say they can, and I say the women stay." Victor's glare was fixed on Laramie. Rafa could almost feel Victor's heart race and palms sweat as he stared at the woman draped in coyote pelts, defiantly glaring back at him.

Please don't challenge him, thought Rafa. That's all Victor needs . . . a woman with an attitude. "Victor," he shouted. "You can't separate the women from their children." As soon as the words crossed his lips, something came to the front of his memory . . . separate the women from their children . . . women from their children. What was it?

"Then I'll take her." Victor was pointing to the same face that Rafa couldn't quite place. The eyes and full mouth – her hair was chopped short, but the eyes and mouth were the same.

Victor moved toward the girl at the same time the shot broke through the frozen air. Rafa crouched instinctively and swung his rifle toward the sound. The whip whirled over Mira's head again and snapped as the ends wrapped around Victor's arm reaching for Lalo. The knife appeared in Lalo's hand so quickly that even Victor was surprised to feel it pressed cold against his throat and the smell of warm blood trickle down his chest. "You can kill me," he whispered, "I'm dying anyway – you'd be doing me a favor, but why would you want to – I just thought you might like it here." The forgotten memory exploded from the past as recognition of a nine-year old boy finally dawned in Victor's eyes and the knife pressed deeper into his throat. "You! I know you!" Fear darkened his swarthy features. "I should have killed you with your sister and mother."

"You did kill me when you killed my mother and sister" cried Lalo, as the tears streamed down his face. "I've waited in the land of the dying to find you and kill you."

"Why, you're nothing but a sissy boy." Victor was betting his life that the boy he mistook for a beautiful young woman wouldn't have the guts to kill him. He didn't notice the yellow eyes of the black wolf, head hung low, on the rocks above him.

It all happened so quickly, Rafa couldn't believe his eyes. Years of searching and undercover work and the child was right in the yard with them now. Only the child was no longer a helpless, timid nine year old boy. The eyes. The full mouth. How many times had Rafa studied the pictures of Senator Logan Lambert's missing son, and now, here, seven years later – he would show up with Roma's family. He couldn't let it end this way. He couldn't let this boy commit cold-blooded murder like Victor had so many times. He had to do something to break the spell of revenge that possessed the boy.

"Logan Lambert!"

Who called him by that name - the one he'd tried so hard to forget? Lalo's eyes darted toward Rafa only for an instant.

"Logan – he's not worth it." Rafa searched for a compelling argument to convince the boy. "If you kill him you'll be just like him." He fished for words to stop the killing. "It's over now. You've found him. You lived. You won, Logan." It was working. The tense muscles of Lalo's face began to relax. Rafa saw a look in Victor's eyes he had never seen before. His evil eyes were no longer challenging and threatening – they were filled with fear. Fear of death at the hand of a child. No, not a child anymore. Rafa knew Lalo had lived harder in his short lifetime than most. He was a warrior.

Lalo lowered the knife and Victor slumped to his knees in a spasm of coughing and choking. "He really is dying," whispered Rafa. Victor's raspy breaths and coughing spasms bore the unmistakable sound of pneumonia. The black wolf disappeared back into the dark shadows.

There was confusion among the men and Rafa knew he better take advantage of it quickly. "There's your fearless leader." They all looked at the dying killer slumped to the ground, covered in his own blood and weak from his last coughing spasm. His men started to move to help him. "He kidnapped a family," interjected Rafa, "and raped the mother, her two year old daughter and nine year old son." He had their attention. "Then he killed the mother and daughter. He would have killed the son too, but the son escaped." Lalo hung his head in shame to hear the truth told.

Rafa embraced both of Lalo's shoulders and forced him to look into his eyes. "You escaped . . . and you lived." Rafa continued. "The son survived. He's tougher than any of us – he survived on the streets knowing his own father sent a killer to murder him, his mother and sister." All eyes were on Lalo. No one but Mira and Laramie knew the details of Lalo's survival. Sharing his courageous battle with Mira helped them both to heal. Laramie's gift had enabled her to hear his soft whispering to Mira, even though his words filled her with his pain.

There's an unwritten law among thieves that says it's not okay to rape. The fight was out of them – the battle was over. They turned one by one and walked back to their units. No one offered to help Victor now and Rafa knew he would be dead by morning. He lost his power and his life at the hands of a boy. Justice!

Rafa watched the young girl tie the whip to her belt and place her arms around Logan Lambert II. It was over. Now the legacy of hate could end.

The defiant woman draped in coyote pelts turned to face Rafa. Her ice-cold blue eyes reflected their hard journey and their unspoken words bore into his soul. Eternity passed as she extended her hand and he held it in his. "My name is Laramie." She never took her eyes from his. "I'm Roma and Dan Zerlich's youngest daughter. And that is Lalo. He's Lalo." Her quavering voice shouted the name as the tears started down her cheeks and she turned and walked away.

Rafa watched her as the somber group gathered their belongings and headed down the road toward the Rocking Z Ranch.

Rafa couldn't unravel all the emotions. It could wait. Everything had changed in the last twenty minutes. It was finally over.

*Chapter 18*

The dramatic showdown at the prison used every ounce of strength and courage they were able to muster, but it was enough and they didn't have to use the guns. The only sound to break the silence was an occasional sob. No one of them could really know Lalo's pain, but as the story unfolded they felt ashamed of humanity for the mean circumstances of his life and marveled at the miracle of his survival. Now they could leave the pain from the past back there – right at that spot in the curve of the dirt road and let the earth absorb it, the wind blow it, seeds sprout from it and life grow there.

Suzan made her muscles push harder on the metal bar of the travois and fought the screams that threatened to escape from her throat – like the screams that erupt from bearing down after the long labor of childbirth – that last bit of energy brought from the depths of your being so the struggle can finally be over.

Jacinth slipped from the top of the travois to walk by her mom. "It's okay honey." Suzan watched their back-trail for Jesse as she drew Jacinth closer to her. "We're almost there now."

"But, where's daddy?" whimpered Jacinth. Suzan's exhausted body automatically moved to the rhythmic sound of wheels and the shuffling of feet over the dirt road.

Where was Jesse? He and Ian should have caught up with them by now. They left them four days ago to hunt. What could have happened? "I don't know where he is honey, but I'm sure he's okay and he knows where we're going. He'll find us." Her gut churned as she said the reassuring words. If she could just make herself believe them. He had to be okay. They had suffered and overcome too much for anything to happen now. Her knotted back and shoulders burned from pushing the travois and she knew the others were just as exhausted. Jane and Laramie guided the catamaran as Lalo, Mira and Levi pushed. The younger children were asleep on the top. They pushed themselves to reach the ranch in the four days since leaving the canyon. They should have paced themselves and camped by the river with the other travelers before continuing, but they were almost there. Just a couple more miles.

Moonlight glistened a silver path on the creek that led to the ranch. Jane searched for landmarks in the valley and recognized the rock outcrop where the puma lived with her kittens each spring. They were so close.

Laramie felt weak from the familiarity of things remembered. The lump that starts in the throat and tightens the chest melted and without warning the tears started to flow as the lay of the land became more familiar and the smell from the wood burning stove grew stronger. The end of their journey was approaching and the bittersweet anguish of finishing overwhelmed them all.

Suzan pushed with all her strength to clear the last curve in the road and dropped to her knees as the soft glow of a window came into view half a mile away. A sharp intake of breath and a low moan sounded in unison as the women stopped and stared at their destination. Cries erupted from their chests and rode on the wind until the hammer and anvil vibrated their existence and Roma appeared at the back porch, holding the lantern high like a guiding beacon. She hung the lantern on its hook and ran down the road, not seeing, only hearing the sounds in her heart, knowing her children were home.

*Chapter 19*

Rafa lay on his cot and stared at the ceiling. He knew Victor would be dead before morning and not one of them would be sorry. It was finally over. The last two years of his life were spent undercover in the prison system to try to find the truth and gain evidence against Senator Logan Lambert. He searched for years for the missing son, knowing he was still alive. How many artists' renderings had he studied memorizing what he would look like as he grew older? And tonight he'd stood five feet away and hadn't recognized him. What a twist of fate to bring the boy face-to-face with his mother's and sister's killer. And Roma's daughters! All three of them had Roma in their faces. All three resembled her in some way.

Rafa remembered his first day at camp. He devised a reason to come to the front office to check out the logistics of the camp administration office. His hand froze on the doorknob when he heard the sound of laughter coming from inside. Wild, hearty, and unabashed laughter. A woman's laughter was what the men missed most while in prison. Memories of mothers, sisters or sweethearts – the softer side of life. He remembered his surprise when he opened the door and saw her standing behind the counter – head tossed back, shoulders bouncing and the melody of laughter wafting through the room. What a sight she'd been – disheveled auburn hair to her shoulders, slender but athletic build, older than he pictured from the first sound of her laughter, but vibrant and quick to smile. And she smiled at him – a warm smile that Roma gave freely to all she met – inmate or not. It was then he decided he could best do his job from this front office and soon managed to become Roma's inmate assistant.

He admired Roma from that first day and found that most of the inmates who had occasion to be around her also respected her. His fellow inmates either desired her or upheld her honor, but none of them disliked her. She had a reputation for being tough, but also for being fair, and on more than one occasion Rafa saw her take money from her own purse to buy some inmate stamps for his letters or offer one of them a cigarette. She attended the AA meetings on Sundays and Wednesdays and was viewed differently than most staff members. She knew them and knew their secrets and was known to hug them after AA meetings – no matter what the rules were. One thing all the inmates who knew her agreed on – she was a beauty, no matter what her age.

On more than one occasion Rafa wanted to confide in Roma, to tell her about his undercover work. He knew he could trust her, and her help on the inside would have made his work much easier, but he couldn't jeopardize her relationship with her peers or the other inmates. Roma had a unique position there and he respected that. His only undercover contact was with a detective that he worked on an assignment with in Mexico City. It was decided that this man would pose as his brother and come to visit him every couple weeks to fill him in on the progress of the case and tell him what his next move would be. The nature of the case was so highly classified that none of the Department of Corrections personnel could be informed that he was undercover in their facility. One knowledgeable glance or indication of preferential treatment would have blown his cover.

The agency kept him pretty close to Victor, so he was transferred three times in the past two years. When Victor was regressed from minimum to medium security, Rafa was regressed too, but without the knowledge of the facility staff it was dangerous and often difficult to stay in the same vicinity as Victor without becoming one of his stooges or whores. Victor didn't allow anyone close to him that he couldn't completely control.

The nature of Rafa's agreed-on-crime – the one that was choreographed in his case management file – put him in a different situation in the camp than most of the inmates. His case was considered *white collar* instead of the violent street crimes more commonly admitted to among the inmates. His file said he was guilty of embezzlement – and indicated that the original charges were more serious, but well-paid lawyers had most of the incriminating evidence disqualified at his trial. It was set-up to look like organized crime, and it worked. His case management files were loaded with articles from newspapers all over the country highlighting the progress of the trial and touting him as one of the financial geniuses of our time. The inmates were impressed, as well as the prison staff, and Rafa's identity was never challenged.

Now, as he lay on the cold cot, he questioned his sanity for staying at the camp for so long. Initially it was because of the weapons. He knew that Victor's men would confiscate the weapons at their first opportunity. He hoped that everyone would leave the camp, but Victor seized the moment and although none of them knew the vastness of the situation at first, controlling the camp seemed the epitome of power. As the weeks passed, he stayed to protect the town from a ruthless band of outlaws. It seemed a valiant cause at first. Most of the men who stayed were the ones who didn't know where else to go. They didn't want to get into more trouble and risk losing their chance of parole. It was so ironic. Most of the men who stayed at the facility – with the exception of Victor's rabble – were the decent, law abiding citizens of the camp who just wanted to eventually go home. After the first few days when it became apparent that things would never go back to *normal*, they all stayed because it was winter and there was plenty of food and medicine at the camp. Spring would be soon enough to search for families and friends that survived.

Now, since Roma's daughters entered the picture with their group of kids and Logan Lambert, there would be no reason to stay to protect the camp, the weapons, the men, the food, or any of it. Victor would die tonight – lying in the cold like the dog that he was. No one would rescue him. No one among them would admit to tolerating a rapist. Now they could put their weapons down and offer to help the people of the town survive. With Victor gone, there was no reason to stay. But where would he go? He had no family – no woman – that's why he had been willing to serve in these odd undercover cases. He didn't know where to go, but knew that now he could.

He decided to check on Dan and Roma soon. Make sure that everyone arrived safely. Maybe he would shoot a deer on the way and take it as an offering of celebration. Maybe he'd be invited to stay and share a meal with them. Maybe that's why he wanted to go – so he could look at Roma's daughter – the one surrounded in coyote pelts with the ice-cold blue eyes – Laramie. Was it her eyes that were ice-cold, or her heart? She sure was defending that boy, Logan Lambert. What had they survived to get here? They all looked tough as nails, come to think of it. But there was something odd about that group – there were no men with them. Surely they hadn't come all that way alone. And where did all those kids come from? Roma talked about her son-in-law many times. James? No, that wasn't it. Jesse! Her son-in-law, Jesse. Where was Jesse now?

Laramie. What a beautiful woman – attitude and all. He racked his memory trying to remember if Roma had ever said her youngest daughter was married. He couldn't remember her mentioning a man in Laramie's life. And why would he be wondering about a man in her life? The only reason he'd stayed at the prison was to defuse the situation to protect the citizens of the surrounding communities. Now he could go anywhere he wanted. He could leave. He'd pack soon, but for now he was too exhausted to worry about where he would go. He was finally out of prison.

The last thing he remembered was the sound of the coyotes yipping – working the ridge – telling their stories and hunting for dinner. And ice-cold blue eyes.

*Chapter 20*

Footsteps quickened and loads became lighter the closer they got to the light. Trouble whined and yelped as she circled the group and recognized familiar scents. It seemed like an instant and Roma was at Suzan's side helping her push the travois while tears streamed down her face.

The back porch loomed just feet away when Suzan stopped, dropped the handles her hands had grown stiff around and collapsed in her mothers open arms. "Oh, Mom! Mom!" she wept. "You smell so good, and I smell like a goat."

"Just let me hold you. From now on I'll always love the smell of goats – it will remind me of such a joyful time." Roma held her daughter away from her and looked at her closely in the lamp light. Her fingers came up and traced Suzan's angular bone structure – her nose, her chin and cheeks – as if trying to make sure nothing had changed, but her daughter was changed. There were painful memories written in new lines around her eyes and mouth.

One by one she scrutinized her daughters and they let her. It was their mother's way of looking into their souls – a silent communion. They were used to it. They had missed it. Roma always read their faces, their eyes, their bodies. She was their mother. The past two months had been brutal and Roma knew they had suffered much. There would be time for talk later.

Dan watched and waited patiently. Roma had been expecting them every day for a week. When each day passed and they didn't come, she knew they would be here the next day, then the next. Each day she would collect the herbs she knew they would need when they arrived – barks for soothing tea, roots and rose hips to stabilize their immune systems and renew their energy, and aspen bark for pain.

He often worried about her – she would be gone for hours. Of course, Trouble was always with her, so he didn't worry about predators. But there was something else. Roma had always been eccentric to the point of frustration, but it was different now. She seemed to be removed from the reality of this life as it was. Sometimes he swore he heard her talking to someone – someone he couldn't see or hear. He was sure it would all change when the family arrived. Surely it was caused from all the worry and stress they were under. At night, when Roma lay on the bed in the middle of the dining room, Dan watched her face as the moonlight moved slowly across her features. He'd loved her his whole life and didn't know what he would ever do without her. Roma was the center. Yes – he was the father, but she was the heart of this family. She nursed him back to life many times in the years gone by and now he wanted to take special care of her.

"Dad – where are you? You seem so far away."

"Jabby!" He put his arms around her and held her close. "My Jabby." For once, Jane didn't object to the nickname she'd inherited years ago. When Laramie was first learning to talk, Jane Abby became *Jabby*. Her dad was the only one in the family that still called her Jabby. Tonight it sounded fine – just fine. Pretty soon Suzan joined in their circle, then Laramie.

"What a sight!" Roma was painfully aware of the dissention between her daughters over the past few years. It nearly broke her heart. She could see it was different now. Maybe the heart wounds had healed. "What a sight!"

"What the hell is that?" Dan swung for his rifle, which always stood in the corner of the porch.

"Dad, that's Black," Laramie quickly interjected. "He's been with us from the first day. He's Jen and Sara's dog."

"Damn! I can see we'll have a whole valley of wolf pups soon."

"Oh, good heavens!" Mira stood in front of her grandmother and withstood the scrutiny she'd watched her mother go through for years. "Oh, my goodness! I can't believe my eyes. Miranda – my Mira! You are such a grown up beauty. It's been just a little over two months since I saw you at Thanksgiving, and you look so much older." Roma was eyeballing her all over and her eyes landed on the whip curled around her belt. "What is this – my baby is now a warrior woman?" Roma looked into Mira's eyes and could see that the little girl was gone and the woman stood before her. "Ah, yes – you are a warrior woman, aren't you." Mira didn't have to reply. "We can have a long talk soon." Mira hugged her grandmother, Granny, as she always called her, and moved aside so that Lalo stood in the light.

"Gran?" Everyone turned in surprise to hear the first words from Mira's mouth in several weeks. "This is Lalo."

Roma saw the handsome boy, but was more fascinated by the look in Mira's eyes. Then the look in "Lalo, did you say?" eyes, told her of their special relationship. Roma saw that love was there. "Lalo, welcome to our family."

Lalo was at a loss. He didn't know how to react to such tenderness. He'd fantasized about families most of his life, and now this one offered him love and acceptance. Tears welled up in his eyes and old, self-conscious shame came flooding back again. Roma took him in her arms and held him.

"You're home now," she whispered, "and everything is okay when you're home. Family loves you, no matter what." The trauma of coming face-to-face with his mother's and sister's killer; the overpowering urge to kill; the shame of having lived and not being able to save his mother and sister; the letting-go of years of hatred; it all came out. The dam burst and tears washed over him like a cleansing baptism, while being held in this grandmother's embrace. Roma felt it too, and held Lalo until his body quit shuddering, his shoulders heaved and a great sigh escaped his throat.

"Gran?"

New tears instantly filled her eyes. "Levi!" She grabbed him and held him to her. "My brave Indian Brave." Roma loved him and spoiled him every chance she got. She'd known his father and had always liked him, but it nearly broke her heart when she discovered he abused Jane and Levi. Jane tried to keep it from her, but Roma knew. That damnable alcohol! It was not meant for the belly! How long had it taken her to figure that out?

"Gran?"

"Oh goodness." Roma drew Jacinth in with her and Levi. *Jacinth is definitely a beauty,* observed Roma. Her dark, short-cropped hair accentuated her sparkling, mischievous eyes revealing a glimpse of the woman-child emerging. "Jacinth, there's something different about you that wasn't there at Thanksgiving, when I last saw you." Roma peered deeply into Jacinth's laughing eyes.

"Gran – quit looking so hard for me. I'm right here in plain sight!"

"Yes, you are in plain sight, but, inside you've changed a lot in the last two months." She looked around at each of them. "I guess we all have, haven't we?"

Kneeling down, she gazed into dark solemn eyes peeking from behind Jacinth. "And who is this beautiful princess?"

"That's Sara." Jacinth yawned and pushed Sara closer to Roma. "Jen and her are sisters and Auntie Laramie found them alone the first day, so they came with us."

"So Auntie Laramie found you, did she? Well, Sara, I'll bet you're hungry, aren't you?" She looked into Sara's eyes and saw the secrets buried deep inside. Roma motioned for the children to come into the house and by the time they gathered around the dining room table where Roma placed the lantern, there were six new little faces staring at her. "My, my, my. Did Laramie find all of you?" The sleepy heads nodded *yes*.

"I was the first son." The cerulean blue eyes startled Roma. Here was an Indian child for sure – with brilliant blue eyes.

"And what is your name – first son?"

"I'm Dominic and I was first."

"Well, Dominic the First," Roma took his hand in hers. "I'm very happy to meet you. I'm Roma – Gran to you." She turned to the next child – a girl sitting next to Sara. "You must be Jen." She touched Jen's face and continued around the table meeting Katie, Tara and Cody. "Cody, huh? Your mother fell in love with a town in Wyoming, too, huh?

"Yes ma'am. My mamma calls me Cody Wyoming."

"Well, Cody Wyoming, you can call me Gran, too."

"Yes ma'am."

Roma looked around the table with pride and gratitude in her heart. "Laramie's got herself quite a little family going here."

"See what happens Gran?" Jacinth stiffled a yawn as she began slicing the loaf of bread. "You turn your back and your daughter comes home with six kids. All these years she's been living a secret life." Jacinth howled at her cleverness.

"Ah, Mistress Jacinth." Roma spoke in her finest British accent. "I see you've left the stage to come slumming with us poor commoners."

"Yes, Grand-Ma-Ma." Jacinth held her imaginary skirt in a broad curtsey. "I wouldn't have missed this day for a king's ransom."

Roma whispered loudly to all the children, "She's always quite considered herself to be of royalty, don't you know." She put her finger to her lips. "Shh, let's not let on that she's just like us." Roma patted her chest. "Her heart wouldn't tolerate it." The children shrieked in delight.

Roma looked up to see her three daughters and Dan standing at the back door. "I see you're encouraging Jacinth's stage career and the kids will be wound up for hours," said Suzan as she quickly started buttering the homemade bread. Suddenly, tears started again as she held the bread close to her face and inhaled deeply of its heavenly aroma. She looked at the knife and now it was she who shrieked in delight. "Mom – this is real butter!" Quickly, she put the end of the knife in her mouth. "Ohhh," she crooned, "I didn't think I would ever taste butter again."

"In the morning I'll introduce you to our milk, cream and butter – Maggie. I'm surprised you didn't see her out in the yard."

"You've got a cow?" Laramie was astonished. "And we'll have milk?"

"Your mom milks her nearly every morning and every night," Dan bragged.

"No!" Jane looked from her dad to her mom. "No way – not Mom." Jane shook her head in disbelief. "Mom would not milk a cow."

"Well," Roma said, "I'll tell you the story of Maggie in the morning – after I milk her." She gazed around the table. "But right now . . . Suzan – quit staring at the butter and get it on that bread so we can get these little ones fed and under warm blankets."

Dan and Roma rolled out the sleeping bags that had been rolled up by the fireplace for a week, while Suzan, Jane and Laramie devoured raspberry jam and butter on homemade bread. They quickly found more bedding for the extra children.

"Oh, Mom," hollered Laramie. "We brought sleeping bags with us."

"Yes," said Roma. "I smelled them while I was helping Suzan push that contraption that got you all here." She laughed out loud. "I'm going to have to get a better look at that thing in the morning." She smiled at Levi. "I saw the travois and I'll bet you had something to do with that because I recognized the Harley gas tanks on it."

Levi beamed with pride. "I designed it and Red and Ian built it just like I told them it should be."

"Ian?" Roma looked at Jane. "Is this someone I should know about?"

"You'll meet him – maybe tomorrow." Jane stole a worried glance at Suzan.

"They should be right behind us."

"They?"

"Ian and Jesse, Mom." Suzan hoped her voice wouldn't belie her anxiousness.

Roma looked around. "I guess I was so excited to see everyone that I didn't count heads. Where is my Jesse? And who's Ian?"

Roma looked at Suzan, but it was Jane who finally spoke up. "Ian is the one who convinced us all to make this trip. He and Jesse left us a few days ago to hunt for deer. They can't be too far behind us."

"You mean you got past the prison camp without your men?" Roma glanced from one face to another and saw anxious eyes shift back and forth.

"We'll save that story for tomorrow, Mom," whispered Laramie.

Suzan quickly interrupted, "We told them we would wait for them at the river, but when they didn't return after the first night, we saw the crowd at the river and in town, and decided not to wait. We ran out of stuff to barter for food." Roma's questioning eyes searched their faces. "Mom, it was my decision," Suzan nearly choked on the words. "I'm sure when they don't find us at the river they will know that we've come to the ranch."

"Of course, honey." Roma comforted. "And you were right to continue on." She looked at each of them and knew they were frightened for Jesse and Ian and doubting their decision to come on without them. "We all have to learn to quit questioning our instincts. You did the right thing and you're all safe now."

"It's the right way."

Roma turned to see which child's voice spoke the wise words. Her gaze rested on Dominic. "Yes, it's the right way." She shook her head in amazement. "It's always the right way, isn't it?"

Excitement of their arrival quickly turned to exhaustion as the weary travelers finally collapsed into clean sleeping bags with cedar chest blankets and Afghans. Baths could be taken in the morning.

Some clothes were burned – along with the lice and fleas. Some were washed bright white with homemade lye soap. Roma insisted the sleeping bags stay outside to be bleached and disinfected by the sun, which insisted on shining – even through the cold winter snow.

The following days were filled with hard work; cleaning, cooking, hunting and tending to the animals. Nights were short stories, prayers, songs of memories and memories of mothers. And each day they watched the road for two weary hunters to return.

## *Chapter 21*

It had been a week since Roma and Dan's daughters passed by the camp. That was one raw looking group, thought Rafa. Where were their men? Surely they didn't come all the way from Denver by themselves. Maybe they did. Those women were pretty mean! What happened to them? Why did they leave Denver? How bad was it?

"Well, they've had enough time to unpack, visit their mamma, and mellow out."

"What?" Willie looked around. "Who you talking to, boy?" Willie had grown close to Rafa. He had protected his back, stood guard at night while Rafa slept and slept during the day while Rafa watched his back. The night Roma's family came through was the turning point for the whole camp. It was as if those women waved a magic wand and transformed a bunch of dangerous criminals, into civil human beings.

He chuckled to himself. It wasn't a woman and it wasn't a magic wand. It was a young girl – womanlike, but still a girl. And she cracked a wicked whip. And the moment froze in time and evil left. It was so evident that Victor even died, right where he stood. He died. He just crumpled and died. And his body disappeared.

They never knew if an animal carried him away – there were no tracks. Some said that Satan himself came to claim his last living son of perdition. Willie didn't try to figure it out. It's just the way it was. It was a good thing.

It had only been a week and Rafa was talking out loud to himself about those women. One in particular – Roma's youngest daughter. Willie would know her anywhere. He studied the picture on Roma's desk every time he came to the office. Strong woman. Bold – unafraid. But soft and womanly – way too white for him, but beautiful – for a white woman. Rafa took the picture that first day and put it away for safekeeping. And now he had a fire he couldn't put out. And a case of heart sickness if he ever saw it. That's what Willie's wife used to call it. Heart sickness. When the heart can't tolerate the loneliness – the separation – from the heart that calls it. Willie's wife died from it. Heart sickness.

"I think we should go check on Roma and Dan's family." Willie watched Rafa from the corner of his eye as he casually finished putting breakfast dishes away.

All the men ate in the kitchen now – together. They took turns cooking and cleaning. Today was their turn to clean. It was a good time for quiet talk.

Many of the men left the day after Roma's daughters passed through. Said if a bunch of women and kids could make it over the passes, they could too. They just peacefully packed their things, took food, medicine, cigarettes; things that were still left in the canteen. Said they were going to find their families. See what was left of their homes. Their old neighborhoods. Their mammas. Men always miss their mammas – even those who don't say so. Even those who never knew them.

The men who stayed talked of planting a community garden in the spring and bartering with the townspeople. Some said they'd stay until the weather got better and then leave. Others hoped to find a woman in town and start over. There were only thirteen of them left now.

"You know, Willie," Rafa beamed. "That's a great idea." He was grinning big. "We could take them some medicine. I know they need medicine with all those kids." Rafa threw a few things in his backpack, grabbed his jacket and was ready to go, but the amused look on Willie's face stopped him cold. "What?"

"I was thinking of maybe putting on my hiking boots, getting my heavier jacket, packing a bite to eat for the walk back. It's six miles to Roma's." He chuckled and shook his head. "Boy, you got it bad. Bad!" Willie walked down to his *house,* laughing all the way.

In half an hour they were on the road. They made a list of things they wanted to ask Dan about; seeds for a garden, where they should go to barter for a horse, how they could best help the townspeople rebuild the community. They wanted Dan to know the camp was no longer a dangerous place and anyone could come and go in safety now.

"Why did you stay?"

"What?"

Rafa shifted his backpack to better distribute the weight of the medicine, first-aid supplies, cigarettes and candy he'd packed to take to Dan and Roma's. "Why did you stay?"

Willie studied the question for awhile before answering. Rafa was always so direct and Willie had learned to trust him and talk openly and honestly, a quality he'd never before developed with a white person, and not too many blacks either.

"Why, I guess I stayed because I didn't know where else to go."

"You could have just as easily left with the others." Rafa watched the gentle eyes as the brows furrowed together thoughtfully. The big man's hands spread wide as he searched for the answer.

"I don't know. I've asked myself the same question." He pointed at Rafa. "You came in and took over so fast that I didn't have enough time to let my brain get me into trouble." His eyes became clouded in memory. "And what was happening was all wrong."

"Wrong? You mean morally wrong?"

"Morally? I don't know about morally. It was more of an inner knowledge that it was all wrong." He looked down at his big hands. "These hands strangled the life out of another man and didn't feel morally wrong, but that morning when everything changed – even the air felt dangerous to breathe. A criminal with guns is a bad thing. It would have been real bad in town and anywhere else they went, if they'd gotten hold of those guns. Thank the Lord there was someone in control with some sense." Willie clucked – "You know Rafa, you've always been about the coolest acting dude in this place. You know – like you never hung with anyone – always by yourself. And so smart the guards even asked your advice about finances and investing. You didn't fit here. You were different and something else has always bothered me."

"And what's that?" Rafa picked the dried flower stalk of last year's yucca plant and a couple twigs of creeping juniper, and brushed the snow off them.

"You always ate and wrote with the wrong hand."

"Didn't know there was a wrong hand to eat with," Rafa answered cautiously.

"You eat and write with your right hand."

"Right – wrong – what difference does it make?"

"The Michael Rafael that I knew was left handed."

Rafa shot him a quick glance. "You know me from somewhere – other than the inside – and you never said anything?"

"No, I said I knew Mike Rafael. I never knew you."

Rafa was numb with shock and didn't know what to say. He picked more remnants of last summer's wild flowers – sage and thistle pods, but Willie continued on.

"Me and Rafa grew up in the same neighborhood as children." Willie's eyes never left Rafa. "It's been so long since I left that neighborhood, that I didn't know if you could really be him or not. I studied everything you did – and you had all the facts right, but Rafa and I got in enough scraps when we were young that I remembered he threw rocks and snowballs with his left hand – and he threw punches with his left hand, too. You got that same scar over your left eye, and you look a lot like him. I gave that scar to Rafa." He paused, remembering. "But you don't have the same cruel look in your eyes." Willie chuckled. "Don't look so worried. I stuck around because I wanted to see how it would all play out. To find out who you really are and what happened to Rafa."

"You never said anything." Rafa stared incredulously.

"I decided I liked this Rafa better – and you didn't try to throw a punch at me when you saw me. That was the real give-away."

"Rafa died in the prison riot at Centennial Prison in 1996."

"I knew he'd been shanked, but thought he pulled through."

"When Rafa died, it was a perfect opportunity. With a little plastic surgery to create the right scars and a whole lot of coaching by Rafa's sister, I came into the system as Rafa and was housed at Shadow Mountain – no man's land – until I could be introduced into medium security as Rafa. Then I trickled down into minimum security and was transferred to Rifle. Not even the guards knew who I was."

"Are you a special cop then?"

"Yea – a special cop." Rafa drew a deep breath. "Yea – I'm a special cop all right. I'm Federal Special Forces."

"Never heard of such a group."

"That was the idea. Very small group of men and women. Only used in high profile cases – usually international or politics in high places – rarely used domestically. Rafa was shipped off to Italy when he was 16 years old and didn't return to the states until he was 25, so we never dreamed someone from his old neighborhood would end up in Rifle with him."

Rafa threw a sideways glance at Willie who picked a sprig of naked rose hips to add to the bouquet. "And wasn't that old neighborhood the Bronx?"

Willie chuckled to himself. "What – you think all the old criminals come from the Bronx? No, man. The old neighborhood was Harlem – right across the street from the Bronx. We both lived on the street that divided the two communities – I lived in Harlem and he lived in the Bronx – on the same street." Willie's laughter rang through the valley – loud and mocking. "Funny, how life turns out."

"Yea." Rafa laughed with the big man at the sight they must be – two grown men picking flower bones in the snow. "Funny."

"Do you hear that mamma?" Laramie turned toward the road and saw the two men walking toward them and laughing loudly.

"Mamma," said Dominic, "they're the men that helped us at the prison."

"So they are," said Laramie as a twinge of excitement went through her. "But we still have our chores to do. Hurry now, we're almost through."

Every day Laramie took Sara, Jen, Katie, Dominic and Cody to gather firewood. They walked through the woods identifying the different animal tracks or birds, while they picked up the deadfall from the aspen and pine trees and put them in the flour sack slings Laramie made them. It had been a cold task every day since they'd arrived at the ranch, but the sun was shining today and the children were eager to be outside, even to do chores, with a few show-ball fights along the way.

Jacinth, Levi, and Tara were in charge of sorting the wood after it was brought down from the hills and stacking it on the south side of the house. There was a nice high pile of assorted sizes neatly arranged in just the short time they'd been there.

Throughout the day the snap and crack of the whip could be heard. Roma often accompanied Mira and Lalo into the forest to bring down the dead trees for firewood. She watched in amazement as Mira cracked the whip above her head, wrapped the tip around the tree branch, and pulled the tree over – all in one graceful movement. She was awestruck at her ability with the uncommon weapon. One day while walking through the dark timber, she asked Mira how she ever learned such a skill. Mira told her about the afternoon she was forced from the cave. She said the next thing she remembered was being underwater – way down deep where it felt safe and warm. She didn't want to come out of the water – she knew it would be cold. She heard a mournful, primal wail that echoed through the water waves and woke her up. Then she heard someone calling her by her given name – *Miranda*. She didn't want to come up but the voice begged her to come back. When she saw Lalo, she chose to return. She had a choice. She remembered the day they were created and each promised to find the other in this life. She said they could hear each other's thoughts and feel each others heart beat. She told how he whispered to her about his life here and how hard it was and that he'd waited a long time to find her. He never stopped whispering words of encouragement to her. He sat behind her and helped her fingers weave the whip. He stood behind her and helped her arm snap the whip until she had the will to hold it herself. Lalo helped her practice everyday – snapping the whip at a twig on a tree, or a stone on a log, until she could pick the stone off the log or snap a leaf from the twig.

Lalo turned to see the two men walking towards the house and winced at the memory of their first meeting. Mira coiled the whip, fastened it on her belt loop and together, they hurried to catch up to the two men.

Rafa sensed he was being followed and whirled to find Mira and Lalo standing in the driveway with a closed hand placed over their hearts in the universal gesture of love, peace, welcome. Automatically, Rafa returned their gesture and Mira and Lalo turned back into the trees before he had a chance to speak.

"What did they call that boy – I can almost remember his new name," murmered Rafa.

"Lalo."

"What?" Rafa turned to find Laramie standing alarmingly close to him. He hadn't heard her approach.

"His name is Lalo." She walked past him and up the porch steps.

The children giggled and cried in unison, "His name is Lalo."

"Guess his name is Lalo," laughed Willie.

"I won't ever forget it again, that's for sure."

"Well, are you coming in or are you going to lolligag out there for awhile?" Laramie disappeared into the open kitchen door.

Roma came to the rescue and waved them inside. "Don't let that wild woman scare you," she hollered, "She's really quite lovely when she pulls in the quills and the hair on your neck lays back down."

Six children raced past them into the house as they entered the kitchen. Willie stood with his arms reverently folded as if he were entering a church. Twelve years passed since he had been in a home. He was overcome with emotion and tears filled his eyes. He looked down and stared into two lovely dark eyes and arms outstretched to him. He plucked the tiny child into his arms and wept openly as Sara tasted the tears on his neck and breathed in the aroma of memories.

"What's your name, child?" She was about the same age his own daughter had been when he last hugged her six yeas ago, right before her mamma died.

"Her name's Sara." Willie sat down in the kitchen chair and swept Jen into his big arm too. "She can't talk."

"No, Sara doesn't talk," said Roma, "But I've heard her sing with the voice of an angel when no one is around." She wiped tears from Sara's face. "Maybe someday she'll feel safe enough to talk to us."

Sara flung her arms up and Roma scooped her up. "She even smiles now."

"Come on kids – outside while the sun is shining. Pretty soon it will be too cold to play and you'll have to come in." Laramie held the door open as the kids chased each other outside.

"Who do all those kids belong to?" Rafa had been counting and trying to figure out who belonged to who.

"They're mine." Her eyes dared him to disagree. "All six of them."

His heart sunk. He could hardly look at her and talk at the same time. It was her eyes – they held him firm.

"They can't . . . uh . . . can't all be yours," he blurted. "They're all about the same age, and different . . . uh . . . colors."

Willie chuckled to himself. He was watching this fearless leader of men being reduced to a stammering, stuttering lump of love-struck boy.

Realizing she was enjoying this way too much, Laramie felt a twinge of shame and the need to rescue him from embarrassing himself any further, especially with everyone standing around them in the kitchen.

"Well, it's a long story and I'll tell it to you someday." Laramie eyed the wad of dried weeds and pods with green pine and juniper sprigs held tightly in Rafa's hand.

"I've got time for a long story now." Rafa followed Laramie's gaze to the bouquet he'd picked for her, given the seasonal restrictions placed upon him. He held them toward her and she timidly took them. She was dumbstruck and didn't know what to say. When her sisters started snickering and Roma couldn't hold back any longer, the whole room burst into laughter and Laramie quickly found her mother's most prized crystal vase and arranged the flower skeleton's in the center of the table.

"Well, since you've provided such a noble centerpiece, you'll have to stay for dinner." Rafa and Willie hemmed and hawed, making excuses about why they couldn't or shouldn't stay.

"So you've got something real exciting to do tonight and have to hurry back? Don't have time to hear a long story after all?"

That woman totally frustrated Rafa and his face turned hot and his hands became clammy.

"Then you can stay for dinner?" Laramie said with her big-eyed innocent look.

Rafa still couldn't speak without tripping over his words.

"Good! We haven't had company for a long time." Laramie almost danced through the house getting the kids cleaned and arranging chairs, stoking the wood stove to set the coals just right for baking. Roma retrieved the hind haunch from the elk that Dan shot the week before and cut generous steaks, Mira brought a piece of honeycomb from the beehive she'd been cultivating, Willie milked the cow, Jane shook the jar of cream until it was butter, and Laramie made the best biscuits ever.

"Dad says the only way to really enjoy steak is to cook it over a campfire and eat by firelight." Laramie licked her fingers, placed her empty plate on the porch and added wood to the glowing coals. "We haven't cooked steak like that for a long time." She enjoyed the casual dinner, the excitement of having a would-be suitor, and the ease of being around this man. Rafa built a fire next to the porch when Laramie suggested they cook the steaks outside, even though afternoon shadows grew long.

"Too cold out here for me", said Jane. "The sun's going down – almost my bedtime. I'll go help the kids get ready for bed." She extended her hand to Rafa. "It's been nice to visit with you." She turned to Willie and shook his hand, too. "You really livened things up today. I've never seen Sara so excited to see anyone. Thanks for coming."

"Yes." Roma hugged them both. "You both are welcome here – come back anytime."

"Thanks for having us. It was the finest meal I've had in years," Willie said, as he started to gather the dishes. "It must be my turn to clean up the dishes," he winked, as he followed Roma and Jane inside, leaving Rafa and Laramie to tend the fire.

They sat in silence for awhile. They didn't rush to fill the quiet. It was comfortable.

"Was it hard?" Rafa started.

"Hard?"

"Getting here, I mean."

Laramie looked far away.

"I mean, you looked pretty beat-up by the time you got to the camp." Rafa immediately felt like an insensitive lump. "I'm sorry," he said hurriedly. "You *were* pretty beat-up, and I know it was hard."

Laramie's eyes penetrated him – absorbed him.

"You're so beautiful." He couldn't believe the words came out of his mouth. He thought he was only thinking them, although he saw his hand reach up and push a lock of hair away from her eyes. Her eyes! Blue in its purest clarity. Everything about her was magnified. More. He hoped time was standing still because he was staring intently at her eyes, through her pupils and into her soul. He could smell her skin, taste her breath, feel her blood rushing. He was filled with the essence of this woman.

"Time is different now."

"What?" Rafa was reeled back to the moment.

"Time happens quickly now – since everything changed." Laramie knew the sincerity of his thoughts, could feel the pureness of his spirit, could see his heat. "There is no need for time anymore."

"Yes. Everything is magnified – time is not the same as it used to be." He could sense her next thought.

"It doesn't take as much time to discern truth." She felt his thoughts mingle with her own.

"Everything is felt at a different level than before." He took her hands in his. His senses were on fire and touching her was electric.

"Energy merges – making everything more together, than it could ever be alone." The current was strong between them, but neither was afraid of what they felt.

"I don't know what has happened, if this is how love feels, or if this is scarier than love, or life, or anything that was before, it's so new."

Laramie shivered at the cold night air. "It's taken us a long time to find each other." Was he the one? The one she'd waited all her life to find?

"If we had met before, I don't think I would have been able to feel this." Rafa pulled the afghan higher around her shoulders. "You're cold. Do you want to go in?"

"I'm afraid if I leave here, all this will go away." Her eyes held him to her.

"I'll never forget how this feels," he said, and gently kissed the palm of her hand. "And I will never be satisfied to feel less."

## *Chapter 22*

Mira and Lalo brushed Litany's winter coat until he shone like glossy copper. Suzan watched them while she and Roma mended ragged clothes.

"Lalo and Mira are almost like twins," said Suzan. "They mirror each other in their actions.

"They are twins . . . spiritual twins," said Roma. "Leave them alone. They remember who they are."

"Mom, they spend way too much time together – alone." Suzan couldn't believe her mother was being so naïve about them. "Mira had her first period last month."

Roma's head came up from her mending. "Yea? – So?"

Silence hung on the memory of what happened to Mira during their journey. Suzan had been so worried that the ugly memory would grow in her belly and a child would be born – daring them all to love it. No one ever talked about what happened that dreadful night.

Suzan cried when Mira brought her the blood-stained panties. The tears were not for Mira's passage into womanhood – which should have been a celebration, but tears of relief that they would not have a living reminder that she would have tried to love. Mira's passage into womanhood happened in violence – something Suzan could not remove from Mira's memory, but she was so relieved that Mira would not have to relive it every time she looked into the eyes of an innocent child.

"She's a woman now – in every sense of the word," Suzan stammered.

"She was a woman long before last month." Roma disregarded the uneasiness in Suzan's eyes. "She was a young woman before you left Denver."

"Mom," stammered Suzan, "I know you've always thought you knew Mira better than anyone else, and maybe you do, but . . ."

"But, what?" Roma nodded toward the corral. "Look at them."

"That's my point, Mom. They're together every waking minute of every day. They're vulnerable and inexperienced. Well – Mira is." She turned from the window to face Roma. "They're too young."

"Too young for what? Suzan – they love each other in a way few of us will ever know."

"Pappa!" Mira's voice carried into the kitchen where Roma and Suzan still debated the correctness of Mira and Lalo.

"Pappa!"

"Someone's here – I don't recognize him, though," hollered Dan. Roma put her sewing down as Dan ran past the kitchen door and caught the rider as he slid off the horse's back.

"Roma, bring some water," shouted Dan.

Suzan was beside herself by the time Roma returned with the water. "Where's Jesse?" She sobbed when she saw the look on Ian's face. "Nooooo!" It couldn't be true. She would have known. She would have felt it. "Where's Jesse?"

"Let the man catch his breath," said Dan. "There, drink up." Ian choked on the first drink, but eagerly drank the rest. "Let's get him inside."

It took all three of them to help him get up the porch steps and into the kitchen. "I take it you must be Ian," said Roma. "And, Jesse's not with you."

"We both went over the edge," Ian whispered. "I hit the wall of the canyon three times that I can remember. I must have blacked out when I hit the bottom." His chest heaved and a long sigh escaped as he continued on. "I don't know how long I was unconscious. From the dried blood and my parched throat and the snow that blanketed us, I would say all day." He gulped the water Roma brought him. "When we fell it was mid-morning. We'd been tracking a buck for a couple hours past dawn and when I woke up the sun was just going down and a thin layer of snow had fallen."

"Was Jesse alive then?" Dan asked. Suzan sat close, unable to believe what she was hearing, twisting her hands in knots.

"Yes." Ian glanced at her questioning eyes. "I couldn't bring him around, and his breathing was shallow, but he was alive."

"Then we have to go find him." She glanced around as if looking for the car keys. Desperation filled her. "I'll just get some things. We can take Litany and Rendi."

"Hold on, honey," Dan grabbed her arm and motioned for her to sit beside him. "Let's hear the rest of this." He stroked her hair. "Let Ian finish telling us what happened, then we can saddle up the horses and go find him."

"Okay." Suzan sat down and tried to concentrate on Ian's words. "I'm okay, Dad."

"When I woke up I was freezing cold one minute and burning up the next. I knew I had a broken arm and a couple of broken ribs, but couldn't find any serious wounds so I knew I was probably suffering from exposure rather than infection." Ian gulped at the air, trying to suck in all the courage he could find.

He looked from Suzan to Dan and back at Suzan as he picked up her hand in his. "I checked Jesse and his lower leg was broken." "The bone was sticking out of his sock – right above his boot line, so I knew he was likely in shock and also suffering from exposure." Suzan gasped as her hand flew to her mouth. "He also had a deep gash and a big bump on the back of his head and had lost a lot of blood. I unrolled our packs and wrapped him up as good as I could and slept close to him all night to keep him warm."

"When I woke up it was nearly light and I knew I'd have to go for help or we would both die." Ian's face was filled with agony.

"I made some tea from bark and twigs that I found, but I couldn't rouse Jesse to drink any of it."

"But he's still alive." Suzan was on her feet again.

"Let's listen to what happened next." Laramie said as she guided her back to the group.

"The sun melted the snow off the day before so I thought it would be a day of good weather. I pulled him under the outcrop of the cliff, so he wouldn't be exposed."

Ian grabbed Suzan's hands in his. "Suzan, you know I wouldn't have left him there alone if I'd had any other choice." His voice cracked. "I tried to pick him up and carry him, but my shoulders and ribs wouldn't let me. I love him like a brother, but I had to leave him to get help."

"Yes, yes." Suzan cried. "Please tell me what happened."

"Okay." Ian's voice lowered to barely a whisper. "I walked all day. It was very slow going. I marked my trail so I could get back to him when I found help. I found a cabin about dusk and knew I couldn't get back to Jesse that night, so I stayed in the cabin and prayed that he would survive the night. The cabin was old and deserted. In the morning, I started out on an old trail – looked like it was a narrow road once. I thought it would run into a town or a better road somewhere. I couldn't find the maps - must have lost them when I fell, but thought I remembered a trail that ran into New Castle." I walked all that day and tried to sleep under a tree and thought I'd freeze to death."

Suzan was softly crying. Roma sat quietly by Dan.

"Ian – do you think Jesse is still alive?"

"I don't think he could have survived that night where I left him. When I woke up there was at least five inches of new snow on the ground and I had walked down-hill most of the time." Ian's head fell into his hands and he began to cry.

"I walked all that day, following a creek and finally found a woman and her two kids hiding in a make-shift shelter. She told me I was about one mile from the Hamilton's ranch down the river. She wouldn't come with me. She had plenty of food, so I continued on to the Hamilton's."

"We know the Hamilton's," Dan said excitedly. "Jed and Mary Lou. Nice people. Surely Jed helped you?"

"Mr. Hamilton died that first day. His missus was barely alive. Didn't want to live very bad, but she fed me and I slept sound that night."

"My God!" Suzan cried. "How many days did you leave Jesse out there?"

"Suzan – I'd give anything if Jesse were sitting here telling this about me."

Suzan looked into Ian's anguished face and felt ashamed. "Oh, Ian," she cried. "I don't mean to blame you. I'm just so worried. Please – please tell me what happened to Jesse." Laramie tried to comfort her, but there was no comfort. Suzan knew where this story was going and she couldn't bare it.

"I know Jesse is still alive. I can feel him." She was wild eyed and frantic. "I'm not remembering him, I'm feeling him breathe and I can feel his blood flowing through his veins." Her voice rose to a shrill. "I know he's still alive."

Roma gently put her arm around her shoulders. "If you feel it, then it's true. He must still be alive." Roma's soothing voice calmed Suzan.

"I took Mr. Hamilton's horse and backtracked to the cabin, but there wasn't enough day-light to continue, so I stayed at the cabin. Mrs. Hamilton packed some dinkum – biscuits, sausage and cheese, so I was feeling stronger. I got up before first light the next morning and backtracked. There was new snow on the ground so my markers were hard to find, but I finally found the spot where I left Jesse. I found the pack I had left – the metallic blanket I'd covered him with was still there too."

"You're saying that Jesse wasn't there?" Suzan's blood rose and she couldn't stay in herself, but, with a surety she knew that Jesse was still alive.

"Suzan, it had snowed and covered up any tracks that may have been there, but there was no new blood, so I know an animal didn't get to him."

"Then, either he left on his own power, or someone rescued him." Suzan's face was resolute. "I know he's still alive."

"I spent the last two days getting here, so I think it's been a week since we fell off the mountain."

Dan listened intently to each word Ian said. "You say the place you left him is two days ride from here?"

"Yes, but I traveled very slowly. I bet you'll be able to get there a lot quicker."

"I'll bet those ribs hurt you plenty, too." Dan gently laid his hand on Ian's back and Ian let out a howl.

"Let's take a look at those ribs." Roma carefully unbuttoned Ian's shirt and blew softly when she saw the purple and blue bruises that covered his upper body. "Looks more like you've been in a train wreck than fell off a mountain." Roma inspected the scrapes and cuts on his arms and hands. "Looks pretty clean – no infection, anyway."

"You say you hit the side of the mountain three times before you hit the ground?" Dan was mentally calculating. "There's only a couple places with steep cliffs that you could ride to in a couple days. Only one of them would take you to the Hamilton's."

"Dad – you know where Jesse is – or was?"

"It's got to be Parker Ridge. That west side is layered with sheer red-stone cliffs." Dan looked at Ian sharply. "You said you walked to an abandoned cabin?"

"It looked like an old summer cattle station. I remember thinking what a wonderful place to bring the cattle in the heat of summer." Ian excitedly shook his head. "Yes – yes! There is a wide high-mountain pasture there – fenced in on three sides. I never found a gate, but I remember thinking it could sure use a good Aussie fence line."

Dan studied this newcomer. Jane's sweetheart – or so he'd been told. And he seems to think he knows something about fences. Thought he was a college professor!

"That's Parker Ridge. Only place you could fall off of, walk to cattle camp, and straight down to Hamilton's. And it's a good two days ride from here – without broken ribs."

Ian winced as Roma tied strips of torn bed-sheets around his chest. "Get a couple aspirin in you and you'll feel much better."

"Where's my Janie-girl?" Ian asked.

"Why – you must have hurt your head when you fell." Everyone turned to look at Dan. "It must have effected your thinking. There's only been one Janie-girl, and she wasn't yours." Dan looked far away. "Come to think of it, she hasn't been mine for a long time." Dan had quietly measured Ian up and down and liked what he saw. Good man! "Maybe she is yours."

Ignoring Dan's possessive fatherly outburst, Roma secured the last knot in Ian's bandages. "Jane Abby took the kids on a field trip to gather fire wood. She thought it would be good to get them out of the house – get their minds off of you and Jesse being gone." Her voice quavered. "She'll be thrilled to see you're back."

"Dad," said Suzan, "when can we go look for Jesse?"

"I think we should let Ian rest up and if he's up to it, we'll leave tomorrow."

"If we leave right now, we can be to the Hamilton's by tonight."

"Yes, and we'd each have a peanut-butter sandwich and a couple of bottles of water. Or," said Dan, "we could take a day to prepare, pack the things we'll need because I can smell a snow storm brewing, gather the horses in, grain them some, let them rest in the corral for the night and then leave in the morning."

Dan put his arm around Suzan's shoulders. "I know you're worried about Jesse. We all are. Ian said there was no blood, so I'm thinking someone found him and is taking real good care of him. He's probably recuperating somewhere nice and warm."

Suzan pulled away from her father. "Or he could just as easily be lying in a ravine somewhere with buzzards flying over him."

"Is that how he feels to you this minute?" Roma asked. Suzan looked puzzled. "You said you could feel him breathing, feel his heart beating." Roma's eye's held Suzan. "What does it feel like – this minute?"

Suzan's eyes closed. "He's quiet." She paused and kept her eyes closed. "He's warm." Peace came over her. "He's safe. I know he's safe."

"Then you're okay with leaving tomorrow?"

"Yes – tomorrow we'll go find Jesse."

"Whose horse?" Jane came in the back door, blowing on her hands. "Boy, it's getting cold – must be a storm coming in." Jane froze in mid stride when she looked past her dad and saw Ian sitting by the fire, all bandaged up.

"Janie-girl!"

"Ian." Jane's eyes filled with tears. "Oh, Ian." She rushed to him and saw the grief in his eyes. "What's the matter?" She looked around. "Where's Jesse?"

"We're riding for Jesse tomorrow," said Dan. "Ian can fill you in on all the details – I'll get the horses corralled and fed."

"Guess I'll start cooking and packing supplies." Roma steered Suzan toward the door. "You better tell your girls where you're going tomorrow."

## *Chapter 23*

"When did they leave to look for Jesse?" Rafa and Willie had become regulars for dinner at the Rocking Z. Laramie always had a sixth sense about when Rafa would show up. Those were the days she took a morning bath in lilac water. Like this morning. Roma told the story over dinner of Ian arriving hungry and tired – and alone. How Dan, Suzan and Ian were out trying to find Jesse.

Roma and Jane brought their coffee to the porch and lit a cigarette together. "Well, I don't want to miss anything," said Willie as he joined them.

"It was six days ago," said Jane. "They should have been back by now."

Jane remembered the dream she had the night before they left. The dream she promised Ian she wouldn't share with anyone until they found Jesse. "It wouldn't serve any purpose to tell them," he had said.

"But remember when I dreamed about Mira and I didn't tell anyone?" she argued.

"Yes, but would it have changed anything if you had told them all?"

Jane closed her eyes and saw the blood and felt the darkness. Deep, bloody claw marks across her face. Blood blinding her, she couldn't see, it was dark and dangerous. The scream of the puma tore through the memory of her dream in a terrifying moment of clarity. The smell – oh the smell was so putrid that when she awoke in a cold sweat, she couldn't get the smell out of her nostrils. She knew immediately that it was about Jesse, but couldn't acknowledge that it meant his death. It didn't feel like it was his death. It felt . . . like she couldn't see him. The blood blinded her. Blood in her eye. The stench of death in her nostrils. And dark – so dark.

"Oh honey, you know how the weather can change up there on the flat tops. They're probably holed up in that old abandoned cabin." Roma tried to be positive, but couldn't keep the concern from her voice. "The storm that blew through here yesterday is bound to be over and done with up there. They're fine. Your dad knows that country as well as he knows this ranch."

"Roma, maybe we can search down the valley for a couple of horses for Willie and me so we can help in the search."

"No, Rafa, thanks, but you don't know this country and there's no sense sending everyone to search. They'll be riding in here tomorrow or the next day."

Dan, Suzan, and Ian hunted for eight days, but never found Jesse. Not a trace. Not a scrap of cloth or footprint. The snowstorm that hit wiped out any clues that may have helped them.

They stopped at the Hamilton's ranch and Mary Lou Hamilton was sitting in the same rocker Ian found her in eight days earlier. It seemed to Suzan that she'd waited until they got there so she could put her mind to rest over matters of this world. Before she died she made Dan promise her he'd move someone into the house who would take care of the ranch – in case her son showed up by chance, and if he didn't come within two years, then Dan and Roma could do with it as they pleased. It was a nice ranch. Only four miles from Dan and Roma's with Harris Gulch and a cow trail between them, it had the best summer pasture around. It bordered the wilderness area, so there wasn't another ranch to the north or east of them for miles. Dan went on a couple of cattle drives up the gulch and past Hamilton's ranch to cow camp. Jed and Mary Lou lived there year round for years, but as they got older the winters nearly killed them.

It took her two days to dig through the frozen ground to bury Jed, and afterwards she just didn't have it in her to go on without him. The cattle were at winter pasture in a little valley not far from Harvey Gap Dam and Dan assured her they would be fine on the open range.

They buried her in the same unmarked grave with Jed and placed piles of rock on top to keep the coyotes from digging up their bodies. Suzan promised herself she'd come back in the spring to place a marker on the gravesite and plant flowers nearby. It snowed all night, covering the grave, the rocks and any clues that may have led them to Jesse.

Early the next morning, they headed east toward the flat tops – 1,000 square miles of the most beautiful and majestic country Suzan had ever seen. Deep mountain valleys carved by ancient glaciers and centuries of melting ice flanked by high mountain mesas were covered with pine, aspen and cedar. Jagged rock ledges towered skyward, standing sentinel for as far as they could see.

It took them all day to reach Parker Ridge and the place Ian had left Jesse. It was as Ian had said - not a single sign that they'd ever been there. Thank God there's no sign of mountain lions, thought Ian, although snow had fallen erasing any hope of finding footprints or tracks.

"Well, there's no trace of blood or clothing, so no animal has carried him away," said Dan. He was trying to comfort Suzan, but his attempt felt hollow - empty. "Bears are still hibernating and mountain lions usually eat their prey at the site of the kill. Leave a hell of a mess, so, no sign is good."

They camped there that night and got an early start in the morning searching every rock crevice and ravine along the way. Dan led the way on Rendi letting the experienced ranch horse pick her own way back to the top of the mesa, all the time searching for signs of human passage.

Finally, Dan said the words out loud that he'd only been thinking. "Honey, I think we have to accept the fact that Jesse is not in this area anymore." Dan didn't want to see the look of anguish on Suzan's face. He would have searched all winter to protect her from the fact that there just wasn't any trace of him or Ian ever having been there. Not even sign of campfires or camping spots.

"What does that mean, Dad? Not in this area anymore," Suzan cried. "What does that mean?"

"It means that someone probably helped him to safety and he's healing somewhere. Maybe someone in Meeker, or New Castle, Silt, Rifle." He hated to say it – "He could be anywhere. Any of those little towns, or the hundred or so hunting cabins peppered in a hundred mile radius of here."

"Dad, I know he's still alive."

"Keep hold of that faith, honey." Dan sighed and pulled his daughter to his chest and held her, like when she was a child. Tears fell down the front of his flannel shirt as Suzan came to the realization that her dad was right. "Know that when he's able, he'll find us. If I thought he was holed up somewhere and in trouble, I'd search until summer. But, someone has helped him to safety. There's not a single sign of struggle, no markers along the way, nothing." He continued to stroke her hair until he felt her body relax in resignation.

"Okay, let's go home." She let out a tired sigh.

"Yea – let's go home."

"Dad?" Her voice sounded small.

"What is it, honey?"

"If he's not home by spring, will you go with me to Meeker? And Silt and Rifle and New Castle, until we find someone who's seen him or heard of him?

"I'm sure he'll be back by spring. But if he's not, we'll go find him together."

## *Chapter 24*

"You know your mother." Suzan looked around the kitchen; the two gallon jar half filled with loose cigarettes – all flavors and colors; the little stack of pebbles on the window ledge – the ones she brought from *Levi's Lake* last summer when she took the kids fishing; the African Violet leaf she'd stuck in a cup of soil that now grew as big around as a dinner plate with leaves the size of silver dollars; and the four turkey wish-bones that hung in the window – one for each grandchild.

"Yes, I know Mom." Suzan's eye's scanned the room. Everything in her mother's home was treasured. The hutch with the collection of tiny cups and saucers that were carried by her great-grandmother all the way from Romania – fine porcelain china – all hand painted and different, and each of them already selected by Jane, Laramie or her. Treasures to be passed from mother to daughter – like the tatted lace dresser scarves that had been in the family for generations and the stemware that they only used on Christmas morning, or her great grandmother's heart-shaped locket. Suzan knew that only a woman would understand the significance of each cherished item and the memory it stored – the tug at the heart when holding your great-grandmother's heart locket – your only connection to that woman who gave life to your mother, who gave life to you. I'm definitely my mother's daughter, thought Suzan. She looked at the memories of a lifetime in each corner or ledge or counter-top of her mother's house and the story they told was clear. After it's all said and done – the only things that really matter are the people you've loved and shared your life with.

"Then you know we have to let her go." Dan looked at Suzan waiting for her to confirm his opinion.

"No, we don't have to let her go!" The words snapped out. "It's too dangerous," she said softly, her eyes pleading with her father. "It's crazy to walk in the mountains alone – in the dead of winter – I don't care what she says." She turned her back so he couldn't see the tears slip from her eyes then fell into his open arms and let go of the sobs that were stuck in her throat. "What's happening to her? Where does she go?" Suzan's face was wracked with pain.

"I wish I had some answers for you honey." Dan wiped at his eyes. "I just don't know."

"Why won't she let me go with her? Or anyone? Why does she insist on going alone?"

"Honey, when you've lived through what we have – and who knows what that really is – a walk alone in the forest brings sanity back."

"But she's been gone since yesterday morning! Where does she sleep? What does she eat?" Suzan was frantic. "And Mira and Lalo are gone too."

"Well, I know they didn't go with her, but they may have followed her."

"Where does she go?"

"I'm embarrassed that I don't have any answers," he said again, shaking his head. "I feel like I should know, but I don't. I only know that when she returns, she's laden down with roots, barks, rocks, twigs, leaves, bird feathers, coyote teeth, deer antlers, even dirt. *Medicine bones*. That's what she calls them."

Dan's eyes searched the ceiling. "And something else. When she returns, she acts like she's only been gone for a half an hour or so." He scratched his head. "I milk Maggie for her if she doesn't get back by dark, then I milk her in the morning. Wherever she's going, it must only be a couple of miles away, because she always shows up at about the same time in the morning – right after milking time." Dan looked miserable as he continued on. "She doesn't stay gone overnight very often – just a couple of times before this, but when she comes in the door, she marches in, puts her treasures of medicines and herbs away, and acts as if she'd just arrived from a trip to the supermarket and she's always different somehow. Fresh. Younger almost. Renewed! I can't quite put my finger on it."

"Boy! Have you seen that girl of yours with that whip?" Roma exploded in the back door, dropped her bundle in the middle of the table and began removing layer after layer of boots, jackets, sweatshirts and thermal underwear, until she stood before them in her jeans, tee-shirt and moccasins. She picked up her bundle and headed toward them as she continued on. "I'd bet my last dollar that she could pick the tick off a dog's ear with that whip of hers." She froze at the incredulous look on Suzan's face. "What?"

"Mom!" Suzan snapped.

"What, honey."

"Mom." Suzan's voice was pleading and filled with pain. "Mom, where have you been?" The tears started and she didn't give Roma a chance to answer as she continued. "I've been worrying all night long. If you don't have enough sense to come home at night so people don't worry about you, I would at least think you'd send my daughter home so I wouldn't worry about her, too."

"Oh Suzan." Roma touched her face. "Would you really think such a thing?" She walked to the table then turned to face Suzan and Dan.

"I didn't know Mira and Lalo followed me until the moon was high. Some herbs shouldn't be gathered until the sun has gone down, especially during the wintertime and it's hard to find them all close enough to the house, pick them and then walk all the way home again, so I usually pick some, sleep some, pick some more and sleep more until it gets light out." Roma's eyes glowed from deep down inside her. "And I lay on the ground and listen to the heartbeat of the earth. I can almost feel her breathing, resting with me, renewing."

She rushed to Suzan and tugged on her arm. "You should go with me sometime and listen." Suzan watched as her mother became animated with excitement. "I can hear the animals feeding and walking through the timber."

She searched Dan's face. "Have you ever heard deer talk to each other?" She didn't let him respond before she continued. "Or mountain lions purring to their kittens?" Roma's eyes got far away while she viewed her memory. "I can hear where they go to eat at night and I can hear what they're eating." She ignored the questions she saw in Suzan's eyes. "I know it sounds crazy," she hurried, before she changed her mind. "I've questioned my own sanity a hundred times in the last two months, waiting for you to get here, waiting for Judd and Dani to get here."

"Mom . . ." Suzan started.

"Don't tell me that they're not coming," Roma interrupted. "I know they're coming, just like I knew you were coming and just like I know that the animals show me what they are eating, so I'll know what to pick to help us survive this winter and stay healthy."

Suzan no longer challenged her mother. She knew it was a lost battle.

"I know mamma." Roma was her mother . . . that's all. She had always been half here and half somewhere else; somewhere magic and mystical. Roma came to this life with a memory of where she'd been before and now that memory was wide awake and becoming more vivid every day. Yes, they would have to let her go. Of course her mother heard herbs grow and listened to what the animals ate and heard deer talking to each other. She always had, only now she knew what she heard and couldn't deny it.

"Let me help you prepare the herbs." Suzan picked up the bundles from the table where Roma dropped them. "You can teach me about them; what they are and what they're good for."

"I don't know about all of them," Roma admitted sheepishly. "Mira can probably tell you more about them than I can." Suzan watched her mother clean the roots and barks she'd gathered. "I know to pick them, but it isn't always clear why until I need them." She eyed her daughter expecting skepticism. "I've used almost all that I gathered in the last bunch, like the barks that we boiled to make tea when you first got here." Suzan duplicated Roma's handling of the cleaned twigs and barks and roots until they were all separated in bundles. "I don't know how you got those kids here alive, but you did."

"Did you know that Mira gathered herbs when the younger children were so sick?" Suzan looked back to that dangerous time. "They probably would have died if she hadn't found the herbs, and I don't know how she knew what to gather."

"She heard the earth tell her." Roma looked squarely at Suzan now. "She told me that she was led to the herbs, that they were buried in the snow most of the time, but she knew where to dig through to find them."

"Yes." Suzan remembered. "And thank God she followed where her instincts led her."

"Don't you see what is happening Suzan?" Roma looked hard at her daughter.

"What do you mean, Mom?"

"You mean you don't know?" Roma stared incredulously. "You haven't figured it out yet?"

"Mom," Suzan pleaded. "Figured what out? Tell me."

"Memory." Roma stated. "We have memory of all things. All we have to do is remember." She hurried before the disbelief could settle into Suzan's eyes. "I can remember what I ate as a rabbit, even though I have never been a rabbit. And I can remember what a carrot sounds like when it's growing, even though I've never been a carrot." Suzan didn't dare interrupt. "It's like remembering the day of creation – like we were there and saw how everything would work and now our memory is coming back."

"Think about all that has happened. Think about how you knew what to pack. The girls said you instinctively knew what would be good to take to barter, how to prepare the food you had to carry, to preserve it, to prepare it and how to stretch it out and balance the nutritious benefits to keep all of you alive and healthy." Roma waited for it all to sink low – somewhere in the gut that knots when distressed and flattens when calm. "How did you know what to do?" Suzan's eyes searched Roma's, looking for the answer and suddenly her stomach sank – low and flat, her eyes sunk past Roma's – into the memory of past lives, past generations, past lifetimes. For that instant, they remembered what they'd forgotten. They saw each other in creation. They remembered.

The tiny window into the past shut as quickly as it had opened. Dan was awestruck as he watched the energy travel between them. He could actually see it, and almost reached to touch it.

"I was trying to tell you honey," Dan said to Suzan, "only I didn't have the words, but I've seen it myself." Dan paused as he tried to recall those first few days. "I don't know how your mom knew what to do to save my life, but she sure as hell did." His eyes narrowed and his voice lowered. "She sewed me up as good as a doctor could have, better, if he was relying on his fancy education." Dan's eyes misted over. "She did things to save me that scared me, but what she did worked. There were a couple times I didn't know where I was, who I was, or who your mother was, but I knew she was dancing, and I could smell the sage burning." Dan swallowed hard, and held Suzan's gaze. "We were not here." He watched his daughter's reaction and continued on. "We were somewhere in the past, where medicine was practiced by medicine women and herbs were as potent as any prescription drug you could buy."

Dan's eyes filled with respect and love as he looked at Roma. "She was the healer." Moment's passed and the tension that filled the air began to dissipate. "Then she was the veterinarian when she went and rescued that range cow and turned her into one of the best milk cows I've ever seen. Why, I'll bet Maggie gives four gallons of milk a day – and that's every dairyman's dream – using all the hormones and drugs modern science could provide him. But she's never been a dairyman. And she's never been a botanist, or horticulturist, or geologist either."

Suzan remembered their trip and how they'd relied on what seemed like serendipity. All the events rushed past her like viewing a video – getting home that first night, Laramie searching out the children, Jane joining them, Jesse finding the insulin, Lalo saving Mira, Rafa being at the camp, Roma finding Dan when he was bleeding to death, the chickens, the cow, Mira's whip, Mira's herbs. It was too overwhelming to comprehend. Suzan's eyes overflowed as she recalled her own memory of experiences previously unknown. She'd never questioned where the knowledge came from, but took it for granted like it had always been there.

Suzan laid the bundle of herbs on the counter and walked out the back door, down the steps and toward the corral.

"No." Roma caught Dan's arm as he went past her to follow Suzan. "Let her go. She needs to remember. She needs to know."

Spring whispered cold on Suzan's wet cheeks. They'd arrived three months ago – almost to the day. Tender green sprouts crawled bravely through soggy soil as each day grew warmer and longer. *Life just keeps happening – whether we care or not. It doesn't know any better – it can't help it.* Laughter mocked her as it found its lilt on the wind. She laughed until there were no more tears left and the despair of the night before was gone, too. She felt lighter, cleaner. Beautiful.

*You can feel it.*

"Feel what?"

*What you feel.*

"What is it?"

*What does it feel like?*

"It feels like . . . like . . . life."

*How do you know?*

"Because I remember."

*Yes!*

Maggie's eyes rolled in acknowledgement as the crazy woman danced in the field. Black valley mud sucked up her hooves keeping time with the low-belly chant of the woman. Bovine heat filled the empty space as milk flowed down crevices until it reached the dancing feet of the woman, mingled with the earth under their feet and mixed the mud to the heart beat of the crazy woman dancing in the field.

And it didn't matter. She didn't care that she was moving to an ancient rhythm beating so clearly. She was glad to hear it. Glad to feel alive – whether anyone cared or not. It didn't matter. It happens whether anyone cares or not – life. She could feel the memory. She reached down and scooped up the milk and the mud and tasted it and remembered when they were born. She was alive!

"Mother!" Suzan burst through the back door, mud up to her calves, trailing it through the porch and into the kitchen.

Roma continued to sort her dried twigs and barks, knotted memories of summer flowers. "I saw you dancing in the mud." Roma watched Suzan, waiting to hear what she already knew. Wanting to hear it from this child of years ago – this newborn woman of memory.

"Mom," tears brimmed Suzan's eyes. "I remember the day she was born, and the first time she calved, and I remember . . . her milk." She became excited, animated, her thoughts running faster than words could speak them. "I could taste her milk before I put it in my mouth. And the earth – it tasted like mole breath and bee pollen and ant saliva." Tears spilled and ran freely down her cheeks. "I remember the sea-shells and tasted the sea salt that was here before the valley was." Her eyes shone like a magnifying glass viewing the past. "I chose this valley before it was here because I knew it would be here when I was. I remember when it was created." Their eyes locked and looked into the past that united them. "I remember now."

"Yes," answered Roma. "It was time."

## *Chapter 25*

"What do you mean, you want to get married in a month? And what's the big rush?" Dan felt panicky inside. What did anyone really know about this man? Roma liked him, but hell, she liked just about everyone, unless she felt a real sense of evil about them – and there had been a few. Since the first day Rafa came to the facility, she'd like him. Dan had to admit that he liked Rafa, too. But, still – Laramie was the youngest – the last daughter to let go to another man. "And besides, the snow hasn't even melted off the mountains. Wait until summer when the weather's nice and folks will feel more like celebrating." Dan knew his argument was weak. "And where would we find a preacher?"

"A preacher?" Rafa almost laughed out loud. "You serious?" He didn't give Dan time to reply. "It's all different now. Everything's different . . . and it's not that there isn't enough time to court your daughter, it's just that there is no need for us to wait." He hefted another bundle of hay between the two hooks and hauled it to the corral with Dan right on his heels. Somehow, the words he'd rehearsed wouldn't come to him and he had to make his case in a hurry.

"Good Lord, Rafa," Dan countered. "You've only known each other for twenty minutes. I've known my daughter all her life. She can charm the skin off a snake, but she can turn into that viper with the next word from her mouth if she feels she's right. She's about the strongest willed woman I've ever met besides her mother. Believe me," he pleaded. "You need to give it some time."

"We don't need to test time to know that it's the right thing for us." Rafa whirled to face Dan who almost ran right over the top of him. "You think I don't know Laramie? You think I couldn't see her high-strung, strong willed nature that first night they passed by the facility? All those kids, three women and no men." Rafa's voice was almost reverent. "And we don't need to wait to find a preacher to sanction it before God." Rafa could see he'd come on a little too strong and he stopped to face Laramie's father. "Look Dan, haven't you ever known something absolutely? Without having to worry it over in your mind, weigh the pro's and con's – you just knew it was right?"

Slowly he met the challenge in Rafa's eyes. "I felt the same way about Roma when we met." His eyes stared back at that summer day 40 years ago. "In fact, the day we met, I knew we would be together forever, if she'd have me."

"There! See?" Rafa continued to haul the hay with Dan following.

"But, it was the proper thing to ask the father's permission to court, then to court for several months so the family could look you over, then to be engaged for a year or so . . . oh." They were facing each other again. "I see your point. There really isn't much need, is there?" Dan began to chuckle. "There really wasn't any need for Roma and I to go through all that, and it's a good thing we didn't carry it out much longer, or her father would have escorted me to the wedding with a shotgun." Dan put his arm around Rafa's shoulder and they both began to laugh.

"I only have a couple concerns."

"Oh, oh." Rafa flinched. "I should have known it couldn't be so easy."

"It's about who you are." Dan hurried to add, "Not that it really matters. My daughter would never judge anyone by their past, but, let's just call it a curiosity factor. Oh, I know what Roma told me your file said, but, I also know what Laramie said about first meeting you; that you somehow knew Lalo from somewhere else and you seemed to know a lot about him. And that you kept him from killing a man."

Dan was uncomfortable with this line of conversation. He'd always believed that a man's business was his own. And his past was past. But Laramie *was* Dan's business and he needed to put these questions to rest – once and for all.

"I don't mind answering your questions, but I'd rather tell it only once, so it won't have to be repeated, unless Lalo wants to talk about it." Rafa looked dubiously toward the house. "I have to talk to Lalo first. I get the feeling that he and Mira have avoided me, just so Lalo wouldn't have to be reminded of the truth or hear it spoken out loud. It's a part of Lalo's life that he's been running from for many years."

"Fair enough." They shook hands and Dan began walking toward the house.

"Dan, wait – what about the other?"

"The other? Oh, yea," Dan chuckled. "Well, that little gal has had a mind of her own since the day she was born." Dan took off his hat, slapped it against his leg and belly laughed all the way to the porch. "I wouldn't try to talk her out of anything she set her mind on doing. I guess I ought to give you a couple horses for taking her off my hands." He laughed so hard he could barely get the words out and left Rafa wondering if he was half serious. "But, I do appreciate you asking my permission," Dan said seriously. "It was the right thing to do, and I appreciate it."

"Well, come on," he roared, wiping his eyes, "we've got to tell Roma." Laughter rolled through the house as he opened the door. "This has been a long winter and it will give the women something to fuss over. Nothing like a wedding to take their minds off the hard times."

Rafa found Laramie waiting by the door, along with everyone else. He picked her up and whirled her around the kitchen as Dan made the announcement.

"I never dreamed I'd ever be so happy in this life," Rafa said huskily.

Laramie's sensuous eyes drew him into her. "We've barely started," she whispered. "I've a feeling happy is much bigger than this."

"Why do we have to talk about it?"

They sat in a circle on the tree stumps in the hay barn, Lalo, Mira, Laramie and Rafa. Lalo looked like a cornered animal, filled with fear and betrayal and Rafa was the archenemy – the one who knew the truth – the stranger. Rafa found him and Mira splitting logs and chopping wood they had dragged from the black timber. Mira's eyes were hooded with a mask of protectiveness, poised to strike. Lalo's instincts came flooding back. He was agitated and defensive, his body tense. All his energy in the last seven years had been spent trying to forget who he really was and to find a safe place to hide, mentally and emotionally. Mira and Laramie were the only people on this earth who knew the truth of his existence. Not that he'd shared anything directly with Laramie, but he knew she had a gift of hearing the fear. That's how she'd found all the children. He didn't care that Laramie knew, because he felt secure that she would never share it with anyone and they'd never discussed it. Now, as he looked into her eyes, he felt her pleading and her compassion.

"Lalo," she said as she took his hands in hers. "You know that we would protect you from your past forever if there was still a need. You needed all that fear and hiding before. You've developed such a strong sense of emotional survival that you were able to give that to Mira when she didn't want to live." Laramie sensed Mira tense at the reminder of that terrible time just a few short months before. "And it's time for Mira to get past that terrible time too." Lalo's eyes softened as she continued to speak. "Maybe it's time for both of you to be free from it forever . . . to let it go . . . give it to the universe . . . give the child permission to live again without the fear and hiding." She could feel the tension leave his body. His head dropped and his shoulders relaxed as the defiance and fear left him. Mira breathed a deep sigh of relief as the volatile moment melted.

"Okay, we can talk now. But not everyone," he quickly added. "Just Dan and Roma. Just them, not the kids."

"No – it wouldn't benefit the kids to know the details, but it might help them to know that you're healing from a really painful time." Laramie continued to hold his gaze. "They've all been through some terrible times. They've lost families too."

Just then the sweet sound of Sara's angelic voice drifted to them – as if on que. They listened for a moment to the melodious sound, trying to identify the familiar song. "Even Sara is healing," Laramie said, taking advantage of the moment.

Lalo quickly looked toward the direction of Sara's voice. "Mira and I always hear her singing to the lake."

"Singing to the lake?"

"Yes," said Mira. "She goes to the lake and sings to it. Why do you think she does that, Aunt?"

"I don't know," replied Laramie. "She must feel safe there, like the lake is not a threat to her. Do you remember," continued Laramie, "not too long ago, you didn't want to speak to anyone either and only recently felt secure enough to talk to the rest of us. I'm sure the lake is her safe place, just like Lalo was your safe place to talk."

"I remember."

"It's very peaceful at the lake," added Lalo. "We like to go there too, that's why we hear Sara singing. Maybe a lot of ghosts are being set free now."

*Chapter 26*

"Where are they going to live?" yawned Roma.

"With all the empty houses close by, I doubt they'll have any trouble finding a place to live."

"That's true enough. The Hamilton place is close, but it's in some pretty mean country when the weather's bad."

Roma rose up on one elbow and looked at Dan through the moonlight streaming through their window.

"We've had a good life, haven't we Roma." Dan was staring intently into her eyes.

"Yes, Dan. It's been a wonderful life and I wouldn't change one single minute of it."

"You mean you wouldn't take back all the mean things you've said to me over the years?" Dan chuckled.

"If I said mean things, you deserved it," teased Roma.

"I would take back all the times I've hurt you and disappointed you," said Dan seriously. "I wish I had been able to give you all the things you ever wanted."

"Oh Dan," Roma's voice broke, "you gave me everything I ever wanted and more." She laid her head on his chest and he pulled her close. "I never dreamed life would be so good to me." Tears fell from her cheeks onto his chest. "I'm so happy that we lived long enough to get to this wonderful time in our lives and I mean it when I say I wouldn't change a single thing. Not one moment of pain, not one word said in anger – nothing." She wiped her face against his nightshirt. "I wouldn't change any of it. How else would I ever have known that anyone could love me so much that they'd forgive me for hurting them so? You are the best part of me. I love my life with you." Quiet sobs shook her shoulders as Dan held her close to him.

"We've got the rest of our lives to make it even better," Dan said to break the serious mood.

"Yes we do, but who knows how long the rest of our lives will be? The other side of life is closer than we think. And sometimes I think . . . . . ."

"Sometimes you think too much," Dan chided playfully. "And sometimes you talk about things that are too serious or out of my realm to discuss." Dan became pensive and quiet. "I can only imagine today and more today's. I know I'm a lucky man and I'm happy when you're happy. I know having our daughters and grandkids home has made us both easier to live with. Someday our son and his family will be here too, but before you get thinking about Judd and Dani, let's finish talking about where Rafa and Laramie are going to live."

"You're right. I got off the subject again." Roma was relieved the conversation didn't go where her thoughts were taking her.

"I've been working side-by-side with Rafa for almost a month now," started Dan. "He's a good man. That story about him being an undercover agent, and Lalo and Senator Lambert was a shocker, and a relief."

"Yes, it's good to know that sometimes justice is served after all." Dan watched Roma as the fire lit in her eyes. "Can you imagine a man having his wife and children killed? She felt everything passionately. "What that poor boy must have lived through for the past seven years!"

"It is a relief to know the truth about Rafa – you know – that man our daughter is going to marry soon."

"I'm sorry Dan. I just can't keep my mind on one subject. I'm all over the map tonight. So many things to think about. Planning the wedding, worrying about Jesse, about Judd and Dani. Our family isn't whole yet and my mind is frantic most of the time."

"Well, let's take one thing at a time. First – Rafa told me he and Laramie have an interest in the Hamilton ranch up Harris Gulch." Roma started to protest and Dan quickly put a finger to her lips. "Now – I know it's pretty far up the mountain, but it's good summer grazing land and they've got horses and mules on the property, and there's practically a straight path down the mountain to our front door." Again, he pressed a finger to Roma's lips. "I know you'll miss them in the winter, but there's not a closer place around here that won't be just as hard to visit in the winter time, and most of the winter the roads will be passable whether they've seen a plow or not."

"Dan, I'm not objecting to them keeping up the Hamilton's ranch. It's exactly what Jed and Mary Lou would have wanted. It's the children. Are they taking all the kids up there with them?"

"They plan to. Rafa and Laramie want to go to the Rifle Library and the elementary school and gather some text books to start school when summer's over."

"That's the problem. There are hundreds of kids in Rifle and Silt and around the area who will need a school to go to." There's the fire in her eyes again, thought Dan. She's off and running now. "We need to have the kids in the community school so they can socialize with each other and get to know the next generation of citizens in this community." Roma was adamant. "It's important that they keep in close contact with one another so they can get to know each other over the years and develop a close community, otherwise this country will regress two hundred years."

"Roma, you're going way too fast and too far for me to keep up."

"I guess we can save that conversation for later too," said Roma resignedly. "I think the Hamilton place is prime property, and I know they only had the one son and if he comes to claim it, he'll be inheriting a working, well-kept ranch. I know Laramie and Rafa will be happy there." She winced under Dan's stare. "And the kids – a couple of weeks after the wedding," added Roma. "I get to keep them for a couple of weeks." A couple of weeks, thought Roma. I'll only have a couple of weeks.

## *Chapter 27*

Torrential rains reshaped the lay of the land. The creek flooded its banks, leaving it wider, gullies deeper, cliffs steeper and the valley a lush green.

Dan, Suzan, Ian and Jane made three more attempts to find Jesse, but to no avail. It was as if the earth had swallowed him up. Suzan was a stubborn woman, but after weeks went by her resolve began to fade and she finally admitted that all their searching hadn't unearthed a single clue.

"Where can he be and why hasn't he come back to us? I'll be searching for him for the rest of my life." She shouted as Roma placed sage tea on the table.

"You have your children to think about." Roma tread carefully as she broached the subject. "Mira is becoming a stranger to all of us, withdrawing into the mountains sometimes for days. She needs you."

"She doesn't need me. She's doing what you do." Suzan shot her mother an accusing glare. "She doesn't tell anyone where she's going and just shows up when it suits her – like you've been doing." She couldn't stop herself and the words came out in lumps between sobs. "She follows animals and eats what they eat." Her voice rose to a frantic scream. "And Lalo follows her around like a puppy." The children stopped their coloring and stared wide-eyed at Suzan. "Who knows what they do when they're gone."

Roma knew all the fear and stress of the last few months was spewing out as anger, but she didn't try to stop her. Maybe if she got it all out, it could become something else.

"Maybe they've got a den of cubs up in the rocks that they have to tend to." Suzan's eyes became wild and fierce. "Why did everything have to change? Why does life have to be so hard?" She stared at her hands. "Look at these!" She shouted the words. "They're not my hands!" Her fingers traced the tanned lines around her eyes and mouth. "My skin feels like leather." She dropped her face into her hands. "And my husband ran away from me." The words practically choked her and came out as barely a whisper.

"Is that what this is all about?" Roma grabbed Suzan by her shoulders. "Is that what you really believe? Suzan?"

"What other answer could there be?" Fear in Suzan's eyes pled with Roma for another answer. "We searched everywhere. There isn't a shred of evidence that he was ever out there."

"Yes, but there are a dozen different reasons why you weren't able to find him."

"No, Mom." Suzan felt relieved to say the words out loud. "He's not coming back."

"Don't you dare give up. Don't you even hint at it. We don't give up." Roma's voice began to tremble, but the forcefulness of her words startled Suzan. "Where is your faith in God? He didn't bring you all this way safely, just to leave you miserable and alone."

Tears slowly coursed down her face. Why couldn't she believe? What had happen to her faith? A couple months ago she was certain that Jesse was still alive. She felt his heartbeat and knew he was warm and safe. She felt defeated and ashamed that she couldn't remember the strong feelings that drove her to look for Jesse so courageously, just a short time ago.

"Oh, Mom," she cried, "I'm so afraid. I feel so dark and deserted inside." She sobbed in her mother's arms until there were no more tears.

"Why don't you go with Mira – up in the hills where she spends her time to renew her courage and find who she is." Tenderness poured out to her daughter and love swelled her heart for the woman that she held in her arms. "Maybe you'll find Suzan. Maybe you'll be able to hear your own heartbeat again."

## *Chapter 28*

News of a celebration at the Rocking Z Ranch spread quickly through the small outlying communities. The timing was perfect. They'd survived! The women especially were ready to visit and cook and find relief from the winter's worry and heartache. Families came from miles around in hopes of bartering for things they needed and a desire to rebuild the community. Women who'd lost their husbands came, and men came in hopes of meeting some of these brave survivors.

Willie drove a team of horses pulling a flat bed wagon carrying four families from Rifle. One of them was a woman with three children that he wanted to introduce to Dan and Roma.

Most folks didn't care and some didn't know that it was a wedding. It had been a long, painful winter and now the days were getting longer and warmer, snow was melting off the mountaintops, and tender green shoots spotted the landscape promising life to the weary survivors. It was time to celebrate!

Spring run-off made a slippery mess of the road leading to the ranch, as it did every year. Dan and Willie made several trips with horse drawn wagons down the muddy road to pick up families and bring them to the ranch. Tents cropped up on both sides of the creek and everyone was ready to celebrate. The women spent five days cooking on open fires and baking in hot rock ovens for the crowd that came from as far as Glenwood, New Castle, Silt and Parachute. Everyone brought something to feed the growing crowd whether it was a jar of preserves, a sack of flour or a side of beef.

"Thanks, Ruth Ann," said Roma as she hugged the frail woman and took the delicately wrapped package from the leathered hands.

"I wore it on my wedding day, and I wanted your daughter to have something borrowed." Ruth Ann's sunken eyes brimmed with tears. "I guess I'll ask for it back, so my Nancy can wear it someday."

Laramie burst through the door as Roma carefully opened the layers of yellowed tissue paper to reveal the most elegant locket she'd ever seen. Rubies set around inlaid pearl in a heart shape. "Oh mamma!" Laramie admired the exquisite piece of jewelry and looked at the woman inquisitively.

"Laramie, this is Ruth Ann. And this is my daughter Laramie – she's the bride tomorrow. I'm so sorry, I don't know your last name Ruth Ann." Roma handed the locket to Laramie. "She brought you something borrowed to wear tomorrow."

"Jesperson. Ruth Ann Jesperson." The woman's eyes shone with pride as she said her name. "We're the Jesperson's from Silt Mesa. Hope you don't mind that we came without an invitation, but my daughter said it was time we got out and the sun was shining, so we came. And I hope you'll wear the locket," she said to Laramie. "My husband gave it to me when we were married, thirty-five years ago tomorrow."

"Our anniversaries will be on the same day," said Laramie.

"I think it's right," said Ruth Ann. "I think tomorrow is the sixth day of April, the same day that Harold and I were married."

"I'd be honored to wear your locket Ruth Ann," said Laramie, "and it was so nice to meet you and I hope you have a good time while you're here."

"Yes," said Roma, "and I hope you'll stay a few days after the wedding so all of us women can get better acquainted and support one another. It's been a hard time, and we need to help each other plant and harvest and prepare for the times ahead."

Ruth Ann's eyes came to life as tears gently slid down her sunken cheeks. "I'd love to stay on for a day or two. It's been so long since I visited with any women friends. So many of them passed the same time my Harold did – that terrible day, but Nancy and I didn't come prepared and didn't bring anything to even feed ourselves."

"Don't you worry about that for one minute," said Roma adamantly. "It's time we all started living again, and everyone's welcome." Roma shaded her eyes from the bright sun and pointed towards the creek. "I see Nancy already making friends with my granddaughters and the other young girls from around the area. You'll see, there will be plenty of room for you and your daughter." Roma quickly added, "And plenty of food too – mostly game. In fact, I'm sure there will be so much food that everyone will be taking leftovers home." Roma knew from the condition of the woman and her daughter that their food supply had dwindled long ago. The daughter was in far better shape than her mother was and Roma suspected that Ruth Ann had missed a lot of meals so she could feed her daughter. Well, she'd see to it that they had plenty to take home with them.

Laramie took the locket upstairs to the *wedding room*, as the kids called it. She remembered the circles around her mother's homemade calendar and knew that the next day was the second of

May, but it didn't matter. She certainly hadn't been able to keep track of the days, and who knows what had happened to Ruth Ann in the last five months. She was like so many of the women, gaunt and worn, but filled with graciousness and hopefulness at the coming celebration. They came to the door, one by one, to present her with something borrowed, blue, or new to wear on her wedding day. All were treasures.

She carefully laid the locket with the other *borrowed* gifts. There were five broaches with priceless gemstones – emeralds, rubies, diamonds, sapphires, and lockets of different sizes and precious metals – some with pictures inside. Thirteen lace garters lay neatly on the oak dresser, along with the pale blue tatted lace garter that her mother and grandmother wore on their wedding days. Several pearl necklaces of different lengths, and solitaire diamonds on thin gold chains hung from pegs on a tie rack. All the jewels saved in secret places were brought to her to wear on her wedding day.

But she liked the broaches the children made the best. They had asked Mira and Lalo what special gift they could make for Laramie. Their sparse supplies left them limited in choices, but Roma always said *necessity is the mother of invention*, so they made dough from flour, water and white school glue, and Mira helped them form delicate petals and leaves. When the tiny pieces dried, they glued them on small disks of painted cardboard and painted the flowers in bright colors. Roma melted glue sticks found in her craft cupboard and attached a pin fastener on the back of each disk. Since each child made several, there were enough to attach around the flowing hem of her wedding dress. Laramie looked at the treasures and was determined to wear them all.

Her gaze went to the wedding dress her whole family worked on during the past month. It was breathtaking! Suzan cut up a crisp, white sheet and covered it with lace cut from the beautiful tatted lace tablecloth that Roma's grandmother brought from Romania in 1919.

"Mamma, we can't cut up your grandmother's lace tablecloth – you've had it all your life," Laramie was overwhelmed at her mother's suggestion.

"Yes, and I can't think of a better use for it than to adorn the wedding dress of my youngest daughter," Roma said as she kissed Laramie's wet cheek. "It would thrill my mother and her mother too, and we'll all have gifted to someone we love." Roma nodded to Suzan to start cutting and the first slice was made into the hand-tatted lace. "Suzan's the best seamstress I know. We'll all take a few stitches so we can all claim a hand in it. That's how my mamma did it, too. Grandmother did the hand stitching, mamma did the machine stitching, and I anchored down the lace and covered the buttons. Three generations of stitching on my dress." Roma's eyes misted remembering her own wedding dress.

Suzan oiled the antique treadle sewing machine that came to life and hummed a sweet tune as she steadily pedaled and carefully guided each stitch. Roma fixed sweet cocoa and Laramie made cornbread while the four of them relived happy memories, buried painful ones, laughed until they cried, and cried until they laughed.

Jane made a pair of calf length shoes from a white elk hide Roma took from the upstairs cedar chest. Mira selected tiny blue and white beads from Roma's craft cupboard and sewed them in an intricate shape of dolphins on the top of the soft shoe. When the shoes were finished they fit Laramie's foot like second skin and were distinctly beautiful.

Roma stitched tiny pearl beads along the delicate pattern of the remaining tatted lace to make a beautiful shoulder length veil.

Now, Laramie looked at the treasures that lay neatly on the bed. She felt like the princess in a fairy tale. Everything was so beautiful. She remembered thinking her mother was crazy when she suggested making a wedding dress from a plain white sheet.

Roma kneaded the soft flour and cornmeal dough as the young girl shook the gallon jar of cream to make butter. The stone ovens were hot enough to bake in now and Roma formed the dough into biscuits.

"I haven't heard my mother laugh since that horrible day when daddy died," said Nancy with tears in her eyes.

"Women need the company of other women," said Roma. "Encourage your mom to visit with other women. It will heal her heart."

"Why couldn't I heal her heart?"

"It takes time to heal and it wasn't your job," said Roma as she placed her arm around the girl's thin shoulders. "Hearts take time to heal and God always puts the right people in our lives when the time is right."

"Is that what's wrong with Mira?"

The question took Roma by surprise.

"I just think Mira must be really sad." She lowered her eyes in embarrassment and added quickly, "But I really like her. At first I was afraid of her – she looks so wild and that whip she carries – she's so good with it. When she saw me watching her, she wrapped it around the gatepost and pull it shut. I followed her and Lalo into the woods and watched her snap it around a dead tree limb and pull it down to use for firewood." Nancy cocked her head at Roma. "Do you think I could learn to use a whip?"

"I think you can do anything you really want to do." Roma felt Nancy's longing to belong. "Why don't you ask Mira how she made it?"

"You mean she made that whip?"

"Yes," answered Roma. "She and Lalo made it together on their way here from Denver."

"They came all the way from Denver?" Nancy looked with admiration toward the creek where Mira and Lalo were fishing. "When did they get here?"

"Oh, gosh," said Roma. "I think it was toward the end of January. It took them a long time to come across the mountains."

Roma saw the look of admiration and longing in Nancy's eyes and took the gallon jar from her hands. "Why don't you go down to the creek and see if there's an extra fishing pole." Nancy hesitated. "Go on. I'll just finish up here – it's almost butter now."

Nancy shyly walked toward the creek and Roma watched as she approached Mira and Lalo. "Those two are so attached, it's hard for anyone else to fit in their world," said Roma out loud.

"What did you say, Mom?"

"Oh Jane Abby – I was just commenting on Mira and Lalo. It's hard to not worry about them. They're like twins. It's uncanny how they are so much alike. With their hair kept so short, they even look alike. I wonder what's in store for those two?" Roma looked at her daughter. "Do you think they'll end up together when they're older? I mean . . . married someday?"

"Mom," Jane chuckled. "They are older and they don't have to get married to love each other like they do."

"Well, I mean . . . you know . . . married."

"You mean – babies! Will they ever be sexual and have babies together."

"Yes, that's what I mean."

"I don't think their love is that way. They are more familiar with each other than most couples I know – married or not, but I don't think they'll ever be sexual with each other." Jane looked at her mom. "They love each other, that's for sure, but I think they understand their purpose is not to create life with each other. . . but to create life *in* each other."

Roma looked at her quizzically. "What do you mean?"

"I mean, I think they were both ready to die – leave this existence. They gave each other the desire to live again. That's got to be the gift of life in the purest sense – not mixed up with sex."

"That's pretty simple," said Roma. "I sure hope you're right."

"Mom," started Jane.

"Yes?" There was no answer. Roma looked at her. "What is it honey?" Jane's face was full of concern. "What's the matter?"

"I was wondering if you'd seen that bear again?"

Roma stared at Jane for several seconds. "Only in my dreams." She was startled by the question, but tried to sound as casual as possible. She'd actually seen the sow several times in the last month but hadn't said anything to the family because she knew it would worry them.

"She visited my dreams too – her and her cubs."

Roma opened the gallon jar and separated the large mound of soft butter from the pale liquid. Darned that daughter of mine and her dreams, thought Roma. "Plenty of time to discuss dreams after all the excitement and celebration is over." She wiped her hands on her apron. "Maybe in a couple of days," she said too casually.

That's all it took for Jane to know she should be terrified.

"Mamma?

"Yes, Dominic?" Laramie said, as she fastened the last colorful pin on her wedding dress.

"That's the one I made for you," he said, pointing to the ones she'd just attached.

"I know. I wanted to find a special place for it, because you're so special." Laramie picked him up and whirled him around the room. "One-two-three, one-two-three, one-two-three," she counted as she practiced her best recollection of the waltz.

"We need the music player from Cody's house. Do you remember when you heard the music?" Dominic looked at her with his clear blue eyes that still surprised her every time she looked into them.

"Yes, I remember. It was *Für Elise*, one of my favorite songs."

"Did you hear music when you found me?"

"No, I didn't hear music, but I got a real funny feeling inside, a real sad feeling before I saw your grandpa."

"And then what happened?" Dominic settled himself on the bed so he could hear the story again. The children's favorite stories were the ones of how she'd found each one of them and how they all became brothers and sisters.

"Right now, I have to finish my chores to get ready for the wedding." Laramie studied the worried look on Dominic's face. "Is there something wrong?" she asked.

"Well, I was wondering where we're gong to live when you and Rafa get married." Laramie looked at him and realized she hadn't told the children the good news.

"I forgot to tell you the surprise," she said. "Why don't you get the kids and I'll tell everyone at one time."

"A surprise?" Dominic beamed. "If you tell me the surprise, I could tell them," Dominic said, trying to bait her.

"Never mind – maybe I won't tell anyone until after the wedding," she teased.

"Okay. I'll find everyone," he said resignedly as he slid off the bed.

"Tell them to go to the kitchen, and we'll have the leftover biscuits with honey," she hollered after him.

"Did I hear biscuits and honey?" Jane stuck her head in the bedroom. "Isn't there going to be a wedding in a couple of hours?"

"Everything's done except my hair and to put on my dress." She flashed her fingernails at Jane. "Had my manicure yesterday."

"It's the least I could do. Thank goodness mom had all the stuff. I guess being a pack rat all these years has paid off. I can't believe all the stuff mom has drug around from house to house all these years. Who would ever have thought to keep hair rollers and bobby pins?"

"You sound a little irritated." Laramie looked directly into Jane's eyes. "What's the matter?" She recognized the foreboding look in Jane's eyes. "You had another dream, didn't you?" Laramie tensed. "Is it about me and Rafa?"

"No, Laramie. It's not about you and Rafa. I'm sure you and Rafa will live happily ever after – just like the enchanted life you have always lived," she teased. "I hate these dreams. Why don't I get the kind of dreams that I can do something to protect the people I love, instead of prepare them for the worst?"

"Thank goodness we can prepare – because of your dreams. Now, tell me about the dream."

"No, today is your wedding day. There will be plenty of time to talk later." She saw the look of protest in Laramie's eyes. "I promise it will be soon."

"After our honeymoon?"

"You'll be so busy after the honeymoon moving up the canyon, you won't have time to visit."

"Oh, I almost forgot – biscuits and honey in the kitchen. I have to tell the kids."

Everyone gathered under the huge cottonwood trees by the creek. Roma guessed there were at least two hundred people there – counting children and babies. It was the perfect spring day. The sun shone brilliantly, but it was cool enough to be comfortable for the large crowd.

Rafa stood on one foot and then the other as he nervously waited with Willie and the other men from the camp. What could be keeping her? Roma was already seated in the front row of chairs that were arranged in the new spring grass. At Suzan's signal the children started singing the wedding march they had rehearsed. La La la-la, La La la-la, La La la-la-la-la-la-la-la-Laaaaaaa. When Laramie heard the music, which was the signal that all was ready, Dan gave her one last kiss on the cheek and dried her eyes with his clean handkerchief. "Well, it's time. Are you ready, honey?"

"Yes, Dad, I'm ready," she sniffed. "And Dad – thanks for the talk. I love you so much."

"You'll always be my little girl," Dan choked out.

"I used to hate when you said that, but now it sounds so comforting." She wrapped her arm through Dan's extended elbow and they walked in step to the music towards the cottonwood trees. Her heart skipped a beat when her eyes met Rafa's. "He is so handsome."

Cheers went up from the crowd as Rafa kissed Laramie, indicating the celebration could begin. Of all the people gathered, there was not a preacher among them, so Rafa and Laramie said their vows before God and a couple hundred witnesses who joined them in prayer at the beginning of the ceremony.

Violins, guitars, harmonicas and saxophones came out of their cases. Musicians tuned and refined their instruments and practiced familiar songs as people lined up on both sides of the tables to pile plates high with venison, elk, fresh asparagus found on the creek bank, rice, beans, biscuits and gravy. Chicory coffee and cornmeal cakes with honey finished the meal. And a special surprise for Laramie would follow for dessert – peach cobbler with real cream!

"It's going to be a long night for this crowd," whispered Rafa in Laramie's ear.

"Why don't we meet everyone and thank them for coming, I'll dance with daddy, you with mom, and then – they'll never miss us."

"Do we have to dance?" His hands tightened around her waist as he pulled her to him and kissed her.

"We better look like we're dancing right now or we'll embarrass ourselves. You know everyone is watching us, don't you?"

"Let's go meet everyone. They came a long way, and I want to thank them for making this day so special." He grabbed Laramie's hand and led her through the gathering crowds all tapping their feet to the beat of the music.

After the dancing, Rafa waited politely for the crowd of women to ooh and aah over Laramie's wedding dress made from a sheet and a tablecloth. He'd noticed the old man sitting alone by the river and remembered him there from earlier in the morning.

"Have you had anything to eat?" he said as he approached the man. "I don't mean to intrude. It's beautiful here along the creek, but I saw you here this morning and wondered if you had eaten yet."

"Yes, and it was wonderful. Nothing like venison roasted over an open fire."

Rafa sat down on his heels to get a better look at the old gentleman. There was something so familiar about him. "Do I know you?" asked Rafa. "Are you from around here?" Rafa met several local people while incarcerated at the facility and tried to remember where he had seen him before.

"I don't think I've ever been here before, even though it smells and sounds very familiar."

Rafa was startled when the man turned his face toward him. Four ragged scars cut across the right side of his face – one dug deep into his forehead and three ripped across his cheek, trailing onto his neck. The man held out his hand in greeting and Rafa was stunned to realize he was blind.

"I'm pleased to meet you. I'm Rafa," he said and was surprised by the man's firm handshake.

"Then you must be the groom. Congratulations." The man's white hair hung limply against his shoulders, giving him the appearance of old age, but half his face looked young. The scars covered one side of his face, but the other side had no wrinkles to go with the white hair. Rafa looked at his hands and noticed they, too, belonged to a younger man.

"Yes, I would be that lucky man." It was his profile that was so familiar. Where did he know him? "Thank you for coming to our celebration. Would you like to move closer to the crowd to better hear the music? Can I get you anything?"

"No, I like the sound of the crowd and the music drifting on the breeze to me. I think I would scare the children if I moved closer. The man I came with is taking good care of me." The man turned his face and the scars again shocked Rafa. "But thank you for asking. I hope you and your bride will be very happy."

"I'm sure we will be. And thanks again for coming . . . um, I didn't get your name."

"They call me *Cat Dancer.* I look like the lion won the battle, even though they tell me I killed the cat. I don't remember it, but I don't think we were dancing.

"It got you good, that's for sure." Rafa rose to leave when he had a sudden thought. "My wife's niece knows about healing herbs and remedies. She's young but she's definitely been given the gift to heal. Would you like to talk to her? The scars look fairly new. Maybe there's something she could put on them that would heal them . . . softer."

"Oh, not today. Today is a day of celebration." He traced in the mud of the creek with the twig he held in his band. "Maybe after all the excitement of the day is over your niece wouldn't mind looking at me if it wouldn't scare her too much. Maybe there is something that would help. The family I'm staying with talked of finding the medicine woman of their tribe to fix a salve for me, but the scars are getting older and stiffer." His voice became lighter with hopefulness of healing the grotesque scars. "Maybe there is something that will help, if she wouldn't mind looking for me. We plan to leave shortly after sunrise."

"Her name is Mira – I'll tell her to find you." Rafa looked around for the man's tent. "Where will you be?"

"Tell her I came with Jim Blackhorn, from the Puma Paw Ranch." Rafa looked at the tracings the man carved in the muddy bank of the creek – coiled lines that resembled a snake. "Mira," he said. "That's an unusual name."

The man made the sign of *peace* with a closed fist against his chest – the same sign Mira and Lalo made the first time he came to the ranch. "I hope we meet again."

"I'm sure we will." Rafa left the man as puzzled as when he first saw him. He still couldn't figure out why he seemed so familiar. Something he'd recognized in his profile, before the scars distracted him.

"There you are," hollered Laramie, as she ran to catch up. "Where did you disappear to?"

Rafa turned toward the creek. "I was talking to Cat Dancer." He looked all along the creek bank, but the man had disappeared. "He was just there."

"Cat Dancer?" Asked Laramie. "Is he from around here? I haven't heard his name before."

"Come to think of it, I don't know where he lives. He said he's not from around here, but he came with Jim somebody from the Puma Paw Ranch, so maybe he's staying there." Rafa shuddered remembering the deep, angry gashes. "Something strange about him. He seems so familiar, but if I had ever seen his face before I would remember."

"What's strange about him?"

"I can't quite put my finger on it. He looked familiar to me, but I don't know why. He has scars on one side of his face that would scare the tar out of you. I told him that I would send Mira to take a look at them – maybe she knows of an herb that would help them heal better." Rafa ran his hand through his recently cut hair. "His hair is white, but his hands are strong and are not aged like an old persons. The other side of his face isn't old, but it's hard to tell because the scars are all you see."

"We can ask Dad about him, and let's remember to tell Mira to look for him."

"Hey," he said as he pulled her to him. "Don't we have a honeymoon to go on?" His lips brushed her ear and she felt his breath in her hair. "Everything's waiting. All we have to do is sneak away – hopefully before dark."

"Did you think I'd forgotten?" Laramie felt his urgency. Yesterday they told everyone they were going on a picnic and took the basket to a special place where Rafa pitched Dan's wall tent. Laramie took sealed containers of prepared food so they wouldn't have to return to the ranch for a couple of days after the wedding. There was even a bottle of wine they'd received as a wedding gift.

After their two days alone, they planned to go up Harris Gulch and fix up the Hamilton's Ranch the way they wanted it. They'd chosen the Hamilton's place because it was close to Dan and Roma and it was already a working ranch. The garden had to be planted and the children settled in their new home. They considered building a log cabin on the Rocking Z, but it would be a shame to let the Hamilton's ranch go unattended.

"Let's tell mom we're leaving."

"What about the kids? And we have to find Mira to tell her about Cat Dancer."

“I've already told the kids we'd be gone for a couple days. They threatened to follow us and find our special place.” Laramie shaded her eyes from the midday sun and searched the crowd merrily dancing to the tune of *San Antonio Stroll.*

“Finding Mira may be a real challenge. I didn't notice her at the wedding,” he said.

“She was there in her finest wild-thing attire. Why don't you look for Mira and I'll go hug my mom.” Laramie quickly kissed him on the cheek.

“I saw Roma and your sisters go toward the house. Probably mixing up more batter. I hear there's going to be peach cobbler and cream later.”

“Peach cobbler?” Laramie stopped in her tracks. “Real peaches?”

“Real peaches!” Roma found several cases of canned peaches in the Hildebrand's cellar and brought them to the ranch for the celebration. “We'll get all the peaches you can eat this fall when we go to Grand Junction to help harvest the orchards. All the peaches, apples, plums, cherries, apricots, pears and grapes.”

“Okay,” Laramie interrupted. “Maybe Mom will save us some cobbler.”

He turned toward the dancing crowd searching for Mira. “Tell Roma I'll be up in a minute. I want to tell her what a great day this has been.”

“It's not over yet. It will get better if you'll hurry up and find Mira.”

## *Chapter 29*

Sawdust drifted slowly through the shaft of sunlight behind her, highlighting her dark form in a brilliant white halo. The handle of the whip she so expertly wielded had been formed by butting together two ash branches and tightly woven in place in intricate design. Now, the sawdust created from the friction of use drifted slowly to earth. Mira saw the tiny particles like sparkling gems and continued to crack the whip to see more of the dancing glitter.

"Mira," whispered Lalo. "It's my dream." He couldn't take his eyes off the display either. "I dreamed that *when the sawdust flies,* you would be better. Healed – whole again." They were like children hypnotized by fireworks. "I saw it just like this – in the sunlight – sifting through the sunlight." They were lost in amazement and didn't notice the stranger by the creek.

Pfffffftttttt - Zzzzzzzaaaap! The white haired man snapped out of his reverie. Pfffffftttttt- Zzzzzzzaaaaap! "Who's there?" Pfffffftttttt - Zzzzzzzaaaaap! "I remember that sound. Please come closer." The sound of the creek flowing over the rocks drowned out his words. "Who's there?" he shouted. He was certain he heard the sound of twigs snapping under foot. There were two of them. He could smell their scent. "Don't be afraid." He stretched his hands out in front of him. "I won't hurt you."

"Did you find Mira?" Laramie stuffed the last of their packages into the pillowcase. Roma had carefully wrapped cornbread, beans, elk steak and peach cobbler for them to take to their honeymoon hideaway. They were so careful to keep it a secret place. They didn't want to think about anything or anyone except each other for the next few days. They discovered the rock ledge by accident while herding cattle up Harris Gulch. From its edge they could see all the way to Rifle Gap Dam, but were well hidden from below. They sat on the ledge and decided it would be their own special place. Tonight it would become their honeymoon retreat.

"Yes, I found her and Lalo down by the creek. She said they would find the old man tomorrow morning."

Rafa wrapped his hands around Laramie's slender waist and lifted her up to face him. "You've got one anxious husband here."

Laramie kissed him long and full on the mouth and felt the warmth of her blood rise. "I'm all packed and ready to go, Mr. Rafa." She felt his hands tremble as he pulled her closer and buried his face in her hair, softly kissing her neck. They had waited to make this night special. As she felt his breath on her neck and smelled his scent she felt every sense quicken. "I'm ready," she whispered. "Let's go tell mom and dad we're leaving. I don't want the kids to follow us." Laramie looked at the sun. "We've only got a couple hours of daylight left."

"Shh!" Lalo and Mira froze in their path to identify where the voice was coming from. Lalo pointed through the willows to the white haired man standing with outstretched arms on the other side of the creek.

"Who's there?" The man repeated. "I know someone is there."

Mira crept closer – something about his voice drew her to him. What she could see of his face was alarming; the deep angry scars – flesh laid open by sharp claws. "This must be the one they call Cat Dancer," she whispered. She knew he stayed with Jim Blackhorn on the Puma Paw Ranch. Mira was asked to bring healing herbs to the ranch just a couple weeks ago. When she got there the man was being treated in a medicine lodge and she had not been invited to enter. Whispered stories of the blind white haired lion fighter had circulated throughout the camp over the last few days. They said he killed the cat with his bare hands, but would live with the mark of the lion for the rest of his life.

"I won't hurt you," the man repeated. "My face is scarred, but I don't mean to scare you."

Something about him. His voice was familiar, but his face was so scary. At that moment the white haired man turned toward them and Mira was dumbstruck. Her whip fell to the ground, her knees buckled and she sank on all fours across the creek from the white haired man. Tears sprang from her astonished eyes as she faced him. Afternoon sun cast ghoulish shadows across his face, making the claw marks appear fresh and bloody. Mira was paralyzed with fear to be face-to-face with this horrible looking man. A man she recognized. A man she had loved her whole life.

"Who's there," the man cried out as he reached with his arms. Lalo knelt beside Mira and placed a trembling arm around her shoulders.

"Please," he stammered, "do you know me?"

Only five feet of creek separated her from the white haired man. Mira tried to speak, but the words stuck in her throat and only tiny gasps escaped. She felt like running away. Surely this man – he couldn't be – not with white hair – and those terrible scars. And he was blind! Lalo pulled her up and in their haste to escape, they stumbled into the creek and Mira fell on the slippery rocks.

"Are you all right," the man cried as he instinctively reached for her. "Please don't go." Mira couldn't stop herself. She ran and threw her arms around him.

Confused, the man stood in silence, his arms rigid against his sides, as Mira's arms tightened around him. She buried her face in his white hair and sobbed. "I should know who you are, but I can't remember things," he cried out. "I don't even know who I am."

Mira backed away and looked at the blank stare on his wretched face. She brushed the wispy white hair from his face, looked into the unseeing eyes and touched the ugly scars on his cheek. "You've always called me Mira."

"Mira?" he questioned.

"Don't you remember me?"

"I'm sorry," he quavered. "I wish I could remember you." He suddenly flashed. "I remembered the sound though. It was the sound of a whip, wasn't it?"

Lalo picked up the whip by the side of the creek where Mira dropped it and laid it in the man's hand. "Mira made this whip. You drew a picture of it earlier – in the mud by the creek."

"So, this is what I drew? I can almost remember sometimes." He turned toward Lalo. "And who are you?"

"I'm Lalo." He looked nervously at Mira. Did he really want this man to remember?

"Lalo – it's a strange name." His hands studied the whip, feeling the supple leather braided together in its intricate design. He placed it at his nose and inhaled deeply. "The smells are so familiar here." His fingers traced the woven leather strands and the supple handle that almost felt alive. "You made this whip? Are you Indians then?" he said.

"No." Mira swallowed the sob that tried to escape from her throat, but Lalo encouraged her to continue. "I'm your daughter," she said softly.

Tears washed down her face as she looked into his unseeing eyes, hoping to find a hint of recognition there. Little girl memories of a strong, protective father tried to erase the image of this white haired man with the terribly scarred face standing before her. How could this man be her father? What happened to him that made him blind? Who stole his memory? Why couldn't he remember her and the life he used to have?

*But Mira, he's here now.*

The shock of finding him so unexpectedly passed as quickly as it came replaced by the excitement and thrill that he was really alive. "I'm Miranda Gant, but you've always called me Mira."

The man's still eyes filled and spilled down his cheeks. "My daughter?" Tears turned to quiet sobs and he clung to Mira as waves of confusion washed over him. "I have a daughter?" Mira understood at that moment that it could take a long time for this man to remember. What if he never did regain his memory?

"You have another daughter, too," Lalo said. "Her name is Jacinth."

Realization slowly dawned on Jesse. "I guess that means I must have a wife." Mira felt her father stiffen and knew he was as overwhelmed as she was. "I should go now." He began to pace back and forth, softly shuffling along the creek bank searching for his walking stick. "I need to get back to the ranch." He was near panic. "I have chores to do," he stammered. "The horses to feed." He found his walking stick and started to back away.

"Don't you want to see Jacinth and Mom?" cried Mira. She couldn't let him just go away. Not now. Not after all they'd been through. All the prayers. All the searching. The anguish and pain she'd watched her mother go through. "Don't you even care that Mom's been searching for you for months?" Mira's voice was shrill as she called after her father. "Don't you even care about us?"

The accusation echoed in Jesse's ears and he slowly turned toward Mira and Lalo. "I came to the celebration hoping I would find someone who knew me." He hung his head. "But, I'm afraid," he stammered. "I don't remember who I am – I don't have a past." He wiped at his blank eyes with the back of his hand. "Jim Blackhorn's nephews found me. They told me I fell off the cliff during a snowstorm. I had a broken leg, broken ribs and was unconscious. When I finally rallied, I couldn't see and didn't remember a thing – not where I was going or where I had been. They took me to Jim's house and he and an Indian woman looked after me. She got some herbs from a healing woman close by and that's all I know – and that's only because they told me. They said I was incoherent and talked about finding my family – a family I don't consciously remember, but somehow my spirit knows. I don't remember the fight with the mountain lion. I don't even know my own name. That's why they gave me the name of *Cat Dancer.* He laughed for the first time and Mira's heart leaped with joy to hear the familiar sound. "I have the mark of the cat and I look like I'm dancing when I stumble around in my blindness."

Mira took his hand and he didn't pull away. "Your name is Jesse," she said. "Jesse Gant."

"Jesse. I like that – Jesse's a pretty good name."

"I can hardly wait to tell Mom and Jacinth. And Gran and Pappa."

"Is your family here? Do they live close by?"

"Pretty close," replied Mira. "And they're your family too." She tugged at his hand to take him to the house, but he pulled away from her grasp.

"I don't think it's a good idea to just march up to the door with me in hand." His skin glistened with nervousness. "Maybe you should wait and tell your mom after the celebration and everything has calmed down." He was fishing for excuses and knew it, but couldn't' stop himself. He was terrified. "Maybe when she's gone back home I could have Jim take me to your house."

"You're at our house," said Mira. "This is Gran and Pappa's ranch, and the celebration is for Auntie Laramie's wedding – mom's sister – your sister-in-law."

"Oh, I see," he said, amused at his little joke. "Everyone usually laughs when I say that."

"I'm angry that you can't see me or remember me. Why would I laugh? It's not funny."

"I guess I had to find something to laugh about this past month. My mind was asleep for a long time. I hope as time passes that I will remember everything. I understand it is already May now. I have only been awake for one month."

Mira remembered taking the herbs to the Puma Paw Ranch only two weeks ago. They heard about the white haired blind man and the thought never crossed their minds to see if it was Jesse. "Then you came to look for us and that's when the cat attacked you?" Mira was beginning to put the missing puzzle pieces together. "You couldn't see anything, but you still tried to find us?"

"There was such a strong urge to find something – family, roots, memories. I didn't know what I was looking for. I just followed the scents."

"The scents?" asked Lalo.

Scents had been so prominent that they all had experienced feelings and memories in the various smells that arose from the recently awakened spring earth. Sprouting mint and herbs in Roma's garden, alfalfa growing in the fields, and patches of new sage were obvious and remembered scents. But rose hips dried on last years bushes, red dogwood branches along the creek banks, asparagus beds that hadn't yet sprouted, and tubers that had long ago given up their tops, were all found through scent. And memories flooded through the smells. Memories so deep that they seemed to have come from the very core of life. It was a phenomenon that surprised and thrilled them. They didn't know if the snow and rain falling through the newly clean air caused the plants to emit stronger scents, or if their senses and memories were sharper. They were so isolated from the rest of the survivors they hadn't really discussed these things. It was as if everyone received a great gift and didn't question why.

"Yes," said Jesse. "The smells were so strong that I thought they would lead me to my past if I could only follow the scents in my memory." His still eyes seemed to look far away. "The smells are so familiar here." His chin dropped against his chest. "I'm afraid I have brought great disappointment and pain to this happy place and time. And now you want to tell your mother that you've found her long lost husband who is now blind and doesn't remember her, but can smell familiar scents that almost spark memories?" He hurried on so Mira couldn't protest. "And who may or may not recover his sight, and may never remember his past life with her?"

"Some people pray to forget their memories."

"Lalo," said Jesse, "Your voice sounds too young to have such a bad past that you would pray to forget it." Immediately he felt he'd insulted Lalo with such a statement. "I'm sorry that I would discount your painful memories by the youthfulness of your voice." Jesse extended his hand, "I'm sorry, Lalo. I've been living in such a self-absorbed world of empty darkness, that I sometimes forget that others have dark places in memories. Can we be friends?"

Lalo stared dumbstruck from Jesse's face to Mira's. Jesse had barely tolerated him since that earth-shattering day in Denver when Lalo's whole world changed when he met Mira. He knew Jesse had reached some kind of understanding and peace after finding him with Mira on that cold mountainside outside the cave. He knew the offering of the knife was a monumental effort for Jesse – but only because he saved Mira's life. This white haired man before him was a changed man. His spirit was softer, his feelings more tender and he could actually talk about them. Lalo was amazed at the man standing before him.

"Yes, I would love to be your friend." Lalo took the outstretched hand and prayed Jesse would never remember the animosity and jealousy he'd felt for him before. "Maybe only the good memories will return to you."

"I think I'm up to a meeting with my past, but only under one condition." Jesse waited.

"What condition," said Mira, "And I don't think you have a choice."

"Oh, we all have choices," said Jesse. "I want you to give your mother a choice."

"This isn't a big decision she'll have to make. You're my father."

"Your mother knew the man she was married to. And I guess I knew her, too. But, without memories of a past – is there really a past? My only memories are of the healing hands of an old Indian woman." He hesitated only briefly before continuing. "And I know I look a lot different than I used to. Not only the scars, but I have white hair and I'm a fairly young man – or so I've been told."

"Maybe if you spend time with the family we can help you to remember everything." Mira couldn't stop the tears of anguish that spilled down her cheeks for the insight of this man before her. She had to admit that he was very changed. He was much bigger now than he was before. Bigger heart, bigger understanding. He found a different way to see . . . not through his eyes, but through his heart. Not the quick-to-judge father she remembered who made her mother cry. He'd changed. And . . . she realized he was right. Her mother did have a choice. And so did he.

Jesse heard the anguish in her voice and his heart broke for this tender child he couldn't yet call daughter. "I'll wait right here until I feel the mist of night come." He found the big rock with his walking stick and wearily sighed as he sat down. "If you don't come back tonight, I'll be here when the birds start their songs in the morning."

Mira and Lalo raced the familiar path down the creek, across the field, through the maze of tents and playing children, and finally burst through the back door and into the kitchen. "Mamma?" she cried. "Mamma?" The house was quiet, which was a rarity.

"Mira?" Dan came bounding down the stairs. "What's the matter, Mira." She was out of breath and couldn't speak. "Lalo – what happened?" Lalo didn't know where to start.

"Jesse."

"Jesse? Dan turned to Lalo. "You saw Jesse?" He searched Mira's face. "It's okay child." Dan couldn't get used to the idea that Mira was growing into a beautiful young woman. "It's okay honey," he held her while she cried into his denim shirt. Lalo stirred the embers under the coffeepot. Mira loved coffee with cream and honey. He watched Mira and Dan could see the love in Lalo's eyes for this beautiful young woman. "Now honey, while Lalo's fixing coffee you can tell me what has you so upset."

Mira's eyes betrayed the fear and apprehension in her heart. It was her mother's choice to welcome her father back into their lives. She knew he would always be in her life no matter where he lived, but Suzan would ultimately decide if this strange man would live with them or not. What if he never did regain his memory or his sight? He was not the same man – no matter how many good and bad memories he could remember from their past. But all of them had changed. Her life had been altered forever. Lalo's life would never be the same. None of their lives was the same as before. Everyone had changed. Even the children were healing from the loss of their parents and separation from dearest loved family members. It was all different now. There was a healing taking place on the whole earth – Mira felt it, and knew it started in the heart. Maybe now her mother's heart could heal, too.

"I saw my father," she started. Dan's eyes jumped with excitement. "No, Pappa," she cried. "It's not that simple."

"You found him, you've spoken with him?"

"Yes, but he's not the same man."

"Of course he's not, he's been gone for almost five months. Everything has changed."

"Pappa!" Dan's eyes riveted back to Mira's. "Pappa, he doesn't remember anything." Fresh tears formed in her eyes. "And he's blind." She had to make him understand how important this moment was for every single day of the rest of their lives. "Where's Mamma and Gran?"

"You know your Gran. She's out there somewhere, making sure everyone has food to take home with them," he said, gesturing out the door.

"I can only tell this once Pappa. We have to get Mom and Gran." Suddenly she remembered the celebration of this day. "Oh, no! Have Auntie Laramie and Rafa already left?"

"About half an hour ago. Your Gran and Mom went to say goodbye to some of the families who are already leaving. Gran's dividing up the leftover food to send home with people, and your mom went down to the creek to help the kids wash up."

"Oh no," Mira shot Lalo a questioning glance. "Could we have passed her on our way to the house?"

"Mira, we took the short-cut across the field. We didn't take the creek path all the way back." Lalo searched his memory. "I don't think we passed her, but let's go to the creek. Maybe we can find her before she sees him."

A faint breeze picked up and Jesse turned his head in the direction of a familiar scent. Suzan froze in her footprints and her eyes looked past the years and scars on Jesse's face to the core of his spirit. She recognized him immediately.

Earlier in the day she saw the lone figure sitting by the creek and felt sorrow that his old man had not joined in the celebration. She meant to approach him and extend a personal invitation, but was stopped by the stories of *Cat Dancer* – the blind man who strangled the cat with his bare hands. While searching for Jesse, they hadn't checked on the strange old man they heard was recuperating at the Puma Paw Ranch because they heard he had long white hair. Her mind quickly put the pieces of stories together and she knew he didn't know her. She saw the blank look in his eyes and knew he couldn't see her. Her heart swelled with the anguish of months of uncertainty of where he was and why she couldn't find him. She'd always known he was still alive, but couldn't imagine why he wouldn't come home.

A lump formed in her throat that she couldn't swallow. The outward scars she saw were the only scars he had. The scars of the spirit were gone. This man was at peace. Her pain had distorted her life, robbed her of the past months of joy that should have been. This man knew no pain – it had been healed – taken from his memory. Even the deep scars of the cat's paw couldn't remove the peaceful spirit she saw in his countenance. Suddenly she felt awkward – staring at this man. He let her stare. He knew she was there. She could have walked away.

Tears streamed down Laramie's face. Rafa saw the alarm in her eyes. They were almost to their special place and were laughing and playfully teasing when Laramie suddenly sat down in the middle of the trail. Something had drastically changed. His bride of six hours was terrified and filled with pain. His mind flashed on the stories Ian had told about Laramie's tears and finding the children. There couldn't be a fearful child within miles of them. Abandoned children had long since been settled with families. No – this was different. He looked deeply through her eyes and knew it was not about a child, but desperate need – someone was calling out to her. She had a gift for healing the soul and feeling the anguish of others that she could not deny. And he had the pleasure, and sometimes pain, of knowing her deepest thoughts. Right now he felt her pain. He knew her heart. Their plans could wait.

Dusk approached quickly, but it was still seasonably warm. The family sat at the window and strained to see the two figures at the creek sitting side-by-side on the big rock where the lone figure had sat earlier. Jane and Ian had excused Dan and Roma from the last of the celebrating, explaining that a family emergency had arisen. The guests took the cue and those who planned to leave anyway, were already gone. Others retreated to their camps and quietly visited amongst themselves, whispering about the woman sitting on the rock with Cat Dancer.

The children felt the seriousness of the moment, but they weren't afraid. Mira and Lalo told them stories and the family offered solemn prayers to a Heavenly Father and Mother they knew were listening. The one thing they were sure of was the powerful presence that had been with them since this all began.

Dominic said, "It's the right way." And it was.

## *Chapter 30*

A cool breeze rippled the tall grass into a sea of dark green waves and the morning dew glistened in the rising sun. Abundant rains turned the landscape into a living palette of deep green. West Rifle Creek snaked its way down the middle reflecting the sun like a crystal mirror. Red and gold rocks, where pumas nursed their kittens added the perfect contrast to the dark timber and a clear turquoise sky completed the canvas.

Carrying the rope bridle she'd taken from the tack shed, Jane walked silently through the knee-high grass, her too-tight jeans wet from the dew. She wanted to ride early before it got too hot, so she'd quietly left the house before anyone was awake except Dan. She drank a cup of Mom's roasted pine and chicory coffee with him at the corral, then headed down the valley to find Litany even though Dan bet her she wouldn't find him. If it took her all day she was determined to catch and ride that stubborn horse. Dan admittedly hadn't taken him for a good long ride since last fall, preferring instead to ride Rendi, the mare. Litany wasn't nearly as good a workhorse as Rendi, but he was the best riding horse in the county, and it was the perfect time to ride. All she had to do was find him. Although Suzan was considered the most accomplished horsewoman in the family, today would be all hers, and she knew Litany would love the ride as much as she would. He was born to run. They had a lot in common.

Last night she'd spotted him high up on the ridge, and she headed that way now, hoping to find him up the next draw. She didn't have to go far before she heard the familiar whinny. She stood still for a long time hoping he would come to her out of curiosity, and sure enough, she saw his red mahogany coat glistening through the Aspen, playfully kicking up his hind feet in a display of greeting. He came closer as she softly called his name and dropped the rope bridle to the ground.

She loved Litany. She'd gone to the Grand Junction auction with her dad when he bought him three summer's ago. His previous owner couldn't break his wild nature and was ready to sell him to the highest bidder, usually the slaughterhouse. Dan recognized his strong Arabian lines, and although Litany didn't have a paper trail, Dan knew he was nearly a purebred, not the workhorse the old farmer needed. So, for three hundred dollars, Dan acquired the most beautiful riding horse in the valley. Yes, he did have a wild nature, but Dan kind'a related to it, too. Jane rode him nearly every day that summer, and she hoped he would remember her scent.

Litany slowly approached and dropped his head onto Jane's shoulder, nudging her with his nose, as she scratched the white star on his forehead, and patted the dust from his thick coat. He looked so scrawny and dull-coated in the spring, they worried he might not make it, so Dan turned him out to roam the ranch to eat when and where he wanted. He was fully recovered now and full of piss and vinegar.

"There, boy, whoa Litany, that's it, boy. You remember me, don't you, boy?" It was a statement more than a question, because it was obvious he wasn't going to shy from her. "You missed all this attention, didn't you, Litany?" She briskly rubbed the middle of his back, getting him used to touch there. "Want to go for a run? Are you ready to run, boy?"

She slowly kneeled to pick up the bridle, all the while talking to him and stroking his powerful forelegs. He was unexpectedly docile as she raised the rope over his nose, reached her right arm over the top of his head and slowly raised the bridle over his ears. She knew he must be anxious to run too, because he stood still as a fence post, until the third attempt to mount him finally placed her securely on his back.

"Oh, yes." Exhilaration coursed through her to see the lay of the land from the back of this magnificent animal. It had been two years since she'd galloped bareback down the valley. She could hardly wait to feel the warm wind whip through her hair, Litany's smooth gait rhythmically rock her, and the valley floor disappear beneath them. Litany didn't have the powerful Morgan traits like Rendi, but he was majestically beautiful. When Jane rode him, she always felt like a blue-ribbon winner. He loved to show off and often pranced, just for the joy of the rhythmic movement. He would have been a perfect show-horse, but without the genealogy paper trail, he was just a mutt. That's what dad called him – *Mutt*, but everyone knew Dan babied and coddled him too much to be a working, ranch horse; he was more the family pet.

"C'mon, Litany, let's see if we've still got it." She reined him towards the shorter grasses of the valley, so his sharp eyes could pick his own way, and she gave him his head. Cautious at first, he gradually broke from a prance to a trot, and then began to gallop. His strength and stamina allowed him to glide easily over half the length of the valley. Slowing to jump the meandering creek, as if it were the trial marker, he broke out in full run, leaving the ground beneath them a faint blur. Rider and horse became one, riding on the early morning breeze, hearing nothing but the beat of their hearts and the rhythmic pounding of hoof on earth.

Ian and Dan watched the show from the front porch, until horse and rider disappeared around the bend. It felt good to be with Dan, drinking the first pot of coffee in silence. Dan and Ian could talk for hours, swapping stories of the Australian outback and the rugged mountains of Colorado ranches, but this morning it was fitting to sit silently and enjoy the morning quiet. Dan had a great respect for Ian's knowledge and admired the rugged quiet in his son-in-law. Dan's thoughts always turned to his son, Judd, during his conversations with Ian. Ian was much older than Judd, but they both had that resolute composure that didn't need talk to convince you of their manliness. This morning, Dan's thoughts were on Judd again, knowing that he and Dani would have a baby by now. He wondered what continent they were on. His greatest fear was that he'd been shipped to Iran or Russia and they'd never see them again. If he could just know they were alive, he would be grateful.

His thoughts were interrupted and his attention was diverted by a sound he hadn't heard for a long time – a motor running. Both he and Ian quickly stood to stretch their necks and get a better view of the road. "Well, I'll be a jumpbuck in a tuckerbag!" Dan hadn't heard that much excitement in Ian's voice since they'd met.

"Well, not me," said Dan as he set his cup of coffee down on the porch railing and pushed back his hat to get a better look. "What in tarnation?"

"It's *Red Man and The Queen*," shouted Ian as he agilely hurdled the porch rail and headed toward the road. "Legend of the Continental Divide, the same Red everybody's been talking about from Denver to California. It's Janie's Red. What a sight for sore eyes."

Dan didn't know what all the excitement was about as he shaded his eyes from the easterly sun, watching the bike coast down the long driveway towards the house. He'd heard of Red, but had never met the man. He knew there was grumbling among his daughters about Jane adopting this man and his family as her own. Well, he'd never been one to pre-judge a man, and now he'd have a chance to decide for himself.

Everyone they met told the story of the wild *Red Man* who pushed a motorcycle over the Continental Divide, and his female companion, they dubbed, *The Queen.* Ian and Jane speculated on who the queen could possibly be, and decided that it was probably some little young thing he picked up on the road. Now they would find out exactly who she was.

The 1938 Indian motorcycle looked no worse for wear. Ian wondered how long it would take for every man, woman and child who heard and saw the bike to head up the road to investigate. He and Red had discussed the old motorcycle that first night in the little house. They both knew that any motor powered by magnetos would run, if they could find good gasoline. No one made a big deal out of it. It was just good for future reference, like now. Red had obviously been able to beg, borrow or steal enough good gasoline to make it here, and the ranch had a full five-hundred gallon drum standing on stilts behind the barn. The collector's item slowly rolled to a stop at Ian's feet and the big biker put the kick-stand down and raised from the seat with a high-five palm-slap for Ian who was grinning from ear to ear.

"G'day, Mate," hollered Red, the pitch of the engine still ringing in his ears.

"You're a sight for sore eyes, matey! And who is this gorgeous traveling companion, nationally acclaimed as *The Queen*?" Ian stuck his hand out and the woman gratefully accepted his warm offering of welcome.

Jane walked casually back towards the corral, letting Litany cool down after their lengthy ride down the valley. She was unaware of the newly arrived guests. As she stopped to let him drink from the creek about a half mile down-valley from the front porch, her love and her parents were gay as larks, enjoying the tall tales of *Red Man and The Queen*.

"Where's the little guy and his hard-hearted mamma?" joked Red, as he too shielded his eyes to scan the bright, sun-filled landscape.

"Oh, I imagine they'll all be here shortly, after hearing the sound of that motorcycle you've got there." Dan liked him right away, and he liked Vi, too. She seemed quite a bit younger than this leathery old man she was with, and had an air of grace lacking in the imposing biker. Well, shoot, thought Dan, that's why they call her *The Queen*. Made sense to him.

Laramie and Rafa were fishing with the children off the bank of the reservoir to hopefully land a mess of fish for dinner. They perked up when the sound of the motorcycle finally reached their ears on the breeze gently blowing across the lake and toward the ranch in its usual north-to-south fashion. Levi recognized the familiar sound first. Laramie had dismissed it as summer-warm clashing with morning-cold and the low grumbling of distant thunder. Levi pulled down his baseball cap to shade his eyes, and trained them south, searching for the motorcycle his memory said had to be there. It could only be one person. He made out the tiny two-wheeler in the distance, let out a whoop, and threw his cap into the air. "It's Red, it's Red." Laramie grabbed at him to load up his fishing pole and worms, but it was too late – he was already racing wildly toward the ranch, whooping and hollering like a banshee.

The gentle breeze carried the sounds of Levi's joy to his mother, who was guiding the gelding back to the corral to brush him down. Searching for Levi, she spotted the old Indian motorcycle in the roadway. Her heart leapt with delight to see Red's huge, hulking frame glowing in the sunlight. Without hesitation she ran toward his outstretched arms, but stopped dead in her tracks when she noticed his female companion. Buried memories leaped forward as she watched Levi fly into Red's arms and wrap his legs around the big man's waist, just like old times. She ordered her legs to move, but they disobeyed as the hard-forgotten memory pushed at the edge of her consciousness. The two women stood fifty feet apart – Jane recalling the smell of burning sage. She couldn't will herself to move and frantically searched for the missing pieces of the memory to emerge and solve the puzzle.

Levi saw her standing there, just watching. "C'mon Mom, it's Red and . . . " Recognition gleamed in his eyes as he squirmed out of Red's hug and wrapped his arms around the woman's waist. She smelled good, like his mom. Her arms encircled him as she held Jane's stare.

"Oh, damn," said Red, "I recognize that look, and it ain't good." Red was looking at Jane intently staring at the woman as memories of that day, six summers ago, returned from the dark grave where she'd buried them. This was the same woman she remembered from the day they buried Levi's father at Eagle's Nest Rock, above the Pecos River, not far from the reservation at Dulce, New Mexico. The memory was so vivid now. The woman even appeared to be wearing the same pair of jeans, same black tee shirt, same yellow headband tied around her forehead and woven Indian-style into her thick braid as she'd worn that day. She was the woman who shook the burning sage all around the cold, bare body to rid the site of any lurking evil, the smoke leading the spirit of Levi's father to ancestors of the spirit world. Now Levi was hugging her and calling her Mrs. Thomas.

"Incredible," said Jane. "Mrs. Thomas, the principal." The recognition hit her as if she'd been slapped across the face – her dream. This is what the dream meant. The smell of sage, the slap across the face – the dream-tellers sign of betrayal. Jane felt as though the burning sage was raging through her like a forest fire as her fists opened and closed and her leaden legs found their power.

Slowly she moved towards Mrs. Thomas.

Red started to intercept Jane when Vi loosened Levi's grip from around her waist and pushed him towards Red. "This is my job," she said quietly, still holding Jane's advancing stare. Red didn't dare object. He led Levi into the house with Dan and Roma close behind, giving the women all the space they needed to clear the air.

The women stared at each other for a long moment before Jane finally broke the silence. "That man was always somebody else's, but you can't have my son."

Vi knew this part would be hard. It would seem to Jane like betrayal, a lie, the straight-laced Mrs. Thomas – the same woman who looked like the biker-bitch at the secret burial. This was the last thing she ever imagined would happen. She had fully intended to stay Mrs. Thomas, the principal, and help anonymously. She couldn't allow it to backfire now. It was time for truth, and she was ready.

Vi sank to her knees in a show of submission and respect, and taking advantage of catching Jane off-balance, she began to speak: "I'm Viya Brown Bear – Viola Thomas. I was raised on the reservation at Dulce, New Mexico, and taken away to the white man's school when I was twelve years old. Mr. Dillon Thomas was forty years my senior when he bought me from my parents and took me away to school in Tempe, Arizona. When he took me from Dulce, I was a dirty little half-breed, not Indian and not white. He provided me the best education money could buy and I married him when I was sixteen years old. When he died five years later, my debt to him was paid, and I returned to the reservation a wealthy widow and taught at the Indian school. All my life I'd been in love with an Indian boy from the time we were both children. Those years away from the reservation, I willed myself to live because I always knew I would return, and we would be together."

The two women sat cross-legged in the dirt, the noonday sun scorching deeper shades of reds and browns on their weathered skin. Jane allowed her ears to hear, but her anger blocked out the painful outpouring of this woman's heart. Vi continued in spite of the stone wall she felt rise between them.

"By the time I returned to the reservation, Levi's father had joined the Army and was stationed in Colorado Springs at Fort Carson. A couple of years went by and I was offered a teaching job in Denver and jumped at the opportunity, knowing I would be closer to him. I dreamed that he would get out of the Army, and we would have a house full of kids. Life would be great. I had money, education, and had learned to live in the white man's world, but he never did. He was discharged from the service, not honorably, not dishonorably, just discharged."

Jane was listening intently now. She didn't know he was in the military, and was beginning to understand there were a lot of things she hadn't known about him.

The wind picked up, carrying the scent of Ian's breakfast cigarette, as he came through the back door, carrying two glasses of cooled, honey-sweetened Mormon tea, and a couple of cigarettes. Jane and Vi drank some of the tea, and both lit a cigarette as Vi continued.

"I always wanted his sons and daughters and thought maybe being a father would somehow change him, but liquor had already worked its black-magic on him. He found the place to disappear that I saw so often on the reservation, and I was afraid to become his *nanita* – his squaw. I bought him his first Harley. That's when we both met Red. I tried for two years to belong, to fit in, but I was too afraid I would lose all the self-respect I had worked so hard to gain. I wouldn't join his lifestyle of fast bikes, free love, and free-flowing drugs. Towards the end, when he ran out of money, booze or drugs, he used to beat me with his fists, or anything else that was close by. You met him the fall of that year and had Levi the following July. Any chance of happiness between us had died long before that. I always stayed in touch with Red, so I knew what was happening in your lives, not in a nosy way, but because I cared. I also know he abused you, too. When I heard you had his son, I grieved the loss of the sons I would never have and often wished I had made different choices. I lost myself in my teaching. Red kept me informed on what a good mother you were and how hard you struggled to create a family for your son. He told me how you raised Levi to be proud of his Indian heritage and I saw you doing all the things I wished I had done."

Vi no longer cared whether Jane was listening or not. The emotions that had been dammed up for so long, overflowed and cleansed the barren years of heartache and longing. Her heart continued its healing confession.

"When Red told me Tommy White Eagle was dead and you wanted to take him above the Pecos River to Eagle's Nest Rock, I said I would arrange it. No one would know or object to our ceremony. I knew he must have shared that place with you, too. It was a sacred place to him. I dressed in my best biker garb to honor his way of life, and that's when you first saw me. No introductions were made, and you were too lost in sorrow to inquire."

Jane was jolted by her words. It was as if this woman could see into her heart. She realized how well Vi knew the man who had fathered Levi, and, how much she had loved him.

"When the offer was made to teach at the same elementary school Levi would be attending, I jumped at the chance just to be close to him." For the first time, tears welled in the proud woman's eyes. "The year he started second grade I became Mrs. Thomas, the principal, and vowed to be satisfied with any relationship that would develop. I was careful to have only limited contact with you, as his mother, for fear you would recognize me from the day we buried his father. That was my deception, but I was willing to live with it."

Vi blew her nose noisily on a bandanna from her shirt pocket. After wiping her eyes and cheeks, she confessed: "On December 9th, when everything changed, I cherished every second I had left with your son. I felt I would never see him again. Out of selfishness, thoughts of taking him with me entered my head, but I knew I loved him too much to ever hurt him or you. You would be surprised how well I got to know you in four years. Levi has always been so proud of you and often shared how well you were doing in school. I am proud of you, too, for sticking out the four years it took to get through school, and your determination to change your life. I knew education would change your life, because it had drastically changed mine."

Their legs began to cramp and the noonday sun grew intense. They retreated to the shade of the old cottonwood trees by the creek where Vi continued her account. "The day after you left, Red came to my home and convinced me to leave the city with him. He shared the things Ian told him and his fears for those who remained in the city. We locked everything up as securely as possible and headed south to Dulce and the reservation to find my family. It was strange to see how little life had changed there. Many people already lived without electricity or running water, although there were many new graves when we arrived. So many died from alcohol, or I should say, the lack of alcohol. When the liquor ran out, DT's caused some to lose their minds, some died, some beat their wives, wives killed their husbands, and there were those who died just because they didn't want to live anymore."

Vi knew Jane's struggle with drugs and alcohol nearly killed her, and she also knew it had destroyed any chance of life with Levi's father. The two women recognized their common bond, having watched helplessly, while the insidious lifestyle of addiction destroyed so much of what each had loved.

"We spent the coldest months of winter right there on the reservation, although it was one of the mildest winters anyone could remember. The People learned to trust Red and to love him. I probably would have stayed on the reservation forever and found some way to make my life content – perhaps teaching the children. And I may go back someday, who knows? But I'm different now. My years with Mr. Thomas and living in the white world changed me. I can't accept their lifestyle anymore. I love the *Indian Way*, but I hate their acceptance of cruelty. I hate how they treat women who have dared to break from the traditional mold of *nanita*. Red and I have been friends for a long time and we've never tried to turn our friendship into something other than what it is. I have no husband, no child, nothing to lose. It has been a real comfort to have him as a traveling companion. Him pushing that heavy motorcycle caused a lot of excitement along the way. Pretty soon, people named us *Red Man and The Queen.* I laughed when I first heard it, wondering who they were referring to as the queen."

A hint of a smile crossed Jane's eyes at the insinuation. A silence lulled between them, and Jane knew she should respond. "Why are you here?"

The retort did not surprise Vi. It did not sound cruel nor was it meant to. It was exactly what she expected – directness, honesty – she liked that in Jane.

"I'm here because Red and I long for our families. Simple. You and Levi are the closest thing to family either of us have left. I'm not here to steal your son, although I admit I've lived vicariously through you for years. But I love him too, and he loves me, in his way. I'll still be Mrs. Thomas to him, but it has always been more than teacher and student. He knew I really cared about both of you. I never pried and we never discussed his father. We only talked about the happy things in his life – the things that made him proud."

"How long are you planning to stay?" Jane's voice sounded worried that Viola planned to stay forever, and she didn't know if she would like that.

"I don't know how long – you know Red – itchy feet when there's nothing to anchor the body and heart. But I could teach the children while I'm here and school would be out when I'm gone. I would always be Mrs. Thomas, the principal. It's really up to you, Jane. I know I've done all the talking, but I wanted you to know the truth and now there are no more secrets."

Jane stood and leaned on the fence post, staring past the stream and up the hill towards the reservoir. Vi gently placed her hand across Jane's forearm. "I also know about birthing." Jane's hand automatically dropped to her stomach and the two women were again locked in each other's eyes. How did she know? She hadn't breathed a word, not even to Ian. "It doesn't show there," said Vi, as she gently took Jane's hand from her stomach and placed it between her breasts. "It shows here."

Not a word passed between the women, and only their eyes acknowledged the truth revealed.

Jane turned away and silently walked toward the corral and the horses. She loved the manure and hay smell of the corral and welcomed the diversion from jumbled emotions – wisely choosing to deal with them later. She commanded the familiar smells to fill her as she clung to Litany's neck and stroked his strong shoulders and chest. Jane said goodbye as she walked him to the gate and opened it to set him free; the symbolic gesture seemed to fit the day. She knew he would come back again as she watched him kick up his back legs and prance down the valley. Jane watched until he was out of sight. She'd taken a risk riding him as hard as she did, but she had always ridden and was in better physical shape than she'd ever been. It was the perfect ride and probably the last one until next summer.

## *Chapter 31*

Sun shining. Cool breeze. Kids playing in the sunshine. So bright. Kids screaming in delight. Brilliant light. Blinding sun. Oh my God! Run! Run away! Hurry, hurry! No mamma! Mamma!

"Mamma? Mamma?" Jane was screaming and couldn't stop herself.

"Janie – Janie girl. Wake up Janie." Ian gently shook her shoulders until her eyes were opened and she recognized him. "My Janie girl, you're dreaming." Gently, he wiped her wet forehead and face. "You're soaked. There my sweet. You're here with me. It's okay – it's only a dream." There was no comfort in his words. He knew there was no such thing as *only a dream* with Jane. Her dreams were ominous warnings of future events. Damn! Why did she have them? They tormented her. And if she had them, why weren't they dreams that she could do something about? Why weren't they warnings instead of revelations? She always felt so powerless to do anything to change the course of events.

Some of her dreams were of wonderful future events, like Laramie's wedding. She knew Red and a lady would come too, she just didn't know who the lady was. And the baby – she dreamed about the baby the night it was conceived – the night they accepted each other as husband and wife on the rocks by the cave. She hadn't shared that dream with Ian. She didn't trust her dreams then and didn't recognize them as revelations. This was the third time she'd dreamed the same dream and she could no longer deny it. The second time was the night before the wedding, but she didn't want to spoil the celebration so she kept it to herself. The first time – she knew her mother shared the same dream. Since the wedding she had dismissed the dream hoping her fears would subside. Now she had to tell Ian.

"I'll make us some coffee," said Ian, "It's almost light anyway – might as well get up." He slipped on his slippers and reached over, kissed her forehead, placed his hands on her swollen belly and kissed it gently. "Good morning my baby." Yawning, he said, "Then we'll talk."

He didn't like her having these dreams. She's going to have my baby, for heaven sake, he thought. What would it do to her and the baby to be in constant turmoil? Jane waited a long time to tell him he was going to be a father. She didn't want him to feel trapped into a lifestyle that he wouldn't have chosen. She knew he wanted to leave before winter set in so he could continue his research – *close the circle* as he put it. She was seven months along now and he wouldn't miss this event for anything. The research could wait, but the cycle of birth wouldn't.

Ian never had a child and the thought of becoming a father thrilled and terrified him. He loved the children at the ranch. They all shared in the parenting. Jane was a wonderful wise mother, whether to Levi or any of the other children. It's what he loved most about this family of fierce women. But he doubted his own ability as a father. His plan had been to get her family safe and settled in for the coming winter and then trek to California – listen to rumors, see how the rest of the world was faring. He never stayed in one place very long since he'd left his parent's station in Queensland. He swore to himself that he'd never be chained to a piece of land like they were since the day they married. Their lives had been hard and cruel. Ian had been careful not to settle in one place for very long.

He was going to have a baby. He couldn't drag Jane off to California now. She wasn't due for a couple more months, and they would have to leave soon after if they were going to beat the cold weather.

Coffee mug in each hand, Ian pushed the door open to find Jane softly crying. "Don't worry so, my love. It will be okay. Whatever the dream was about, we'll get through it like we've gotten through the rest of them." He held her in his arms for a long time.

"The coffee's not very hot now, but it's good. Please, let's go sit on the porch and drink our coffee and you can tell me all about the dream and we'll see what we can do about it."

Jane had quit smoking and was determined to stay healthy so she could breast feed her child. Tobacco – the last drug addiction. How many had she overcome, and now this last one was really the nastiest of all. She knew her child would need every advantage she could give it in this new life. There were no vaccines for measles and polio, or booster shots for diphtheria, tetanus, typhoid and all the other strains of virus, and bacteria that had become so resistant to antibiotics. But, at this moment, she desperately wanted a cigarette.

She put on Roma's bathrobe to join Ian on the front porch, enjoy her coffee and tell him about her dream.

They saw Dan already in the corral milking Maggie. "That cow gives the best milk and cream. I've never seen a cow give so much at one milking."

"Mother charmed her," said Jane matter-of-factly.

"I'm beginning to believe you. She really is the *Grande Dame* of the family."

"She loves it when you refer to her as the *Grande Dame*." Jane put her coffee down and tucked the robe over her feet. "I feel a nip in the air. It will soon be time to harvest and make sure all our preparations are made for winter."

Ian looked down the valley from the porch. "The summer was busy, every bit as hard work as I remember as a child. Way too much energy spent on survival."

"Oh, as opposed to what – not surviving?"

He knew she was teasing – her gentle teasing of his intellect, always a reminder that he'd rather have his head in books and doing calculations, looking through the telescope, charting through unlocked puzzles, dilemmas, catastrophes around the world, his life's work that abruptly came to an end. Was anyone writing this in history books, capturing this great change in the entire earth's history? The only thing he knew was what had happened since they left Denver and the disaster he saw evolve in the human race. That's not true, he thought. It was all very predictable. All except the exact time it would happen.

"Surviving?" He waved his hand towards the valley beneath them. "I'm looking at survival." He scooted his chair closer and put his cheek next to hers and his hand on her stomach. "Behold, my little-one. See what man has created in such a short time." Jane loved when he talked to their baby. "The greenhouse built over the creek. We built it there so you would always have a place to grow food year-round. The water flowing under the floor will humidify it and the sun will warm the humid air creating a perfect greenhouse to grow lettuce, melons, tomatoes, sprout wheat and alfalfa, and every green thing to keep you healthy. There's even a place to grow the herbs to keep your immune system strong, and to season your food; echinacea, rose hips, fennel, dill, chamomile, elderberry, mint, chives, rosemary, oregano, parsley, basil. "

"That was a wonderful idea – the greenhouse. And I love the swimming pool, but it's always ice cold. Couldn't you think of a way to make the creek water run through solar panels to warm it up first?"

"Your mommy's very funny," he continued. "She has a wonderful sense of humor, but sometimes she expects miracles from this common man. You go to sleep now sweetheart."

He kissed Jane's tummy and looked at her intently. "Do you want to talk about your dream now?"

## *Chapter 32*

Roma and Dan whispered softly so they wouldn't wake everyone. They often woke in the middle of the night and had lengthy conversations before falling back to sleep.

"I'll plant all the late-crop seeds tomorrow." Roma had planted the cold-weather crops of peas, radishes, lettuce, spinach, cauliflower, cabbage, and her favorite – Swiss chard, shortly after the wedding. Then the warm night crops of tomatoes, beans, melons, squash and cucumbers were planted. Now it was time to plant for fall crops of lettuce, spinach and peas. "Laramie and Rafa said they would stay down here through August. We'll all go to harvest in Grand Junction in September, then they'll head up to the Hamilton Ranch."

"I'm glad you've got it all figured out," yawned Dan.

"Well, didn't you talk to some people in town and agree that we would all go to Junction the first week in September to help harvest the peaches, apples and pears? And didn't I also hear there's a bumper crop coming on?"

"Wears me out just to think about it. I haven't had to sleep in that old wagon for years. Then, if we fill up the wagon with fruit to bring home, I'll have to sleep in the tent."

"Oh, don't borrow trouble. Maybe we'll just stay down there and can all the fruit over big fires like we used to. If we stay into September, can dry the grapes there and just bring home boxes of raisins." Roma knew it would be hard on everyone, with gardens to get in and harvesting to do in Grand Junction. There wouldn't be an easier way to do it, and it would be fun to socialize some – maybe have a Harvest Moon Ball – like in the good 'ole days.

"I hear those wheels turning. You're planning a dance – aren't you?"

"Dan Zerlich – I have more important things to think about than dances." She laughed out loud. "Besides – it will be fun. We'll be ready for another celebration by mid-September. Maybe Suzan and Jesse will even feel like dancing together again."

"I saw Suzan and Jesse dancing in the barn the other night." Dan chuckled at his secret.

"No!" Roma poked at him. "And you didn't even tell me."

"Maybe we should just stay home and have a barn dance. Seems to be everyone's favorite place to frolic. I even caught Laramie and Rafa in there the other afternoon."

Roma laughed. "Guess we better stay out of the barn, huh? Or our kids will be finding us in there."

In a more serious tone, Roma said, "I'm so thrilled that Suzan and Jesse are getting to know each other again. It could have ended so differently, you know."

"Yes, if Jesse hadn't agreed to stay here at the ranch for a time, they may never have gotten together again. I hear that *old* Indian woman that nursed him back to health all those months turned out to be a young and attractive woman that had her heart set on him. The Blackhorn family is still brooding over his decision to stay here, but I understand the woman trekked over to Arizona to stay with other members of her family."

"Yes," said Roma, "I heard she loved him enough to let him go. Can't blame the Blackhorn family for being disappointed. Jesse was always a wonderful man, but he's not the same troubled person we used to know." Now Roma was yawning. "I've always believed that God could change the heart of man or woman in the twinkling of an eye, but it's the first time I've actually witnessed it. Not only has Jesse changed, but Suzan has changed overnight as well."

"Yes, Suzan's happier than I've ever seen her. Ever!" Dan pulled Roma over to cuddle up to him in her favorite position. Guess all your prayers worked! Can't decide if you women do prayers or spells – but whatever it is, it's powerful and it works. And I love you."

Jane and Ian lay in bed making plans to go to California soon after the baby was born.

"Are you sure you wouldn't rather wait and go to California next spring?" Jane was pensive tonight and Ian wasn't sure why. Jane was such a direct woman, he didn't know what to think of this solemn, sometimes brooding mood that came over her lately.

"Janie, we've discussed this so many times, my love." He pulled her closer to him and inhaled deeply of her wonderful scent. He couldn't get enough of his Janie-girl. She filled him completely. They had to settle this. "Are you worried about your family not being able to get along without us for the winter?"

"Maybe, a little." She snuggled closer into his chest. "No, I guess not. Jesse has been found, and it looks like he and Suzan are on their way to real happiness now."

"Dad and Mum are doing fine, Laramie and Rafa are married and happy as two newlyweds should be." There was something bothering Jane and Ian couldn't quite get it out of her.

"You're right. It's silly. We'll go whenever you want to leave."

"You've had another dream, haven't you?" Ian practically shouted.

"Not a new dream – an old dream – my bear dream."

"Ah yes." Ian hated the burden her dreams placed on her. She always felt so responsible for everyone's future and yet, telling the dreams didn't change anything. They were her dreams – warning dreams perhaps, but more like the future unfolding while she slept. She felt so helpless to stop the events no matter what precautions she took. Her dream about the fire before they left Denver – she couldn't stop the evil around her, but she was able to save one child. She dreamed about Mira, but after everything that happened, she came to realize that she couldn't have stopped it. If she had warned everyone and altered the course, Jesse and Suzan probably would have been killed instead of that horrible man.

But the bear dream was a recurring dream. She didn't have a good feel for when it would happen, but it would happen. She knew it would happen.

"I can't shake it. I have to do something, I just don't know what."

Jesse's steady breathing reassured Suzan that everything was *the right way,* as Dominic would say. The girls were absolutely thrilled when their father agreed to stay – just for a trial, to see if they could spark past memories or re-kindle their romance. They spent hours each day telling him all the great times they remembered. They were re-building his past life, and never discussed unpleasant memories.

Suzan wanted this new man to stay. She hoped for Mira and Jacinth's sake that memories would return, but she loved this man – whether he could see her or not, whether or not he ever remembered their life together. It no longer mattered. In fact, as she watched him sleep, she realized that deep down she hoped the old Jesse would stay wherever he had left him. This Jesse wasn't afraid of her fears, hopes, dreams or spiritual insights. He trusted life and loved every day. He viewed the future with excitement rather than apprehension, and didn't measure love out in portions or resent anyone else who wanted a part of hers. This man was proud of her capacity to love others and encouraged it.

Suzan blossomed overnight. She had always been the dependable one, the one in charge – who knew instinctively what to do for any situation. But there'd always been an undercurrent of unhappiness about her, making those around her feel oddly responsible for the sacrifice they imagined she was making for them. Always giving away her own happiness so others would be happy. Well, her self-appointed martyrdom was over. She was filled with love and hope for the future. A surge of power and self-assuredness overcame her and everyone felt this newly loved person emerge from the protective shell she had lived in for so long. She was reborn. And she loved being here for the first time that she could ever remember. Life no longer felt threatening or burdensome. She was no longer responsible for everyone's happiness, for in finding her own she realized she couldn't make anyone else be happy. It came from the inside. How many self-help books had she read over the years? It was so simple. Being truly loved allows the spirit to soar. She was soaring and didn't ever want to put her feet on the ground again.

The first couple of weeks were hard, although not as hard on her as they'd been on Jesse. She came to realize that the Indian woman who cared for him meant more to him than he realized. He truly cared for her and missed her. Then there was the adjustment to his new physical surroundings. His favorite place was by the creek at the rock where they spent most of that first night together. It was their place now. The place they went to sort things out, to re-ignite the feelings of hope felt on that first meeting. It was there that Jesse decided he had to stay with the family he couldn't remember. Suzan would never forget the fear she felt when he said he would stay. She had given up hope that he would ever be in their lives again, and now, this white haired man with the scarred face was going to stay.

Her finger traced the scars as he slept. She knew them intimately, kissed them often and memorized them in her heart. Mira still placed healing herbs on them everyday – poultices that even she didn't understand how the chemical mixtures would react. But the scars lessened each day and now, in three short months, they appeared white and flat. They would always be visible, but the angry gashes were smooth, clean lines now. "Thank you for this man you've sent me," she whispered. "And thank you for the woman I've become."

## *Chapter 33*

Roma sat at the kitchen window, evaluating the garden, the fields, and lazily watching others work – a rare occasion. The fields were ripe with alfalfa, ready to harvest. She watched Rafa, and Dan wield scythes while Ian worked on the reaper. The gasoline in the storage tanks was old and turning bad. If they could just get the motor to turn over, they could keep it running to cut the alfalfa. The first cutting had filled the loft, but this second cutting would hold them through the winter. They would haul a wagonload up to the Hamilton Ranch for Rafa and Laramie, although the alfalfa growing up on the mountain was just as plentiful as it was in the valley.

Last month Laramie and Rafa had packed the horses up Harris Gulch and found the Hamilton Ranch intact and comfortable. A good cleaning was all it really needed. There was plenty of room for the kids. It was the perfect place. Winters could be hard there, but the Hamilton's had built the house themselves using energy efficient techniques of their time. The walls were thick, made with concrete blocks hauled up the mountain during the summer months. The well was gravity-fed, like Dan and Roma's, so even without the generator working there would still be plenty of water.

It took them four years to build their home while they lived in the barn, which was built first. They hauled tile made in Albuquerque by the Indians, and Mary Lou braided rugs from old worn out jeans she'd saved over the years and couldn't throw away. The floors that weren't tiled and covered with rugs, were hardwood and rugged. Laramie counted thirteen braided rugs in various shades of faded blue denim.

When the house was finished, Mary Lou adorned it with afghans, tablecloths, bedspreads and quilts in varying shades of wheat, sunshine, and earth, all hand-made over the years. In every room and corner were manifestations of her love for her home. Laramie loved it as much as Mary Lou had and left every quilt, tablecloth and afghan as Mary Lou had laid it. She often walked through each room and imagined Mary Lou patiently creating each beautifully handcrafted item.

Laramie's favorite room was the sewing room, surrounded by large, sun-filled windows facing south. There was an antique treadle sewing machine sitting under the window, next to a new Singer with all the fancy stitches. The treadle had been well maintained and purred when she tried it. A large cedar chest was filled with quality cotton fabric, probably purchased for future quilt making. As all ranch women do, Mary Lou stockpiled threads, zippers, buttons, yarns and quilt batting, so Laramie felt well prepared. She imagined outfits for little girls and boys and knew that someday she would sew on that old treadle sewing machine for her own children.

The cattle they'd taken to the ranch in the spring were easy to find and the herd had grown by half from spring calving. Laramie was determined to wean one of the calves so she could have a Maggie milk cow like Roma's. Roma knew there would never be another Maggie. She was always happy to be milked and the quality was like no other she'd ever tasted – rich with cream.

Roma's thoughts turned to Jesse and Suzan as she watched them in the garden by the tarnished copper sundial, picking ripe tomatoes to can in jars that she brought from the cellar. How happy they were. Her daughter had finally found peace. It took a lot of love and a little time – Roma's personal recipe for all problems. Mira and Jacinth blossomed under their mother's new found acceptance of life. Suzan discovered it didn't have to be perfect, and she learned to relax and let life happen. I wonder why it takes us so long to figure that out, thought Roma.

This year's garden was the biggest and best Roma ever had. The weather had cooperated; enough rain, enough sun, just the right amount of weeding. Strawberries were coming on again and the raspberry canes were so heavy with fruit they had to build clothes lines to tie them to. In another week they would go to harvest in Grand Junction. How they'd been blessed. They were alive and together. She was overcome with emotion and tears ran down her cheeks as she watched her family work together.

She tried not to think about it, but every once in awhile it crept into her thoughts – a reminder that every living thing has its season. The dream of the bear. The same emotions, the same actions, the same reasons, all happening in perfect, harmonious synchronization. Most of the time she saw it in slow motion; heartbeat racing, legs running, mouth wide open – screaming. Both of them. She didn't know the day, but she knew the season. It was the season of young cubs, when their mothers take them out for romps and teach them how to find food to prepare for their long winter sleep. She saw the old barren bear a few times every year. Never had she seen cubs with her until this spring. The cubs were quite small the first time she saw them. Roma knew they were born sickly and nurtured through their precarious infancy to become quite robust, but still very small and dependent on their mother. She hadn't seen them now for a couple of months, but knew she would see them soon.

Suddenly she heard the delighted hollering of the children. They were chasing after Viola. "Oh, she got the honey comb out of the hive!" They had hiked up to the old elm where Viola found the huge hive. The children ran single file behind Viola all the way to her teepee.

Roma was thrilled that Viola agreed to stay and teach the children, and the kids loved to be in the teepee for lessons. Viola built it quite large, with Red and Dan's help. Its walls were made of buffalo hides and the inside was cozy with hides and skins she brought with her from the reservation. They were the only things besides her books that she packed on the motorcycle, on her back and in her arms. She had only a few clothes, but she was about the same size as Laramie and Roma and between the three of them they had quite a wardrobe.

Red left soon after the teepee was finished. He and Viola had been friends for years but knew there could never be more than friendship between them. Viola lived alone in the teepee. It's how she wanted it and she was welcome for as long as she wanted to stay.

It became quite clear to Roma, the role this wise Indian woman would play in all their lives – if they'd let her. Jane had even embraced the idea of her staying on at the ranch and teaching the children. Now that Jane was going to have a baby, it sounded like a good idea to have a teacher, too. Roma laughed out loud at the idea of having a baby at the ranch again. It had been a long time since Jane lived with them when Levi was little. The baby was due any day now and even though Roma knew they would be there only a short time after the birth, she was very excited. Soon there would be the harvest and the dance. And then winter would come with its long sleep and spring would start the re-birthing cycle again.

Ian and Jane had just recently told Dan and Roma they would be going to California, depending on when the baby came. Ian was desperate to see how the rest of civilization was surviving – what ingenious creations people were inventing to live in this new world. Ian knew there were other like-minded thinkers out there and he was determined to find them. His plan was to head to California to see what shape the coastal cities were in, but knew he would meet visionaries all along the way. He'd be drawn to them. Every town would have them. And Levi would get a first-hand education in all the latest ideas and inventions. How fortunate they felt to have Ian as part of their family. They promised to return next summer, but would be sorely missed.

"Oh, how I'll miss my Levi – my brave Indian Brave."

Thinking of Ian drew her gaze to the greenhouse over the creek. An Ian invention. Perfect climate control, perfect temperature control, perfect for growing any herb, vegetable or fruit they had seed for. Ian, Dan and Rafa drove the wagon to the abandoned lumber yard in town and came home loaded with storm doors, screens and lumber. The doors were placed across two-by-four frames and used for roof, walls and doors. Perfect for the short days of winter and easy to prop open during long summer days.

Ian had hundreds of ideas, drawings and designs to help people to survive and re-build. He built the greenhouse, the solar panels and the windmill, all from designs he brought with him from Australia. Roma's favorite creation was the swimming pool in the creek. First he diverted the water when the winter water-flow was low, then he dug a large hole with two-by-sixes across the bottom end and lined the hole with concrete that Dan had in the barn. When he allowed the water to flow into it again, it filled to the level of the two-by-sixes creating a perfect swimming pool. The overflow spilled out and continued down the creek.

Today, Roma's greatest worry was for Judd and Dani, their son and daughter-in-law. She didn't know where they were, but she knew they were alive. They received a letter from them in November and knew they were expecting a baby in April. It's the last communication they'd had with their only son. Mothers always have to be prepared to give up their sons, thought Roma. But it was heavy on her heart. She didn't know if Judd had been sent to Saudi Arabia and Dani and the baby were still in North Carolina or if they were all in Russia or Italy – maybe even Iran or Africa. She tried to prepare herself during the years he was an Army Ranger and then in the Army Special Services. She knew that the places he was sent to do his work were the most dangerous places on earth for a mother's son. Her heart broke when she thought she may never see them again. Lately, though, she'd find herself standing on the front porch, shielding her eyes from the sun while watching the road from town – looking for them, expecting to see them walk up the gravel road. Dan tried to discourage her, to spare her the pain, but he'd learned that anything is possible – especially if Roma believed it.

"Gran?"

"I'm in the kitchen – lolligagging." It was Mira. She showed up unexpectedly quite often lately.

"Where's Mom and Aunt Laramie? I thought they were in the garden." Mira helped herself to a glass of mint tea – her favorite.

"I saw your mom and dad in the tomatoes, but I didn't see Laramie." Laramie and Rafa were staying at the ranch until after the harvest and Roma was so happy to have them home. They were so joyful with each other and their new life together. Come to think of it, they were probably in the barn.

"Viola stole the honey comb from the beehive and we wanted Auntie to make some cornbread." Mira was animated in her excitement. "Gran, she didn't even get stung – not once." Mira looked up to Viola and learned all she could about the Indian way of life. "I watched her and I think they didn't sting her because they knew she wasn't afraid. She practically had to get naked to do it though, so the bees wouldn't get caught in her clothes and sting her."

"You only got stung once the last time you took the honey comb."

"Yea, but next time I'm getting naked – then I won't get stung at all," Mira said teasingly.

"Okay." She knew Mira was baiting her.

She looked closely at Mira for signs of unhappiness or anxiety. She and Lalo had come a month ago for a *grandmother talk*, as they called it. Lalo was an unusual boy – actually he was a man, but seemed so child-like and innocent to Roma. She knew he had terrible childhood experiences from what Rafa told the family several months ago.

"Gran," Lalo had said, "You know I love Mira with every part of me."

"Yes," replied Roma, "I do still recognize that look in your eyes when you look at her."

"You know I would never do anything to hurt her, don't you?"

"Of course you wouldn't – you risked your life for her."

"Gran, he not only risked his life," interrupted Mira, "He brought me back to life. I remember I was dead – or wanted to be. He talked me into coming back. He promised me he'd always stay with me and protect me." Lalo was embarrassed to hear her speak the words he whispered to her that tragic night.

"We want to be together forever," Lalo continued, looking nervously at Mira.

"Do you mean you want to be married?" Roma had asked. "Let me say something before you answer," she said. "You can be together forever no matter what." She hurried on before they could protest. "You will always love each other the same way you love each other today." She was coming to the hard part and didn't know how to tell Lalo what he already knew to be true. "Lalo, you lived your life in a much different way than you live it today."

Lalo hung his head. He knew what was coming and he knew it had to be said. He even knew it was true. He and Mira had already had this discussion. He knew their decision was reckless and selfish.

"Yes, but we've already talked about it. We wouldn't have children. We'd just be together forever."

"I don't think for one minute that either one of you believe that. It's wishful thinking, it's irresponsible thinking." Roma knew she sounded stern, but had to hold her ground. Roma then encircled them in her arms and they had all cried together. "I know you don't want Mira to get sick. I know it would kill you to watch her die, but you know that's what could happen."

"I haven't gotten sick yet." He backed down. "Well, not so sick that I didn't get better. I'm getting stronger all the time – I can feel it." His eyes pleaded with her to understand. "If one of us dies, the other one will follow."

"Are you talking about a suicide pact?" Roma tried to remain calm. It was a volatile conversation and she was glad they trusted her enough to talk about it, but she knew what was right and they were terribly blind-sided by love for each other. "Just the fact that you've discussed it, shows me you know the risks. It's not a *maybe Mira won't get it*. It would be a miracle if she didn't." The devastation in their eyes was apparent.

"Gran, you believe in miracles. I'm not afraid to get it, or to die from it – if we can be together."

"Mira, my beautiful Mira." Roma held her granddaughter's face in her hands while the tears streamed down. "Do you think this is what anyone who loves you would plan for you, even as much as we love Lalo?" She continued. "Do you know that you have been blessed with knowing love that few ever get to experience in their lifetimes – the pure innocent love of souls found?" Mira started to protest, as Roma knew she would. "Sweetheart, would you let that love destroy the very object that you adore?" Mira's heart was breaking and Roma saw it, but had to continue. "Would either of you want the other to kill themselves, if one of you got sick and left this world?"

"No Gran, I wouldn't want Lalo to kill himself if I died, but if he died, I wouldn't want to stay here without him. I know that."

"Mira, you have been allowed to experience the gift of pure love. I know you haven't walked over the line into a sexual relationship yet, but if you do, then both of you know you will be re-creating the horrible disease that has ravaged your generation. Today, there's an opportunity to destroy it – unless it's carried on to the next generation. It's a huge responsibility, but it's yours. It may not be fair. In fact, it's tragic. But it's yours."

"Gran," Lalo's voice was filled with grief. "What if we went away and lived in the mountains – away from everyone but each other?"

"Would that make your problems go away, or just make you suffer them alone? Would you end up resenting each other because you would be isolated to protect the others that you love? Would you break my heart by not letting me ever see you again – afraid that you could infect me with the virus? Is it worth all that? Would you want to kill your own child to prevent the disease from spreading?"

They were devastated. It had to happen sooner or later. Roma suspected the signs a few months ago, although he seemed perfectly healthy now. And she knew that Lalo knew he had the virus that had taken the lives of so many young and old around the world. Her knowledge was limited and she knew it. But she also knew the earth had been cleansed. Potential for evil would always be with them, but they had to do what they could to rid the earth of disease. Everything was healthier – the plants and vegetables, trees, even the barren bear had a litter of twins this year. Surely God wouldn't abandon them to disease without any defense? Maybe Lalo was becoming healthy again and the virus would die without taking him with it.

"I may have a solution," said Roma. Instantly the light of hope came into their eyes.

"Promise me you'll wait for two more summers." The light flickered, but held. "If Lalo stays healthy and you both feel the same way, then get married. But only if you stay healthy Lalo. Promise me."

They looked at each other and Roma knew that no one had ever looked at her like that – not even Dan. She watched as the pure love of old souls flashed between them. She knew they had known each other through the veil of worlds. They would fulfill whatever they had been called here to do and they knew it.

Holding hands with Mira, Lalo said, "I would wait for her forever. I know the way I love Mira is much bigger than the physical part of love." He looked deeply into Mira's eyes again and Roma saw the same electricity pass between them – almost visible – like lightening flashes.

"I love you whether or not I ever touch you in that way," said Lalo. I will always love you – whether we are ever known here as man and wife. I love you too much to ever rob you of experiencing all that life has to offer you – especially having children." His whole body convulsed with the pain of his words. "I know how important children and family are to you." He wiped his wet face with his shirt. "Promise me, if anything happens to me in the next two years that you'll continue on to do everything that is placed before you."

Rivulets of tears washed white streaks down Mira's face.

"Promise me you'll find love again and have all the children who want to come to you," cried Lalo.

"Why would you ask this of me?" she choked on sob-filled screams. "Wwwwhhhhyyyyyyyyy???"

"Because we have so much love." He picked up the tail of her shirt and wiped her tears. "We were so lucky to find each other here. I would be happy until the day I die just knowing you love me."

They searched each other's souls in the long silence that followed. "Lalo, I would do anything for you. I can't promise that I will be happy here without you, but I can promise you that I will always live life as if you were beside me, experiencing it with me – and I wouldn't want you to miss a thing." Her eyes never left Lalo's who was shaking his head in agreement as tears flowed unabashedly down his face.

"Yes," a smile slowly spread across his face. "Two more summers – this time in two years." He was joyous – he had something wonderful to look forward to. "You'll be sixteen and I'll be eighteen. I'll get healthier and stronger and we'll love each other even more in two years."

"Thank God," Roma had whispered.

▮"I can make cornbread for you," said Roma. "You bring the honey and I'll bring the cornbread." Roma forced herself to leave the window, the quiet reminiscing and soul-searching.

"Okay, but we're going to have it in Viola's teepee," said Mira.

"That's good," said Roma. "I won't have honey dripping from one end of the kitchen to the other."

Roma saw in Mira's eyes that she was back to enjoying the everyday delight of just being alive, and was reminded again that anything can happen in two years.

*Chapter 34*

thump-THUMP, thump-THUMP, thump-THUMP

She was running as fast as her legs would go!

thump-THUMP, thump-THUMP, thump-THUMP

She couldn't make it!

thump-THUMP, thump-THUMP, thump-THUMP

"Nnnnnnooooooooooooooooo!"

thump-THUMP, thump-THUMP, thump-THUMP

"Run – children ! Run!"

thump-THUMP, thump-THUMP, thump-THUMP

"Nnnnnnooooooooooooooooo!"

thump-THUMP, thump-THUMP, thump-THUMP

"Run away!"

thump-THUMP, thump-THUMP, thump-THUMP

"Janie! Janie-girl!" Ian shook her. "My Janie-girl" He held her close and rocked her.

"Ian!" she shouted.

"It's okay Janie-girl." He held her tighter to him. "It's okay girl, I've got you." He was terrified. "Is it the baby Janie?"

"Ian!" Jane was drenched in nightmare sweats. "Ian!" she screamed again. "Nnnnnnooooooooooooooooo!" The mournful wail filled the air with her nightmare memory.

"Janie – it was a dream, wasn't it?" He held her tightly and cursed under his breath. "Those damned dreams!" Why were they sent to her? The dreams haunted her. He had to get her away from this place! Maybe they would stop if he could get her away.

"Oh Ian, Ian, Ian," Jane wailed.

She was back to this life. "Thank God!" said Ian. He was terrified the vivid nightmare terrors would leave her there and she wouldn't be able to find her way back from them. "Janie, I don't know what I would ever do without you," Ian whispered. "I've got to get us away from here."

"No, Ian. I have to stay, because of the dream." She rubbed her fingers through his hair as he lay his head across her belly. She knew their baby would be born soon.

"Can you tell me about it now?" He gently caressed her belly and listened as her heartbeat returned to its natural rhythm. He didn't pressure her in the silence that followed. He didn't want to upset her.

"This is the last dream," started Jane. "I know I'll have other dreams, but I will never be helpless again to change the events they foretell. And, don't be afraid for the baby. Our baby is strong and will be here soon." She felt her child move in response to her voice.

"Wow, that was a strong reaction, all right." Ian concentrated on the movement under his hands. "It's a big one, Janie girl."

"A big boy."

"A boy?" Ian's face lit up. "Are you sure?"

"Pretty sure. I think we should decide on a name for your son."

"Oh, my Janie. I can hardly wait."

Ian was a wonderful father to Levi, but Jane knew how much the birth of this child meant to him. When she'd first told him, she wasn't sure he was happy about it, but the impression was fleeting, instantly replaced by elation. Every man should feel this happy about having a son, she thought. They'd thought of names for both boys and girls – Jane would love to have a daughter, but more and more she was impressed that she carried a son.

"I thought we already chose a name for a son," said Ian.

The name Ian liked for a boy was Joshua – after the Joshua Tree and the prophet Joshua. Mormon pioneers had given the tree its name. They thought the long scraggly limbs looked like the prophet Joshua waving them on to the Promised Land. Their son, Joshua, would be named for this new Promised Land that God had given them. Ian hoped to see the Joshua Tree in the desert when they trekked to California.

"Are you ready to get up, Joshua?" Ian whispered to his child. "I've got to get up – I don't want to go back to sleep," he said. "Come on Janie," he urged. "Come watch the sun come up with your husband and your sons."

"Sons?"

"Yes, we may as well wake Levi, too. Let him know he's going to have a new brother soon – Joshua Jayne."

"Seems a terrible thing to do to such a small thing – naming him Joshua Jayne." Jane laughed. "Maybe we should change his last name." Jane protested the look of defense on Ian's face. "Well –

Jane Jayne is bad enough for your mother's name – but Josh Jayne? Think about it!"

"No one would dare to tease my son because of his name and certainly not because of his mother's name. That would not be wise." He pulled Jane to him and kissed her passionately.

"Don't start anything, mister." Jane loved Ian's passion for her. She loved that he loved her.

"I'll go wake Levi. We'll celebrate! I'll even make him some coffee." He reconsidered. "Maybe a little coffee with some warm milk. I might even share my coffee with you."

The mood of the morning had changed. Thank goodness, thought Jane. Her dream terrified her. It would happen soon. But not this minute. She loved when this wonderful, serious man became playful.

Dan slept soundly beside her, as if nothing in this world could disturb him, he looked so peaceful. The bed was soaked and so were her nightclothes. She sat on the edge of the bed remembering the scream she'd heard a few moments ago. Jane's scream from her bear dream – the same scream she'd heard in her own nightmare. They'd shared this dream before. Jane knew.

"Roma?"

"Well, that was quick. You were sound asleep a second ago."

"Something woke me – I thought it was your snoring."

"You know I don't snore!" she teased. "But since you're up, we may as well get up and watch the sun come up. Someone else is already up and fixing coffee."

"It has to be Ian. I don't think anyone loves coffee more – especially your special blend."

"Well, we better get more chicory if we can find it, when we go to harvest, because it's almost gone."

Roma was fully dressed for the day and downstairs having her first cup when Dan came downstairs.

"You're walking a mite gingerly this morning," said Ian.

"Yea – I think I twisted my back trying to lift that hay yesterday." Roma poured him a cup of coffee. "Guess I'll just have to work it out today. Plenty more alfalfa to move, and as good a crop as I've ever seen."

Roma and Jane's eyes met and Jane knew her mother had the same dream. Again. She had a hard time fighting the tears. It would be difficult. She had to be strong. They didn't speak to each other. Emotions were too high.

Dan and Ian noticed the tension, but were distracted by Levi. "Where's my coffee?" He looked at Ian. "You said I could get up and have coffee with you." Ian looked at Jane in mock puzzlement. "You said you had some great news to tell me. C'mon – you know what I'm talking about."

"Okay, okay," said Ian. "We thought you might want to know you're going to have a new brother and his name will be Joshua."

"Really?" Levi's faced beamed with pleasure. He'd hoped he would have a brother and now he knew. "How do you know it's a boy? It might be *Joshette*," he said, relishing his joke.

"It's a boy and I know just like I knew you were a boy," said Jane, hugging him.

"Alright! I'll be able to teach him to play ball," he hollered.

"Okay – who's the wise-guy that started this day so early?" Said Laramie, as she and Rafa came in the back door. They were staying in the cook tent until after harvest when they would return to their ranch. Laramie poured coffee for her and Rafa. "Where's mom? I thought I heard her."

Roma stood at the porch, shielding her eyes from the sun, searching the road from town.

"Mom?" Laramie took their coffee and joined her.

"Hi sweetheart. It was so nice out here, I thought I'd catch the sunrise." A brilliant outline that stretched pink and purple across the range was just creeping up. "Have you ever seen anything so beautiful?"

"Yes," said Dan, who had joined them. "You're just as beautiful."

"Dad," said Laramie. "I love that you love my mother so much. And I love that you let us know you love her."

"Me too," said Jane as everyone piled out to the porch. "My gosh, what a beautiful sunrise."

"Oh, has anyone ever seen such a beautiful sunrise?" Suzan and Jesse walked hand-in-hand up the porch steps. Now they were all here.

"Mom said that when you see something so beautiful, that God made it just for you," said Levi.

"Well, aren't we the lucky ones, then," said Ian, as he stood behind Jane with his arms around her and his hands on her belly. "Did we tell you we are having a son and his name will be Joshua?"

"Josh Jayne?" chided Laramie. "You're actually going to do that to a little baby?"

"Oh, this baby is anything but little," said Ian good-naturedly. "Maybe we'll just have to call him *Joshua Tree* Jayne."

They laughed until they cried and their laughter echoed down the valley. Soon all the children and Viola too, were laughing, kidding and drinking coffee on the front porch. Dan milked Maggie and they drank more coffee with her warm creamy milk. Viola went to the teepee to retrieve the honeycomb and Laramie put a big batch of cornbread in the oven for breakfast while Roma stood on the porch and shielded her eyes from the sun as she searched the road from town.

"Did you hear that?"

"Hear what? The raven caw?"

"No. Listen." They stood quietly until the crisp morning breeze shifted. "There! Did you hear it?"

"Sounds like laughing."

"It is laughing."

"Haven't heard that for awhile."

"You'll hear a lot of it from now on."

"I hope so."

## *Chapter 35*

"Dan?" Roma said excitedly.

"Yes, honey." He saw the look on her face. "What is it?"

"They're coming Dan." She shielded her eyes from the sun and searched the road from town. Dan followed her stare.

"I don't see anyone, Roma. C'mon and join the fun. Cornbread will be done in a minute." It broke his heart to see her like this.

"No. I mean – I can't see them either, but I know they're coming."

"Well, I guess we should take a little ride down the road to greet them." Dan knew better than to argue. She was definitely convinced someone was coming.

"Okay," said Roma. "But I guess it can wait until after the cornbread." With all this talk about having a son, maybe she was just feeling homesick for her own son. "Yes, we can go after the cornbread."

The smell filled the kitchen and drifted out to them. The butter was ready. The honeycomb dripped in a bowl on the table. Soon the steaming cornbread was piled high and every child had a piece in hand with butter and honey dripping to their elbows.

"Take it outside," said Laramie. "No sense dripping it all over Gran's floor." They'd been exiled to the yard and the sunshine and they loved it.

"Dan. Let's go now."

"Okay. I'll go saddle up Litany and Rendi.

"I'll wait here on the porch."

Roma shielded her eyes from the sun and searched the road from town. Dan called to her and as she walked down the steps she caught the movement from the corner of her eye – the children playing in the field by the fence. They squealed with delight as the two small cubs galloped down the hill toward them. Roma's reaction was swift and instantaneous. She'd rehearsed it too many times not to know what to do.

thump-THUMP, thump-THUMP, thump-THUMP

She was running as fast as her legs would go!

thump-THUMP, thump-THUMP, thump-THUMP

She couldn't make it!

thump-THUMP, thump-THUMP, thump-THUMP

"Nnnnnnooooooooooooooooo!"

thump-THUMP, thump-THUMP, thump-THUMP

"Run – children ! Run!"

thump-THUMP, thump-THUMP, thump-THUMP

"Nnnnnnooooooooooooooooo!"

thump-THUMP, thump-THUMP, thump-THUMP

"Run away!"

thump-THUMP, thump-THUMP, thump-THUMP

No one saw the old barren bear racing to protect her children. Her reaction was swift and instantaneous.

thump-THUMP, thump-THUMP, thump-THUMP

She was running as fast as her legs would go!

thump-THUMP, thump-THUMP, thump-THUMP

She couldn't make it!

thump-THUMP, thump-THUMP, thump-THUMP

"Nnnnnnooooooooooooooooo!"

thump-THUMP, thump-THUMP, thump-THUMP

"Run – children ! Run!"

thump-THUMP, thump-THUMP, thump-THUMP

"Nnnnnnooooooooooooooooo!"

thump-THUMP, thump-THUMP, thump-THUMP

"Run away!"

thump-THUMP, thump-THUMP, thump-THUMP

Before Ian could stop her, Jane raced toward the mother bear. Her reaction was swift and instantaneous. She'd rehearsed it too many times not to know what to do.

thump-THUMP, thump-THUMP, thump-THUMP

She was running as fast as her legs would go!

thump-THUMP, thump-THUMP, thump-THUMP

She couldn't make it!

thump-THUMP, thump-THUMP, thump-THUMP

"Nnnnnnooooooooooooooooo!"

thump-THUMP, thump-THUMP, thump-THUMP

"Run – children ! Run!"

thump-THUMP, thump-THUMP, thump-THUMP

"Nnnnnnoooooooooooooooooo!"

thump-THUMP, thump-THUMP, thump-THUMP

"Run away!"

thump-THUMP, thump-THUMP, thump-THUMP

Roma felt the old bear's protectiveness and knew they both shared the same instinct. Maybe they had even shared the same dream. Sara and Dominic had just thrown handfuls of cornbread to the cubs when they heard Roma scream and watched her running toward them. They didn't see the mother bear until she butted Sara with her head and started for Dominic. Sara jumped up and ran shrieking past Roma just as the bear stood on her hind legs and screamed her most ferocious warning. Roma froze and for an instant thought this might end differently than the dream. Dominic stared at the bear in paralyzed terror and Roma diverted the old bear's attention by shouting and thrashing her arms wildly.

The last shriek escaped from Roma's throat when she saw Jane fall to the ground.

"Nnnnnnoooooooooooooooooo," Jane screamed as she watched the powerful claws slash into Roma and toss her across the field.

Searing pain burned through Roma's chest. The forceful blow knocked the air out of her and she struggled for breath. She knew she was hurt, but could still move and tried to crawl.

"Mamma – stay still. Don't move," hollered Jane.

Roma froze where she lay and felt the hot breath on the back of her neck as the old bear rushed to her, sniffed her still body and raised her huge paw to attack again.

No one saw Trouble race through the tall grass until she lunged at the old sow's throat, clamping with her powerful jaws. Within seconds Black attacked the back of the bear's neck. The startled sow screamed in pain and frantically clawed at Trouble's body, ripped her from her throat and threw her onto the ground. Black clung to the back of the massive neck as the bear hurled herself around and around, trying to release the painful grip that was slowly paralyzing her.

It happened so fast – not in slow motion at all, Roma thought, as she lay there staring into Trouble's eyes. A strong musk scent filled the air. Roma knew from Trouble's short, ragged breaths that her beloved wolf pup was dying. "You got her, girl." Roma reached her hand to the pup's head and felt her life drain away. "Thank you, Trouble," she whispered. "You changed the dream."

Trouble closed her eyes and Roma wept. She painfully lifted her head to see Black release his powerful grip from the old sow's neck and the bear and cubs slowly lumber up the hill and disappear into the safety of the tall timber. Black sniffed and probed Trouble with his nose, and whined as he frantically circled her body.

The children cried – all huddled together on the porch – Viola had them. Jane lay on the ground ten feet from her mother and couldn't stop what happened, but was relieved that the dream had been altered. She should have known that Black would be close to the children and Trouble close to Roma.

Dan was the first to reach Roma. She groaned when Dan carefully turned her over. Broken ribs, he thought, but was shocked to see the front of her blouse already soaked with blood. Roma looked past Dan's shoulder and smiled.

"Mamma?"

"Oh, Judd!"

"Hi mamma. I'm home."

"Yes, you're home," barely squeaked from Roma's dry lips. "I knew you were coming."

He knelt and tenderly picked up his mother's limp body and carried her up the yard, across the porch and into the living room where he laid her on the mattress where Mira usually slept. "Don't try to talk, Mom." He wiped her face with the cloth baby diaper that lay on his shoulder. The question on his mother's face prompted him to motion for Dani and the baby. "Mamma, this is Roman Zerlich, your newest grandson. We call him Romy."

Tears welled in Roma's eyes as her gaze went from Dani to Roman and she strained to speak. "He looks like you, Dani, except he has red hair." Dani was a blonde beauty and this new grandson had curly, coppery-red hair. Red hair was a Zerlich trait even though it had skipped a generation. Roma stared into Dani's eyes and saw the strong resolve there – saw the pain of childbirth in a cold barren room in April and the protective feelings that every mother recognizes – like in the old bear's eyes. "He's a beautiful child Dani. Big, too."

"Let's get mom's shirt off to see how badly she's hurt," said Suzan.

"We need to get this bleeding stopped. Thank God she's alive." Dan quickly unbuttoned Roma's shirt and gasped when he saw her chest.

"Dad?" It was Judd. He'd seen many chest wounds before and quickly assessed the situation. "Dad – go get your suture kit and all your medical supplies."

Dan ran as Judd knelt close to Roma and wiped at the blood that oozed with every beat of her heart. Ragged gashes ran across her chest and her right breast was almost ripped off and the left side didn't look much better, although the wounds weren't as deep. One of her lungs was likely punctured, from the sounds he could hear coming from her chest. He hoped it was only one. You can survive with only one lung. "Laramie, is there anything like tubing around?"

Searching quickly through kitchen cupboards and drawers, she found a box of straws and handed one to Judd. "Get some alcohol."

Suzan ran to the bathroom and came back with a bottle and poured it on the straw, which Judd carefully inserted into the hole in her lung. "Give me another straw." Again they sanitized the straw and inserted it into another puncture wound in her lung.

Judd put his ear to Roma's chest and listened for telltale signs of air escaping. He pulled the straws and wiped her chest with alcohol. She didn't flinch – Judd knew she was in shock and that her body's own defenses were protecting her now.

He stood up to look at his father who carried a large bucket of medical supplies, including his suture kit. Dan dropped the bucket when he saw the look in Judd's teary eyes. As Dan bent to reach for Roma, Judd pulled him up to face him. "Dad," he started, "we need to work fast." Judd's words trembled as he spoke. Dan swallowed hard. "She's in shock so she's not in any pain. The bleeding has slowed, but the damage is done." His eyes held his fathers. "We've got to operate on her and hope she doesn't die from shock." He hurried to interrupt the protests he saw coming from his father. "If we don't do this, she'll die for sure." He saw the reality of his words sink into his father like a leaden weight. "I think only one of her lungs is punctured and all we can do about that is pray that it heals up and doesn't get infected." His voice broke.

How many times he'd seen this on the battlefield, in Saudi Arabia, Iran, Bosnia, Africa. He'd traveled so far and now his mother lay like another casualty of war. How was it that they'd arrived at just the same moment the attack happened? He'd quickly assessed what was happening and pulled his gun to kill the bear, but by the time he had a clear shot the bear retreated and hurried her cubs up the hill. It was over as quickly as it started.

"If we don't remove the shredded breast tissue and get her stitched up, infection will surely kill her." Tears welled in his eyes. "I've done this on the battlefield – emergency life saving techniques, but I'm not a doctor and I need your help."

Dan couldn't keep the fear from his voice. "You just tell me what to do. We'll do whatever it takes to save her life."

Suzan and Dani immediately began preparations – boiling water to sterilize scalpels, scissors, and needle nose pliers – strips of cloth for bandaging – Betadine, alcohol, peroxide, iodine, all lined up on the kitchen table.

Laramie held Roma's hand and continually talked to her mother even though she was now unconscious. Soothing words of comfort telling her everything they planned to do, and fierce words demanding that she fight with them to save her life. She monitored the ragged pulse and shallow breathing, willing them to continue in spite of the shock that tried to take Roma's life.

"Janie's water broke," Ian whispered to Suzan. "We'll be upstairs in the bedroom." His eyes were filled with concern. "I'm sure we have a time to go before the baby comes – it's not early or anything, so everything should go okay. It looks like everything's being done and there are plenty of hands to help, but please come and get me if there's anything I can do to help with Roma."

"And you call me if Jane needs anything, or if her labor pains get serious," whispered Suzan back to Ian.

"I'll help Ian," said Jesse.

"Jesse!" Their eyes held each other.

"Yes, I can *see* you," he started. "As I hurried toward the commotion I slipped and fell. I tried to catch myself, but must have hit my head on the step."

Suzan ran into Jesse's arms and he buried his face in her hair, as he whispered, "I heard Roma scream and a light flashed behind my eyes. When I raised myself, I could see the field before me – all gray and shimmering – like forms moving in a fog." He held her away from him and looked into her eyes. "I tried to get up – to help, but I couldn't move – I couldn't believe the unbelievable scene trying to come into focus." He shook his head. "When the fog thinned, I saw . . . the bear." His feelings were so conflicting – his elation at being able to see and the trauma of witnessing the brutal attack of the bear. "I closed my eyes and as my mind slowly cleared, I opened them and saw Judd holding Roma."

There was no time to celebrate the joy she felt. Seeing the love in Jesse's eyes was enough. "Thank you, God."

Roma lay on a sheet on the dining room table – in front of the sliding glass doors to get the best light. "Everything's ready," said Judd. "I'm not a surgeon and we don't have time to take all the internal stitches that would be done in a hospital, but let's get started."

Dan stood on one side of Judd to hand him instruments and Suzan stood on the other side to wipe the blood away. Dani was in the living room, quietly nursing Romy . Viola took the children to her teepee where sage scented smoke curled from the top and prayer songs filled the air.

Roma watched it all in amazement as the drama unfolded below her. Is this the part where the bright light comes and I walk toward it, she thought. She watched her son carefully cut away the ragged shreds of her breast and take a stitch deep into the remaining tissue. She'd always loved her breasts.

She watched Suzan dab at the blood that still oozed from her wound. "God bless you sweetheart. You've had a long struggle, but I can see the happiness in your eyes. Now I know you remember." Her heart filled with love for this first daughter who'd learned to let the fantasy go and love the reality. She'd always been the second mother – had stepped in when Roma couldn't mother. Roma had always known they'd been great friends before this life.

She heard Laramie talking to her. "Laramie," she whispered. "You're so much like me, it's scary."

"I know mamma, but I like it." Laramie answered her! Could she hear her or were they speaking to each other's souls? "I know I'll see you again, mamma." Laramie cried softly. "But, I hope while I'm here, I can love my life as much as you've loved yours. I want to love every minute of it."

"You go girl!" whispered Roma.

A sob escaped Laramie's tight throat. "And Mom – I want you to stay here. Please don't leave."

"I'll always be close, Laramie. Always close."

"No Mom," Laramie sobbed, "I don't want you to leave. Fight to stay. You have a choice – don't you remember?"

Roma heard the black timber wolf's mournful howl from the top of the ridge, smelled the burning sage, tasted the salty tears of her youngest daughter, felt the bearing-down pains of childbirth and met the new spirit entering this world. "Ah yes," she told Jane. "The perfect daughter to teach you and Ian all the things you still have left to learn here." She laughed at her little joke with Joshua Tree.

"Yes, Laramie. I remember." But the dream! She knew she left this world in the dream. There is a plan, thought Roma, better than anything I could plan. "And I do have a choice."

"Mamma," whispered Jane. "Trouble intervened for you so you could stay."

"Yes, she did." Roma gently scruffed at the thick fur of the wolf pup's neck. "It's so ironic, Jane, that you would be the wise woman of us." Roma wiped her daughter's tears. "You've learned so much already. You are the perfect mother for this strong new spirit."

"And you were the perfect mother for me – your strong, willful, defiant daughter." One last push and the bellow that erupted from Jane's throat was heard simultaneously with the first cries of her strong new daughter. Ian lifted his tiny wailing baby and placed her across Jane's belly. Tears mingled with afterbirth as he cut the cord and thanked God for allowing him the pleasure of the greatest experience of his life.

"Thank you, Ian, for loving our Jane Abbey and our brave Indian Brave."

"My pleasure, Roma."

Two hours had passed since Judd took the first stitch and Suzan wiped the sweat that trickled into his eyes as he took the last one. "We've done all we can do. It's not pretty, but the bleeding has stopped and she's still alive. The rest is up to God. All we can do now is pray."

Tears streamed down his face as relief from the trauma washed over him. He came all this way – months of walking – to try and save his mother's life. He quickly went outside and let his dad and sisters finish bandaging her. This was all wrong – not how he'd planned his homecoming. After all they'd been through. The scream heard down the valley tore from his throat like a wounded animal. The old barren bear recognized the cry and hurried her cubs back to the safety of their den. She had to protect her children.

Roma recognized the cry as well and whispered to Judd, "I knew you were coming, and I also knew the bear was coming." He looked in her eyes and saw his mother. "Mom," he started, but couldn't continue.

"Sweetheart." Roma's eyes filled with tears. "You're the only son of my body. I'm so happy I could see you again." What could she say to this man that she birthed – the little tow-headed boy she adored? He was always so gentle, and sensitive, and loving. He'd brought such joy to her heart. Now he was a man with a son of his own. Dani stood on the porch with tears in hers eyes. She understood the love that Roma felt for Judd – for she too, loved a son.

The mournful howl of wolves rang continuously from ridge to ridge and mingled with the yipping of coyotes. Sleeping children lay on animal skins heavily scented with sage smoke and Lalo followed Mira through the forest collecting herbs by the light of the moon.

Spirits lingered close waiting for Roma. The extraordinary outpouring of love from her family held her to this world. Oh Dan! "My life with you has been splendid. I have loved every minute of it - no regrets. You have honored me." How could she leave him? When she felt life fading, she lingered to be with Dan – just one more hour, one more day. She couldn't leave him. Their love was given with no holding back – they loved as much as was humanly possible. Dan held her in his arms and fed her the strengthening herb tea Mira steeped and bathed her with the herbs boiled for cleansing and healing. Roma passed through the thin veil that separated them many times before finally returning to him. She knew she had a choice and that she wouldn't die. Not now.

Two weeks passed since the bear attack. The healing ceremony continued in the teepee day and night. Vi and the children ate and slept there, waking at odd hours to offer prayers to the Great Spirit, pleading for Roma's life.

Mira and Lalo buried Trouble on the hillside overlooking the valley, the creek, the garden spot, the back porch – all her favorite places. The wolves continued their mournful howling until the day Roma opened her eyes – the day Black proudly led the four wolf pups down from the ridge to the garden. Black sniffed the depressed spot under the peach tree where Trouble used to lay and the pups whined at the remembered scent of their mother.

"Well, I'll be damned," said Dan as he stood with Ian and Jesse on the front porch and witnessed the procession. "I knew this valley would fill up with wolf pups and I guess this is the first of them." They watched as the smallest of the litter whined and sniffed her way to the porch. Dan opened the front door and it timidly entered the living room where Roma lay, waiting to return to this life. Roma's eyes opened wide at the remembered sound and the familiar feel of the cold nose on the back of her hand. That's the only time the pup ever entered the house.

From that first day back, Roma insisted she recuperate on the front porch so the sun could heal her. She didn't know where the pup stayed at night, but she was there everyday nudging Roma's hand to play the favorite game of tag she'd once played with its mother. Roma laughed at the description of the *pup parade,* but never did get to glimpse the other three pups Dan described. Black took them back through the forest to the rocky ridge. Roma was thrilled that this pup bore the same markings and had the same mannerisms as Trouble and sometimes became confused between memories and real time, forgetting all that had happened in between the two wolf pups.

Life happened on the porch. Dan and Roma slept there and mothers nursed their babies on the porch. Dani and Judd's house built-up before Roma's eyes – right down the valley from the porch. Suzan and Jesse gathered seeds for planting next year and harvested the fruits of this year. Roma watched as seeds of love were planted, nurtured and matured in the fertile place of their hearts, as well. She watched from the porch as Dan and Rafa cut the last of the alfalfa and hauled it to the hay barn for the coming winter while Laramie whispered comforting words as she massaged Roma's healing body.

Everyday the children brought pretty rocks to Roma. Jane placed a small purple stone in the tight little fist of Joshua Tree to add to the pile. What a wonderful surprise she'd been – Joshua Tree. Ian was elated to have a daughter and Levi adored her. Jane prayed that she and her daughter would share a love for each other like she knew with Roma.

Roma blessed the days and felt her strength return. The pile of rocks on the porch grew as she accepted each child's earthy gift, knowing that every one was personally selected to heal her. Did they know that gifts from the heart could heal the body as well as the soul? These children know, thought Roma. They remember.

Love healed Roma. Tears washed down her cheeks as she closed her eyes and wept with joy. Everything was the right way.

## From the Author

I live in Highlands Ranch, Colorado with my best friend and husband of thirty-seven years. We have three daughters and one son who also live in the Denver area with their families.

I started writing this book in 1991 and didn't feel an urgency to complete it by a specific deadline. Every year I feel anxious about winter; food, heat, power, gasoline, all those things that seemingly keep this world going. I agonize over the natural disasters that throw thousands of peoples' lives into chaos and despair in the flash of an eye, while my life seems to go on as usual. Then I turn on the TV and it's right in front of me. What would I do if a natural disaster happened here – in Denver, Colorado? What if life didn't get back to normal?

Over the months while writing, the story continued to unfold and as the significance of the events and characters evolved, it became more important to complete this project.

I feel a great spiritual strength organizing on the earth. It feels urgent. It feels important. I am compelled to write about our survival. Please enjoy this story.

I am currently working on the sequel to . . . *and mother earth wept*.

Sincerely,

J.A. Schrader